FORBIDDEN COLOURS

Yukio Mishima was born in Tokyo in 1925. When he graduated from the Peers' School in 1944, he received a citation from the Emperor as the best honour student. He then attended the Tokyo Imperial University School of Jurisprudence until 1947. In his teens, he became a prolific writer of great talent. These works include some fifteen novels (many of which have been made into films), thirty-three plays, several travel books, numerous essays and countless short stories. Among his books published in England are *After the Banquet*, *Confessions of a Mask*, *Death in Midsummer* and *The Sailor Who Fell from Grace with the Sea*. *The Sound of Waves*, published in Japan under the title *Shiosai*, won the 1954 Shinchosha literary prize.

Mishima revered and mastered the martial arts of Japan. He was a devotee of body-building exercises and also accomplished in the arts of *kendo* and *karate*. He always firmly upheld the traditions of Japan's imperial past – a legacy from his samurai forbears – and believed that these values were being eroded by Western materialism.

On November 25, 1970, at the peak of his brilliant literary career, he astonished the world by committing ritual suicide, or *hara-kiri*, by disembowelment. Mishima had written much about suicide and early death and often expressed the wish to die young. His last work was the tetralogy, *The Sea of Fertility* which is published by Penguin. This comprises *Spring Snow*, *Runaway Horses*, *The Temple of Dawn* (in two parts) and *The Decay of the Angel* and was finally completed on the morning before his death. Just before his suicide he wrote to friends that he felt empty, having put everything he thought or felt about life into this mammoth undertaking, later hailed as a masterpiece. His writing has been widely acclaimed, compared to that of Proust, Gide and Sartre, and Arthur Miller once said of him that 'He had the economy of means to create enormous myths – his novels are compressed visions.'

Yukio Mishima

Forbidden Colours

**Translated from the Japanese by
Alfred H. Marks**

Penguin Books
in association with Secker & Warburg

PENGUIN BOOKS

Published by the Penguin Group
Penguin Books Ltd, 27 Wrights Lane, London W8 5TZ, England
Viking Penguin, a division of Penguin Books USA Inc.
375 Hudson Street, New York, New York 10014, USA
Penguin Books Australia Ltd, Ringwood, Victoria, Australia
Penguin Books Canada Ltd, 2801 John Street, Markham, Ontario, Canada L3R 1B4
Penguin Books (NZ) Ltd, 182–190 Wairau Road, Auckland 10, New Zealand

Penguin Books Ltd, Registered Offices: Harmondsworth, Middlesex, England

First published in Japanese as *Kinchiki*
This translation first published in Great Britain by
Martin Secker & Warburg Ltd 1968
Published in Penguin Books 1971
10 9 8 7 6

Copyright © 1951, 1953 by Yukio Mishima
Translation Copyright © Alfred A. Knopf, Inc., 1968
All rights reserved

Printed in England by Clays Ltd, St Ives plc
Typeset in Linotype Times

Contents

1

The Beginning

Yasuko had grown accustomed to coming and blithely seating herself on Shunsuké's lap as he rested in the rattan chair at the edge of the garden. This brought him great joy.

It was the summer of 1950. Mornings Shunsuké received no visitors. If he felt like it, he would work. If he didn't, he would write letters, or have his chair set out in the garden and stretch out in it with a book, or close his book on his lap and do nothing, or ring a bell and have a maid bring him tea, or if for some reason he had not had enough sleep the night before, he would pull his blanket up to his chin and drop off for a little while.

Although he was five years past sixty, he had no diversions, nothing worthy of being called a hobby. In fact, he didn't believe in them. He was entirely deficient in the quality so important to a hobby: appreciation of the concrete relationships that tied him fast to other men. This acute deficiency in objectivity, accompanied by clumsy, convulsive stabs at establishing a relationship between his inner world and that which lay outside it, imparted a certain freshness and naïveté even to the works of his later years, but they took their toll. They took the strength from the very vitals of his fiction: the dramatic incidents, born of the collision of human wills; the humorous portrayals; the urge to limn human character – all nurtured by the rivalry between the human being and his world. On this score, two or three of the crustier critics still hesitated to acclaim him a great writer.

Shunsuké's right knee was plagued by seizures of neuralgia. Before each onset he would feel a dim pain deep inside it. It was doubtful that his ageing, brittle kneecaps could stand the warm weight of a young woman upon them for very long. As the pain increased, however, an expression of joy slyly stole across his features.

Finally he said, 'My knee hurts, Yasuko. Let me move my leg over like this, and you sit there; so.'

Yasuko opened her eyes wide and looked at Shunsuké with concern. He laughed: Yasuko loathed him.

The old novelist understood this loathing. He stood up and grasped Yasuko by the shoulders. Then he took her chin in his hand, tipped it back, and kissed her on the lips. Then, his duty to her thus hurriedly completed, he felt a sudden flash of pain in his right knee and slumped back in his chair. When he was finally able to lift up his face and look around him, Yasuko had disappeared.

A week afterwards, he had still not heard from Yasuko. While taking a walk one day, he dropped by her house. She had gone with two or three school friends to a hot-springs resort on the southern coast of the Izu Peninsula. After jotting down the name of the resort in his memo book, he returned home and began making preparations for a trip. There was a stack of proofs urgently calling for his attention, but he took care of them for the time being by saying that he suddenly felt the need to take a midsummer vacation.

Concerned about the heat, he took an early morning train. Nevertheless, the back of his white suit was soon soaked with perspiration. He took a sip of the hot tea in his thermos bottle. Then he put his slender hand, dry as bamboo, into his pocket and took out some of the advertising brochures for his next collected works, given him by one of the people at his publisher's.

This new collection of *The Works of Shunsuké Hinoki* would be his third. The first one was assembled when he was forty-five.

At that point in time, I recall, he thought to himself, that in spite of the great accumulation of my works acclaimed by the world as the epitome of stability and unity and, in a sense, having reached the pinnacle, as many predicted, I was quite given over to this foolishness. Foolishness? Nonsense. Foolishness could never be connected with my works, with my soul, with my thinking. *My works are certainly not foolishness.*

(Italics were often a sign that he was speaking ironically.) Not only that, I was above using thought in mitigation of my foolishness. In order to maintain the purity of my thinking, I kept free from my foolish activities enough spirit to allow my thoughts to form. Sex was, however, not the only motivating force. My foolishness had nothing to do with sex or spirit. My foolishness lay in a wild ability to handle abstractions, which threatened to make me misanthropic. It still threatens, even now in my sixty-sixth year.

With a sad smile on his lips, he studied the picture of himself on the cover of the prospectus he held in his hand.

It was a picture of an ugly old man. That was the only way to put it. However, it was not difficult to see in it certain dim and delicate traces of the spiritual beauty so acclaimed by the world. The broad forehead; the clipped, narrow cheeks; the broad, hungry lips; the wilful chin: in every feature the traces of long, hard work and of spirit lay open to the light. His face, however, was not so much moulded by spirit as riddled with it. It was a face in which an excess of soul was laid bare, causing the onlooker to shrink from looking at it directly, as if it talked too openly of private things. In its ugliness his face was a corpse emaciated of spirit, no longer possessing the power to retain its privacy.

It was their doing. Shunsuké's features were termed beautiful by that admirable group which, having been poised by the intellectual hedonism of the times, having replaced concern for humanity with individualism, having extirpated universality from the sense of beauty, had larcenously and violently torn beauty from the arms of ethics.

Be that as it may, on the back of the prospectus that boldly bore the features of an ugly old man, rows of testimonials by numerous prominent men presented a strange contrast to what was on the front. These great men of intellect, this flock of bald parrots prepared to sing a loud song wherever and as directed, were singing of the uncanny beauty of the works of Shunsuké.

One renowned critic, for example, a well-known Hinoki scholar, summarized the entire twenty volumes of the works as follows:

9

This great shower of works cascading into our hearts was written in sincerity and finished in mistrust. Mr Hinoki states that if he didn't have that instinct of mistrust in his works he would have thrown them away as soon as written. Was ever such a row of corpses laid before the eyes of the public?

In Shunsuké Hinoki's works, the unexpected, instability, the unlucky, misfortune, the unseemly, impropriety – all the minus quantities of beauty – are depicted. If a certain historical period is to be used as background, without fail a decadent period is chosen. If a love story is needed for subject matter, without fail the emphasis is placed on the hopelessness and the tedium of it. In his hands the healthy, flourishing form is a passionate loneliness in the human mind exploding with the intensity of an epidemic raging in a tropical city. All the fierce hatreds, the jealousies, the enmities, the passions of humankind, he does not seem to be concerned with. Not only that, he finds much more to write about, much more living, essential value, in a single capillary of warmth in the corpse of the passions than in a living period of human feelings.

In the midst of coldness comes a clever shudder of feeling. In the midst of immorality appears an almost ferocious morality. In the midst of coldness, a heroic unrest makes itself felt. What masterfully wrought style must this be to intrude into the purlieus of paradox? It is a rococo style, one out of the old Heian times. It is a human style in the real sense of the word. It is a clothed style for the sake of clothing. It is the diametrical opposite of a bare style. It is filled with lovely tucks and pleats, like those in the sculptures of the Fates in the gable of the Parthenon, or those in the clothing of the Nike by Paeonius. Flowing pleats, flying pleats, not simply those that follow the motions of the body and so subordinate themselves to its lines. These are pleats that flow of themselves, that of themselves fly to heaven ...

A smile of irritation flickered about Shunsuké's mouth as he read. Then he muttered, 'I don't get it at all. He missed the boat completely. It's a fabricated, flowery eulogy; that's all it is. After twenty years, he turns out tripe like this.'

He turned to look out of the broad window of the second-class coach. The sea was in view, and a fishing boat, its sail spread, was heading for the open water. The white canvas, its womb not quite filled with wind, clung to the mast, languidly flirted with it. At that instant a sliver of light glinted from the base of the mast; then the train sliced into a grove of red pines, their trunks bright in the morning sun of summer; then it entered a tunnel.

Well, Shunsuké thought, I wouldn't be surprised if that glimmer of light came from a mirror. There must be a fisher-woman aboard that boat who's in the middle of making herself pretty. In her sunburnt hand, stronger than a man's, she is probably sending off sidelong signals towards the passengers of each passing train, in order to retail her secrets. In Shunsuké's poetic fancy the face of the fisherwoman changed to that of Yasuko. The ageing writer shook his thin, sweaty frame.

*

All the fierce hatreds, the jealousies, the enmities, the passions of humankind he does not seem to be concerned with.

Lies! Lies! Lies!

The process in which a writer is compelled to counterfeit his true feelings is exactly the opposite of that in which the man of society is compelled to counterfeit his. The artist disguises in order to reveal; the man of society disguises in order to conceal.

Another result of Shunsuké's reticence was the attack on his lack of intellectuality by the people who sought to bring about the unity of the arts and the social sciences. It stood to reason that he would have no part of the silly display of philosophy in the epilogue of a work, much like a burlesque girl pulling up her skirt and exposing her thighs. Just the same, there was something in the thinking of Shunsuké, in his attitude towards art and life, that persistently invited sterility.

What we call thought is not born before the fact but after the fact. It enters as the defence attorney of an action born of accident and impulse. As defence attorney it gives meaning and theory to that action; necessity is substituted for chance, will for impulse. Thinking cannot heal the wounds of a blind man who has walked into a lamp-post, but it can show that the lamp-post and not the blindness was at fault. To one action after another theory after the fact is applied until theory becomes the system. The agent of actions becomes nothing more than the probabilities within all actions. That's what threw the scrap of paper in the street. It thought and threw the scrap of paper in the street. In this way he who possesses the power of thinking, seeking to extend that power beyond all limits, becomes himself the prisoner of thought.

Shunsuké drew a sharp line between thought and foolishness. As a result of this he blamed his foolishness without extenuation. The ghost of his foolishness, rigidly excluded from his works, nightly stalked his rest. Surely his three disastrous marriages might be glimpsed once or more in his works. In his youth that fellow Shunsuké's life had been a succession of debacles, a chain of miscalculations and failures.

He knew nothing of hatreds? A lie. Nothing of jealousy? A lie.

In contrast to the serene resignation that floated within his works, the life of Shunsuké was filled with hatred, with jealousy. After the breakdown of his third marriage, after the clumsy resolutions of ten or so love affairs – the fact that this old artist, beset by an ineradicable detestation of womankind, had never once decked out his works with the blossom of that detestation was an achievement of immeasurable self-restraint, of immeasurable arrogance.

The women who entered the pages of his numerous books appeared to women as well as men among his readers as annoyingly pure. One curious scholar of comparative literature placed his heroines alongside the ethereal heroines of Edgar Allan Poe, namely, Ligeia, Berenice, Morella, and the Marquesa Aphrodite – more marble than flesh. Their easily wearying passions were like the transient light of the afternoon sun reflecting here and there off carved features. Shunsuké was afraid to endow his heroines with deep feeling.

One good-humoured critic pointed to Shunsuké and said that his position of eternal feminist was absolutely charming.

His first wife had been a thief. In their two years of married life she cleverly stole and sold a winter overcoat, three pairs of shoes, material for two spring suits, and a Zeiss camera – just on a whim. When she went out, her neckband and her sash were studded with jewels. Shunsuké was, after all, a rich man.

His second wife had been mad. Obsessed by the notion that her husband would kill her in her sleep, she grew so weak from lack of rest that she became hysterical. One day Shunsuké returned home and was greeted by a strange odour. His wife stood at the door, barring the way, refusing to allow her husband to enter.

'Let me in,' he said. 'What's that strange smell?'

'No, you can't come in,' she said. 'I'm doing something very exciting.'

'What?'

'You're always leaving me and going off somewhere, so I snatched the kimono off the back of your mistress, and I'm burning it. My, it feels good!'

He pushed his way in, and saw pieces of charcoal smouldering all over the Persian rug. His wife walked back to the stove and, daintily holding back her long sleeve, in perfect composure, scooped out the burning charcoal and sprinkled it on the rug. In dismay, Shunsuké restrained her. With terrible strength, his wife struggled to free herself. Like a captive bird beating its wings to the full extent of its power, she resisted. Her whole body, sinew and flesh, had gone rigid.

His third wife had been with him until her death. This woman of great sexual need gave Shunsuké a taste of every variety of husbandly agony. He clearly remembered the first morning of that agony.

Shunsuké's work always had to wait until after the act, but its pace had picked up enormously. About nine o'clock at night he and his wife would go to bed. After a while he would leave her and go up to his study on the second floor, work there until three or four in the morning, and then go to sleep again on the little bed in the study. He kept to this routine rigidly. From the previous night until about ten in the morning he never saw his wife.

Late one summer night he felt a strange impulse to shock his wife out of her slumber. His strong desire to go on with his work, however, led him to resist the impulse and the mischief it entailed. Until five o'clock that morning, in fact, as if to punish himself, he worked without let-up.

He had lost all desire to sleep. Surely his wife was still sleeping ... Noiselessly he crept down the stairs. The bedroom door was open. His wife was nowhere to be seen.

In that instant Shunsuké was struck with the feeling that

this was what usually went on. That must be why I've been keeping myself to this schedule, he thought to himself. 'I must have known it; I must have feared it.'

He soon got himself under control. His wife must have thrown her black velvet robe over her nightgown, as usual, and gone to the bathroom. He waited. She didn't return.

Shunsuké walked uneasily down the hall towards the downstairs lavatory. Under the kitchen window, at the kitchen table, the black-robed form of his wife quietly rested, propped forward on its arms. It was not yet dawn. He could not tell whether the dim figure was sitting or kneeling. Shunsuké hid behind the thick damask curtains that led to the hall.

As he did so he heard the sequel of the wooden gate twenty-five or thirty feet from the kitchen door. He heard a low, musical whistle. It was time for the milk delivery.

From the yards near by the dogs barked, one after another. The milkman wore sneakers. Over the stone walk wet with the night's rain he bounded joyously, his body flushed from labour, his bare arms extending from his blue polo shirt and brushing the wet leaves of the eight-finger shrubs, the cold wet stones passing behind him. The clear note of his whistle bespoke the freshness of his young lips in the morning.

She stood up and opened the kitchen door. In the grey night a black human shape could be seen. His teeth, white as he smiled, and his blue polo shirt showed faintly. The morning wind came in and shook the tassels of the curtain.

'Thank you,' said Shunsuké's wife.

She took two bottles of milk. The sound of the bottles clinking together and the silvery clink of her ring against the glass reverberated softly.

'You'll give me something for it, ma'am, won't you?' the young man said, insolently bantering.

'Not today,' she said.

'How about tomorrow noon?'

'No, that's out, too.'

'But only once in ten days! Have you found somebody else?'

'Don't talk so loud!'

'Day after tomorrow?'

'Day after tomorrow . . .?'

Shunsuké's wife pronounced that 'Day after tomorrow' as if she were coyly placing a piece of fragile china back on the shelf. 'In the evening, though, my husband is going to a meeting. It will be okay to come then.'

'Five o'clock?'

'Five o'clock.'

His wife opened the door, which had been shut. The young man made no move to leave. He struck the doorpost two or three times, softly.

'How about now?'

'What are you saying? My lord and master is upstairs. I hate people who don't have any sense.'

'Okay. Just a kiss.'

'Not here. If somebody sees us we've had it.'

'Just a kiss.'

'You're a nuisance. Just a kiss.'

The young man closed the door behind him and stood in the entranceway to the kitchen. She stepped down to him in her rabbit-fur bedroom slippers.

The two of them stood together, like a rose beside a pole. A wavelike undulation passed from time to time from her back to her hips down her black velvet gown. His hand groped out and loosened her belt. Shunsuké's wife shook her head, resisting. They scuffled silently. Until this moment her back had been towards Shunsuké. Now it was the man's back. Her open gown was towards him. She had nothing on underneath. The young man knelt down in the narrow entryway.

Shunsuké had never seen anything so white as the naked body of his wife standing there in the grey dawn. It was not standing, that white embodiment; it was floating. Like the hand of a blind man, her hand moved, feeling for the hair of the kneeling young man.

What could the eyes of his wife be looking at now, first gleaming, then clouding, then opening wide, then staring half-closed? At the enamelled pans on the shelves? At the cupboard doors? At the view of the trees in the dawn through the window? At the glint of the sun bouncing off the doorpost? The intimate silence of that kitchen, like that of a sleeping barracks before the activity of the day, could surely conceive nothing within the eyes of his wife. Yet something was clear in those eyes, and it was somewhere in this curtain. And as if they were conscious of it, they never once met the eyes of Shunsuké.

They are eyes that have been instructed from childhood never to look at one's husband – Shunsuké shuddered as this thought came over him. At the same time the wish to propel himself suddenly out there vanished. He was unable to utter a word and, what was more, knew no way to get revenge.

After a time the young man slid open the door and departed. The garden was turning white. Silently Shunsuké retreated to the second floor.

This writer, gentleman beyond measure, had only one way of getting rid of the resentments his life brought him. It was his French diary, in which on certain days he would write pages. (He had never been abroad, but he had mastered French. Three works of Huysmans – *La Cathédrale, Là-bas,* and *En Route!* – as well as Rodenbach's *Bruges-la-morte* he had transmuted into splendid Japanese just to get his hand going.) Were this journal made public after his death, there would probably be much discussion as to whether it were more valuable than his works *per se*. All the important elements that his works were deficient in flourished in the pages of this diary, but transferring them verbatim into those works ran counter to the wishes of Shunsuké, who hated the naked truth. He held firmly to the belief that any part of one's talent, be it what it may, which revealed itself spontaneously was a fraud. Not only that, at the root of the lack of objectivity in his works lay his creative attitude, his excessively stubborn adherence to subjectivity. He hated the naked truth to excess and made his works sculptures of the raw flesh of its naked body.

As soon as he got back to his study he plunged into his diary, into the painful description of that assignation in the dawn. It was written in the wildest hand, almost as if he intended that he himself would not be able to read it when he came back to it a second time. As with the diaries of decades past piled on his shelf, the pages of this diary too were filled with curses directed against women. If the curses had no effect, it was in the last analysis because the one doing the cursing was not a woman but a man.

It is easier to quote fragments, such as the following one, from this memorandum filled more with jottings and aphorisms than entries in diary form. Here is the record of one day of his youth:

Women can bring nothing into the world but children. Men can father all kinds of things besides children. Creation, reproduction, and propagation are all male capabilities. Feminine pregnancy is but a part of child rearing. This is an old truth. [Incidentally Shunsuké had no children. It was half a matter of principle.]

Woman's jealousy is simple jealousy of creativity. A woman who bears a son and brings him up tastes the honeyed joy of revenge against creativity. When she stands in the way of creation she feels she has something to live for. The craving for luxury and spending is a destructive craving. Everywhere you look, feminine instincts win out. Originally capitalism was a male theory, a reproductive theory. Then feminine thinking ate away at it. Capitalism changed into a theory of extravagance. Thanks to this Helen, war finally came into being. In the far distant future, communism too will be destroyed by woman.

Woman survives everywhere and rules like the night. Her nature is on the highest pinnacle of baseness. She drags all values down into the slough of sentiment. She is entirely incapable of comprehending doctrine: '—istic', she can understand; '—ism', she cannot fathom. Lacking in originality she can't even comprehend the atmosphere. All she can figure out is the smell. She smells as a pig does. Perfume is a masculine invention designed to improve woman's sense of smell. Thanks to it, man escapes being sniffed out by woman.

Woman's sexual charm, her coquettish instincts, all the powers of her sexual attraction, prove that woman is a useless creature. Something useful would have no need of coquetries. What a waste it is that man insists on being attracted by woman! What disgrace it brings down upon man's spiritual powers! Woman has no soul; she can only feel. What is called majestic feeling is the most laughable of paradoxes, a self-made tapeworm. The majesty of motherhood that once in a while develops and shocks people has in truth no relation to spirit. It is no more than a physiological phenomenon, essentially no different from the self-sacrificing mother love seen in animals. In short, spirit must be viewed as the special characteristic that differentiates man from the animals. It is the only essential difference.

Essential difference (it might be better to call it the peculiarly human capability of fictional creation) ... it might be discovered upon the features in the picture of the twenty-five-year-old Shunsuké that was inserted in the diary. They were ugly features, yet there was in their aspect a certain man-made ugliness, the ugliness of a man who strove day by day to believe himself ugly.

In that year's diary, carefully written in French, might be found various random, outrageous doodles. There were two or three rude sketches of the vagina, roughly scratched over with a cancelling X. He was cursing the vagina.

Shunsuké did not marry a thief and a madwoman because no other brides were available. There were enough 'spiritual women' who could find this promising young man interesting. But the creature that was the 'spiritual woman' was a monster and not really a woman. The only women who could be unfaithful to Shunsuké were the ones who refused to understand his lone strong point, his one beautiful feature, his soul. These indeed were the original, the true, the genuine women. Shunsuké could only love these beautiful Messalinas, sure of their beauty, who did not require spirit to round out their charms.

The lovely face of his third wife, three years dead, floated into Shunsuké's mind. At fifty, she and her lover not half her age had committed suicide. Shunsuké knew why she had taken her life. She feared the prospect of an ugly old age spent in his company.

Their dead bodies were thrown up together on Inubo Point, deposited by the waves high on the rocks. It was no easy task to get them off. Fishermen fastened ropes to them and passed them from rock to rock in the white spume thrown up by the booming surf.

Nor was it easy to separate their corpses. They had melted together like wet tissue paper, their skin seemingly shared in common. The remains of Shunsuké's wife, forcibly pried loose, were sent to Tokyo for cremation, according to her husband's wishes.

It was a magnificent funeral; the ceremony was over, and

18

the time had come to start the procession. The aged husband took his leave of the deceased, who had been carried into another room. No one else entered, as he instructed. Above her tremendously swollen face, buried with lilies and pinks, the roots of her hair seemed to glisten in blue striations out of a semitransparent hairline. Without apprehension Shunsuké stared at this ugliest of all faces. Then he sensed the malice in that face. It could cause her husband no more pain; her face no longer had to be beautiful. Was not this the reason it was ugly?

He took his treasured Nō mask representing young womanhood and placed it over her face. Harder and harder he pressed against it, so that the face of the drowned woman buckled under the mask like so much ripe fruit. (No one would know what Shunsuké had done; in an hour or so all traces of it would be consumed in flame.)

In pain and indignation, Shunsuké went through the period of mourning. When he recalled that dawning day that marked the beginning of his pain, his response was so fresh that he found it hard to believe his wife was not still alive. He had had more rivals than he had fingers, and their youthful arrogance. their hateful good looks. . . .

Shunsuké had taken a stick to one of them, and his wife had threatened to leave him. So he apologized to his wife and bought the boy a suit of clothes. Later the fellow was killed fighting in North China. Drunk with joy, Shunsuké wrote a long passage in his diary; then, like one possessed, he went for a walk down the street.

It was jammed with soldiers departing for the front, with all their well-wishers. He joined a crowd of people round a soldier saying good-bye to a lovely girl, obviously his fiancée. Somehow Shunsuké found himself joyfully waving a paper flag. A cameraman happened to be passing at the moment and caught him, so Shunsuké's picture appeared prominently in the newspapers, waving the flag. Who could have known? Here was this eccentric author waving a flag, sending off a soldier to die on the battlefield – the very battlefield on which had recently died the detested young soldier whose death he was really celebrating!

*

19

These were the thoughts passing through the mind of Shunsuké Hinoki during the hour-and-a-half bus trip that was the last leg of his journey to the shore where Yasuko was.

Then the war ended, he thought. She committed suicide the second year afterwards. The newspapers were polite; they called it a heart attack. Only a small number of my friends knew the real facts.

After my mourning period was over, I fell in love with the wife of a former count. My life of ten-plus love affairs was fulfilled, it seemed, with this love. At a critical moment, her husband appeared demanding 300,000 yen. The former count had a sideline, with his wife as a partner: blackmail.

The memory made him laugh. The blackmail episode was funny, though the humour made him uneasy.

I wonder whether I am still capable of hating women as fiercely as when I was young.

He thought of Yasuko, this nineteen-year-old girl who had come to see him several times since they met in Hakoné in May. The old writer's breast heaved.

In the middle of May, when Shunsuké was working at Nakagora, a girl staying in the same hotel asked, through the maid, for his autograph. He met the girl eventually near the garden. She was on the way to meet him, one of his works under her arm. It was a lovely evening; he had been out for a walk and met her on the way back, as he climbed the stone steps.

'Is it you?' Shunsuké asked.

'Yes. My last name is Segawa,' she said. 'How do you do?'

She was wearing a pink dress, the kind a child would wear. Her arms and legs were long and graceful, perhaps too long. The skin of her thighs was tight, like that of a fresh-water fish. It was white skin, with gamboge depths, gleaming out from under the hem of her short skirt. Shunsuké guessed she was seventeen or eighteen. From the expression around her eyes, though, one would guess her to be twenty or twenty-one. She was wearing *geta*, revealing her trim heels – small, modest, firm, birdlike.

'Where is your room?'

'Way back there.'

'That's why I haven't seen you. Are you alone?'

'Yes – today, that is.'

She was convalescing from a bout with pneumonia. It pleased Shunsuké that she was a girl who was only able to read novels 'for the story'. Her companion, an elderly woman, had gone back to Tokyo for a day or two on business. He could have gone back to his room with Yasuko, autographed her book, and returned it to her at once, but he wanted to arrange to meet for the book the following day, so they sat down on one of the ugly benches by the garden. There they talked about this and that – there really was no topic that could speed intimacy between this shy old man and this proper young woman. 'When did you come?' 'What's your family like?' 'Do you feel better now?' Things like that Shunsuké asked, and she answered with a quiet smile.

Thus it was surprising how soon the garden seemed to become wrapped in twilight. In front of them, the soft shapes of Myolo Peak and Tateyama to the right of it grew darker and quietly sidled their way into the thoughts of those watching them. Between the two mountains sank the Odawara Sea. The flashing of the lighthouse glimmered like the evening star somewhere in the area where the twilight sky and the narrow seascape dimly merged. The maid came to announce dinner, and they parted.

The next day, Yasuko and her elderly companion came to Shunsuké's room, bringing with them some sweets from Tokyo. He brought out the two volumes, which had already been signed. The old woman did all the talking, affording Yasuko and Shunsuké the luxury of silence. After Yasuko and the woman left, Shunsuké took it into his head to take a long walk. He panted as he scrambled irritably up the hill.

'It doesn't matter how far; I can do it. I'm still not tired. See how I can walk,' he told himself.

Finally he came to a grassy spot shaded by a tree. There he stretched out, as if unconscious. Suddenly a huge pheasant launched out of a bush at one side. Shunsuké started. Then he felt his heart leaping with a restless joy born of over-exertion.

It's been a long time since I had this feeling. How many years? Shunsuké thought to himself.

He chose to forget that 'this feeling' was for the most part of his own making, that in order to create 'this feeling' he had designedly taken this unusually vigorous hike. Surely such forgetfulness, such wilfulness, could be attributed to his advanced age.

*

The bus route from the nearest railroad station to the town where Yasuko was staying passed close to the sea at several points. From the top of the cliffs one got a bird's-eye view of the flashing summer sea. A transparent and therefore barely visible incandescent glow lit up the surface of the sea.

It was still long before noon. The two or three passengers in the bus were local people, but they spread out side dishes wrapped in bamboo sheaths and started eating their balled rice. Shunsuké barely knew what it was like to be conscious that his stomach was empty. When he was thinking, he would eat and then forget he had eaten, then wonder why his stomach was full. His viscera as well as his mind were oblivious to the vicissitudes of daily life.

The K— Park stop was two stations away from the terminal point, K— Town Hall. Nobody got off there. The bus route sliced through the centre of this great park, which covered about a thousand hectares between the mountains and the sea. One side had the mountains as its focal point; the other side had the sea. Through the thick shrubbery, noisy in the wind, Shunsuké caught glimpses of the deserted, silent playground, and of the sea, its blue enamel expanse broken here and there in the distance, and of sundry park swings that threw motionless shadows on the shining sand. For no reason that he could fathom, that great park, silent in the midsummer morning, intrigued him.

The bus stopped at a corner of the jumbled little town. Around the town hall there were no signs of life. Through the open windows the white tops of the desks, on which nothing was piled threw out gleams of light. The welcoming party from the hotel bowed.

Shunsuké gave them his baggage and slowly climbed the stone staircase they had pointed out beside the shrine. Thanks to the wind off the sea, the heat was barely noticeable. The voices of the cicadas came down from overhead languidly – warm sounds wrapped in wool. Halfway up the stairs, Shunsuké took off his hat and rested a while. Below him in the little harbour a little green steamer rested; it let off steam noisily, as if prompted. Then it stopped. As it did so, the all-too-simple curve of the still harbour seemed all at once filled with a doleful sound as of countless wings, like the buzzing of a persistent fly; no matter how often one chases it, it will not be driven off.

'What a fine view!'

Shunsuké said that as if to get the idea out of his mind. It was certainly not a fine view.

'The view from the hotel is better, sir.'

'Is that so?'

The old author's dignity stemmed from the fact that he was too lazy to take the trouble to indulge in teasing and ridicule. It wearied him to break his composure even for a moment.

They had given him the finest room in the hotel, where he asked the maid the questions he had prepared on the way and found so difficult to phrase with requisite casualness. (To make matters worse, he feared he had lost all casualness.)

'Has a young lady named Segawa checked in?'

'Yes. She's here.'

His heart was pounding, so he pronounced the next question slowly.

'Does she have someone with her?'

'Yes; they arrived four or five days ago. In the Chrysanthemum Room.'

'Maybe she's here now? I'm a friend of her father's.'

'She just went to K— Park.'

'Did she go alone?'

'No, she is not alone.'

The maid did not say, 'They went with her.' Under the circumstances, Shunsuké was filled with dismay. He did not know how to ask with proper indifference how many friends there were and whether male or female.

If her friends were male, what if there was only one of them? Wasn't it strange that this very natural question had never even entered his head until now? Foolishness preserves its own undeviating equilibrium, does it not? Until it gets its way it advances, suppressing every proper intelligent consideration.

He felt his attendance was more commanded than invited as he was subjected to a lavish welcome by the hotel. Throughout his bath and his meal, until the business was over, he was given no rest. When he was finally left alone he was overcome by excitement and moved about restlessly. His anxiety impelled him to do something a gentleman should not do. He quietly entered the Chrysanthemum Room.

The suite was in perfect order. He opened the Western-style clothes closet in the smaller room and saw a man's white trousers and white poplin shirts. They were hanging next to Yasuko's Tyrolean appliqué white linen one-piece suit. He turned his eyes to the dressing table and saw pomade and a stick of hair wax beside the powder, cream, and lipstick.

He left the room, returned to his own, and rang the bell. When the maid came he ordered a car. While he was putting on his suit, the car arrived. He was driven to K— Park.

He told the driver to wait, and entered the gate of the park, which was deserted, as usual. It had a new, natural-stone arch. From it, one could not see the sea. In the wind, the heavy branches of the trees, covered with blackish green leaves, soughed like the distant surf.

Shunsuké decided to go to the beach. There, he had been told, they swam every day. He left the playground. He passed the corner of the little zoo, in which a badger was huddled, dozing, the shadow of the cage sharp upon his back. In its grazing area, at the point where two kaede trees grew close together, a long black rabbit slept quietly, beyond the heat. Shunsuké descended a stone staircase covered thickly with grass and saw, on the other side of a vast patch of shrubbery, the expanse of the ocean. As far as his eyes could see, there was only the movement of branches. The wind slowly made its way towards him. It twisted nimbly from branch to branch, seeming to approach like an invisible small animal. The roughest blasts of wind that came at times were like the frolicking of an invisible large animal. Over all this the unfailing sunlight reigned; the unfailing buzz of the cicada prevailed.

What path should he take down to the beach? Far below, he could see a grove of pines. The grass-covered staircase seemed to lead down there by a roundabout route. He was bathed in the sun that forced its way through the trees, dazzled by the fierce glare off the grass, and he came to realize that his body was covered with perspiration. The staircase curved. He struggled his way on to the edge of a narrow corridor of beach at the foot of the cliff.

There was nobody there. Exhausted, the ageing writer seated himself on a boulder.

Anger it was that had brought him this far. Living as he did encompassed by his great reputation, the religious veneration in which he was held, his multifarious business affairs, his miscellaneous friendships, and all the related unendingly venomous essentials, he generally required no escape from life. The most extreme escape for him would be to come closer to it. Within the amazingly broad sphere of his acquaintanceship, Shunsuké Hinoki performed like a great actor, through whose skill thousands of spectators were made to feel that he was close to each of them alone. An adroit skill it was, seemingly in disregard of all the laws of perspective. Neither their praise nor their criticism touched him. That was because he was deaf to everything. He was trembling now in anticipation of being hurt, fiercely desired to be hurt; only in this sense did Shunsuké in his own inimitable way seek an escape. In short, he sought consummation in a climactic reception unto himself of clear, unequivocal injury.

Now, however, the unusually close, undulating broad sea seemed to soothe Shunsuké. As it craftily and nimbly came in between the rocks again and again, the sea soaked him, it flowed into his being, it instantly painted him with its blueness. Then it fell away from him again.

Then a ripple appeared out in the middle of the ocean. A delicate, white splashing like an advancing wave developed. The ripple advanced rapidly in the direction of this part of the shore. As it reached the shallows and seemed about to break, suddenly in the middle of the wave a swimmer stood out. Quickly his body seemed to erase the wave. Then he stood up. His sturdy legs kicked the ocean shallows as he walked forward.

It was an amazingly beautiful young man. His body surpassed the sculptures of ancient Greece. It was like the Apollo moulded in bronze by an artist of the Peloponnesus school. It overflowed with gentle beauty and carried such a noble column of a neck, such gently sloping shoulders, such a softly broad chest, such elegantly rounded wrists, such a rapidly tapering tightly filled trunk, such legs, stoutly filled out like a heroic sword. The youth stopped at the water's edge and twisted his body to inspect his left elbow, which seemed to have struck against the corner of a rock. As he did so, he bent his face and his right arm in the direction of the injury. The reflections on the waves, retreating past his feet, lit up his downturned profile as if an expression of joy had suddenly stolen across it. Quick, narrow eyebrows; deep, sad eyes; rather thick, fresh lips – these made up the design of his extraordinary profile. The wonderful ridge of his nose, furthermore, along with his controlled facial expression, gave to his youthful good looks a certain chaste impression of wildness, as if he had never known anything but noble thoughts and starvation. This, together with the dark, controlled cast of his eyes, his strong white teeth, the languid way in which he unconsciously moved his wrists, the bearing of his quick body, brought out in full relief the inner nature of a young, beautiful wolf. 'That's it! Those looks are the beautiful features of the wolf!'

At the same time there was in the soft roundness of the shoulders, the innocent nudity of the chest, the charm of the lips ... in these bodily features there was a mysteriously indefinable sweetness. Walter Pater mentioned, in connection with the lovely thirteenth-century story 'Amis and Amile', a certain 'sweetness of the early Renaissance'. Shunsuké saw signs of a later and unimaginably mysterious and vast development of that 'early sweetness' in the lines of the body of the youth before him.

Shunsuké Hinoki hated all the beautiful young men of the world. Yet beauty struck him dumb whether he liked it or not.

Mostly, he had the bad habit of immediately connecting beauty with happiness; yet what silenced his resentment here was perhaps not the perfect beauty of the youth, but what he surmised to be his complete happiness.

The youth glanced in Shunsuké's direction. Then he unconcernedly stepped out of sight behind a rock. After a time he appeared again, in white shirt and conservative blue-serge trousers. Whistling, he started up the same stone steps Shunsuké had just descended. Shunsuké got up and followed him. The young man turned once again and glanced at the old man. Perhaps it was the effect of the summer sun shining across his eyelashes, but his eyes were quite dark. Shunsuké wondered why the youth, who had shone so resplendently earlier in his nakedness, had now lost his air of happiness, if nothing more.

The youth took another path. It was going to be difficult to keep up with him. The exhausted old man started down the path doubting he had the energy to trace the young man's steps much farther. Then, however, somewhere in the vicinity of a grassy clearing within the wood, he heard the clear, vigorous sound of the young man's voice.

'Are you still sleeping? You amaze me. While you were sleeping, I swam way out into the ocean. Come on, get up and let's stroll back.'

A girl stood up there under the trees. Shunsuké was shocked at how close she seemed to be as she stretched her slim arms above her head. Two or three of the buttons in the back of her blue, girlish Western dress had come undone. For the first time he was able to see the youth as he fastened the errant buttons. The girl brushed from her skirt the pollen and soil she had collected during that quite indecorous nap on the grass. As she turned her hand to brush herself off, she showed her profile. It was Yasuko!

Spent, Shunsuké slumped on the stairs. He took out a cigarette and lit it. It was not an uncommon thing for this expert in the art of jealousy to be filled with a mixture of admiration, jealousy, and defeat, but this time Shunsuké's heart was involved not with Yasuko but with that youth whose beauty was such a rarity in this world.

In that perfect youth were concentrated all the dreams of the ugly writer's young days – dreams he had hidden from the eyes of men. Not only that, he rebuked himself for them. The spring-time of intellect, the time when it begins to grow – that was the poison, he felt, that caused the young man to lose his youth even as he watched. Shunsuké's youth was spent in the frenzied pursuit of youthfulness. What foolishness, indeed!

Youth tortures us with all kinds of hopes and despairs, but at least we do not realize that our pains are the normal agonies of youth. Shunsuké, however, spent his whole youth realizing it. He rigidly excluded from his thinking, from his consciousness, from his theorizing on 'Literature and Youth', everything connected with permanence, universality, common interest, everything unhappily subtle – in short, romantically immortal. To some extent, his foolishness lay in facetiously impulsive experimentation. At that time his one fond hope was that he would be so fortunate as to be able to see in his own pain the perfect, consummate pain of youth. Not only that, he wished to see in his own joy the consummate joy. In sum, he saw in it a power indispensable to humankind.

This time, being defeated won't bother me a bit, he thought to himself. He is the possessor of all the beauty of youth; he dwells in the sunshine of human existence. Never will he be polluted by the poisons of art or things of that sort. He is a man born to love and be loved by woman. For him, I shall gladly retire from the field. Not only that, I welcome it. So much of my life has been spent fighting against beauty; but the time is approaching that beauty and I should shake hands in reconciliation. For all I can tell, Heaven has sent these two people for me to see.

The two lovers approached single file down the narrow path. Yasuko was the first to see Shunsuké. She and the old man confronted each other. His eyes showed pain, but his mouth was smiling. Yasuko grew white and dropped her glance. Still looking at the ground, she asked, 'Have you come here to work?'

'Yes. I just got here.'

The youth looked at Shunsuké inquiringly. Yasuko introduced them – 'This is my friend Yuichi.'

28

'Minami,' he said, supplying his surname.

When he heard Shunsuké's name, the youth did not seem at all surprised. Shunsuké thought to himself: He's probably heard about me from Yasuko. That's why he is not surprised. I would be delighted if he had never so much as looked at my complete works in three editions and had never heard my name.

The three climbed the stone park staircase in the dead calm, chatting idly about how deserted the resort seemed. Shunsuké felt expansive. He wasn't one easily given to joking like a man of the world, but he was cheerful enough. The three got into his hired car and went back to the hotel.

They ate supper *à trois*. It was Yuichi's idea. After the meal they separated and went to their rooms. Later, Yuichi, tall in his hotel robe, appeared at the door of Shunsuké's room.

'May I come in? Are you working?' he called through the door.

'Come in.'

'Yasuko was taking a long time in the bath and I got bored,' he said, by way of excuse. His dark eyes, however, had grown more sad since the daytime. Shunsuké's artistic instincts told him that some kind of confession was forthcoming.

For a time they talked about insignificant matters. Then it became apparent that the youth was impatient to get something off his mind. At last he said: 'Are you going to stay here for a while?'

'I expect so.'

'I, if I can, would like to leave by the ten o'clock boat this evening, or by tomorrow morning's bus. In fact, I want to get away from her tonight sometime.'

Surprised, Shunsuké asked, 'What about Yasuko?'

'That's what I've come to talk to you about. Can I leave her with you? I've thought perhaps you would like to marry her.'

'I hope you are not being held back by something that is not true.'

'Not at all. I can't stay here another night.'

'Why?'

The youth answered in sincere, rather frozen tones: 'Do

you understand? I can't love a woman. Do you know what I mean? My body can love them, but my interest in them is purely intellectual. I have never wanted a woman since the day I was born. I have never seen a woman and wanted her. Just the same I have deluded myself about it, and now I have deceived an innocent girl in the bargain.'

A strange light came into Shunsuké's eyes. By nature he was not sensitive to this problem. His inclinations were quite normal.

He replied, 'Then what can you love?'

'I?' The youth's face reddened. 'I only love boys.'

'Have you told Yasuko about this?' Shunsuké asked.

'No.'

'Then don't tell her. It won't work. There are some things that are good to tell a woman, and some things not. I don't know much about your particular problem, but it seems to be something women wouldn't understand. When a girl appears who loves you as much as Yasuko seems to, it would seem best to marry her, since you have to get married sometime. Don't take marriage as being anything more than a triviality. It's trivial – that's why they call it sacred.'

Shunsuké began to take a fiendish delight in the encounter. Then he caught the young man's gaze and, out of deference to the world, decorously whispered: 'And these three nights ... didn't anything happen?'

'No.'

'That's fine. That's how women should be taught.' Shunsuké's laugh was loud and clear. None of his friends had ever heard him laugh like this.

'I can tell you from long experience that it never pays to teach a woman pleasure. Pleasure is a tragic masculine invention. Don't take it as anything more than that.'

An ecstatic, parental affection floated in Shunsuké's eyes. 'You two will have an ideal married life, I am sure.' He didn't say 'happy'. As far as Shunsuké was concerned it was splendid that this marriage seemed to hold in store such complete unhappiness for the woman. With Yuichi's help he felt he could send a hundred still-virgin women off to nunneries. In this way Shunsuké for the first time in his life knew real passion.

2

Mirror Contract

'I can't,' Yuichi said, hopelessly. What man content with the advice he had been given would make so shamefaced a confession to a perfect stranger? The suggestion that he get married was pure cruelty, the young man felt.

Now that he had told all, he felt a certain sense of regret; the mad impulse to confess had vanished. The pain of those three nights during which nothing happened had almost torn him to pieces.

Yasuko would never make the first advances. If she had he would have told her everything. Yet there in the darkness filled with the sound of waves, inside the pale green mosquito netting shaken from time to time by the wind, the recumbent form of the girl at his side staring at the ceiling, holding back the sound of her breathing, was enough to cut his heart to pieces in a way he had never known.

The window thrown open, the starlit sky, the shrill whistle of the steamboat ... for a long time Yasuko and Yuichi lay awake, not daring to stir. They did not speak. They did not move. It was as if they feared that a movement of so much as an inch would provoke an entirely new situation. To tell the truth, they were both wearied with waiting for the same action, the same situation – in short, the same thing; but Yuichi's embarrassment was perhaps a hundred times more fierce than the shyness under which Yasuko quivered. He asked only to die.

Her coal-black eyes wide open, hand to her breast, her body motionless and faintly perspiring, the horizontal figure of the girl beside him was death to Yuichi. If she moved one inch in his direction, that itself would be death. He hated himself for having been ignominiously enticed to this point by Yasuko.

Now I can die, he thought to himself over and over. Soon,

I'll get up, rush down the stone staircase, and throw myself off the cliff overlooking the sea.

When he thought of death, in that instant everything seemed possible. He was drunk with possibility, filled with cheer. He pretended a yawn and said aloud, 'My, I'm sleepy.' He turned his back to Yasuko, curled up, and feigned sleep. After a time, he heard Yasuko emit a slight, delicate cough and knew she was not asleep.

Then he got up courage to inquire, 'Can't you sleep?'

'Yes, I can,' she answered, with a low voice like the sound of flowing water. With that, the two set about feigning sleep, hoping to fool one another; doing so, they fooled themselves into falling asleep. He dreamed that God had turned over to the angels his plea that he be killed. It was such a happy dream that he burst out crying. Of course, the tears and sobs were not real. Then Yuichi realized that he was still ruled by vanity and he felt better.

For the eight years or so since puberty Yuichi had set himself against sexual desire, which he detested. He kept his body pure. He involved himself in mathematics and sports – geometry and calculus, high jumping and swimming. He did not realize particularly that this option of his was a Greek option; mathematics somehow kept his head clear, and athletic competition kept his energies in tune.

Nevertheless, once when he was in the locker room and a lowerclassman came in and took off his sweaty shirt, the odour of young body distressed him. He ran outside and threw himself down on the darkening field and pressed his face into the firm summer grass. There he waited for desire to pass. The dry sound of bat on ball where baseball practice was still going on echoed off the colourless evening sky and came to him from the ground. Yuichi felt something strike his bare shoulder. It was a towel. The white, rough, thorny threads bit into his flesh.

'What are you doing? You'll catch cold.'

Yuichi lifted his head. It was the same lowerclassman, now in his school clothes, standing there smiling out from under the visor of his cap.

Yuichi stood up, snapping out a 'Thank you.' With the

towel flung over his shoulder, he returned to the locker room, conscious of the eyes of the lowerclassman following him. He did not, however, turn around. He had recognized that the boy loved him; consequently, by all the logic of purity, he had decided that he could not love the boy.

If I, who, though I cannot love women wish only to love women, loved the boy – after all a man – would he not become transformed into some unspeakably ugly, woman-like creature? Love brings about all kinds of unwished for changes in the one who is loved, does it not?

In these confessions of Yuichi a desire that was not yet real came out of his phrases to nibble away at what was real. Would he and reality some day meet? In the place where he and reality might come together, not only would these harbingers of his desire already in existence eat away at reality, reality itself would eternally bring forth fictional forms dictated by his desire. He would never find what he wanted. Everywhere he went he would meet only his desire. Even in this abortive confession of those three nights of pain. Shunsuké could, as it were, hear the gears of this youth's desire turning.

Was not this, however, the epitome of art, the very model of the reality of artistic creation? In order for Yuichi's desire to come into reality, either his desire or his concept of what was real must perish. In this world it is believed art and reality live quietly side by side; but art must dare to break the laws of reality. Why? In order that it alone may exist.

It is a shame, but the *Complete Works of Shunsuké Hinoki*, from their first lines, renounced war against reality. As a result his works were not real. His passions simply brushed against reality and, repelled by its ugliness, shut themselves up in his works. Thus his incessant foolishness moved to and fro between his passions and reality like a dishonest courier. His style, peerlessly ornate in its decorativeness, was, after all, no more than a design for reality; it was no more than a curious, worm-eaten figure of speech in which reality had consumed passion. With all frankness one may say in conclusion that his art, his thrice-published complete works, did not exist. Why? Because not once did they break the laws of reality.

This old writer had already lost all the muscles necessary for creation; he had tired of the labours of careful craftsmanship. Now, left only with the task of interpreting aesthetically his past productions, what an irony it was that a youth like Yuichi should appear before him at this time!

Yuichi had all the gifts of youth the old writer lacked, but at the same time he had that supreme good fortune the artist had always hypothesized as the object of his heart's desire. In short, he had never loved a woman. This prefiguration of a paradoxical ideal: in the life of Shunsuké the desirable qualifications of youth without the awful chain of tragedies caused by love and woman; an existence somehow merged in the mind of Shunsuké with the inescapable conviction that he had been unlucky; an existence in which the blood of the dreams of his youth mixed with the disappointment of his old age. This was Yuichi! If Shunsuké had been like Yuichi in his youth, what joy there would have been in his love of women. And if like Yuichi he had not loved a woman – suppose, better yet, he had come to live without women – what a happy life his would have been! In this way Yuichi became transformed into Shunsuké's idea, his work of art.

All style, it is said, ages beginning with the adjectives. In short, adjectives are flesh. They are youth. Yuichi is an adjective; that's what, Shunsuké went so far as to think.

With a thin smile playing on his lips as if he were a detective in the middle of an investigation, he propped his elbows on the table, raised one knee under his bathrobe, and listened to Yuichi's confession. When it was over he insensitively said again: 'Fine. Get married!'

'But how can someone get married if he doesn't want to?'

'I'm not joking. Men marry logs; they can even marry ice boxes. Marriage is man's own invention. It is something he can do; desire isn't necessary. At least in the past one hundred years, mankind has forgotten how to act with passion. Just make believe she's a bundle of sticks, a cushion, a side of beef hanging from a beam in the butcher shop. You'll surely be able to conjure up a counterfeit passion to excite her and make her happy. Nevertheless, as I told you before, to teach a woman pleasure is to incur a hundred liabilities and not one asset. The

34

only thing to be careful about is never to acknowledge at any time that she has a soul. Even the dregs of a soul are out of the question here.

'All right? Never think of her as anything but inanimate matter. From my long and painful experience, let me tell you, as you take your wrist watch off when you take your bath, get rid of your soul when you come near a woman. If you don't it will soon become so rusty you won't be able to use it. I didn't, and I lost countless watches. I was driven to making the manufacturing of watches my life's work. I've collected twenty rusty watches and have just brought them out under the title *Collected Works*. Have you read them?'

'No, not yet.' The youth's face grew red. 'But what you are saying makes sense, sir. I'm thinking it all over. About why I have never once desired a woman. Whenever I have thought I might be counterfeiting this spiritual love of mine, I have leaned towards believing that spirit itself is counterfeit. Even now it's always on my mind. Why am I not like everybody else? Why do none of my friends separate the flesh and the spirit the way I do?'

'Everybody's the same. People are all the same.' Shunsuké raised his voice: 'But it's the prerogative of youth to think it's not so.'

'Just the same, I'm the only one who's different.'

'All right. I'm catching hold of your conviction and becoming young again,' said the old man slyly.

As far as Yuichi was concerned, he was puzzled by the fact that Shunsuké was interested in, in fact envious of, his secret tendencies, the tendencies that had tortured him with their ugliness. However, Yuichi was exhilarated by a sense of self-betrayal after this first confession of his life, this turning over to another of all his secrets. He felt the jog of one who, driven by a hated master to sell seedlings, happens to meet a customer he likes and betrays his master by selling all the seedlings he has at a bargain price.

Briefly he explained his relationship with Yasuko.

Yuichi's father had been an old friend of Yasuko's father. He had studied engineering, had gone to work as a technician, had become a director, finally the head of a subsidiary of Kikui

Zaibatsu, and had then died. That was in the summer of 1944.

Yusuko's father had graduated from a business course and gone to work for a well-known department store, where he was now an executive. Thanks to an agreement made by the fathers, Yuichi and Yasuko were betrothed at the beginning of this year, when he became twenty-two.

Yuichi's coldness filled Yasuko with yearning. Her periodic visits to Shunsuké's were made at times when she had failed to induce the youth to respond to her advances. Finally, this summer, she got him to go with her on this trip to K—.

Yasuko suspected he was interested in someone else and suffered as any girl her age might. There was something ominous about such a suspicion harboured against a fiancé, but the fact was Yuichi loved no one else.

He was now commuting to a certain private college. He lived with his mother, invalided with chronic nephritis, and their maidservant in a once-sound household now bankrupt in which his shy filial affection was a source of torment to his parent. Although there were plenty of girls besides his fiancée who, she knew, were attracted to this handsome young man, his mother believed that his failure to commit even one indiscretion was based on financial concern and devotion to her in her illness.

'I never planned to make you into such a pennypincher,' she said candidly. 'If your father were living, how he would grieve about it! From the time your father was in college he ran after women constantly. Thanks to that, when he matured he settled down and with my help lived peacefully.

'You are so sober in your youth that I worry about the plight of Yasuko in her mature years. I never expected that of you, who inherited your father's face, so attractive to women. The only gift your mother wants to see is a grandchild some day soon, and if you don't like Yasuko we'll break that engagement in a hurry and even let you pick out someone you like and bring her home. Providing you don't make a fool of yourself, I don't mind if you play around with ten or twenty girls before you decide.

'The only problem is that your mother doesn't know how

long she'll last with this illness, so let's have a wedding soon, can't we? A man needs to look his best, you know, and if you need some money, we're poor, but at least we eat. I will give you double your allowance this month, but don't spend it on books.'

He had used the money for dance lessons. He had become a good dancer needlessly. Yet his dancing, which was artistic in comparison with the modern utilitarian dance – nothing but calisthenics for the development of lust – took on the loneliness of a smooth machine in operation. His figure, emotions held quietly in check, made observers feel that within his beauty his energies were constantly being crushed to death. He entered a dance contest and took third place.

The third prize was two thousand yen. He decided to deposit it in his mother's bank account. When he looked at the bankbook, however, he discovered that a terrible error must have been made in the computation of the balance, which he had been told by his mother amounted to 700,000 yen.

Since the time when deposits of albumin in her urine had forced her periodically to take to her bed, his mother had turned the responsibilities of the bankbook over to their maid, kind old Kiyo. Whenever his mother asked her for the balance, this faithful spinster would bring out her abacus, deliberately total up the two columns in the book, and announce the result. Somehow, since they had been given a new bankbook, their balance had remained at 700,000 yen no matter how much they withdrew. Yuichi checked further and found that it was now down to 350,000.

Securities were bringing them in about 20,000 yen a month, but they were having a depression, and this income could not be depended on. Living costs, his school expenses, his mother's doctor bills and hospital bills were quickly making it necessary to sell their home.

This discovery, however, oddly enough delighted Yuichi. The marriage he had felt he must go through with no matter what could now be evaded, if it became necessary to move to a house big enough for only three. He decided to take over the management of their finances.

It grieved Yuichi's mother to see her son stick his nose into the household account book as if he enjoyed it; besides, as he said lightly, it was a practical application of his schoolwork in economics. In truth, it appeared to her that his present activity was somehow brought on by her earlier frank discussion with him, and fearing that he was taking her words to mean something she had not wished to suggest, she said to him once, apparently for no good reason, 'It seems to me that there's something abnormal about a student's developing an interest in the household account book.'

Yuichi grimaced fiercely. His mother was content that her words of vexation had roused her son and evoked a reaction, but she did not know which of her words had cut him so. Anger, however, had set Yuichi free from his usual sense of decorum. He felt that the time had come to blast some of the idle romantic fancies his mother cherished on his behalf. They were fancies completely without hope, so far as he could see. Her hopes were an affront to his despair.

'Marriage is out of the question. We have to sell the house,' he told her. Out of consideration for his mother he had hidden from her his discovery about their financial straits.

'You're joking. We still have seven hundred thousand yen in the bank.'

'You're off by three hundred and fifty thousand yen.'

'You must have figured wrong – either that or you've embezzled it.'

Her disease was slowly introducing albumin into her reason. Yuichi's disclosure had the uncalculated effect of propelling her feverishly into fantastic scheming. In expectation of Yasuko's marriage portion and what income Yuichi would get from the job he had been promised in her father's department store, he should get married quickly and at the same time somehow manage matters so that he could hold on to this house. She had long dreamed that her son and his wife would come to live here.

The more the gentle Yuichi thought about this the more he felt trapped into getting married. Then his conscience came to his rescue. Supposing he did marry Yasuko (when he grudgingly went along with this supposition he always exaggerated his misfortune), surely it would become known soon that her marriage portion had saved his home. People would think he married not for love but out of vulgar self-interest. This young man of integrity, who pardoned not the slightest meanness in himself, was willing to marry out of filial piety, but he feared that his action would not be completely pure where love was concerned.

'Let's consider together how we can best realize what you want,' Shunsuké said. 'I maintain that marriage has no meaning. Therefore you can get married without a sense of responsibility, or even soul-searching. For your sick mother's sake, it seems advisable. As for the money, however –'

'Oh, I wasn't talking to you with that in mind.'

'But I heard it this way. The reason you're afraid of a marriage for money is that you have no confidence that you can divert your wife from the conviction that your love for her is sullied by ulterior considerations. You hope things work out so that you can betray this marriage you have entered less than wholeheartedly. In general, young people insist on believing that love can vindicate self-interest. Now, there is something you can depend on in the integrity of a mercenary man like me. Your squeamishness comes from some fuzziness in your own integrity. Take the marriage portion and save it for alimony. That money doesn't obligate you. From what you said before, if you had four or five hundred thousand, you could keep your present house and bring your bride home there. Forgive me for suggesting that you let me handle that matter. Better keep it a secret from your mother, though.'

It happened that there was a black mirror stand opposite Yuichi. The round mirror had been knocked askew by the robe of someone walking past it, but there on its back, as it were, it reflected full in the face of Yuichi. While they talked, Yuichi felt as if his own face stared at him from time to time.

Shunsuké strung his words together impatiently.

'As you know, I am not a rich man who can afford to throw four or five hundred thousand yen to every fellow that passes, as if in drunken spree. I want to give it to you for a very simple reason. In fact, for two reasons –'

He hesitated, as if embarrassed.

'First, you are the most beautiful youth in the world. When I was young, I always wanted to be what you are. Second, you do not love women. I still wish I could be that way, but that's beyond remedy. You have been a revelation to me. Please. Live my youth again in another way. In short, be my son and avenge me. You're an only son and you cannot take my name, but I would like you to become my son in spirit. (Ah! That was a forbidden word!)

'For countless foolish actions – my lost children – mourn for me. For this I will spend any amount of money. I didn't save it up so that I might be happy in my old age, by any stretch of the imagination. In return for it, please don't tell anyone else your secret. When I ask you to make the acquaintance of some woman, do it. If ever there breathes a woman who won't fall in love with you at first sight, I'd like to see her. You can't feel desire for a woman. I will teach you, point by point, how a man who has felt desire behaves. I will teach you the coldness of a man who, while he desires a woman, lets her die yearning for him.

'At any rate, let's proceed according to orders. Will somebody see that you can't love women? Leave it to me. I will use all kinds of tricks to prevent anyone from finding you out. And lest by some mischance you settle down in a peaceful married existence, I wish you would look into the practice of masculine love. In that I shall provide opportunities for you to the very best of my small ability.

'Don't, however, give it away in the world of women. Don't confuse the stage with the dressing-room. I shall introduce you to the world of women. I shall bring you before the sets freshly made up with cosmetics and eau de cologne, sets before which I have always performed my mimicries. You will play the part of a Don Juan who never touches a woman. From time immemorial even the worst Don Juans don't get into bed on stage. Don't worry. I have served an apprenticeship in backstage machinations.'

The old man had just come to his real intention. He was outlining the plot of a novel he had not yet written. At the same time he was hiding the embarrassment he felt in his heart's core. This mad charity performance costing 500,000 yen was a memorial service held on behalf of what was perhaps his last love; the love that had propelled this home-loving old man down to the southern tip of the Izu Peninsula at the height of summer; the love which again out of sad foolishness had ended in pitiful disappointment; his tenth stupid lyric of a love affair.

He had loved Yasuko without intending to. In return for leading him into this blunder, for causing him to taste this affront, Yasuko must somehow become the loving wife of an unloving husband. Her marrying Yuichi sprang from a kind of ferocious logic that trapped Shunsuké's will. They had to marry.

Now this unhappy writer, past sixty and still unable to find within himself the power to stand guard over his own will, was using money to eradicate the foolishness that could still cause him trouble under the delusion that he was spending it on beauty. Is there any intoxication more false? Was it not true that Shunsuké had anticipated this indirect betrayal he held against Yasuko now, this crime whose pain tore his heart so exquisitely? Poor Shunsuké, always unhappy, never once the party to blame.

All the while Yuichi was taken with the face of the beautiful youth that stared at him out of the mirror in the lamplight. The deep, mournful eyes under the intelligent brows stared fixedly in his direction.

Yuichi Minami tasted the mystery of that beauty. The face he had always known, filled with the energy of youth, carved with the depth of masculinity, bearing the unhappy bronze substance of youth – it was his own. Until now Yuichi had felt only loathing in his consciousness of his own beauty. The beauty of the boys he loved, on the other hand, filled him with longing. As men in general do, Yuichi forbade himself ever to believe that he was beautiful. But the fervent praise of this old man before him now rang in his ears; and that artistic poison, the powerful poison of his words, loosened those inhibitions that had persisted so long. He now permitted himself to believe that he himself was beautiful. Now for the first time Yuichi saw himself in all his beauty. Within that little round mirror appeared the face of a surpassingly beautiful youth he had never seen before. The manly lips exposed a row of white teeth that involuntarily broke into a smile.

Yuichi could not have known the passion of Shunsuké's rankling, indeed poisonous vindictiveness. Nevertheless his curious, hasty proposal demanded an answer.

'What do you say? Will you make an agreement with me? Will you accept my help?'

'I don't know. Right now there are some things I can't figure out that might cause trouble later.'

Yuichi said this as if out of a dream.

'It won't hurt if you don't answer now. If you decide to accept my offer just send me a telegram saying so. I'd like to get things going soon and I wish you'd let me make one of the speeches at your wedding reception. Afterwards I want you to move in accordance with our plan. It will be all right. Not only will you never have any trouble, you'll also get the reputation of being a husband who runs after women.'

'If I'm married —'

'If so, then I shall be absolutely necessary,' said the old man, cocksure of himself.

'Is Yuchan here?' said Yasuko, from the other side of the sliding door.

'Come in,' said Shunsuké.

Yasuko slid the door open and met the glance of Yuichi, who looked up without realizing he was doing so.

She saw in his face the enchanting beauty of a young man's smile. Consciousness had changed his smile. Never before had Yuichi radiated such beauty as he did at this moment. Yasuko blinked as if dazzled. Then, in the manner of women who have been touched, in spite of herself she felt a presentiment of happiness.

Yasuko had washed her hair in the bath, and while her hair was still wet she had found it impossible to get Yuichi out of Shunsuké's room. Leaning out of the window, she had dried her hair. The passenger ferry, which started at O— Island, then came to K—, and tomorrow morning in the false light before dawn would dock at Tsukishima, was now entering the harbour, its lights gleaming off the water.

There was not much music in the town of K—. Every time a boat docked, the sound of a popular song could be heard through the summer air from the loudspeaker on the upper deck. The lights of the official greeters from the inns flocked about now, down on the docks. After a time the sharp sound of the docking whistle pierced the night and entered Yasuko's ears like the cry of a startled bird.

Her hair was drying rapidly and made her feel cold. A few stray strands of hair across her temple felt as if they were not hers but were the touch of cold wet leaves. There was something frightening about the feel of her own hair. The touch of her hand against her drying hair gave her a startling sense of death.

I just can't figure out what Yuchan is fretting about, Yasuko thought. If he tells me about it and it's something he must die for, I won't find it difficult at all to die with him. Surely that thought was part of my intention in getting him to come here with me.

Thus, for a time, while doing her hair, her mind ranged over many things. Suddenly she was seized by the unhappy thought that Yuichi was not in Shunsuké's room but in some place she was not aware of. She got up and hurried into the hall. She called and opened the door, and then she met that smile. It was natural that she feel a presentiment of happiness.

'Am I interrupting anything?' she asked.

The old man averted his gaze, conscious that her concern, her cocked-head coquetries, were clearly not intended for him. He imagined Yasuko at the age of seventy.

There was a stiffness in the air. As anyone might do at such a time, Yuichi glanced at his watch. It would soon be nine o'clock.

Suddenly the house telephone in the alcove started ringing. All three stared at the instrument as if it had stabbed them. No one moved a finger.

At last Shunsuké picked up the receiver. Then he looked in Yuichi's direction. It was a long-distance call from Yuichi's home in Tokyo. He went down to the office in order to take the call; Yasuko went with him not wishing to be alone with Shunsuké.

After a time the two returned. Yuichi's eyes had lost their composure. He explained quickly, without being asked: 'My mother is suffering from atrophy of the kidney, they believe. Her heart is getting weaker and she's terribly thirsty, they tell me. Whether they take her to a hospital or not, they want me home right away.' Excitement enabled him to deliver this news, which ordinarily he could not have uttered.

'She keeps repeating all day long that she'd be content to die after seeing my bride. Sick people are just like children, aren't they?' As he said these words he realized that he had decided to marry. Shunsuké sensed this resolution. A dark joy floated in Shunsuké's eyes.

'At any rate, you'd better get back, hadn't you?'

'We can still make the ten-o'clock boat. I'll go with you,' said Yasuko. She ran to her room to pack. There was joy in her steps.

Mother love is an extraordinary thing, thought Shunsuké, whose mother had found it impossible to love him, ugly as he was. With all the power of her kidneys she came to the rescue of her son in his moment of danger. Somehow something told her that Yuichi wanted to return sometime tonight.

As Shunsuké marvelled, Yuchi was deep in reverie. Looking at his narrow downturned brows, his eyebrows cast in graceful masculine shadows, Shunsuké shuddered slightly. This is really a strange night, he thought. I must be careful about introducing a pressure that wouldn't go well with his concern over his mother. Never mind. The boy is coming around to my way of thinking.

They barely made the ten-o'clock embarkation. The first-class cabins were taken, so they were given two places in a second-class cabin for eight, Japanese-style. When he was told about this, Shunsuké nudged Yuichi, 'You'll surely sleep well tonight,' he said.

As soon as the two young people got on board, the gangplank was raised. On the pierhead two or three men, dressed only in their underwear, held up miner's lamps and made indecent remarks to a woman on the deck. She answered back with all the power of her shrill voice.

Yasuko and Yuichi were embarrassed by this exchange. Smiling fixedly, they waited until the boat was a fair distance from Shunsuké. Between the boat and pier a silent expanse of water, gleaming evenly as if oiled, slowly widened. Then it grew, gradually and silently, like a living thing.

The author's right knee hurt slightly from the night air. The pain of neuralgic seizures provided the only passion of many of his months and days. He had hated those months and days. Now he did not hate them at all. The unpredictable pain in that right knee became for him at times a secret refuge for his passion. He sent the clerk with his lantern ahead and slowly returned to the inn.

A week later, immediately after he got back to Tokyo, Shunsuké received Yuichi's wire consenting to their arrangement.

3

The Marriage of a Dutiful Son

The wedding date was set for a lucky day between the twentieth and thirtieth of September. Two or three days before the ceremony Yuichi decided that once he was married he would have no opportunities to eat alone. Actually he almost never ate alone anyway; but on the half-formed pretext to do so he walked down the street. On the second floor of a Western restaurant which gave off a back street, he took his supper. Surely this luxury was something a wealthy man with 500,000 yen could afford.

It was five o'clock, rather an early hour to dine. The place was quiet; the waiters moved about sleepily.

His glance fell on the street, bustling in the lingering afternoon heat. Half of the street was extremely bright. Across the way, under the awnings of the stores selling Western goods, he could see the rays of the sun extending into the back of the show windows. Like a shoplifter's hand, the sun's rays slowly approached the shelf on which jade seemed to be resting. While Yuichi waited for his food to arrive, that one point on the shelf shimmering in the silence struck his eye from time to time. The lone youth felt thirsty and sipped at his water continually. He was quite uncomfortable.

Yuichi did not know the common truth that a multitude of men who love only men marry and become fathers. He did not know the truth that, though at some cost, they use their peculiar qualities in the interest of their marital welfare. Fed to satiety with the overflowing bounty of woman in a single wife, they don't so much as lay a hand on another woman. Among the world's devoted husbands men of this kind are not few. If they have children, they become more mother than father to them. Women who have known the pain of being married to philanderers find it wise, should they marry again, to seek out such men. Their married lives are a kind of happy, peaceful, unstimulating, in short, essentially frightful self-desecration. Husbands of this sort find their ultimate justification in the fact that in all the human details of life they rule with a sneer that proclaims their complete self-reliance. To their women, crueller husbands do not exist, even in their dreams.

It takes age and experience to figure out these subtleties. In order to endure such a life, some breaking-in is necessary. Yuichi was twenty-two. Not·only that, his utterly crazy patron was consumed by notions that were unworthy of his years. Yuichi had at least lost the tragic conviction that had lent intrepidity to his appearance. He didn't much care what happened.

His food seemed to be a long time coming, and he began to look idly around the walls. As he did so he became conscious of a gaze fixed upon his profile. When he turned to intercept that gaze, which had come to rest like a moth upon his cheek, it fluttered away. In the corner stood a fair, slim young waiter of nineteen or twenty.

On his breast were two curving rows of buttons in the latest style. His hands were turned backwards as if his fingers might have been tapping lightly on the wall. There was something abashed about the way he stood at attention, evidence that he had not been waiter for long. His jet-black hair gleamed. The languid grace of his limbs went well with the innocence of his small features; his lips were like a doll's. The line of his hips showed that his legs had the streamlined purity of a boy's. Yuichi felt unmistakably the stirrings of desire.

Someone called from the back and the boy left.

Yuichi smoked a cigarette.

Like a man who has received his draft notice and spends every effort to use the time until he is inducted in a riot of pleasure and finally ends up doing nothing, he was bored by the endless preliminaries his pleasure seemed to require. As on ten or twenty occasions he had already known, on this one too Yuichi anticipated his desire would vanish without a trace. Some ash fell on the polished knives on his table; he blew it off, and a few flecks collected on the rose in the bud vase.

His soup arrived. The boy he had noticed earlier – napkin on his forearm – brought it in a silver tureen. When the waiter removed the lid and held the tureen over his soup plate, Yuichi drew back from the cloud of steam rising from it. He lifted his head and looked the boy full in the face. They were extremely close. Yuichi smiled. The boy revealed a white canine tooth and for an instant returned the smile. Then he left. Yuichi turned to the brimming bowl of soup before him.

This brief episode, seemingly full of meaning, or perhaps void of any meaning, remained vivid in his memory. Afterwards its meaning would become clear.

*

The wedding reception was held in the annex of the Tokyo Kaikan. The bride and groom, as was customary, sat together in front of a gold screen. It was not fitting, to say the least, that a widower such as Shunsuké sit with them in the role of matchmaker. He was present as the famous and honoured guest.

The old man was smoking in the lounge when he was joined by a couple dressed like all the others in formal kimono and morning clothes. The woman, however, stood out above all the others in the lounge with her dignity of mien and her slender, coolly beautiful face. Her serious, clear eyes unconcernedly observed all that was going on around her.

She was the wife of the former count who, with her as accomplice, had extorted 300,000 yen in blackmail from Shunsuké. To one who was aware of this, the affected detachment of her glance had the aspect of a search for further quarry.

Her stout husband was beside her, squeezing, it seemed, a pair of white kid gloves in both hands. His sidelong glances lacked the quiet confidence of the philanderer as. his eyes moved like wary predators about the room. Man and wife had the demeanour of explorers dropped by parachute in an unexplored region. This absurd mixture of pride and fear was a thing rarely encountered among pre-war nobility.

The former Count Kaburagi saw Shunsuké and held out his hand. He fumbled with the other scoundrelly hand at one of the buttons of his suit, inclined his head slightly, and, with a broad smile, said, '*Go kigen yo!* – Cheers.' Since the institution of the estate tax, snobs had misappropriated this greeting, while it was the silly penchant of the middle class to avoid it completely. Since underhandedness was the outward evidence of the count's noble arrogance, his '*Go kigen yo*' gave a perfectly natural impression to whoever heard it. In short, through charity, the snob becomes barely inhuman; through crime, the nobleman becomes barely human.

There was, however, something indefinably revolting in the looks of Kaburagi. Something like a stain in a garment that will not come out no matter how often cleaned, a mixture of discomfiting weakness and audacity, along with a weird, tightly constrained voice – giving one the impression of a carefully planned naturalness. . . .

Shunsuké was suddenly filled with anger. He remembered the Kaburagis' blackmail scheme. He certainly had not reason to be obligated to Kaburagi because of the polite greeting.

The old man barely acknowledged the greeting. Then he thought that response childish and decided to amend it. He got up from the sofa. Kaburagi was wearing spats over his patent-leather shoes. When he saw Shunsuké stand up he retreated two paces on the polished floor as if he were dancing. Then he remembered that he had not seen one of the ladies here for a long time and greeted her as if sensible of having neglected her. Shunsuké had arisen but now had no place to go. Mrs Kaburagi immediately came over and led him to a window.

She was usually not given to long-winded greetings. She moved briskly, her kimono moving in correct folds about her ankles. As she stood before the window in which the lamps of the room were reflected clearly against the twilight, Shunsuké was amazed that not a wrinkle marred the beauty of her skin. She was, however, ingenious at selecting just the right angle and just the right lighting at a moment's notice.

She did not touch on the past. She and her husband worked according to the psychology that if you show no embarrassment the other party will.

'You're looking well. In this place, my husband looks much older than you.'

'I'd like to age quickly, too,' said the sixty-five-year old writer. 'I'm still committing a lot of youthful indiscretions.'

'You naughty old man. You're still romantic, aren't you?'

'And you?'

'How dare you! I still have a long time to live. As for today's groom, before you marry him off to play house with that mere child of a bride, I wish you would send him around to me for two or three months of instruction.'

'What do you think of Minami as a bridegroom?' As he nonchalantly threw out this question, Shunsuké's eyes, muddy with yellow blood vessels, observed the woman's expression attentively. He was absolutely sure that if her cheek quivered ever so slightly, if she displayed the faintest glint in her eye, he would not fail to catch it, enlarge it, dilate it, set it flaming, develop it into the highest state of irresistible passion. In general a novelist does just that: he is a genius at stirring up someone else's passion.

'I never set eyes on him before today. I've heard rumours about him, though. He's a much more beautiful young man than I thought. But when a young man like this at twenty-two takes an uninteresting bride who knows so little about the world, I foresee a pretty stale romance, and when I do, I get more and more upset.'

'What do the guests he has invited say about him?'

'He's all they talk about. Yasuko's classmates, though, are green with envy and finding fault. All they can say is "I don't like his type!" I can't say enough about the groom's smile. It's a smile filled with the fragrance of youth.'

'How about bringing all this up in your congratulatory speech? Who knows, it may do some good. This marriage is, after all, not the kind of love match that's so fashionable nowadays.'

'Just the same, that's what they're giving it out as.'

'It's a lie. It's a wedding of the noblest kind. It is the marriage of a dutiful son.'

Shunsuké's eyes flicked to the overstuffed chairs in a corner of the lounge. Yuichi's mother was sitting there. The powder that lay thick on her rather swollen face made it difficult to determine the age of this cheerful middle-aged woman. She was making every effort to smile, but her swollen face prevented it. Heavy, twitching grimaces were continually appearing on her cheeks.

This was the last happy moment of her life. Happiness is so ugly, thought Shunsuké. At that moment the mother made a gesture as if to run her hand, on which an old-fashioned diamond ring gleamed, over her hip. Perhaps she was saying that she wished to urinate. A middle-aged woman near by, in a wisteria-coloured dress, bent her head towards her and whispered something, then gave her hand to Yuichi's mother and helped her up. They made their way through the crowd, throwing greetings to the guests, and proceeded to the hall towards the rest rooms.

When he saw that swollen face so close by, Shunsuké was reminded of the dead face of his third wife, and he shuddered.

'It's not something we see often nowadays,' said Mrs Kaburagi coldly.

'Shall I arrange for you and Yuichi to meet sometime?'

'It's rather difficult right after the wedding, isn't it?'

'How about when he gets back from the honeymoon?'

'Promise? I'd like to have one long talk with that bridegroom.'

'You don't have any preconceived notions about marriage, do you?'

'Other people's marriages. Even mine isn't my marriage but someone else's. I don't have anything to do with it,' said this coolly poised lady.

The attendants, at a signal, began to announce dinner. The crowd of about a hundred guests surged towards one of the dining rooms in a body. Shunsuké was placed at the main table with the honoured guests. The old writer bitterly regretted that, from his seat, he could not watch the expression of discomfiture that had been flashing on Yuichi's face since the ceremonies began. Perceptive onlookers could tell that the dark eyes of the bridegroom were surely an outstanding feature of the evening.

The banquet moved along without interruption. As was customary, the bride and groom were applauded as they rose from their seats. The couple serving as matchmakers spared no effort in helping this grown-up yet childish pair of newlyweds. Yuichi had great difficulty with the tie of his travelling suit and had to retie it several times.

Finally, he and the matchmaker were standing near the car for them at the entrance, waiting for Yasuko, who was still getting ready. The matchmaker, a former cabinet minister, importuned Yuichi to have a cigar. The young bridegroom clumsily lit the cigar and looked down the street.

They did not wish to wait in the car; it was too warm, and they were a little tipsy from the wine. So the two men leaned against the shiny car, its surfaces lit intermittently by the headlights of passing traffic. They chatted idly.

'Don't worry about your mother,' said the matchmaker. 'I'll take good care of her while you're away.'

Yuichi listened to these kindly words from this old friend of his father's with joy. Though he thought he had become altogether cold-hearted, he was still quite sentimental about his mother.

At that moment a slender man, not Japanese, crossed the sidewalk from a building opposite. He wore a suit of eggshell colour and a bright bow tie. He approached what seemed to be his own late model Ford parked in the street and inserted the key. As he did so a young Japanese appeared behind him and stood for a time on the stone staircase, looking about. He wore a slim, double-breasted suit, obviously tailor-made, with a checked pattern. His necktie, which was vivid yellow, was visible even in the dark. In the light from the building his oily hair glistened as if sprinkled with water. Yuichi looked again and started. It was the young waiter of a few days ago.

The Westerner called to the youth, who jumped into the front seat with practised ease. His companion joined him, sliding beneath the steering wheel and slamming the door with a loud bang.

'What's wrong?' said the matchmaker. 'You're white as a sheet.'

'Yes, I guess I'm not used to cigars. I smoked only a little of it, but I feel terrible.'

'That's not good. Give it to me, I'll dispose of it.' The matchmaker put the lighted cigar in a silver-plated cigar-shaped receptacle and closed the lid with a snap. The noise caused Yuichi to jump again. At that moment Yasuko, in a travelling suit and wearing lace gloves, appeared among a crowd of well-wishers at the entrance.

The two went to Tokyo Station by car. From there they took the seven-thirty train bound for Numazu, on the way to Atami, their destination. Yasuko's happiness was such that she was barely conscious of her behaviour; it made Yuichi uncomfortable. His gentle spirit had always been capable of including love, but now it had become a thin vessel, not really meant for so volatile a substance. His heart was like a dark storehouse filled with ceremonial notions.

Yasuko handed him the popular magazine she had been reading. From its table of contents the word 'Jealousy' flashed out in bold type. For the first time he felt able to attach that motive to his own dark impulses. Jealousy was what seemed to be the source of his unhappiness.

Of whom?

He thought of the youth, the waiter he had seen a short time earlier. Here he was bound on his honeymoon journey, in the company of his bride, and he was feeling jealous of a youth he had barely seen. He recoiled at the thought of himself. He must be some strange creature indeed, he thought, without shape or semblance of anything human.

Yuichi rested his head against the line-draped chair. He watched Yasuko's downturned face distantly. Surely he could not make her out to be a boy! This eyebrow? This eye? This nose? These lips? He clucked at himself like an artist who had failed in sketch after sketch. Finally he closed his eyes and tried to think of Yasuko as a man. Something perverse in this imaginative process, however, made of the lovely woman in front of him something less lovable than a woman – in fact, more and more the image of something ugly and impossible to love.

4

Forest Fire in the Distant Twilight

One evening early in October, Yuichi ate supper and went to
his study. He looked around him. It was a student's quarters,
simply furnished. The concentration of its only occupant
loitered there chastely, like an unseen sculpture. This was the
only place in the house not yet wedded to woman. Only here
could the unhappy youth breathe freely.

Ink bottle, scissors, pencil vase, knife, dictionary – he loved
to see them glitter brilliantly in the lamplight. Things are solitude. When in their happy circle he hazily conjectured that
surely this was what the world meant by 'family circle'. The
ink bottle looked at the scissors and said nothing about
whether it had yet taken certain steps regarding their mutually
independent reasons for being. The clear, inaudible laughter of
that circle. The circle's only qualification for mutual security...

When that word 'qualification' entered his mind, it gave him
pain. The outward peace of the Minami household was like an
accusation levelled against him. The smiling face of his
mother, who, fortunately, was not suffering because of her
kidney condition and had not been hospitalized; Yasuko's
misty smile that hovered on her face night and day; this repose
... Everybody was asleep; he was the only one awake. He felt
uneasy that he should be living with a sleeping family. He was
tempted to arouse them deliberately out of their sleep. But if
he did ... indeed his mother, Yasuko, even Kiyo would wake
up. And from that instant they would hate him. It was a kind
of betrayal for one to be awake while the others slept. The
night watchman, however, guards by betrayal. By betraying
sleep he protects sleep. Ah, this human watch, maintaining
truth beside the sleeping! Yuichi felt a hatred towards the
night watchman. He hated his human role.

It was not time for exams. All he had to do was look over his notes. Economic history, public finance, statistics – all his notes were arranged there, transcribed meticulously in tiny characters. His friends were amazed at the preciseness of his notes, though it was a mechanical precision. Mornings in the sunlit autumn classroom, amid the rustling agitation of hundreds of pens, the machine-like character was what particularly marked Yuichi's pen. What made his passionless jottings look almost like shorthand was his habit of treating thought as nothing more than an exercise in mechanical self-discipline.

Today he had gone to school for the first time since the wedding. School was a real refuge. Then he had returned. There was a call from Shunsuké. From the receiver came the dry, clear, high voice of the old man.

'It's been a long time. Aren't you well? I haven't wanted to bother you. Can you have dinner with me tomorrow night? I wish I could invite your wife, too, but I'd like to hear how things are going, so this time just you alone. Better not tell her you're coming here. When she answered the phone, she said something about coming over with you to see me on Sunday; you'd better act on that day as if it were your first visit since your honeymoon. So come tomorrow. The time? Well, five o'clock. Someone else will be here that I want you to meet.'

When he thought of that phone call, he felt as if a great, importunate moth had tumbled across the surface of the page he was studying. He closed his notebook. 'It's another woman,' he muttered – that alone was enough to make him feel thoroughly worn out.

Yuichi feared the night like a child. Tonight was a night when he could at least feel liberated from his sense of duty. This one night, he would stretch himself out luxuriously on his bed; he would receive the coveted reward of rest for having, until the night before, repeatedly performed his duties. He would awaken on pure, unrumpled sheets. This was the greatest of all rewards. Ironically, however, this night his repose was denied him by the promptings of desire. Desire lapped and retreated at the dark edges of his insides, like water on the shore; it retreated and then it quietly stole back again.

Grotesque, passionless acts, over and over. The icy play of

sensuality, over and over. Yuichi's first night had been a model of the effort of desire, an ingenious impersonation that deceived an inexperienced buyer. In short, the impersonation had succeeded.

Shunsuké had instructed Yuichi carefully about contraceptive methods, but Yuichi feared that these methods would get in the way of the vision he had worked hard to construct, and he abandoned them. Reason told him to avoid conceiving a child, but he feared more the embarrassment he would suffer if he failed in the act with which he was immediately concerned. The next night, too, out of a kind of superstition, he came to believe that the success of the first night was facilitated by his avoidance of contraceptive measures, and fearing the obstacles they might place in his path, he repeated the blind actions of the first night. On the second night the successful impersonation became a faithful impersonation of an impersonation!

When he thought of those hazardous nights – cold from beginning to end – he had somehow struggled through, Yuichi shuddered. First night of mystery in that Atami hotel, bride and groom overcome by the same fear. While Yasuko was taking her bath, he went out on the balcony, far from calm. The hotel's dog barked in the night.

There was a dance hall down below the hotel, where all the lights lit the vicinity of the station. He could clearly hear the music from it. When he looked carefully he could see black human shapes within the windows, moving, stopping when the music stopped. When it stopped he could feel his pulse quicken. He recited Shunsuké's words to himself as if invoking a charm.

'Just make believe she's a bundle of sticks, a cushion, a side of beef hanging from a beam in the butcher shop.' Yuichi ripped off his necktie and laced it like a whip against the iron railing of the balcony. He needed to act, to use his power.

Finally, when the lights were out, he had to fall back on his imaginative powers. Impersonation is a superlative act of creativity. While involved in impersonation, however, Yuichi felt that he had nothing to impersonate. Instinct intoxicates man with a commonplace originality, but his anti-instinctive, excruciating originality did not intoxicate him in the slightest.

'Guys who do this are never alone, before or after. I am alone. I have to think it up, then do it. Every moment waits, holding its breath for the command of my imagination. Look! At the cold scenery of another of my will's victories over instinct; at how a woman's joy blows up like a tiny, dusty whirlwind in the middle of this desolate landscape.'

For all that, it was not right that there was not another beautiful male in Yuichi's bed. A mirror was needed between him and the woman. Without help, success was doubtful for him. He closed his eyes and embraced the woman. In doing so he embraced his own body in his mind.

In the dark room the two of them slowly became four people. The intercourse of the real Yuichi with the boy he had made Yasuko into, and the intercourse of the makeshift Yuichi – imagining he could love a woman – with the real Yasuko had to go forward simultaneously. From this double vision at times a dreamlike delight spurted. This gave way immediately to a boundless exhaustion. Yuichi several times saw a vision of the empty athletic field of his school after hours, with not a soul visible. In the face of this rapture he would throw himself on the ground. With this momentary suicide the act was over. Beginning with the next day, however, suicide became a custom.

Overwhelming weariness and nausea stalked their honeymoon's second day. They ascended towards the top of the town, which hung over the sea at a perilous angle. Yuichi felt as if he were displaying his good fortune before men.

They went out on the wharf and for amusement peered through the three-minutes-for-five-yen telescope. The sea was clear. On top of the cape on the right they could see clearly an arbour in Nishikigaura Park, bright in the morning sunlight. A twosome crossed the arbour and melted into the gleam of a patch of pampas grass. Another couple entered the arbour and drew close together. The forms of the two became one. On turning the telescope to the right they saw a stone-paved road sloping gently upward where, at various points, several groups were ascending. The shapes of each group were etched sharply on the stone pavement. Yuichi was overwhelmed with relief to see these identical shapes following his footsteps.

'They're just like us, aren't they?' said Yasuko. Stepping away from the telescope, she leaned on the parapet, exposing her forehead to the sea breeze. Now, however, envious of his wife's certainty, Yuichi was silent.

Returning from his unhappy thoughts to the present, Yuichi gazed from the window. The tower windows opened on a view of the Tokyo horizon on the other side of the trolley tracks and the shantytowns where the factory chimneys bristled. On clear days, that horizon seemed to ascend just a bit higher thanks to the smoke. Nights – perhaps from the night shift, or perhaps, too, from the faint glow of neon lights – the skirts of the sky in that vicinity were tinged from time to time with red.

Tonight's vermilion, however, was somehow different. The edge of the sky was quite clearly intoxicated. Since the moon had not yet risen, that drunkenness stood out in the light of the faint stars. Not only that, the faint vermilion was fluttering. Striped in smoggy apricot, it looked like a mysterious flag fluttering in the wind.

Yuichi recognized it as a fire.

At the same time there was a darkening of the white smoke around the flame.

The beautiful youth's eyes were cloudy with desire. His flesh throbbed languidly. He did not know why, but he could stay here no longer. He got up from his chair. He had to get out. He had to get rid of the feeling. He went out the front door and tied the belt of the light navy-blue trench coat he wore over his school uniform. He told Yasuko that he had remembered a reference book he needed and was going to find it if he could.

He went down the hill. On the trolley street, into which the feeble light filtered from the meagre shanties, he waited for the car. He would go into the centre of town with no particular destination in mind. Soon the glaring streetcar staggered around the corner. There was not a seat to be had; the dozen or so standing passengers were distributed along the aisle, leaning against the windows or hanging on straps.

Yuichi leaned against a window and lifted his glowing face

directly into the night wind. The distant fire was invisible from here. Was it really a fire? Was it, on the other hand, the glow of a worse, even more unfortunate catastrophe?

There was nobody by the window adjacent to Yuichi's. At the next stop two men got on and moved in beside him. All they could see of Yuichi was his back. For no reason at all Yuichi circumspectly looked them over.

One was abour forty, looked like a store clerk, and wore a grey jacket that had been made over from a suitcoat. He had a little scar behind his ear. His diligently combed hair was larded disgustingly with grease that made it glisten. The clay-coloured cheeks of his long, oval face were covered with thick, long hairs, like weeds. The other was an ordinary office worker, by the looks of him, dressed in a brown suit. His face reminded one of a rat, though he was extremely fair, even pallid. His shrimp-brown, imitation tortoise-shell glasses accentuated his pallor all the more. His age Yuichi could not estimate.

The two conversed in low tones. Their voices buzzed with a nameless, sticky intimacy and a lip-licking joyful secrecy. Their conversation entered Yuichi's ears relentlessly.

'Where are you going now?' said the man in the brown suit.

'Men have been pretty scarce lately,' said the clerk. 'I really need one. When such a time comes, I just walk around.'

'Are you going to H— Park today?'

'That has a bad reputation. Call it the "Park", in English.'

'Oh, excuse me. Do nice boys come around?'

'Once in a while. The best thing is right now. Later on there are only foreigners.'

'I haven't been there in a long time. I'd like to go again sometime. Today's out, though.'

'You and I won't be looked at suspiciously by professionals. They are jealous of those who are younger and prettier than we are because they stand in the way of their business.'

The squeal of wheels broke in on their conversation. Yuichi's breast was turbulent with curiosity. The ugliness of these kindred spirits he was seeing for the first time, however, wounded his self-respect. Their ugliness struck him right where his long-cultivated agony at being different festered. Compared with them, he thought, Hinoki's face is venerable, and at least his is a masculine ugliness.

The trolley had arrived at the transfer point for centre-bound cars. The man in the jacket parted from his companion and stood at the door. Yuichi followed him and got out. He was moved more by a sense of duty to himself than by curiosity.

The intersection was fairly busy. He waited for the next car, as far away as possible from the man in the jacket. In a fruit store in front of him the autumn fruits were piled in abundance under the overbright lamps. Here were grapes; purple under their darkish bloom, they mingled sunny autumn brilliance with the Fuyu persimmons near by. Pears also, along with early green mandarin oranges. There were apples. The heaps of fruit, however, were as cold as corpses.

The man in the jacket looked towards Yuichi. Their eyes met; Yuichi looked away unconcernedly. The man's gaze, intolerably persistent, did not falter. Will it be my fate to sleep with this man? Perhaps I don't have any choice. Yuichi shuddered at the thought. Mingled with the shudder was an unclean, putrescent sweetness.

The trolley arrived, and Yuichi swiftly boarded it. Perhaps during their earlier conversation they had not seen his face. It wouldn't do for them to think him one of their sort. In the eyes of the man in the grey jacket, however, desire burned. Standing on tiptoe, he stared intently, searching Yuichi's face. Complete face; intrepid, young wolf's face; ideal face...

Yuichin, however, turned the broad back of his navy-blue trench coat and looked at the placard painted in fall colours: 'Go to N— Hot Spring in the Fall.' The advertisements were all like that. Hot springs; hotels; rooms by day or week; you can rest here; see our Romance Room; best facilities, lowest prices ... In one poster there was the silhouette of a naked woman on the wall and an ash tray with a cigarette wafting smoke. 'For a souvenir of one night this fall, stay at this hotel,' the caption read.

These advertisements pained Yuichi. He was coming to the inescapable conclusion that society is governed by the rule of heterosexuality, that endlessly tiresome principle of majority rule.

The car soon came to the centre of town and ran under the light from windows of buildings already closed or about to close. There were few pedestrians; the trees along the street were dark.

There was a car stop in front of the park. Yuichi got off first. Fortunately there were many others getting off with him. The other man was behind them all. Yuichi crossed the street with the others and went into a little corner store across from the park. Picking up a magazine as if to read it he studied the park. The man was standing restlessly in front of the public rest room just off the sidewalk. Clearly, he was searching for Yuichi.

The man went into the rest room; Yuichi left the store and, cutting through a tide of flowing traffic, swiftly crossed the street. The rest room was dark under the trees. There was, however, a suggestion of a multitude walking softly, a stealthy bustling, a certain unseen assemblage. It was, for instance, as if at a public banquet, when all the doors and windows were tight shut and the faint sound of music, the clatter of dishes, the plop of corks being pulled, all issued indistinctly – this was how it seemed. Actually, it was a toilet, under a cloud of evil odours. As far as Yuichi could observe, no one was in sight.

He entered the dim, clammy lamplight of the rest room, and saw what is called an 'office' among the fellowship. (There are four or five such important places in Tokyo.) It was an office where the tacit office procedure is based on winks instead of documents, tiny gestures instead of print, code communication in place of a telephone. This was the dimly lighted, silent office whose activities here greeted Yuichi's eyes. He saw nothing definite, though, beyond a group of at least ten men – many for this hour – exchanging furtive glances.

All at once, they saw Yuichi's face. Then many eyes glistened, many eyes stared in envy. Under their glances the beautiful young man felt himself torn eight ways by fear. Then he wavered. There was, however, a kind of order in the movements of the men. It was as if they were held by a restraining power so that the pace of all their movements was carefully regulated. They moved like a clump of seaweed untangling slowly in the water.

Yuichi fled from the doorway of the toilet to the shelter of the eight-finger shrubs in the park. As he did so, he saw the glow of cigarettes here and there on the paths ahead of him. Lovers who strolled arm in arm along the narrow paths at the rear of the park, in daylight or before sundown, surely never dreamed that a few hours later they would be put to a completely different use. One might say that the park had changed faces. Another side of the face than that which appeared during the daytime now manifested itself.

As a human banquet at midnight might become in the final act of a Shakespearan play a banquet for ghosts, the bench where lovers from the office casually sit and chat and enjoy the view becomes at night something that can be termed a 'First-class Stage'. The dark stone stairway which grade-school children on a hike find too steep and must run up so as not to fall behind has its name changed to 'Runway for Men'. The long road in back of the park has its name changed to 'First Sight Road'. All are night names.

The police knew these names well as part of their jurisdiction which they neglected, since there were no laws by which they might crack down. In London and in Paris, of course, parks serve this purpose as a practical necessity, but it is a sign of some ironic charity that a public place like this, symbol of the principle of majority rule, should benefit such a small number of people. H— Park has been used as a gathering place for men of this sort since the time of the last emperor, when a part of its area was a military drill field.

At any rate, Yuichi, without realizing it, was standing at the edge of 'First Sight Road'. He went up the road the wrong way. The men stood in the shadows of the trees or walked along the sidewalk.

This company – this choosing, craving, pursuing, joyfully seeking, sighing, dreaming, loitering company – this company with sentiments whetted by the narcotic of custom – this company whose desire had been changed to something ugly by an incurable aesthetic disease exchanged fixedly sad stares as its members roved under the dim light of the street lamps. In the night many, many, wide-open, thirsty glances met and melted into each other. At the bend of the path, hand in hand, shoulder against shoulder, eyes over shoulders, while the night breeze softly rustled the branches; now coming, now going again, the appraising looks sharply cast crossed in the same place ... insects sang under the bushes where either the moon or the street lamps formed patches of light and shadow under the trees. The sound of the insects and the light from the cigarettes blinking on and off here and there in the darkness deepened the silence so heavy with feeling. At times the headlights of automobiles zipping by beyond or within the park set the shadows of the trees shivering and momentarily launched into view the shapes of hitherto unseen men standing there.

They are all my comrades, Yuichi thought as he walked. Rank, occupation, age, beauty notwithstanding, they are a fellowship welded by the same emotion – by their private parts, let us say. What a bond! These men do not have to sleep together. *From the day we were born we have slept together.* In hatred, in jealousy, in scorn, coming together for a short moment of love just to keep warm.

What is there about the walk of that man over there? His body is all affectation – his shoulders narrowed, his wide hips swaying, his neck at a posturing angle. His walk reminds one of the peristaltic glide of a snake. Closer than parent or child, more than wife, brother, or sister, they are my comrades ... hopelessness is a kind of repose.

Yuichi's despair had lightened a little. It was partly because, even in so large a group of his own kind, none displayed a beauty that surpassed his. Still, he thought, I wonder what happened to that fellow in the jacket. I don't know whether he was still in the toilet. I got so scared, I took off without seeing him. Is that him I see standing around under the tree?

The superstitious fear came back, the frightening conviction that, having encountered that man, he must end up sleeping with him. To settle his agitation, he lit a cigarette. At that moment a youth approached with an unlighted, perhaps deliberately pinched out cigarette, saying, 'Excuse me. Can you give me a light?'

He was dressed in a well-tailored grey double-breasted suit, a fine felt hat, necktie in the best of taste ... Silently, Yuichi handed him his cigarette. The youth turned his oval face. Seeing that face more distinctly Yuichi shuddered. The veins in the man's hand, the deep wrinkles at the corners of his eyes, were those of a person well past forty. The eyebrows were meticulously blackened; the ageing skin lay masked beneath the theatrical make-up. His unnaturally long eyelashes, too, could not possibly be genuine.

The aged youth lifted his round eyes as if about to say something. Yuichi, however, turned his back and walked away. As he did so – slowly, so as not to appear to be escaping the man, who had aroused his pity – the other men, who had seemed intent on approaching him, also turned. There were five or more. Separately, each nonchalantly changed direction. One, Yuichi perceived clearly, was the man in the jacket. Unconsciously, he walked faster. These silent admirers, however, followed closely, as if bent on gazing at that beautiful face.

When he reached the stone staircase, Yuichi estimated the distance and counted on finding an escape route at the top. He did not know its night-time name. The moonlit night glittered at the head of the stairway. As he climbed, he saw someone coming towards him, whistling carelessly as he descended. It was a boy in a tight white sweater. Yuichi looked at his face. It was the same boy he had seen in the restaurant.

'Oh. Big brother!' the boy said, extending his hand as he moved impulsively towards Yuichi. The uneven surface of the stones caused him to sway momentarily. Yuichi grasped his slim, firm waist. This physical encounter had a strange effect upon him.

'Do you remember me?' the boy asked.

'Yes, I remember you,' Yuichi replied.

He held back the memory of the pain that had troubled him at seeing the boy on his wedding day. Their hands were still clasped in greeting. Yuichi could feel the rough setting of the ring on the boy's little finger. It recalled the sensation of coarse fibres of the towel thrown against his shoulder by a schoolmate back in high school.

Hand in hand, the two hurried out of the park. Yuichi's breast heaved. He drew the boy, with whom he had somehow locked arms, along with him. There on that quiet night path, where lovers often strolled, they ran.

'Why are you hurrying so?' the boy said, gasping for breath. Yuichi flushed and stopped short.

'There's nothing to be afraid of. You're just not used to it, big brother, are you?' the boy said.

The three hours they spent soon afterwards in a hotel of doubtful reputation was to Yuichi like a bath in a hot waterfall. He divested himself of every human restraint; his soul was stripped naked in those three drunken hours. How delicious is it to strip the body to nakedness! In that moment when his soul doffed and discarded its robe and stood naked, Yuichi's ecstasy was lifted by a fierceness so intense that it seemed almost as if there was no room left for his body.

It must, however, be set straight immediately that it was not Yuichi who bought the boy so much as it was the boy who bought Yuichi. In other words, a skilful seller bought a clumsy buyer. The boy's skill made Yuichi tremble violently with pleasure. The reflection of the neon signs against the window curtains was like a fire. Amid those reflecting flames a pair of shields – Yuichi's beautiful manly breast – floated. Somehow in the night a strange chill affected his allergy-sensitive constitution, and in several places on his breast hives appeared in red lumps. With a sigh, the boy kissed the spots one by one.

Sitting on the edge of the bed, drawing on his trousers, the boy pleaded, 'When will I see you again?'

Yuichi was to see Shunsuké the following day.

'The day after tomorrow is all right. Not in the park, though.'

'You're right. We don't have to do that. Ever since I was a child I have yearned for the man whom I met for the first time tonight. I have never seen a man so lovely as you, big brother. Surely, God sent you, didn't He? Didn't He? Please, don't ever get tired of me.'

The boy rubbed the nape of his slim neck against Yuichi's shoulder. Yuichi rubbed the boy's neck with his fingertips and closed his eyes. At this time he took pleasure in the anticipation that he might someday discard his first lover.

'Day after tomorrow, as soon as the restaurant closes, I'll

come. Near here there is a coffee house where only the fellows come around. It looks like a club, though, and some regular people who know no better come in for coffee. So it's all right if you go there. Now let me draw you a map.

'All right. You'll find it right away, I think. Oh, from now on my name is Eichan. What's yours?'

'Yuchan.'

'That's a nice name.'

Yuichi was slightly irritated by the compliment. He was shocked that the boy was much more at ease than he.

They parted at the street corner. Yuichi caught the last trolley and went on home. Neither his mother nor Yasuko asked where he had been. Asleep beside Yasuko in his bed, Yuichi felt relaxed for the first time. He had already scored a victory. Having been thrown into curiously sinful pleasures, he compared himself to a prostitute who had come to the end of a happy holiday and was now returning to her daily employment.

There was, however, a deeper meaning in the comparison he had formed, half in fun. It was a first impression of the unexpected influence that the modest, powerless Yasuko would someday exert on her husband; in fact, it conveyed a presentiment of its eventual domination.

When I compare my body stretched out beside that boy, thought Yuichi, with my body now stretched out beside Yasuko, I feel so cheap. Yasuko does not give her body to me; I give mine to her, and I do it free. I am an unpaid prostitute.

These self-deprecating thoughts did not hurt him as before; somehow they delighted him. Tired, he slowly sank into slumber – like a lazy prostitute.

5

The First Steps Towards Salvation

The smiling face of Yuichi, brimming with happiness, that appeared at the door the next day disconcerted Shunsuké first of all, and later the woman caller whom Shunsuké had invited Yuichi to meet. Each had anticipated that the badge of misfortune would fit this youth best. It must be said they were wrong. Yuichi's beauty was universal. There was no badge, as it were, that did not become him. With a woman's quick, appraising glance, Mrs Kaburagi saw this immediately. This youth is cut out for happiness, she thought. A youth who can wear happiness as one might wear a black suit is a being that must be termed precious in our day.

Yuichi paid the lady the courtesy of thanking her for her presence at his wedding reception. The artless cheerfulness of his manners was enough to make any friendly woman affect mincing familiarities with a young man. His smiling face, she told him, was enough to set the flag of 'Just Married' fluttering from his forehead. She warned him of her fear that if that flag were not removed when he left the house he would not be able to see where he was going and be hit by a trolley or car.

The old man listened to his answer with an open smile; Yuichi seemed oblivious of her banter. Shunsuké's perplexity revealed the foolish look of a man trying to hide the fact that he had been betrayed. For the first time, Yuichi began to despise this pompous, ancient man. Not only that, he tasted the joy of the swindler in the fantasy that he had bilked him of 500,000 yen. Thus, the meal shared by the three was unexpectedly animated.

Shunsuké Hinoki had a long-standing admirer who was a skilful chef. His culinary art filled the china collected by Shunsuké's father with delicacies that became them. Out of his constitutional lack of interest Shunsuké was fastidious about neither the style of his china nor his cookery, but when he had people over he usually sought the aid of this man, who begged to be of service.

This is what this second son of a Kyoto textile merchant, a pupil of Kitsu Issai in the Kaiseki school, prepared for this evening's board: à la Kaiseki, a *hassun* tray of hors d'oeuvres made of mushrooms with pine needles, fried lily roots, Hachiya persimmons sent by a friend in Gifu, soybeans from the Daitokuji, and calico-fried crab; followed by red *miso* broth combined with the flesh of small birds ground with mustard; and then, in elegant Sung dynasty red plates in a peony pattern, sliced raw flatheads prepared blowfish-style; the fried course was spawning sweetfish broiled in soy, served with *hatsutaké* mushrooms in a blue Aoae dressing and ark shellfish in white sesame and bean-paste dressing. The boiled course was pickled bracken in bream bean curd, served with a steaming broth containing red madders. After the meal they were served Morihachi, 'little rising monks', white and pink dolls individually wrapped in tissue paper. Even these rare delicacies, however, did not serve to loosen the youthful tongue of Yuichi. It was an omelette he craved.

'This meal isn't much to your liking, is it, Yuichi?' said Shunsuké, noting the youth's lack of appetite. He asked him what he would prefer. Yuichi simply answered what was on the top of his mind. That single, artless word 'omelette', however, went straight to the heart of Mrs Kaburagi.

Yuichi was deceived by his own joy. He forgot that he was incapable of loving women. The exposure of fixed ideas sometimes cures fixed ideas; but it was only the idea and not its cause that was cured. His false sense of being cured, however, left him free for the first time to revel drunkenly among hypotheses.

Assuming everything I've said is a lie, Yuichi thought to himself with more or less euphoric gaiety, suppose I really loved Yasuko and, strapped for cash, had cooked up a cock-and-bull story for this philanthropic old novelist; then I'd really be in a fine position now. Then my triumph, my lovely-spot-in-the-country happiness, might boast that it was built on an unquiet grave. My unborn children would hear stories of an old skeleton buried beneath the dining-room floor.

Now Yuichi felt embarrassed by the excess of truth that comes with confession. Last night's three hours had changed the quality of his sincerity.

Shunsuké filled the lady's saké cup. The saké overflowed and ran over on to her shiny jacket.

Yuichi drew a handkerchief out of his coat pocket and wiped it.

The bright white gleam of the handkerchief somehow made her feel a delicious tenseness.

Shunsuké wondered what it was that made his old hand shake so. He had frozen in his jealousy of the woman, whose eyes did not stray from Yuichi's face. Even though self-indulgence would spoil everything for Shunsuké, and it was necessary for him to suppress all emotion, Yuichi's unexpected cheerfulness made the old man act irrationally. He reflected about it for a moment: it is not true that it is the beauty of this youth that has caught me and moved me; it is only that I have fallen in love with his unhappiness, I suppose....

As for Mrs Kaburagi, she was moved by the warmth of attention shown her by Yuichi. With most men she quickly surmised that their kindnesses were for their own benefit; only Yuichi showed her kindnesses she could not help believing were genuine.

Yuichi, on the other hand, felt embarrassed by the rashness with which he had brought out the handkerchief. He felt he had been insincere. It was as if he were becoming sober after a period of drunkenness and was now struck by the thought that his words and actions might be taken as flirtatious. The habit of reflection had at last reconciled him with his unhappy self. His eyes darkened, as usual. Shunsuké noticed it and felt relieved at the joy of seeing something to which he had been accustomed. Not only that, it was as if the luminous youthfulness Yuichi had exhibited earlier was all an artifice designed to help Shunsuké achieve his objectives. The look the old man now turned towards Yuichi had in it a mixture of gratefulness and of understanding.

The original mistake occurred when Mrs Kaburagi visited the Hinoki home an hour before the time at which Shunsuké had invited her. That hour which Shunsuké had set aside to find out how things had gone with Yuichi she purloined in her usual offhand way, greeting Shunsuké nonchalantly with, 'I didn't have anything to do, so I thought I'd come over right away.'

Two or three days later she would write Shunsuké a letter. One line would bring a smile to his face: 'At any rate, that young man was elegant.'

This was not the reaction he expected from a well-bred lady who admired wildness. Was Yuichi frail? Never. It seemed likely, therefore, that what she wanted to convey with the word 'elegant' was her objection to what she perceived as a courteous indifference in the way Yuichi treated women.

Now, away from his women, alone with Shunsuké, he was obviously relaxed. Shunsuké, long accustomed to stiff, polite young admirers, enjoyed watching him. This was what Shunsuké would have called elegant.

When it came time for Mrs Kaburagi and Yuichi to go home, Shunsuké suggested that Yuichi come with him to his study to help find the book he had promised to lend him. Yuichi looked mystified for a moment; Shunsuké winked. It was his method of getting the youth away from the woman without being rude. Mrs Kaburagi had never read so much as one book.

The sixteen-by-sixteen-foot library, whose windows were festooned outside with masses of the hard, armour-like magnolia leaves, was next to the study wherein the diary once filled with hatred and the works overflowing with magnanimity were still being turned out. Few people were ever admitted here.

The beautiful youth followed unconcernedly into the very heart of the odour of mildew and leather and dust and gold foil. Shunsuké felt that even the most important works of his large and imposing collection were blushing in shame. Before life itself, before this gleaming, living work of art, most of his works seemed useless and therefore embarrassing.

The gold on the covers and spines of his specially bound collected works had not lost its brightness, but the gold on the cropped edges of the assembled pages of expensive paper almost reflected the features of a human being. When the young man took out one of these works, Shunsuké felt as if the deathly odour of the accumulated documents was purified by the youthful face in the shadow of this great quantity of pages.

'Do you know of anything in the Japanese Middle Ages like the worship of the Virgin Mary in European medievalism?' Shunsuké asked. Taking it for granted that the answer would be negative he continued: 'It was a worship of the catamite. It was a time when the catamite was given the seat of honour at the banquet and was the first to receive the Lord's saké cup. I have a reproduction of an interesting and esoteric book of that period.' Shunsuké took a manuscript of slender Japanese binding from the shelf at hand and showed it to Yuichi. 'I had a copy made from a book in the Eizan library.'

Yuichi couldn't read the characters on the cover – 'Chigo-kanjo' – and he asked the old man about them. ' "Chigo-kanjo", the *Anointment of the Catamite*, that is. This book is divided into the *Anointment of the Catamite*, and *The Mysteries of the Great Cult of Catamite Worship*, with the name Eshin under the title *The Mysteries of the Great Cult of Catamite Worship*, but of course that is a barefaced lie. He lived in a different time. What I want you to read is a section of *The Mysteries of the Great Cult of Catamite Worship* that goes into detail concerning the miraculous ceremony of the caress. What subtle technical terminology indeed! The organ of the boy that was loved became the "Flower of the Law", the organ of the man loving him was called the "Fire of Darkness". What I'd like you to understand is this idea of the *Anointment of the Catamite*!'

He nervously riffled the pages with his aged fingers. He read one line aloud: ' "Thy body is the deep seat of holiness, the ancient Tathagata. Thou art come into this world to save the multitude."

'The word "thy" here,' said Shunsuké, 'shows that a child is being addressed. "From today forward we shall add the character Maru to your name, and you shall be called so-and-so Maru." After the naming ceremony, it was customary to recite that mystical phrase of praise and admonition. However' – Shunsuké's laugh had a tinge of irony – 'let's talk about how our first step towards salvation has gone. It's a success, it seems.'

For a moment Yuichi failed to understand.

'When Mrs Kaburagi sees a man who interests her, it is said that within a week something happens. That's the truth. There are countless instances. The intriguing thing, however, is that even if a man whom she is not interested in pursues her, something will come just that close to happening. At the last critical stage, though, there is a certain fearful contrivance. I got caught by it. In order not to disturb your illusions about this lady, I won't tell you what it is. Just wait a week and you and she will come to a critical moment. But you will cleverly escape – of course, with my help. And let another week go by. There are all kinds of ways to tantalize her so that she won't give you up. Just let another week go by. Then you will achieve a terrific power over that woman. In short, you will take my place and save her.'

'But she's someone else's wife,' said Yuichi innocently.

'That's just what she says. "I am someone else's wife," she announces. She doesn't appear to be separated from her husband, but she isn't faithful to him either. Whether her failing is her inconstancy or her eternal fidelity to a husband like hers, a third party simply cannot distinguish.'

When Yuichi laughed at this irony, Shunsuké teased him with the comment that he was laughing like a happy fool today. Since marriage had worked out well, surely he now liked women, the highly suspicious man probed. Yuichi told him what had happened. Shunsuké was amazed.

As the two descended to the Japanese room, Mrs Kaburagi was whiling away the time by smoking. Her cigarette was held tightly between her fingers as she pondered. She was thinking about the large young hands she had just been looking at. He had told her stories about sports – about swimming and high jumping, both solitary sports. If the word solitary was not right, they were at least sports that could be participated in without a partner. Why did this youth choose such sports? And what about dancing? Suddenly Mrs Kaburagi felt a pang of jealousy. She had thought of Yasuko. She forced herself to concentrate upon the solitary image of Yuichi.

Somehow, she thought, that man is like a wolf that avoids the pack. It is not that he is like a renegade; surely the energy locked up inside him is not rebellious or subversive. What is he made for? Surely for some intense, vast, deep, absolutely dark, useless something. Beneath that man's clear, transparent laughter, a metallic despair lies submerged like a weight.

That simple, warm palm, enfolding security like a farmhouse chair ... I'd like to sit on it. Those brows like narrow-bladed swords ... his double-breasted blue suit becomes him. His movements, like those of a graceful, alert wolf when he senses danger, twists his body and points up his ears. That innocent drunkenness! As a sign that he couldn't drink any more, he put his hand over his cup, and as he twisted his face at an angle and looked down drunkenly, his glossy hair fell right over his eyes. I felt the wild urge to reach out and grasp that hair. I wanted his hair oil to cling to my hand. My hand seemed as if it would suddenly reach out ...

She lifted the languid gaze that had become second nature to her towards the two men who had just come down. On the table stood a bowl filled with grapes and half-filled coffee cups. She felt too independent to say, 'You have been away a long time,' or 'Would you help me get home?' or words of that sort. So she greeted the two of them without a word.

Yuichi looked at the solitary figure of the woman so engulfed by rumour. He felt for some reason that this woman and he were doubles. With nimble fingers she stubbed out her cigarette in the tray, peered a moment in the mirror in her handbag, and stood up. When she left, Yuichi followed her.

The woman's actions amazed Yuichi. She never said a word to him. She took the liberty of calling a cab; she took the liberty of ordering it to the Ginza; she took the liberty of escorting him to a bar; she took the liberty of entertaining him with the help of the waitresses; and she took the liberty of escorting him back towards his home.

At the bar, she deliberately took a seat apart from him and stared at him as he sat in the midst of a swarm of women. Unused to a place like this, unused also to his suit, Yuichi now and then, with a charming gesture, pulled from his coat sleeves the white cuffs that kept hiding themselves. Mrs Kaburagi enjoyed it greatly.

In the narrow space between the chairs, the two danced for the first time. Under a palm in the corner of the bar, the hired musicians played. Dance that threaded its way through the chairs, dance that threaded its way through the cigarette smoke and the endless laughter of the drunks ... the woman touched the back of Yuichi's neck with her fingers. Her fingers brushed against his hair, tough as summer grass. She lifted her eyes. Yuichi's eyes were turned away. She was excited by that. For a long time she sought those haughty eyes that never would look at a woman unless she fell on her knees ...

When a week had gone by he had received no word from her. Shunsuké, who had got that elegant note two or three days later, heard of this miscalculation from Yuichi and was appalled. On the eighth day, however, Yuichi received a long letter from her.

6

The Vexations of Womanhood

Mrs Kaburagi looked at her husband beside her. Not once in the past ten years had she slept with him. What he did, nobody knew, least of all his wife.

The income of the Kaburagi household was the natural result of his laziness and his villainy. He was a member of the board of directors of the Racing Society. He was a member of the Council for the Protection of Natural Wonders. He was the president of the Far East Marine Products Corporation, which produced moray leather for handbags. He was the titular head of a dressmaking school. On the side he speculated in dollars. When his funds ran short, he took advantage of harmless suckers like Shunsuké and practised some gentlemanly villainy. To him it was a kind of sport. From his wife's foreign lovers he exacted consolation money on a sliding scale. Some who feared scandal, like a certain buyer, produced 200,000 yen without being asked.

The love that joined this couple together was a model of connubial affection; it was the love of partners in crime. The sexual loathing in which she held her husband was an old story. Her present transparent hatred born of worn-out sexuality was no more than the tightly knotted bond of criminals. Since chicanery constantly isolated them, it was necessary that they live together as they lived in the air, by random, long-term habit. Nevertheless, at the bottom of their hearts the two longed to be divorced. The reason they had not yet managed to break apart was only that they both wished to do so. For the most part divorce occurs only when one side does not want it.

The former Count Kaburagi always laboured to maintain his fine complexion. His too meticulously groomed face and moustache gave the unwitting impression of man-made filth. His somnolent eyes moved restlessly under their double lids. His cheek rippled now and then like water in the wind, so he was in the habit of clutching the skin of his smooth cheek with a white hand. He prattled to his acquaintances with a cloying aloofness. When he addressed people he did not know well, his high and mighty attitude put them off.

Mrs Kaburagi looked at her husband again. It was a bad habit. She never looked at his face. When she was thinking, when she was attacked by boredom, when she was visited by disgust, she looked at her husband as an invalid stares at a wasted hand. One blockhead who noticed this look, however, started the rumour that she was still as crazy about her husband as ever.

They were in the lounge that gave off the ballroom of the Industrial Club. Five hundred members of The Monthly Charity Ball Society were gathered there. In accordance with the false splendour of the occasion, Mrs Kaburagi wore over the bodice of her white chiffon evening gown a necklace of imitation pearls.

She had invited Yuichi and his wife to the ball. In the bulky letter that accompanied the two tickets were ten or so sheets of blank paper. She wondered just how he must have reacted on seeing those blank pages. He would not have known that she had inserted in the envelope the same number of sheets that made up the passionate letter she had written first and then burned.

Mrs Kaburagi was an impetuous woman. She did not believe in the vexations of womankind. Like the heroine of Sade's novel *Juliet*, who it was predicted would come to no good end, thanks to the indolence of vice, she unfortunately arrived at the opinion that she was somehow loafing on the job since that uneventful evening spent with Yuichi. She was, in fact, indignant. She had wasted so many hours with that boring young man. Not only that, she rationalized that her laziness was to be ascribed to the fact that Yuichi was quite deficient in charm. This way of thinking set her free to some extent. She was shocked to realize, though, that all the other men of the world seemed to have lost their charm.

When we fall in love we are filled with the sense of how defenceless human beings are, and we tremble at the daily existence we have led in blissful obliviousness until this time. For this reason people are occasionally made virtuous by love.

As the world sees it, Mrs Kaburagi was almost old enough to be Yuichi's mother. Perhaps for this reason she was conscious that Yuichi might be held back by the taboo against love between mother and son. She thought of Yuichi in the same way the world's women might think of their dead sons. Were not these symptoms evidence that her intuition had perceived in his haughty eyes how impossible were her wishes and that she had fallen in love with that impossibility?

Mrs Kaburagi, proud that she never dreamed about men, saw in her dreams the innocent lips of Yuichi speaking and shaping themselves as if in complaint. She interpreted those dreams to mean that she was to be unlucky. For the first time she felt the need to protect herself.

This was the only reason that this woman, who had the reputation of becoming sexually intimate with any man within a week's time, had accorded Yuichi such exceptional treatment. In the effort to forget him, she had made up her mind not to see him. On a whim, she wrote him a long letter she had no intention of mailing. She wrote it with a smile on her face, stringing together half-jesting, seductive phrases. When she read it over, her hand began to tremble. Afraid to read more, she struck a match and set fire to the pages. They flamed up more violently than she had expected, so she hastily threw open the window and cast them into the rain in the garden below.

The flaming letter fell halfway on the baked earth under the eaves and halfway in a puddle. It burned for a while longer – it seemed a long, long time. For some reason or other she put her hand to her hair. A white substance came away on her fingertips. The fine ash from the burning paper had tinged her hair as does remorse.

Rain? she wondered ... the music had stopped while the bands changed. The sound of countless approaching feet advanced like rain. Through the wide-open doors leading to the balcony, one had a quite ordinary view of a city evening – the starlit sky and the sprinkle of lights from the windows of tall buildings. The white shoulders of crowds of women, warmed by dancing and wine despite the night air, moved smoothly and imperturbably back and forth.

'It's young Minami. Mr and Mrs Minami, over there,' said Mr Kaburagi. His wife picked them out at the congested threshold where they stood scanning the lounge.

'I invited them,' she said. Yasuko led the way as they threaded through the crowd and approached the table. Mrs Kaburagi greeted them with perfect composure. When she had seen Yuichi without Yasuko, she had felt jealousy towards her. Why she breathed easier when Yasuko stood beside him, Mrs Kaburagi could not explain.

She barely looked towards Yuichi. She directed Yasuko to the chair beside her and praised her charming couture.

Yasuko had secured the imported cloth cheaply from the buying office of her father's department store and had ordered it early for her fall wardrobe. Her evening gown was of an ivory-coloured taffeta. The billowing skirt did justice to the effect of the stiff, cold, voluminous taffeta, on which the grain of shifting light flowed and opened up its quiet, silver, dead, long, slender eyes. Colour was provided by a cattleya pinned to her bodice. The faint yellow, pink, and purple velum, surrounded by violet petals, imparted the coquetry and shyness peculiar to members of the orchid family. From her necklace of little Indian nuts strung on a yellow gold chain, from her loose lavender elbow-length gloves, from the orchid on her bodice, the fresh odour of perfume like the air after a rain wafted its charms.

Yuichi was shocked that Mrs Kaburagi had not looked at him once. He greeted the count. The count, whose eyes were fairly light for a Japanese, greeted Yuichi as if he were reviewing troops.

The music began. There were not enough chairs at the table. Young people from the other tables had taken away all those not in use. Someone had to stand. Naturally. Yuichi stood, sipping at the highball Kaburagi had ordered for him. The two women had crème de cacao.

The music overflowed from the ballroom; like a mist it pervaded the hall and the lounge, restricting the conversation of the guests. The four said nothing for a time. Suddenly Mrs Kaburagi stood up.

'Oh, I'm sorry; there you are standing up alone. Shall we dance?'

Count Kaburagi languidly shook his head. He was amazed that his wife could propose such a thing. They never danced at these dances.

Her invitation was fairly clearly directed to her husband, but Yuichi noticed that her husband refused as a matter of course. He could only surmise that Mrs Kaburagi must have anticipated that refusal. Must he not out of politeness immediately ask her himself? It was clear that she wished to dance with him. Perplexed, he looked towards Yasuko. Her decision was polite but childish: 'That's too bad. Let us dance.'

Yasuko nodded to Mrs Kaburagi, placed her bag on the chair, and stood up. Yuichi turned his back to the chair beside which Mrs Kaburagi was standing, and for no reason grasped the back of it with both hands. As Mrs Kaburagi sat down again her back lightly pressed against his fingertips and held him thus for an instant against the back of the chair. Yasuko didn't observe it.

The two made their way through the crowd towards the dance floor.

'Mrs Kaburagi has changed lately. She has never been subdued like that,' Yasuko said. Yuichi remained silent.

He knew that Mrs Kaburagi was watching him without expression from a distance as he danced, almost as if escorting him, just as she had once done in the bar.

Yuichi exercised great care not to crush the orchid, and they danced somewhat apart. Yasuko felt that she was to blame; Yuichi was grateful for the obstacle. When he thought, however, of the manly joy of crushing that high-priced flower with his chest, the ardour of that thought swiftly darkened his heart. When an act committed without passion cost so little, should he restrain himself out of the false consideration that people watching might consider him decorous and parsimonious? To crush that flower when he felt no passion – by what code was it wrong? While he pondered, the great, lovely flower stood proudly between them, and the brutish idea of destroying it grew into a sense of duty.

The centre of the dance floor was extremely crowded. Lovers in great numbers striving to bring their bodies close to one another gave themselves the pretext of doing so by huddling here in increasing masses. As a swimmer cuts the water with his chest, Yuichi cut through the top of Yasuko's flower during the *chassé*. Yasuko moved nervously in order to spare the orchid. This natural womanly attitude of preferring to preserve her flower to dancing with her husband's arms tight around her simplified things for Yuichi.

If that was the way she was going to act, Yuichi was entirely willing to play the part of the passionate husband. The tempo of the music was fast, and so the young man, his head filled with his unhappy mad notion, feverishly pulled his wife hard against him. Yasuko had no time to resist. Mercilessly crushed, the orchid drooped.

In many ways, however, Yuichi's impulse had a good effect. Of course Yasuko felt happy about it after a time. She glared accusingly at her husband and, like a soldier displaying his medals, flaunted that broken flower and walked back to their table with the steps of a little girl. 'Oh, your cattleya has been spoiled the first dance!' she hoped people would say.

When they got back to the table, Mrs Kaburagi was laughing and chatting with four or five friends around her. The count yawned and drank in silence. Mrs Kaburagi, even though she surely noticed the crumpled flower, surprised Yasuko by saying nothing about it.

She puffed at her long women's cigarette and studied the crushed orchid dangling from Yasuko's breast.

*

As soon as he started dancing with Mrs Kaburagi, Yuichi said, candidly and eagerly: 'Thank you for the tickets. There was nothing in the letter, so I came with my wife. I hope that was all right.'

Mrs Kaburagi avoided the question. 'Wife, indeed. How shocking! That's not the proper word yet. Why don't you say "Yasuko"?'

He was shocked that she used his wife's given name, but did not know what to make of it.

Mrs Kaburagi discovered once more that not only was Yuichi's dancing skilful, it was also light-footed and without frills. Was it a vision – the youthful haughtiness she found so beautiful each instant? Or his candour, was it a kind of abandon?

The usual men of the world, she thought, attract a woman with the text of a page. This young man attracts with its margins. I wonder where he learned the technique.

After a time Yuichi asked the reason for the blank sheets in the letter. The unsuspecting innocence of his query now caused her embarrassment.

'That was nothing. I was just too lazy to write. Actually there were at the time twelve or thirteen pages of things I wanted to say to you.'

Yuichi felt that her nonchalant reply was an evasion.

What bothered him really was that the letter came on the eighth day. The one-week limit Shunsuké had mentioned was to be regarded as the mark of success or failure in this test. At the end of the seventh day, when nothing had happened, his self-respect was considerably wounded. The self-confidence he had acquired through Shunsuké's encouragement was gone. Although it was certain that he did not love her, he had never before wanted someone to love him so much. That day he almost suspected that he was in love with Mrs Kaburagi.

The blank letter made him wonder. The two tickets she had enclosed because somehow she feared his reaction if she asked him without also asking Yasuko made him wonder all the more. When he phoned Shunsuké, whose curiosity would carry him to the limits of self-sacrifice, he promised that he would go to the ball, though not to dance.

Had Shunsuké arrived?

When they returned to their seats, bus boys were already bringing a number of chairs, and ten or more men and women were gathered around Shunsuké. He saw Yuichi and smiled. It was the smile of a friend.

Mrs Kaburagi was amazed at seeing Shunsuké, but those who knew him, besides being amazed, were soon exchanging all kinds of rumours. This was the first time Shunsuké Hinoki had ever appeared at the Monthly Ball. Who had the power to get him to invade this strange place? Only one who did not know what was going on could ask that question. Sensitivity to out-of-the-way places is a talent essential to the novelist, though the intrusion of his talent into the centre of activity was something Shunsuké avoided.

Yasuko, heady with wine, to which she was not accustomed, innocently babbled something about Yuichi. 'Yuchan has been getting to be pretty vain lately. He bought a comb and he keeps it in his inside pocket. I don't know how many times he combs his hair. I'm afraid he'll soon be bald.'

Everyone commented agreeably on Yasuko's influence on him, but Yuichi, laughing good-naturedly, pondered on the implication of her words. His purchase of the comb, indeed, was associated with a habit he had acquired without realizing it. Even during boring college lectures, he would at times unconsciously take out his comb and groom his hair. Now, before all these people, Yasuko's words made him aware for the first time that he had changed to the extent of carrying a comb concealed in his inside pocket. He saw that as a dog carries a bone from another house to his own, so this insignificant comb was the first thing he had carried home from that alien world.

Nevertheless, it was natural that Yasuko would think the metamorphosis of her husband so soon after the wedding was related entirely to herself. There is a game in which one adds thirty or forty strokes to a picture and changes the meaning of the picture until gradually a quite different image emerges; if one happens to look at it after adding only the first three or four strokes he will see only a meaningless triangle or rectangle. No one can say that Yasuko was a fool.

Shunsuké could not ignore Yuichi's absent-mindedness. 'What's wrong?' he asked softly. 'You have the appearance of one troubled by love.'

Yuichi arose and went out in the hall. Shunsuké followed him casually. 'Have you noticed the faraway look in Mrs Kaburagi's eyes?' he said. 'What surprised me is that she has turned spiritual. Perhaps this is the first time in her life she has ever been connected with anything spiritual. It might be said further that with you there has appeared another of the mysterious side effects of love, a reaction produced by your very lack of spirit. It has gradually occurred to me that although you think you can love women spiritually, that is not true. Human beings have no such facility. You can't love women spiritually or physically. Just as natural beauty reigns over mankind, by the same process you rule over women in the complete absence of spirituality.'

Shunsuké at this time was not conscious of the fact that he was looking at Yuichi as no more than a spiritual puppet of Shunsuké himself. That was, nevertheless, in the way of being the highest aesthetic praise.

'People always love best those for whom they are no match. That's particularly true of women. Today's Mrs Kaburagi, thanks to love, looks as if she had completely forgotten her physical charm. This was something that, until yesterday, she found harder to forget than any man you can name.'

'But the interval of one week has expired, hasn't it?'

'An exceptional favour. The first exception I've seen. In the first place, she can't hide her love. Did you notice before, when you two returned to your seats, how she picked up the Saga brocade opera bag – embroidered with peacocks, no less – from the chair where she had left it and placed it on the table? She looked at the table top carefully and meticulously put it down. And she coolly set it right in the middle of a puddle of beer! Anybody who says this woman usually gets excited at a dance is mistaken.'

Shunsuké offered Yuichi a cigarette and went on: 'This business will take a long time, I think. For the time being you can rest easy; your charms have had their effect and now you can relax, no matter what. First, you have the usual protection you get from being married, and newly married at that. But really I have no wish to protect you. Wait a minute. There's someone else I want you to meet.'

Shunsuké glanced around. He was looking for Kyoko Hodaka, who had thrown him over, just as Yasuko had, and married more than ten years ago.

Yuichi suddenly looked at Shunsuké as if he didn't know

him. Here in the middle of this young and splendid world, Shunsuké looked like a dead man standing in search of something.

Shunsuké's cheeks were leaden-coloured. His eyes had become dull, and between his black lips the chalkiness of his too-even false teeth gleamed unnaturally, like the white wall of a ruined castle. Yuichi's emotions, however, belonged to Shunsuké. Shunsuké knew what he was doing, for when he saw Yuichi he decided to crawl, very much alive, into his coffin. When he was involved in creation the world seemed clear, and men's affairs transparent, because in such moments he was undoubtedly dead. Shunsuké's many foolish actions were nothing more than the products of the clumsy efforts of a dead man trying again and again to return to the mainstream of life. As he did in his works, he was taking Yuichi's body and populating it with his spirit, and with it had decided to cure all his gloomy jealousies and grudges. He sought perfect rehabilitation. In short, he wished to be reborn in the world as a corpse.

When one looks at the world with a dead man's eyes, with what clarity the sublunary world bares its activities! With what accuracy one can see through the loves of one's fellows! In this unprejudiced free condition, how the world becomes transformed into a little glass mechanism.

Within this dead man ugly with age, however, certain nagging things were in motion, battering at his self-imposed restraints. At the time he heard that Yuichi had nothing to report after seven days, within his fear of failure and in his confusion over missing the mark he took a certain slight joy. It had the same root as the unhappy pain that seized his heart when at the earlier time Mrs Kaburagi's face displayed the unmistakable signs of love.

Shunsuké got a glimpse of Kyoko. A publisher and his wife approached him, however, and their polite effusions prevented him from reaching Kyoko's side.

Kyoko was the beautiful woman in Chinese dress beside a desk heaped with raffle prizes to be given out during the entertainment. She was engaged in a lively, indeed effervescent, conversation with an elderly white-haired foreigner. Whenever she laughed her lips softly swelled and contracted like waves around her white teeth.

Her Chinese dress was satin, with a dragon pattern embossed on a white background. The collar clasp and buttons were gold; the dancing slippers under the trailing skirt were gold also. Her jade earrings trembled, each a flash of green.

When Shunsuké tried to approach her, another middle-aged woman in evening gown detained him. She kept bringing up artistic topics, but Shunsuké extricated himself without so much as paying her the courtesy of being impolite. As she walked off, Shunsuké's gaze followed her retreating figure. On her plain, naked back, the unhealthy hue of a grindstone, her shoulder blades protruded grey under a plaster of white powder. Why, Shunsuké wondered, do those people always talk about art just to cover up their ugliness and their offences against the world?

Yuichi approached uncomfortably. Shunsuké noticed that Kyoko continued talking with the foreigner, so he motioned Yuichi over with his eyes and spoke to him softly.

'That woman. She's a pretty, cheerful, and ostentatiously virtuous wife, but lately she and her husband have not been hitting it off too well. Someone told me that they came here separately. I'm going to introduce you to her as having come alone, too, without your wife. Now you must dance five numbers in a row with her. No more, no less. When you've finished those and leave, tell her apologetically that your wife actually came but that you lied to her because you thought if you told the truth she wouldn't have danced all this time with you. Put all the sentiment you can into it.

'She'll forgive you. The impression you make is a miracle, surely. Also, it's wise to flatter her a little. The most effective flattery is to tell her she has a beautiful smile. When she got out of girls' school, her gums used to show when she smiled. It was pretty funny. About ten years after that, though – years filled with practice – she had trained herself so that no matter how she laughed she never showed her gums. Praise her jade earrings. She thinks they set off the white skin on the nape of her neck.

'Don't pay her erotic compliments. She likes clean men.

85

And when it comes to that, it's because her breasts are small. That lovely bosom is a contrivance. It's made of fine sponge. Deceiving men's eyes seems to be good form among beautiful things, isn't it?'

The foreign gentleman engaged himself in conversation with a group of other foreigners, so Shunsuké came forward and presented Yuichi to her.

'This is Minami. He asked me to introduce him to you long ago but I never had the opportunity. He's still a student. What's more he's married – unfortunately.'

'Really? And so young? Everybody's getting married early these days.'

Shunsuké went on in that vein. 'He asked me for an introduction to you before he got married, and now Minami is pretty upset with me about it; but he told me that he saw you for the first time at the earliest party of the fall season.'

'If so' – Yuichi watched Shunsuké's face while Kyoko hesitated over her words – 'if so, he's only been married three weeks. That party was held on a hot day, isn't that so?'

'That's when he saw you for the first time,' Shunsuké said, in a peremptory tone, 'and that's when this man was seized with a childish whim. Before he got married he wanted to dance five numbers in a row with you. That's right, with you! Don't blush. If he could accomplish that, he felt he could get married without regret. Finally he married his fiancée without fulfilling his ambition. But he has never got over it, and so he has been after me now. He has been saying I have forgotten I know you. Today, you see, he has come here alone, without his wife. Won't you grant him his wish? If you dance five numbers in succession with him he'll be content.'

'That's an easy request,' Kyoko said, consenting magnanimously in a tone that concealed the riot of her emotions, 'but I hope you haven't chosen the wrong partner.'

'All right, Yuichi, dance!' Shunsuké urged, conscious of the people in the lounge. The couple walked into the dimness of the ballroom.

At a table in a corner of the lounge Shunsuké was stopped by a friend and his family. There he sat in a chair that offered a direct view of Mrs Kaburagi, three or four tables off. Just then he saw Mrs Kaburagi return to her table from the ball-room, escorted by a foreigner. She nodded to Yasuko and sat down facing her. The picture these two unhappy women made, when seen from a distance, had all the elegance of an old tale. There was now no cattleya on Yasuko's breast. The woman in the black dress and the woman in ivory, with nothing to do, exchanged silent glances.

The unhappiness of other people when viewed through a window is more beautiful than when viewed from within. This is because unhappiness seldom crosses the window frame and springs upon us.

The despotism of music reached out to the gathered throng; its discipline worked. The music, like a deep-seated sense of fatigue, moved them indefatigably. In the flow of this music there was a kind of vacuum that the music could not infringe upon. Through the window of that vacuum Shunsuké now felt, he watched Yasuko and Mrs Kaburagi.

At the table where a family sat, with Shunsuké, the young-sters were discussing the movies. The eldest son, who had been with the Special Attack Forces, was dressed in a becoming suit and was explaining to his fiancée the difference between the automobile motor and the aeroplane engine. His mother was telling a friend about an ingenious widow who took orders for dyeing rugs and made stylish shopping bags. The friend was the wife of a former Zaibatsu who, since her only son had died in the war, had immersed herself in psychic phenomena. The head of the family was insistently filling Shunsuké's beer glass and repeating: 'How about that? My family could be made into a novel, couldn't it? If you took it and described it just as it is – as you can see, beginning with my wife we're a fine set of characters.'

Shunsuké smiled faintly and looked around at this run-of-the-mill family. Unfortunately, the father's pride was mis-guided. There are many such families – families so much alike that there is nothing they can do but read detective stories avidly in order to cure themselves of the sickness of humdrum health.

He must get back to his own table. If he stayed away too long people would suspect him of being in collusion with Yuichi.

When Shunsuké reached the table he found that Yasuko and Mrs Kaburagi had risen in response to requests to dance. He sat down at the side of Kaburagi, who had been left alone.

Kaburagi did not ask where he had been. He silently poured Shunsuké a highball and said: 'Where did Minami go?'

'Oh, I saw him in the hall a little while ago.'

'Is that so?'

Kaburagi folded his hands on the table and stared at the tips of his index fingers, which he held up vertically.

'Look at this, won't you? They don't tremble at all, do they?' he said, referring to his hands.

Shunsuké didn't answer but looked at his watch. He estimated five numbers would take twenty minutes. Counting the time he was in the hallway, that would be thirty minutes – not an interval to be easily borne by a new wife who had come here to dance with her husband.

After one dance number Mrs Kaburagi and Yasuko came back to the table. The two of them were rather pale. Both had been forced by what they had seen to make an unhappy judgement about themselves, and since they had reason not to discuss it, they were left with little to say.

Yasuko was thinking of her husband, who had just finished two dances with a woman in a Chinese dress. She smiled at him when they danced near, but perhaps because he didn't see her Yuichi didn't smile back.

The jealousy and suspicion that had plagued Yasuko while they were engaged and which led her to say to herself, 'Yuichi has another girl,' were dispelled once they were married. To be more exact, she dispelled them herself with her newly gained rationality.

Idly Yasuko fidgeted with her gloves – now holding them in her hand, now drawing them on. Wearing gloves of itself gives a person the look of being lost in thought.

Yes. Thanks to her newly acquired rationality, she had cleansed herself of suspicion. Back there in K—, Yasuko had been filled with anxiety and presentiments of misfortune by

Yuichi's melancholy. But when she thought about it at all after their marriage, in her innocent girlish pride she held herself responsible for everything and decided that the reason he had lain awake worrying was her lack of responsiveness to his advances. Looked at in this way, those three nights of limitless torture for Yuichi during which nothing happened were the first evidence that he loved her. He was fighting against desire; there was no doubt about it.

With his extraordinarily strong self-respect, he certainly had feared rejection and froze. She felt she had won the proud privilege of ridiculing, of despising her former childish suspicion that Yuichi had another girl friend while they were engaged. There was, after all, no clearer proof of his purity than that he had refrained from laying so much as a hand on the innocent girl lying beside him silent as stone, her body rigid, for three nights running.

Their first visit to her home was happy. Yuichi seemed in Yasuko's parents' eyes to be a completely endearing, conservative youth, and his future in her father's department store, where he would be especially useful with women customers, was assured.

He seemed to be a dutiful son, upright, and on top of that, inclined to be careful of his reputation.

It was on the first day he went back to school after the wedding that he had started to come home late, after dinner. He could not get around treating some bad companions, was his excuse. Yasuko did not need instruction from her deeply experienced mother-in-law to tell her that this was the way it would be with a newlywed husband and his friends . . .

Yasuko now took off the lavender gloves. Suddenly something made her distinctly uneasy. She was horrified to see, right in front of her, exactly like herself in a mirror, Mrs Kaburagi, wearing the same distraught look. Perhaps Yasuko's despair was a contagion caught from Mrs Kaburagi's inexplicable melancholy. Perhaps that's why I feel a certain kinship with this woman, she thought. Before long both of them were invited to dance.

Yasuko saw that Yuichi was still dancing with the girl in the Chinese dress. This time she looked past him without a smile.

Mrs Kaburagi also observed the couple. She did not know the woman. Mrs Kaburagi's derisive spirit detested the outrageous pretext of charity, a detestation she expressed in her imitation pearls. She had never come to this dance before and so did not know Kyoko, one of the organizers of the affair.

Yuichi finished the five dances as agreed.

Kyoko returned to the table occupied by her group, accompanied by Yuichi, and introduced him. He was plainly fidgety, because he had not yet made up his mind when it would be well to confess to the lie that his wife had not come. Then a school friend, a cheerful young man who had talked with him at the Kaburagis' table, came by and, catching his eye, settled matters by saying: 'Oh, you deserter! Your wife has been sitting for the longest time alone at that table.'

Yuichi looked at Kyoko's face. She returned his look; then she averted her eyes.

'Go, I humbly beg of you. The poor thing,' she said. This counsel, given courteously and in a quiet tone, made Yuichi turn beet red with humiliation. Once in a while a sense of honour serves in place of passion. Impelled by a vigour that surprised himself, he ran to Kyoko's side.

'I want to talk to you,' he said and led her to a corner. Kyoko was filled with a cold fury; however, if Yuichi had been aware of the weight of passion the fierceness of his actions indicated, he would have known why this beautiful woman got up from her chair and followed him as if she had surrendered. His black eyes accentuating the impression of sincerity and with the air of one deeply in love, Yuichi said: 'I lied; I have no words to apologize for it. I couldn't help it. I thought if I told the truth, you'd never dance five numbers in a row with me.'

Kyoko's eyes opened wide at his forthrightness. Moved almost to tears out of the womanly generosity that makes for self-sacrifice, she quickly forgave Yuichi, and while she watched his retreating form hurrying off to the table where his wife waited, this impressionable woman memorized the shape of his back down to the tiniest wrinkle in his suit.

Back where he had left them, Yuichi found Mrs Kaburagi exchanging jokes with the men with new-found hilarity and

Yasuko half-heartedly joining in, along with Shunsuké, who was preparing to leave. Shunsuké wished at all costs to avoid a confrontation with Kyoko before these people. When he saw Yuichi returning, therefore, he hastened his departure.

Yuichi felt uncomfortable there and offered to accompany Shunsuké as far as the stairs.

Shunsuké laughed with delight when he heard how Kyoko had acted. He tapped Yuichi on the shoulder and said, 'Tonight, please forget about playing around with your boy. This is a night when you had better do your husbandly duty and get your wife in a good humour. Kyoko is going to meet you somewhere again in a few days completely by accident. I'll let you know when.'

The old man gave him a youthful handshake. He descended the red-carpeted staircase leading to the main exit, and on the way put his hand in his pocket, where he felt something jab his finger. It was an old-fashioned opal necktie pin. Earlier he had dropped by the Minami home in order to give Yuichi and his wife a ride. They had already departed, but Yuichi's mother invited this famous friend into the living room and courteously gave him a memento of her dead husband.

Shunsuké happily accepted this gift from a bygone era. He imagined the motherly sentiments she would probably pass on to Yuichi later on: 'When you give something like that away, you can look at people with pride.'

He looked at his finger. A drop of blood had congealed there like a jewel. It had been a long time since so much colour had appeared on his body. He was amazed at the trick of fate that permitted an old person with kidney disease to do him so unwitting a bodily injury just because she was a woman.

7

Entrance to the Stage

In that place nobody asked Yuichi Minami his address or his station. They called him 'Yuchan'. It was the place where he went to meet 'Eichan', who had drawn him the childish map.

It was an ordinary tea shop named Rudon's, opened after the war on a corner of Yuraku Cho. Sometime later it became a club for men of this persuasion. Men who didn't know what it was came in there in groups, drank coffee, and left none the wiser.

The proprietor was a second-generation Eurasian, a small, neat man of forty. Everyone called this clever businessman Rudy. Yuichi started calling him Rudy the third time he visited there, imitating Eichan.

Rudy had been around the Ginza area for twenty years. Before the war he had a place in West Ginza called the Blues. He had girls there and two or three beautiful young waiters. Homosexuals, therefore, came to Rudy's place from time to time.

The men who were in the know had the instinct of animals to smell out their own kind, and as an ant is attracted to sugar, so they did not miss a place that had the slightest sign that what they were after was brewing there.

It is hard to believe, but not until after the war did Rudy know that a secret world of this sort existed. He had a wife and children, but when it came to other objects of affection, he felt that nothing more than his own peculiar aberration existed. He simply indulged a penchant for installing beautiful boys in his restaurant. When he opened Rudon's in Yuraku Cho immediately after the war, he arranged so it was always possible to see five or six such waiters there. Thus the place became very popular among the people of that world and finally became a kind of club.

When he realized this, Rudy refined his business tactics. He recognized that when these men came here once to bring warmth into their lonely lives they would never again succeed in separating themselves from the place. He divided his guests into two types: the young, charming, magnetic guests, whose appearance there could bring him success; and the generous, wealthy guests drawn by the magnetism of the place to spend money like fools. Rudy worked harder to take care of the members of the first group, but once, when one of the regular young guests was invited by one of the well-paying guests to go to a hotel, and fled after going only as far as the hotel door, Yuichi heard with his own ears Rudy's imprecations: 'You're giving Rudy a bad name, aren't you? All right. You just see if I ever help you to meet any nice men now!'

It was said Rudy took two hours to put on his make-up every morning. He too had the homosexual's peculiar public habit, not to be condemned, of boasting: 'Men made eyes at me and embarrassed me.' Rudy took it for granted that men who gazed at him were all homosexuals. Even kindergarten children, seeing him on the street, must have turned around in amazement. This man of forty wore circus suits; and his Ronald Colman moustache changed its width and its direction with his mood whenever he trimmed it.

The crowd got together as a rule at sundown. There were always dance records on the restaurant jukebox – it was important that private matters not be noised around for all to hear. When a flush, flashy guest had been served, Rudy would move from the corner table, where he always stationed himself, to the counter in order to look at the check. Then, in respectful tones the proprietor himself would intone: 'Your check, sir.' With such courtly practice, the guest had better be prepared to pay double.

Whenever a man entered, all the guests would look up. The man coming in would instantly be bathed in glances. Who could guarantee that the ideal sought for for so long would not suddenly take shape and appear through that glass door? Much of the time, however, the light in those glances suddenly faded and went out in disappointment. Appraisal ended in the first moment. When a young guest who knew nothing about the place entered he would be startled to hear, if the jukebox happened to be silent, appraisals of his person murmured at every table. 'What's he? Not much,' they would say, or, 'That one; he's been rolled everywhere,' or, 'His nose is small; probably his tool is too,' or, 'I don't like the way his lower lip sticks out,' or, 'He has good taste in neckties,' or 'His sex appeal, though, is in short, zero.'

Every night these box seats looked out on the stage of an empty night street on which some miraculous manifestation was sure to be seen. Religious, one might call it, for it was not far different. One might savour in purer, more direct form the atmosphere of piety and expectation of miracles in the cigarette haze of a homosexual club than in one of today's indifferent churches. Spreading outside that glass door was their ideal society, a great city conceived in accordance with their outlook. Like the many roads that lead to and from Rome, so countless invisible streets lead from individual beautiful youths scattered like stars in a night sky to clubs like Rudy's.

According to Ellis, women are fascinated by male strength, but they have no opinions about male beauty. Insensitive almost to the point of being blind, they have a discerning eye for male beauty not greatly different from that of the normal male. Sensitivity to the peculiar beauties of the male is the exclusive property of the homosexual. The establishment of the system of male beauty in Greek sculpture in the field of aesthetics had to wait for the advent of Winckelmann, who was a homosexual. When at first the normal boy encounters the fever of homosexual glorification (women are incapable of according to the male such fleshly praise), he becomes transfigured into a dreamy Narcissus. Expatiating on his own beauty, which has become the object of his praise, he imagines an ideal image based on the aesthetic ideas of males in general and becomes a full-fledged homosexual. The natural homosexual, on the other hand, cherishes these ideals from infancy. His ideals are those true angels, undifferentiated as to carnal or intellectual; they are akin to the ideal of the Eastern theology which completed its religious carnality through the so-called Alexandrian purification.

The time when Yuichi was to meet Eichan was nine p.m.,

the busiest hour at the place, and when he entered the door wearing his maroon necktie with the collar of his navy-blue-trench coat turned up, he was something of a miraculous advent. Although he did not know it, in that moment he established his supremacy. Yuichi's entrance on the stage would be a source of legend at Rudon's for a long time to come.

That evening Eichan left his place early, and as soon as he passed the door of Rudon's he said to his young friends: 'I really met a terrific one in the park day before yesterday. We spent a little time together that night and I've never seen anyone so pretty. He's coming soon; his name is Yuchan.'

'How's his face?' said Kimichan, who felt that no youth had a face like his own; he wanted to find fault. Originally he had been a bus boy at the Oasis Dance Hall. He wore a double-breasted, emerald-green suit a foreigner had bought for him.

'How's his face? He has a manly, deep-cut face. His eyes are sharp, his teeth are white and even, his profile is rather fierce. And you should see his body! He's an athlete, sure.'

'Eichan, if you get carried away you'll be ruined. How many times did he do it in that little time?'

'Three times.'

'Amazing! I never heard of someone coming three times. You end up in the sanitorium that way.'

'He's really strong, though. How good he was in bed!' He joined his hands together, then put the back of each hand against his cheeks and postured coquettishly. The jukebox happened to be belting out a conga, and he leaped to his feet and spun about in a wild dance.

'Well, Eichan, did you get taken?' said Rudy, who had been eavesdropping. 'And he's coming here? Who is he?'

'Now, now, the dirty old man gets into it right away!'

'If he's a nice boy, I'll treat you to a gin fizz,' said Rudy, whistling innocently.

'You want to bring him around with a gin fizz, don't you?' said Kimichan. 'If there's anything I hate it's a usurer.'

The word 'usurer' is part of the patois of this world. The idea of selling one's body for money is at times transformed in this way into the idea of selfish interest.

This was a good time at the place, and it was filled with

homosexuals who knew one another well. If an ordinary patron came in the door, he would not notice a sign of anything different except that there happened to be no women. There was an Iranian buyer and two or three other foreigners. There were middle-aged men. There was an affectionate pair of youths of about the same age. They would light their cigarettes, take a drag, and then exchange them.

It is not true there was no sign. Someone once said that homosexuals have on their faces a certain loneliness that will not come off. Besides, in their glances flirtatiousness and the cold stare of appraisal are combined. Although the coquettish looks that women direct at the opposite sex and the appraising glances they direct at their own sex have quite separate functions, with the homosexual both are directed at one and the same person.

Kimichan and Eichan were invited to the Iranian's table as a result of his whispering something in Rudy's ear.

'There, you've got a client,' Rudy said, pushing them from behind. Kimichan was quite reluctant about it. 'He's a mad foreigner; I can't bear him,' he grumbled. When they got to the table, he asked, in his normal voice: 'I wonder if this man can speak Japanese.'

'He doesn't look it.'

'I wouldn't be surprised if he could, the way things are lately.'

Recently the two had been invited to the table of a foreigner and sang him a toast: 'Harro, dahring blockhead. Harro, dahring dirty old man,' they sang in chorus, with the insulting words in Japanese. The foreigner laughed: 'Dirty boys and dirty old men get along well together,' he said in perfect Japanese.

Eichan was far from composed. His eyes moved repeatedly towards the door that exposed the night street. He thought of that fierce, sad profile, carved from rare alloys – the boy had the feeling he had seen it on one of the foreign coins he had once collected. He suspected that he had met his owner in an old tale.

Then the door was pushed open with youthful vigour. A surge of refreshing night air poured in. All raised eyes towards the door.

8

The Jungle of Sentiment

Universal beauty had won all with the first cast.

Yuichi floated on desire. The look they gave him was like that a woman feels when she passes among men and their eyes instantly undress her down to the last stitch. Practised appraisers' eyes usually do not make mistakes. The gently sloping chest Shunsuké saw back there in the spray, the slightly tapering, chastely mature trunk, the long easy sinewy legs. When one took these and added them to the matchless, pure, youthful, statutesque shoulders, the eyebrows like narrow blades, the melancholy eyes, the truly boyish lips, the white, orderly, correct teeth, and the beautiful head they composed, the potential lovely harmony between what one saw and could not see seemed as perfect as a product of the ratio of golden section. That perfect neck belonged to a perfect beautiful artistic restoration.

Even the normally carping critics at Rudon's were struck dumb. Before their companions, or the boys who were serving them, they refrained from putting into words the inexpressible admiration they felt. Their eyes, however, were taking the most beautiful visions of the countless young men they had caressed and placing them beside the naked body of Yuichi they had just sketched in their minds. There the vague shapes of the imaginary youths, the warmth of their flesh, the odour of their bodies, their voices, their kisses floated. But when these visions were placed beside the naked form of Yuichi, they shyly stole away. Their beauty was captive in the castle of individuality; Yuichi's beauty, overriding individuality, gleamed resplendent.

Their arms folded, they sat in silence, their chairs tilted against the walls in the dim distance. Conscious of the weight of those concentrated glances, he stood with downcast eyes.

Thus his beauty took on the semblance of the innocent standard-bearer at the head of the regiment.

Eichan left the foreigners' table guiltily, went to Yuichi's side, and touched his shoulder. 'Let's sit down,' Yuichi said. They sat facing each other, conscious of more glances than they dared face. They ordered cake. Unselfconsciously Yuichi opened his mouth wide and stuffed it with a huge piece of shortcake. Strawberries and cream were demolished by those white rows of teeth. To the boy watching, it was as if his own body were being swallowed to his boundless enjoyment.

'Eichan, won't you introduce the master?' Rudy said. The boy couldn't help but introduce them. 'How do you do? We hope you'll come here often. All of our clientele are fine people,' said the proprietor, as if he were stroking a cat.

After a time Eichan left for the men's room. Just then a flashily dressed middle-aged man came all the way over to the cashier's table to pay his check. In his face a certain indefinable childishness, a pent-up childishness, was evident. In the thickness of his eyelids especially, and in the region of his cheeks, the air of infancy was heavy. Bloated, isn't he? thought Yuichi. The man acted as if intoxicated. The distinctness of the raw lust that gleamed in his eyes contrasted strongly with his assumed role. As if he were groping for the wall, he let his hand fall on the youth's shoulder.

'Oh, excuse me,' he said, removing his hand. Between these words and the act of taking away his hand, however, in that instant's hesitation, there was what could be called a kind of groping. The somewhat unpleasant hiatus between word and action left an imprint on the youth's shoulder like a muscular stiffness. The older man looked towards the youth a second time; then, like a fox in flight, he broke off his gaze and departed.

When Eichan returned from the men's room, Yuichi told him what had happened. The boy was dumbfounded: 'What? Already? That's quick! That fellow was making a pass at you!'

To Yuichi, this staid restaurant was rather like the park; he was shocked at how soon it went through its formalities.

At that moment a small, dark, dimpled youth entered, arm in arm with a handsome foreigner. The youth was a ballet dancer who had recently been given a wide audience; his companion was his teacher, a Frenchman. They had met just after the war. The youth's reputation at present was largely due to the work of that teacher. For several years the sunny, golden-haired Frenchman had shared his quarters with his companion, twenty years his junior. It was rumoured that the Frenchman had recently fallen victim to a terrible whim, which came on him while drunk. He climbed the roof and tried to lay an egg.

This golden-haired chicken instructed his protégé to stand beneath the eaves with a basket and then asked all his invited guests to step out into the moonlit garden. Then he climbed a ladder and went out on the roof, bent over like a chicken. He turned up his tail, flapped his wings and cackled and cackled. As he did so, an egg dropped into the basket. Then he flapped again and cackled. A second egg fell.

His guests held their sides with laughter. Then they clapped their hands in applause. When the scene ended, however, and the host escorted them to the door, they saw a fifth egg, which he had forgotten to lay, rolling from the cuff of his trousers and splash its contents on the stone step. This chicken's cloaca was capable of holding five eggs – no mean feat.

When Yuichi heard the story he laughed and laughed. Then, as if someone had frowned at his mirth, he was silent. After a time he asked the boy: 'That foreigner and the ballet dancer – how long has it lasted?'

'Going on four years.'

'Four years!'

Yuichi tried to imagine a period of four years with this boy across the table and himself. Why did he feel certain that the rapture of the night before last would never be repeated in that four-year period?

The body of a man was something that spread out like the contour of a plain, a vast unbroken expanse. It had none of the fresh little marvellous springs, the mineral caves where exciting crystalline structures were to be seen as with the woman's body, which held out something new at each encounter. It was a simple exterior, the embodiment of pure, visible beauty. In the first fever of curiosity, love and desire were wagered.

99

Afterwards love invaded the spirit or simply and lightly stole away to another body.

After only one experience, Yuichi had already acquired the right to think: If only in the first night my love makes itself manifest, it would be no more than dishonest to both me and my lover to repeat my clumsy carbon copies of that first night. It will not do for me to judge my own sincerity by the sincerity of my lover, but the reverse of that. Perhaps my sincerity will take the form attained through an unlimited number of first nights spent with a succession of lovers encountered in turn. My constant love will be the common thread in the ecstasies of countless first nights, nothing other than the intense contempt of single encounters unchanging no matter whom I meet.

Yuichi compared this love with the synthetic love he accorded Yasuko. Both loves drove him without surcease. Loneliness gripped him.

While Yuichi sat silent, Eichan loked idly over at the table occupied by a group of youths. They sat leaning against each other. They seemed to be conscious of the transience of the ties that held them together and, rubbing shoulders and touching hands, to be barely resisting this sense of uneasiness. The tie that bound them seemed like the mutual affection of comrades-in-arms, who sense they will die on the morrow. As if this was too much to bear, one kissed another on the neck. After a time they hurriedly departed, their smooth-shaven napes alongside each other.

Seated in his double-breasted checked suit and toying with his lemon-coloured tie, Eichan opened his mouth slightly and watched them. Yuichi's lips had once searched his brows, his eyelids, even his mouth like that of a male doll. Yuichi had looked him over. Looking was cruel in the extreme. Every corner of the boy's body, even to the little mole on his back, Yuichi felt he knew. Once having entered this simple, lovely room, he remembered how it was made. There was a vase, and over there was a bookcase. Surely, until the room crumbled, the vase and the bookcase would remain in the same places, unmoved.

The boy took in that cool gaze. He suddenly grasped Yuichi's hands under the table. Cruelly, Yuichi wrenched his hand away. The cruelty was to a certain degree intentional. Over-burdened by the resentment against his wife which he would not reveal, Yuichi yearned for the right to be unequivocally cruel to someone he had loved.

Tears mounted in the boy's eyes.

'I know how you feel, Yuchan,' he said. 'You're tired of me already, aren't you?'

Yuichi denied it vehemently, but Eichan, as if speaking from experience of a different level from that of his older friend, went on maturely and decisively: 'Yes. I knew it from the moment you came in. That's the way it must be. That's the way we are, one-step men. I'm used to it and can take it. But I hoped that you above all would continue to be my big brother for the rest of our lives. Now I'll be satisfied for ever that I was your first lover. You won't forget me, will you?'

Yuichi was greatly moved by this tender entreaty. In his eyes, too, tears welled. He sought the boy's hand under the table and gently squeezed it.

At this moment the door opened and three foreigners entered. Yuichi remembered having seen the face of one of them. It was the slender foreigner who had come out of the building across the street at the time of his wedding reception. His suit was different, but he wore the same polka-dot bow tie. His hawk's eye roved the room. He seemed to be drunk. He clapped his hands smartly and called: 'Eichan! Eichan!'

His pleasant, sweet voice reverberated from the walls.

The boy looked down so that his face could not be seen. Then he clicked his tongue maturely and professionally: 'Oh my, I told him I wasn't coming here tonight.'

Rudon flapped the hem of his sky-blue jacket and leaned over the table. Then he said in a peremptory voice: 'Eichan. Get over there. It's your gentleman, you know.'

The atmosphere of the place was filled with sadness.

Rudy's insistent plea added to it. Yuichi was ashamed of the tears he had just shed. The boy glanced at Rudi and stood up motioning as if he were going to throw something at him.

Moments of decision sometimes provide balm for the soul's hurts. Yuichi now felt pride in the composure with which he could watch Eichan. His gaze collided with the boy's uncertainty. Then as if to try again and mend all, their eyes met again, but to no avail. The boy walked away. Yuichi looked in another direction, where he noticed the beautiful eye of a youth winking at him. His heart moved without hindrance, as easily as a butterfly, to meet that look.

The youth was leaning against the wall opposite. He was dressed in dungarees and a navy-blue corduroy jacket. He wore a dark-red necktie of coarse netting. He seemed to be a year or two younger than Yuichi. The flowing line of his brows and the wavy richness of his hair imparted a legendary cast to his face. Sad as a one-eyed jack, he winked in Yuichi's direction.

'Who is he?'

'Oh that's Shigechan. He's the son of a grocer over by Nakano. He's rather pretty. Shall I call him over?' said Rudy. He signalled, and that prince of the working classes rose nimbly from his chair. He alertly saw that Yuichi had just taken out a cigarette, and he struck a match with practised grace and held it within his palm. Translucent in the light of the match, his hand glowed like agate. It was a big, honest hand, however – legacy of his father's toil, one might surmise.

*

The dislocation in the thinking of the men who visited this place was subtle indeed. From his second day there, Yuichi was called 'Yuchan'. Rudy treated him more like a close friend than a customer. The patronage of Rudon's had increased suddenly, after all, the day after he showed up there, as if word of this new face had been deliberately broadcast. On the third day, something happened to swell Yuichi's reputation even more – Shigechan appeared at the place shaved bald as a monk. Since Yuichi had shared his bed with him the night before, he had, with no regret, cut off his beautiful, abundant hair as a token of his love.

Numerous fantastic stories of this kind circulated rapidly in the world of this persuasion. By the code of the secret society, stories were not carried one step outside, but once a miraculous story got started on the inside it replaced all earlier secrets of the boudoir. For, after all, nine tenths of the daily conversation was taken up with erotic reports of one's own and others' experiences in the bedroom.

As Yuichi's knowledge broadened, he came to be amazed at the unexpected scope of that world.

Muffled in a straw poncho, this world idled through the daylight hours. There was friendship, the love of comrades, philanthropy, the love of master and protégé; there were partners, assistants, managers, houseboys, leaders and followers, brothers, cousins, uncle and nephew, secretaries, amanuenses, drivers – there were numbers of other capacities and stations of diverse kinds: executives, actors, singers, authors, artists, musicians, high and mighty college professors, white-collar workers, students. In the world of men they idled, muffled in all kinds of ponchos made of straw.

They asked for themselves the advent of a world of supreme benison; bound by the spell of their common fate, they dreamed a dream of a simple truth. That dream was that the truth that man loves man would overthrow the old truth that man loves woman. Only the Jews were a match for them when it came to fortitude. In the abnormal degree to which they held fast to a single, humiliating point of view they were like the Jews. The emotion proper to this tribe gave birth to fanatical heroism during the war. After the war it embraced a pride at being in the van of decadence. It thrived on confusion. In that riven ground it grew clumps of tiny, dark violets.

Across this world of men only, however, a tremendous female shadow lay. All tossed in nightmare under this unseen feminine umbra. Some defied it; some resigned themselves to it; some resisted and in the end were defeated; some worshipped it from the beginning. Yuichi believed he was an exception. Then he prayed that he was an exception. Then he strove that he might be an exception. He worked that he might at least limit the influence of that awful shadow to trivial matters – such as looking in the mirror frequently, or the little habit of turning to look at his form reflected in windows at street corners, or, when he went to the theatre, the insignificant, functionless habit of walking affectedly in the hall during intermission. These are, of course, habits common among normal young people.

One day in the hall of the theatre Yuichi saw a singer who, though famous in that world, was married. He had a manly face and figure. He led a busy professional life and, as an avocation, boxed assiduously in a ring he had installed in his home. He had a sweet voice and possessed everything that girls clamoured for. Now he was busily surrounded by four or five ladylike young creatures. It happened, however, that a gentleman of about his own age called to him from near by. He might have been a schoolmate. The singer roughly grabbed his hand and shook it. (They looked for all the world as if they were getting ready to fight.) He shook the friend's right hand in great swings and pounded the friend's shoulder vigorously. His thin, serious friend staggered slightly. The young ladies looked at each other and laughed decorously.

This scene pierced Yuichi's heart. It was the exact opposite of what Yuichi had seen in the park – these fellows in all their coquettishness, hips swinging, shoulders drawn together, something so directly opposed that the hidden similar numbers came floating up like invisible ink, touching something disgusting that had been brought to live within him. Were he a spiritualist, surely he would have called it fate. The singer's empty, artificial coquetries directed at women; his entire life concentrated, his entire peripheral nervous system bent, intent, taut, totally engaged – that strenuous 'virile' performance capable of evoking tears was unbearably bitter to watch.

Afterwards 'Yuchan' was wooed incessantly. In short, intimacy was forced upon him.

In a few days a romantic middle-aged merchant came to Tokyo all the way from Aomori because he had already heard of Yuichi and longed for him. One foreigner offered, through Rudy, a suit of clothes, an overcoat, shoes, and a watch – a generous offer for one night's favours. Yuichi was not interested. One man moved into the chair next to Yuichi when it happened to be vacant and, feigning drunkenness, pulled his hat brim down over his eyes. Then he pushed his elbow far over the armrest and poked Yuichi meaningfully in the ribs several times.

From time to time Yuichi had to take a roundabout route home to avoid people covertly following him.

All that was known about him, however, was that he was still a student. His station, his history – above all the fact that he was already married, his lineage, his home, his house number – not a person knew. The being of this beautiful youth, therefore, was soon charged with the fragrance of divine miracle.

One day a palm reader who dealt primarily with homosexuals came into Rudon's. He was an old man, wearing a threadbare overcoat of the old Japanese style. He scanned Yuichi's palm and said, 'You have two choices, see. Like the two swords of Musashi Miyamoto, see. Somewhere away from here you have left a woman in tears, and you are here acting as if you don't know about it, right?'

Yuichi shuddered slightly. Revealed before his eyes was a certain pettiness, cheapness, in his exotic charm. It lacked a frame in real life.

That was true enough. The world that gathered at Rudon's supported no more life than the torrid zone, a life like that of practically exiled colonial administrative employees. In short, there was nothing more than the bare essentials of sentiment, the violent discipline of sentiment in that world. And if this was the political fate of the tribe, who could resist it? There, plants of extraordinary tenacity grew; it was the jungle of sentiment.

The man who lost his way in that jungle became affected by noxious exhalations and eventually turned into a kind of unsightly monster. No one had a right to laugh. The difference is only a matter of degree. In the world of homosexuality, no man has the power to resist the mysterious force that drags people down willy-nilly into the wallow of sentiment. A man might, for instance, resist by turning to a busy occupation, or intellectual pursuit, or art and cling to the higher intellectual levels of the masculine world. No man, however, can withstand the flood of emotion that cascades into his life; no man has been able to forget the connection that somehow exists between his body and this morass. No man has been able to cut his hand away summarily from the damp familiarity he has with the creatures of his kind. There have been countless attempts. The outcome of each, however, has been only this damp handshake again, only this sticky winking come round once more. Men like this, who essentially are incapable of maintaining a home, can find something like a household fire only in the gloomy eyes that say: 'You, too, are one of our kind.'

One day Yuichi's early morning lecture had ended, and in the interval before the next one began, he strolled around the fountain in the university garden. Paths stretched out in a grid pattern enclosing patches of lawn. The fountain stood out against a background of trees eloquent with the loneliness of autumn; as the wind changed, it drooped to leeward and wet the grass. Its fan, fluttering in the sky, at times seemed to have lost its pivot. Outside the gate, the superannuated intra-city trolleys sent the sound of their passing echoing off the mosaic walls of the lecture halls under the cloudy sky.

He did not choose one friend above another, and as far as the world was concerned he had no need of anyone to relieve his constant loneliness other than a few incorruptible souls with whom he could exchange notes. Among these steadfast friends, Yuichi was envied for his lovely wife, and the question as to whether marriage would cure his philandering was seriously argued. It was an argument that seemed to know what it was driving at, and it arrived at the conclusion that Yuichi was a woman chaser.

As a result, when he suddenly heard himself called by the name 'Yuchan,' his pulse quickened like that of a fugitive.

It was a student sitting on a stone bench caught up in ivy beside one of the paths where the sun now gently slanted. Bent over a large electrical engineering textbook open on his knees, the student had not been in Yuichi's field of vision until he called.

Yuichi stopped and regretted that he had done so. It would have been better to act as if it were not his name. Again the student called, 'Yuchan,' and stood up. He slapped the dust from his trousers carefully. He had a cheerful, round face, an animated face. His pants looked as if they got their crease by being placed under his mattress nightly. They stood straight and stiff as if they had been cut and hung up. He pulled up his trousers at the waist, and as he adjusted his belt, he exposed the broad pleats of his bright, immaculate white shirt.

'Are you speaking to me?' said Yuichi, pausing.

'Yes. I met you at Rudon's. My name is Suzuki.'

Yuichi looked at the face again. He didn't recall it.

'I guess you've forgotten. There are a lot of kids that wink at Yuchan. Even kids who have come there with their gentlemen wink at him. I haven't winked yet, though.'

'What do you want?'

'What do I want? Yuchan, of all people! Don't be uncouth. How'd you like to play around now?'

'Play around?'

'You don't understand, eh?'

The two youths slowly drew closer.

'But it's still broad daylight.'

'Even in the daylight there are loads of places to go.'

'Yes, for a man and a woman.'

'No, not that. I'll show you.'

'But ... I don't have anything on me.'

'I do. And if Yuchan will come play around with me, it's my pleasure.'

Yuichi cut that afternoon's lecture.

With what he got from working somewhere or other, the younger student treated to cab fare. The cab went through a dreary, burned-out mansion district of Takagicho, in Aoyama. Inside a gate of which only the stone wall had not burned down, before a house bearing the name 'Kusaka' and a barely visible new temporary roof, Suzuki ordered the cab to stop. There was a wicket gate in the entrance and an old-fashioned door that was shut tight. Suzuki rang the bell, and for no apparent reason unhooked the neckband of his student uniform. He turned to Yuichi and smiled.

In a short time the sound of garden *geta* moving with short, quick steps approached the entrance. A voice that was either a man's or a woman's – one could not tell which – asked who was there.

'It's Suzuki; open up,' the student said. The door opened. A middle-aged man in a bright red jacket greeted the two youths. The garden was strange to look at. It was possible to go to the outbuildings, connected with the main house by a covered way, on a path of steppingstones. The garden trees, however, were practically all gone. The spring had dried up. As if part of a wilderness in microcosm, fall plants were flourishing luxuriously everywhere and anywhere. Among the plants, foundation stones – remnants of a fire – gleamed whitely. The two students stepped up into a new four-and-a-half-mat outbuilding that still smelled of lumber.

'Shall I heat your bath?'

'No, thank you,' Suzuki said.

'Would you like a drink?'

'No, thank you.'

'Well,' the man said, grinning sagely, 'I'll lay out the bed. Young people are always in a hurry to get to bed.'

The two waited in the adjoining two-mat room until the *futon* was laid out. They said nothing. Suzuki offered Yuichi a cigarette. He accepted. With that, Suzuki put two cigarettes in his mouth, lit them, and gave Yuichi one with a smile. In the exaggerated composure of this student, Yuichi could not help but think there were traces of a childish innocence.

There was a sound as of distant thunder – the storm doors in the other room were being closed even though it was daytime.

They were called into the bedroom. A light was burning in the lamp by the bed. From the other side of the sliding doors, the man said, 'Rest well.' His retreating footsteps sounded from the covered passageway. It was a daytime sound – the creaking of the boards in the passageway – yet they made one think a feeble sun was shining.

Suzuki undid a breast button and lay down on the quilts. Propped on one elbow, he smoked his cigarette. As the sound of footsteps faded, he jumped up like a young hunting dog. He was somewhat shorter than Yuichi. He sprang to embrace Yuichi around the neck and kiss him. The two students kissed for something like four or five minutes. Yuichi slipped his hand inside the other boy's tunic, under the button that was loose. The heartbeat he felt was violent. The two separated, turned from each other and hastily tore off their clothing.

As the two naked youths embraced each other, the sound of

the trolley cars and the crow of roosters, inappropriate at this time, came to them as if it were the middle of the night.

Through a gap in the storm doors, however, a ray of the westering sun made the dust dance. Spots of coagulated resin in the centre of the knots in the wood were turned by the sun's rays into the colour of blood. A thin ray of light glinted off the muddy water that filled the vase in the alcove. Yuichi sank his face into Suzuki's hair. His hair was slicked down by lotion instead of oil and the smell was agreeable. Suzuki buried his face in Yuichi's breast. In the outer corners of his closed eyes, traces of tears glistened faintly.

The sound of a fire siren came dreamily into Yuichi's ears. As it faded in the distance it was followed by a second. Finally he heard a third, heading somewhere in the distance.

Another fire ... He pursued the slippery train of thought. Like the first day I went to the park. In a big city, there are always fires somewhere. And there are always crimes with fire, where, too. God, despairing of burning away crime with fire, perhaps distributed crime and fire in equal quantities. Thus crime is never consumed by fire, while innocence can be burnt up. That's why insurance companies prosper. My guilt, however – in order that it might become a pure thing immune to fire, must not my innocence first pass through the fire? My complete innocence where Yasuko is concerned.... Didn't I once ask to be born again for Yasuko's sake? And now?

At four o'clock in the afternoon the two students shook hands in front of Shibuya Station and separated. Neither had the feeling he had conquered the other.

When he got home, Yasuko said: 'You're home unusually early. Are you going to stay home all evening?'

Yuichi said he would, but that evening he and his wife went to the movies. The seats were narrow. Yasuko leaned against his shoulder. Suddenly she pulled her head away. Her eyes narrowed wisely, like the ears of a dog coming to a point.

'You smell good. You put on hair lotion, didn't you?'

Yuichi started to deny it, but he caught himself and said she was right. Yasuko, however, seemed to realize that it was not her husband's scent. And what if she did? It was not really a woman's scent either.

9

Jealousy

'I have made a terrific find,' Shunsuké wrote in his diary. 'To have found such a perfect living doll as this! Yuichi is truly exquisite. Not only that, he is morally frigid. He isn't addicted to circumspection, of which other youths smell like incense. He doesn't take responsibility for his actions in the slightest. The morality of this youth says, in short, "Don't do anything." Thus, once he starts to do something he rules out morality. This youth decays like radioactive material. He is truly the thing I have long wearied of searching for. Yuichi does not believe in the modern distress.'

A few days after the Charity Ball, Shunsuké laid plans to have Kyoko and Yuichi meet accidentally. He heard the story of Rudon's from Yuichi. It was his suggestion that they meet there in the evening.

That afternoon Shunsuké Hinoki delivered a speech, which he hated to do. He was reduced to it by the necessity of promoting his *Complete Works*. It was an afternoon in which the coolness of early autumn was noticeable. The gloomy figure of the old writer in his Western suit lined with silk floss intimidated the people assisting with the lecture. He stood at the rostrum still wearing his cashmere gloves. He had no reason for doing so. The impudent young man running the lecture had been careful to inform Shunsuké that he had forgotten to take off his gloves, so he went ahead with them on, just to annoy.

The audience that filled the hall numbered about two thousand. Shunsuké looked at lecture audiences with contempt. Among the members of lecture audiences, there are the same fads that are current in modern photography. There is the watch-for-a-chance method, the unguarded-moment method, the reverence for naturalness, the faith in the unvarnished truth, the over-valuation of daily life, the interest in anecdote – all crazes that take into account only men put together of such worn-out materials. The photographers say: 'Relax,' or 'Keep talking,' or 'Smile, please.' The audience asks the same things. They are addicted to earnestness and the unpainted face. Shunsuké hated the preoccupation with modern psychology that judged his casual, offhand remarks or his daily actions as betraying his identity or ideas with better clarity than did his highly polished sentences.

To countless curious eyes, he exposed his familiar face. Before this throng, convinced beyond a shadow of a doubt that individuality was better than beauty, he felt not the slightest sense of inferiority. Shunsuké indifferently smoothed the creases out of his thin note-paper and placed the cut-glass water pitcher on them by way of a paperweight. The moisture ran into the ink and turned the notes to a lovely indigo. It made him think of the ocean. With that, somehow he had the feeling that in that jet-black audience of two thousand, Yuichi, Yasuko, Kyoko, and Mrs Kaburagi were buried from sight. Shunsuké loved them, because they were not people who would come out to a lecture or anything of the kind.

'True beauty makes men dumb,' began the old man, in spirit-less tones. 'In the days when this faith had not yet been destroyed, criticism was a profession unto itself. Criticism strove to imitate beauty.' With his cashmere glove, Shunsuké stroked the air and gestured with his fingers. 'In short, criticism, like beauty, sought above all to strike men dumb. We can't call this an objective so much as an anti-objective. Criticism's method was to evoke silence without calling on beauty. It depended on the power of logic. The logic that is criticism's method, with beauty's coercive power, must impose silence forcibly. This silence must depend for its effectiveness, as the end product of criticism, on creating the delusion that here beauty exists. A vacuum must be given shape as a surrogate for beauty. In this way only, criticism succeeded in being of use in the process of creation.

'At some time, however, the faith that beauty must strike dumb became a thing of the past. Beauty has not only failed to silence people, it has gotten so even when it passes through the middle of a banquet people don't stop talking. Those of you who have gone to Kyoto do not fail to go to the Stone Garden at the Ryoanji Temple. That garden, though, is never a problem; it is beauty, pure and simple. It is a garden to strike man dumb. The amusing thing, though, is that the fine people who are so kind as to fare forth to view this august garden are not satisfied simply to be silent. Saying that it would not do not to say a word, they screw up their faces trying to squeeze out a haiku.

'Beauty has become a stimulus to garrulity. It has gotten so that on confronting the beautiful one feels duty-bound to say something in a great hurry. It has gotten so we feel we must convert beauty right away. If we don't convert it, it's dangerous. Like explosives, beauty has become a difficult thing to own. The power of possessing beauty through silence, this majestic power for which one would lay down his life, has been lost.

'With this the age of criticism began. Criticism came to function not as the imitator of beauty, but as the converter of it. Criticism marshalled its forces in the direction opposite to that of beauty. Critics who earlier were followers of beauty now became the stockbrokers of beauty, the process servers of beauty. To wit, as the belief that beauty would strike men dumb went into decline, criticism had to flaunt its sad sovereignty as surrogate, standing in for beauty. Beauty itself struck no man dumb; much less so did criticism. Thus today's evil times of talk begetting talk, of ears being deafened by it, began. Beauty makes men everywhere chatter. In the end, thanks to this loquaciousness, beauty is artificially [What a strange way to express it!] propagated. The mass production of beauty has begun. Thus criticism, turning to these numberless imitation beauties – born from essentially the same place as itself – had heaped vile oaths upon them. . . .'

After the meeting was over, and Shunsuké entered Rudon's at nightfall to meet Yuichi, the guests who observed the entrance of this fidgety, lonely old man took one look and averted their eyes. Just as when Yuichi entered, everyone was silent, but here it was not beauty but lack of concern that struck men dumb. It was, however, not a forced silence.

112

As if he knew him well, the old man bowed to Yuichi, who sat in a corner talking to the young men; he found a place at the somewhat isolated table to which he had invited Yuichi. Every eye showed unusual interest.

Yuichi joined Shunsuké, exchanged a few words, then excused himself for a moment. When he returned to Shunsuké he said: 'It seems that everybody thinks I'm your boy friend. They asked me if that was so; I told them it was. That way you'll have no trouble coming around here. Since you're a novelist you must surely find much of interest in a place like this.'

Shunsuké was shocked, but because he preferred to let matters in this place take their course he did not reprove him for his rashness.

'If you are my boy friend, how am I supposed to act towards you?'

'That's a problem, isn't it? If you just look quietly happy, it will be fine.'

'Me, happy?'

It was uncanny – Shunsuké, the dead man, portraying happiness! He was perplexed by this strange role he had been pressed into by this unexpectedly forceful director.

Taking the opposite tack, he tried to make a wry face. That was difficult, however. Thinking he was making a fool of himself, he gave up trying to act anything. He was aware that now an expression of happiness radiated his countenance.

Since he could think of no proper explanation for his lightness of heart, Shunshuké assumed it was from his customary professional curiosity. Long deprived of his literary powers, he was embarrassed by his false fervour. For ten years now, how many times the impulse to create had flooded over him like a tide, but when he took brush in hand, the brush would not write so much as a line. The artistic impulse that in his young days nagged at him like an illness in everything he did now was only a barren half-starved curiosity.

How beautiful Yuichi is! the old author thought, watching him from a distance when he left his seat again. Among these four or five beautiful boys, he alone stands out. Beauty is something that burns the hand when you touch it. Thanks to him there must surely be a lot of burned homosexuals.

Now, before his eyes, a rather tense scene began.

Yuichi had been called over to the table of two foreigners. The table happened to be separated from Shunsuké's table by a water tank in which fresh-water fish were swimming. It served as a screen. In the tank green lights had been placed that gleamed through the clumps of seaweed. Set off by the lights, the ripples threw patterns on the face of the bald-headed foreigner. His companion was a much younger foreigner who seemed to be his secretary. The older man spoke no Japanese, and the secretary interpreted everything he said to Yuichi.

The rhythmic Boston English of the older man, the fluent Japanese of the secretary, and the short answers of Yuichi all made their way to Shunsuké's ears.

First the old foreigner poured Yuichi a beer; then he praised his beauty and his youth over and over. These flowery words and phrases made for a rare translation. Shunsuké listened attentively. The gist of the conversation was becoming clear.

The old foreigner was a trader. He was looking for a young beautiful Japanese youth as a companion. It was the secretary's job to select that person. The secretary had recommended many young men to his employer, but they had not appealed to him. He had, in fact, come here several times. This evening for the first time, however, he had discovered the ideal youth. If Yuichi wished, a purely platonic association would be satisfactory for the time being, but, the request went, would he enter into some kind of arrangement?

Shunsuké noticed that there was a strange gap between the original statement and the interpretation. Subjects and objects were being intentionally muddied. At no time could it be called unfaithful, but the tone of the interpretation struck Shunsuké as being a sweet, flirtatious circumlocution. The young secretary had a fierce, Germanic profile. From thin lips he pronounced his sharp, dry, clear-as-a-whistle Japanese. Shunsuké glanced under the table and started. Both the secretary's feet were locked tightly about Yuichi's ankle. The old foreigner seemed quite unaware of this barefaced coquetry.

At last the old man began to understand what was going on.

114

There was no duplicity in the letter of the interpretation, but the secretary was doing his best to get one foot ahead of his employer in Yuichi's esteem.

By what name can the unspeakably painful emotion be called that now overcame Shunsuké? Shunsunké glanced at the shadow thrown by Yuichi's eyelashes on his downturned cheek. These long eyelashes, creating conjectures of how beautiful they must be in bed, suddenly fluttered. The youth's smiling glance flashed in the direction of Shunsuké. The old author shivered. Then a deeper, twofold, unfathomable despair gripped him.

You must be jealous, he said to himself, judging by this pain in your breast.

- He was reminded of each detail of the feeling that tortured him when long ago he was shown the prurience of his wanton wife in the kitchen door in the dawn. There was the same pain in his breast, an emotion that had no outlet. In this feeling, the only thing that was worth all the emotions of the world, the only prize, was his ugliness.

That was jealousy. In shame and anger this dead man's face flushed. In a piercing voice, he called: 'Check!' He stood up.

'Well, that old man is singeing in jealousy's flame,' whispered Kimichan to Shigechan. 'What does Yuchan see in him? How many years, I wonder, has Yuichi been hooked up with that old guy?'

'He even followed Yuichi here, didn't he?' said Shigechan, his voice ringing with hostility. 'He's really a shameless old man.'

'He looks like a profitable client.'

'What does he do? He looks as if he's got a penny or two.'

'Maybe he's an alderman or something.'

At the door, Shunsuké realized that Yuichi had arisen and was coming quietly after him. On the street Shunsuké stretched himself, then pounded himself over and over on the shoulders, alternating hands.

'Are your shoulders stiff?'

Yuichi spoke in a gentle, reassuring tone, giving the old man the feeling that his inner depths were open to view.

'The same thing will happen to you someday. The shame gradually gets inside you. When young people are embarrassed, their skin turns red. We feel embarrassment in the flesh, particularly the bones. My bones hurt because I was taken for one of the fraternity.'

The two strolled about for a time, side by side through the crowds.

'You don't like youth, do you?' Yuichi came out with this suddenly. They were words Shunsuké had not anticipated.

'What do you mean?' he said, affronted. 'If I don't like youth, how did I ever beat my old bones into coming here?'

'Just the same, you don't like youth.' Yuichi said it again with finality.

'Youth that is not beautiful. "Beautiful youth" is an annoying twist of phrase. My youth was ugly. That's something you can't imagine. I spent my youth wishing to be born again.'

'Me, too.'

'You mustn't say that. When you say that, you violate a taboo, or something. It is your fate never to be able to say that. By the way, I hope I didn't get you into trouble with that foreigner by walking out so suddenly just now.'

'No, not at all,' said the youth unconcernedly. It was close to seven o'clock. The throng was at its height on the street at this time, which had been the hour of early closing during the war. It was a very misty evening, and the outline of the distant shops was like a copper-plate lithograph. The smell of the twilit street busily teased the nostrils. It was the best time of the year for subtle olfactory excitement. The smells of fruits, flannels, newly printed books, evening papers, kitchens, coffee, shoe polish, gasoline, and pickles mingled and created a translucent picture of the business of the street. The noise of the elevated train battered at their conversation.

'There's a shoe store,' Shunsuké said, pointing to a brightly decorated window. 'It's a high-priced shop, called Kiriya. Tonight that store is going to have the dancing shoes ready that Kyoko ordered. Kyoko is coming for them at seven. At that time I want you to be going in and out, looking at men's shoes. Kyoko is a fairly punctual woman. When she comes, act surprised and say, "Oh!" Then invite her for tea. She'll take care of the rest.'

'And you?'

'I'll be at the little restaurant over there, having tea,' the old man said.

Yuichi was perplexed by the strangely narrow and twisted view this old man had of youth. He supposed it came from the poverty of his own youth. Yuichi imagined the tiny bit of youthful ugliness that might have come back into Shunsuké's cheek while he walked about checking the time of Kyoko's appointment at the shoe store. He could not, however, think of it any longer as alien to himself. At the same time, thanks to his abnormally close contact with the self in his mirror, he was already slave to the habit of taking his own beauty into account on every occasion.

10

The False Accident and the True

For the past twenty-four hours, Kyoko Hodaka had thought of nothing but her chartreuse dancing slippers. Nothing else in the world mattered to her. Whoever looked at Kyoko would think fate had surely touched her lightly. Like a person who had thrown himself into a salt lake and then found himself buoyed up and rescued in spite of himself, Kyoko never ever under any circumstances got to the bottom of her emotions. For that reason, although her sunny disposition was instinctive, it seemed to be something imposed upon her by conscious policy.

There were times when Kyoko was feverish; people were always seeing the calm hand of her husband in the background, fanning this false passion. In truth, she was like a well-trained dog, an intelligence built up from nothing more than force of habit. Those impressions gave to her own natural beauty the beautiful aspect of a plant made painstakingly by hand.

Kyoko's husband was tired of her complete lack of sincerity. In order to increase the heat of his wife's passion he resorted to every technique of lovemaking. In order to make her serious, he played philanderer, very much against his inclinations. Kyoko wept often. Her tears, however were only showers. Start a serious story, and Kyoko would giggle as if tickled. Just the same, she lacked the superabundance of wit and humour that could have redeemed her womanliness.

In her bed by the morning, if ten great ideas occurred to Kyoko, by nightfall it would be surprising if she remembered one or two. Her plan to change the picture in her living room might thus be put off for ten days. The few things that did happen to remain in her mind had to wait until they became nagging nuisances before they got done.

The fold of her rather Caucasian eyelids would sometimes show an extra fold. Her husband hated to see this, for it became shockingly evident at those moments that there was not a thing on her mind.

That day Kyoko had gone to the near by stores shopping with a former servant. In the afternoon she entertained two of her husband's female cousins. The cousins played the piano and Kyoko merely sat, not listening. When it was over she clapped and meted out effusive compliments. Then they talked about some shop in the Ginza where Western pastries were cheap and delicious, or how a watch that one of them bought with dollars was selling at three times the price in a store in the Ginza. Then they talked about the fabrics they were getting ready for winter, and after that they came to the best-selling novel. Then the fair argument was advanced that the reason novels were cheaper than Western fabrics was, naturally, that they couldn't be worn about. All Kyoko was thinking about then was her dancing slippers, but the cousins, who noticed her absent-mindedness, thought she must be in love. It was doubtful, however, that Kyoko was capable of loving anything more than dancing slippers.

For this reason, Shunsuké's expectations notwithstanding, Kyoko had cleanly forgotten about the beautiful youth who had made such a fuss about her at the last ball. When Kyoko came face to face with Yuichi on her way into the shoe store, her mind was full of the idea that she would soon see her shoes. She was not particularly surprised at running him and she greeted him perfunctorily.

Yuichi suddenly realized the meanness of the part he was playing. He decided to leave, but anger held him back for the time being. He hated that woman. He had even forgotten his hatred of Shunsuké, evidence that the passion of Shunsuké now possessed him. He whistled unconcernedly as he passed inside and looked at the window displays from that vantage point. His whistle reverberated with his disappointment. Occasionally his eyes flicked back to the woman behind him trying on her shoes, and as he did so a dark competitive spirit developed in him.

'All right! I'll really make that woman unhappy.'

The style of the dancing slippers was exactly what Kyoko wanted. She had the clerk wrap them up. Her fever slowly subsided.

She turned and smiled. Then she became really aware of the lone, beautiful youth for the first time.

This evening her good fortune was like a faultless bill of fare. Though it was not her way to extend an invitation to a man she did not know well she went up to Yuichi and ever so gently said: 'Would you like to go somewhere for a cup of tea?'

Yuichi nodded in silence.

It was past seven, and a great number of shops had already closed. The tea shop in which Shunsuké was sitting was still brightly lighted. As they passed it, Kyoko started to enter, but Yuichi headed her off. After that they passed two places with drawn curtains; then at last they came to one that looked as if it might be open.

They sat down at a table in the corner, and Kyoko casually pulled off her lace gloves. Her eyes were glowing. She looked at Yuichi steadily and inquired: 'Is your wife well?'

'Yes.'

'Are you all alone today?'

'Yes.'

'I see. You're going to meet your wife here, and it'll be nice if I keep you company until she comes.'

'I'm really alone. I just came over here on a little business at a friend's office.'

'Is that so?' The note of caution vanished from her voice. 'I haven't seen you since that time.'

It came back to Kyoko slowly: the way that youth's body, like an animal, filled with majesty, had pressed her body into the corner; the way his fierce eyes begging her pardon seemed more intent on some design of their own; his rather long sideburns forming a point under the temples; his passionate cheeks; his simple child's lips, pouting as if caught in the midst of a complaint.

Then another definite recollection insisted on returning. She decided to test it with a trick. She pulled the ash tray towards her. Now when the youth wanted to tap off his ashes he had to bend his head before her, like that of a young bull. She inhaled the aroma of his hair cream. It was a scent throbbing with youth. That was the scent!

That scent she had caught again and again, even in her dreams, since the evening of the ball. One morning this scent of her dreams enveloped her tenaciously even after she had awakened. She had some shopping to do in the city, and about an hour after her husband went to his job at the Foreign Office, she boarded a bus jammed with people who started work later than most. There she got a strong whiff of that same pomade. Her breast was in tumult. When she got a look at the profile of the youth wearing it, however, she was disappointed to realize that though the pomade had the same scent as in her dream the face bore no relation to it. She didn't know the name of the pomade, but from time to time in crowded trolleys or stores, the aroma was wafted to her from she knew not where, over-powering her, she knew not why.

That's it! That's the scent! Kyoko looked at Yuichi un-waveringly with new eyes. She had discovered in this youth the dangerous power he was plotting to wield over her, a dazzling power.

Yet here was a truly frivolous woman, and she found amusing the power that every man worthy of the name ex-erted. Be they ugly or handsome, men all had in common this master-slave absurdity they call desire. For instance, the man does not exist who from the time he ceases being a boy is not ruled by the theme of those stories—the trite theme that goes: 'Woman is never intoxicated by her own happiness at any time so much as when she sees desire in a man's eyes.'

How ordinary is this young man's youthfulness, thought Kyoko, still full of self-reliance in her own youthfulness. It's a youthfulness you find everywhere. It's a youthfulness aware that it is at the age most prone to confuse sincerity with desire.

In perfect consonance with the misapprehensions Kyoko was thus arriving at, Yuichi's eyes brimmed with the cloudi-ness of a somewhat dissipated passion. Those eyes had not forgotten however, their natural blackness, and when she looked at them she felt as if a torrent was roaring through a conduit.

'Have you been dancing anywhere since I saw you last?'

'No, I haven't.'

'Doesn't your wife like dancing?'

'She rather likes it.'

How noisy it was! This restaurant was really a quiet place. Nevertheless, the low sound of records, of shoes, of plates, of laughter from the patrons at infrequent intervals, as well as the telephone, all commingled and amplified, irritating the ear. As if bearing them ill will, the sound drove a wedge into their already stilted conversation. Kyoko felt as if she and Yuichi were talking under water.

When she tried to approach him in their conversation, he seemed to move away. Happy-go-lucky person that she was, Kyoko was just beginning to realize the great gulf that lay between her and this youth who seemed to desire her so much. I wonder if my words are getting across to him, she thought. Maybe it's because the table is too big. Without realizing it, Kyoko was exaggerating her own emotions.

'Now that you've danced with me, you don't seem to want anything more to do with me, do you?'

Yuichi's expression seemed to be one of discomfort. If this sort of give and take, this unpremeditated acting in departure from the script, had become second nature with him, it was largely attributable to the power of that wordless youth in the mirror. The mirror had schooled him in the expression of the various emotions that all the angles and shades of his beauty spoke of. After a time his beauty had, by conscious effort, become independent of Yuichi himself, and thus made itself freely available to him.

Perhaps for this reason Yuichi no longer felt the constraint as with Yasuko before they were married. In fact, he had succeeded by this time in freely revelling with almost sensual gusto in the presence of women. A vague, abstract sensuality, it was the feeling that had intrigued him once in swimming and high jumping. In possession of this freedom unfettered by the great adversary that is sexuality, he felt that his own existence was like a delicately versatile mechanism.

For want of something better, Kyoko gossiped about people she knew. She mentioned various names, but Yuichi didn't recognize any. Kyoko thought that amazing. As far as Kyoko knew, romance was a thing that could only happen to her or her acquaintances. Even they, however, were always paired in perfectly predictable patterns. In short, the arranged romance was all they believed in.

After a time, Kyoko did hit on a name Yuichi knew: 'Did you know Reiko Kiyoura, who died three or four years ago?'

'Yes; she was my cousin.'

'Why, then you're called Yuchan by your relatives, aren't you?'

Yuichi started; then he smiled calmly.

'I guess I am.'

'So you're Yuchan.'

Kyoko looked at him so fixedly that Yuichi felt uncomfortable. She explained why. Of her classmates, Reiko had been her closest friend. Before she died, Reiko had entrusted her diary to Kyoko. It was a diary in which she had written up till a few days before the end. The only thing this poor long-suffering woman had felt that mattered in her life was the occasional sight of her young cousin's beautiful face.

She loved this youth, who visited at infrequent and irregular intervals. She would ask to kiss him, but he, fearing contagion, would shudder and hold back. After all, Reiko's husband had passed his own infection on to his wife before he died.

Reiko tried to let the youth know how she felt, but she never succeeded. Now a fit of coughing, now reticence stood in the way of her confession. To her this young eighteen-year-old cousin was like a young tree catching the sun in the garden just outside her sickroom. She saw in him all that shone, all that stood opposed to sickness and death. His health, his bright laughter, his beautiful white teeth, his freedom from pain and misery, his naïveté, the way vernal youth touched him in dazzling brightness: all she seized upon. She feared, however, that her confession of love, if it awakened sympathy in him, or if it made him begin to love her, would mark his cheek with pain and misery. She preferred to go to her grave remembering only the fierceness of his profile and his almost unconscious youthful capriciousness. Every day's entry in her diary began with the invocation: 'Yuchan.' She took an apple he had brought one day, cut his initial out of it, and kept it hidden under her pillow. She also teased him for his picture. He modestly turned her down.

Kyoko had reason to find the name Yuchan more appealing than Yuichi. Not only that, she had come to love this name, as she had built it up in her fancy since Reiko's death.

Listening to her, Yuichi toyed with his silver-plated spoon. Her revelation stirred him. He was learning for the first time that his bedridden cousin, ten years his senior, had loved him. Also, he was amazed at how far mistaken her idea of him had been. At the time he had been groaning under the weight of aimless, abnormal sexual desire. He also envied his cousin her then not very distant death.

I had no reason at that time to pull the wool over Reiko's eyes, Yuichi thought. It just happened because I hated to lay my heart bare. Reiko, furthermore, had the mistaken notion I was a simple uncomplicated boy; and I, for my part, was quite unaware of Reiko's love. I suppose everybody finds in a mistaken notion about another person his one reason for living. In short, this youth, permeated with the virtue of pride, was trying to persuade himself that his dallying with Kyoko was sincerity itself.

Kyoko sat back and observed Yuichi. She was already in love with him. The motivation of her shallow heart sprang from, one might almost say, a faint mistrust of her own passions. When, therefore, she had before her a witness to the passion of the dead Reiko, she was able to affirm the validity of her own passion.

Besides, Kyoko miscalculated. She felt that Yuichi's heart had been inclined towards her from the beginning. She had therefore only to come half a step.

'I wish we could find a place to talk quietly. Is it all right if I call you?'

Yuichi, however, was usually not at home at any definite hour. He suggested he do the calling, but Kyoko informed him that she herself was seldom at home. She was therefore delighted to find that they must arrange for their next meeting then and there.

124

Kyoko took out her appointment book and grasped the delicate pencil fastened to it by a silk cord. She had many appointments. It filled her with secret pleasure to cancel the one that was most difficult to break. Across the date of a reception for a certain international figure which required her attendance at the Foreign Office with her husband, she lightly drew the point of her pencil. It would provide the very secrecy and excitement her next meeting with Yuichi would require.

Yuichi agreed. The woman grew bolder; she suggested he see her home this evening. The youth hesitated, and she told him that she only said it to see the troubled look on his face. Then she gazed at his shoulders, much as one would gaze at a mountain peak. Hoping he would speak, she kept quiet for a time; then she started chattering again. She went so far as to demand herself by saying: 'Your wife is lucky. You're really considerate of her.'

Having said this, she slumped in her chair as if worn out completely.

Suddenly a thrill went through Kyoko. She had guests coming to the house this evening! They were waiting for her. She decided not to meet them. She got up to telephone an excuse.

The call went right through, but the voice came from far away. She could not hear the maid's words distinctly. Interfering with their exchange was a sound in the phone like that of falling rain. She looked out of the great plate-glass window. It was raining. Unfortunately she had not brought any rain gear with her. She felt very daring.

On the way back to her place, she saw a middle-aged woman sitting beside Yuichi. Kyoko drew her chair away as she sat down. Yuichi introduced the woman: 'This is Mrs Kaburagi.'

Each woman perceived the hostility of the other at a glance. This accidental meeting was something Shunsuké had not reckoned with; Mrs Kaburagi had in fact, been watching the two from a distant corner for some time.

'I came a little early for our appointment. I didn't want to interfere until you'd finished with your business. I beg your pardon,' Mrs Kaburagi said. In that instant, in the act of telling that little-girl fib, Mrs Kaburagi showed her age as infallibly as did her too youthful makeup. Kyoko saw the ugliness of those years with relief. Convinced of her advantage, she saw through the lie. She smiled in Yuichi's direction, with a wink to indicate that she understood.

What prevented Mrs Kaburagi's noticing the contemptuous wink of the younger woman was the fact that jealousy had robbed her of pride. Kyoko said: 'I must beg your pardon for having kept you waiting with my ceaseless chatter. Well, I must be going now. Would you get me a cab, Yuchan? It's raining.'

'Raining?' Embarrassed at being addressed as Yuchan, he pretended to be astonished by the rain, as if it were a momentous event.

As soon as Yuichi was outside the door, a cruising cab drove up. He signalled towards the restaurant. Kyoko said good-bye to Mrs Kaburagi and arose. Yuichi saw her off, waving his hand in the rain. Without a word, she departed.

Yuichi returned to Mrs Kaburagi and sat down. His wet hair clung to his brow like seaweed. Then he saw that Kyoko had left a package behind in her chair. Swiftly he picked it up and started to run outside. He had forgotten that the cab had departed. This concern he was showing for someone else filled Mrs Kaburagi with dismay.

'Did she forget something?' she asked, forcing a smile.

'Yes, her new shoes.'

Both believed that Kyoko had forgotten no more than a pair of shoes. Actually she had left behind something that, until she met Yuichi today, had been the sole concern of this day in her life.

'It might be a good idea to go after her. You might still overtake her.' Mrs Kaburagi said this with a bitter smile, obviously to annoy him.

Yuichi made no reply. The woman said nothing more, but over her silence the flag of defeat fluttered plainly. Her voice rose in excitement, almost tearfully. 'I've made you angry, haven't I? I'm sorry. I have a bad habit of doing mean things like that.' While she spoke, she kept thinking that the next day Yuichi would deliver the shoes to Kyoko and would explain Mrs Kaburagi's lie.

'No, I'm not angry at all.'

Yuichi's smile was like a patch of blue sky on a cloudy day. He could not have imagined how much strength Mrs Kaburagi derived from that smile. Drawn by that youthful smile, so like a sunflower, she was buoyed to the peak of happiness.

'I'd like to give you something to show you how sorry I am. Can we leave?'

'Never mind being sorry. Anyway, it's raining.'

It was an intermittent shower. Since it was night, they couldn't tell whether it had cleared. A slightly intoxicated man happened to leave just then; he called out near the doorway: 'Oh, it's stopped. It's stopped raining.' Patrons who had come in to seek shelter from the rain hurried out again into the clear night air. Urged by Mrs Kaburagi, Yuichi picked up Kyoko's package and followed her, turning up the collar of his navy-blue trench coat.

Now, Mrs Kaburagi's mind busied itself blowing up out of all proportion the bit of luck that had led her to this happy encounter. Since that last time she had struggled with jealousy. Her self-restraint was stronger than that of most men, and it gave her the power to keep her resolve not to make advances to him. She started going out for walks all alone. She went to the movies alone. She ate her meals alone. She had tea alone. She was alone, but, paradoxically, she felt that she was gaining freedom from her emotions.

Nevertheless, wherever she went, Mrs Kaburagi felt the gaze of Yuichi's proud contempt following her. That gaze would say: 'Get on your knees. At once – down on your knees before me!'

One day she went to the theatre – alone. During the intermission she witnessed the awful crowding in front of the mirror in the ladies' room. The ladies' faces were almost in collision – every woman for herself; they pushed out their cheeks, they pouted their lips, they protruded their foreheads, they stroked out their eyebrows – so as to apply their rouge, their lipstick, their eyebrow pencil, to rearrange a stray hair, to make sure that the curls so carefully rolled this morning had not committed the unspeakable sin of coming undone. One woman had shamelessly taken out her teeth. Another, choking on powder, was making a terrible face. If one were to put that mirror in a painting, he would certainly hear the dying screams of slaughtered women coming from the canvas. Mrs Kaburagi saw that in all this pitiable turmoil, her face alone was cool, white, and composed. 'Get on your knees! Down on your knees!' – blood gushed from her pride's wounds.

Now, however, drunk with the nectar of submission – pathetically going so far as to believe that this sweetness was the boon of her own cunning – she cut into the rain-wet tracks of the automobiles and across the street. A broad, yellow leaf fallen from one of the trees along the street clung to the trunk and fluttered like a moth. A wind had sprung up. Silent, as she had been on the evening she first met Yuichi at the Hinoki home, she led him into a certain tailor's. The clerks in the store treated Mrs Kaburagi with deference. She had them bring out winter materials and placed them over Yuichi's shoulders. Thus she was able to inspect him with care.

'It's uncanny. Any pattern goes well with you,' she said, holding piece after piece of material across his chest. Yuichi was in despair, imagining that the store clerks thought him a complete fool. Mrs Kaburagi chose one pattern, and had them take his measurements. The old and experienced owner of the firm was amazed at the youth's ideal measurements.

Yuichi thought uneasily of Shunsuké. The old man was surely still in that tea shop, patiently waiting. Just the same it would not be good policy to have Mrs Kaburagi run across Shunsuké this evening. One could not say, furthermore, where Mrs Kaburagi might still want to go. Yuichi was gradually coming to need Shunsuké's help less and less, and, like a schoolboy developing an interest in detested, enforced homework, he was becoming infatuated with the excitement of this inhuman comedy with womankind as antagonist.

In short, the Trojan horse in which Shunsuké had imprisoned this youth, this replica of the violent power of nature itself, this fearful mechanism, was miraculously beginning to move. Whether the fire that had been building up between the two women would become hotter or cooler was entirely a matter for Yuichi's pride to decide. His cold rage had begun to assert itself. He was possessed of a self-confidence completely devoid of compassion. He looked at this woman who, having just ordered a new suit of clothes for him, was now drunk in her small and conventional joy of giving, and thought how like a monkey she was. Truthfully, this young man found it impossible to see any beautiful person, so long as she was a woman, as more than a monkey.

Mrs Kaburagi would laugh and be defeated, keep quiet and be defeated, chatter and be defeated, give things away and be defeated, from time to time look at his profile as if stealing and be defeated, act cheerful and be defeated, pretend despair and be defeated. Before long this woman who never cried would even be defeated in tears, of this there was no doubt.

Yuichi flung his coat on roughly; the comb fell out of his pocket. Before Yuichi or the tailors could retrieve it, Mrs Kaburagi nimbly stooped for it. She herself was amazed at her own condescension.

'Thank you.'

'My, it's a big comb. It looks as if it does the job.' Before she returned it to its owner, she passed it quickly through her hair a couple of times. The pulling of the hair in the comb made her eyes twitch a little and brought moisture to the tense outer corners.

After parting from Mrs Kaburagi at a bar, Yuichi went to the restaurant where Shunsuké had been waiting, but it was closed. Rudon's stayed open until the last trolley, so he went there, and Shunsuké was waiting, Yuichi told all that had happened. Shunsuké laughed aloud.

'It's probably best for you to take the shoes home and act as if you don't know anything about them until you hear from her. Kyoko will probably call your house and leave word at least by tomorrow. Now your date with Kyoko is for October twenty-ninth, isn't it? That's still a week off. Before that you'd better see her again, return the shoes, and explain what happened this evening. Kyoko is a clever girl, and she undoubtedly saw through Mrs Kaburagi's story right away. After that...'

Shunsuké paused. He took a calling card from his case and wrote a simple note of introduction. There was a slight tremor in his hand. Yuichi looked at that hand, wasted by age, and associated with it the pale, somewhat swollen hand of his mother. These two hands and nothing else had awakened in him a passion for forced marriages, vice, phoniness and falsehood, and had induced him to embrace them. These two hands were close to death, had formed a secret alliance with death. Yuichi suspected that the power that had taken possession of him was the power of the nether world.

'On the third floor of the N— Building, in Kyobashi,' Shunsuké said, handing over the card, 'is an establishment that sells stylish imported women's handkerchiefs. If you show this card they will sell to Japanese. Buy a half dozen matching handkerchiefs. All right? Give two of them to Kyoko as a token of apology. The other four give to Mrs Kaburagi the next time you see her. Since coincidences like today's don't happen often, I'll have to arrange for you and Kyoko and Mrs Kaburagi to get together. Then those handkerchiefs will really have a part to play.

'Next, I have a pair of agate earrings at home that belonged to my dead wife. I'll give those to you. Then I'll show you how we'll use them. Now, just wait and see. Each of the women will come to think you're intimate with the other and that she is being left out. Let's add a handkerchief for your wife. She'll think you're carrying on with these two women. That's just what we want. Your freedom in real life will then be a clear road before you.'

At this time at Rudon's the activity seemed to be at its height. The youths at the rear tables were laughing over their endless dirty stories. If the topic happened to come around to women, however, the listeners all knitted their brows and looked askance. Rudy, unable to wait until eleven p.m., when his young lover arrived every other day, stifled a yawn and glanced intermittently towards the door. Shunsuké yawned in sympathy. His yawn was clearly different from Rudy's – a rather sickly yawn. When he closed his mouth, his false teeth clashed. This sound echoing within the core of his body frightened him terribly. He felt as if he was hearing from his insides the unhappy sound of the violation of his flesh by matter. Flesh is at heart matter. The sound of his false teeth clashing was nothing more than a clear revelation of the real nature of his flesh.

130

It's my body, but I'm already somebody else, Shunsuké thought.

More important, my soul is somebody else. He stole a look at the beautiful face of Yuichi. The form of my soul, at least, is as beautiful as this.

*

Yuichi came home late so frequently that Yasuko exhausted herself working up all kinds of suspicions about her husband. She finally decided to believe him, but that decision was of late causing her undeniable pain.

In the character of Yuichi, Yasuko saw a nameless riddle. That riddle, rather involved with the side of him that seemed easy to understand, was somehow not easy to solve. One morning he saw a cartoon in the newspaper and burst out laughing, but Yasuko, who came over to look, couldn't figure out what he saw that was humorous in that not-at-all-funny cartoon. He started to explain, blurting out: 'The day before yesterday –' and closed his mouth. He had thoughtlessly started to mention one of the topics of conversation at Rudy's.

At times Yuichi seemed quite frustrated, filled with pain. Yasuko would wish to find out the reasons for his pain, but the next moment Yuichi would explain that he had eaten too much cake and his stomach ached.

Her husband's eyes seemed constantly to be yearning for something. Yasuko went so far as to believe that it was his poetic nature. He was morbidly fastidious about the rumours and gossip of society at large. Belying the good opinion of her parents, he seemed to have a strange prejudice against society. A thinking man seems to be a mysterious thing in a woman's eyes. Woman can face death refusing to say anything like, 'I adore snakes.'

One day the following happened: Yuichi was away at school. His mother was taking a nap; Kiyo had gone shopping. Yasuko was at the end of the veranda, knitting. She was knitting a winter jacket for Yuichi.

The front door bell rang. Yasuko got up, went down to the entrance, and unlocked the door, kneeling to greet the visitor. A student carrying a Boston bag entered. She did not know

131

him. He smiled affably and bowed; then he closed the door behind him. He said: 'I go to the same school as your husband and I'm working my way. How would you like some very nice imported soap?'

'Soap? We have enough right now.'

'Don't say that until you've seen this. Once you see it, you'll surely want it.'

The student turned his back and, without a by-your-leave, sat down on the step leading into the house. The black serge of his back and the seat of his trousers shone with age. He opened his bag and took out a sample of soap in a gaudy wrapper.

Yasuko said again she didn't need any, that he would have to wait until her husband came home. The student laughed as if there were something funny about that. He handed the sample to Yasuko to smell. Yasuko took it and the student grasped her hand. About to cry out, Yasuko looked the youth in the eye. He laughed, undaunted. She started to scream, but he covered her mouth. Yasuko struggled fiercely.

As luck would have it, Yuichi appeared. His lecture had been cancelled. As he was about to ring the bell, he sensed that something was wrong. His eyes were accustomed to the light outside, and for a moment he did not discern in the half darkness a writhing, obscure shape. There was one point of light – the wide-open eye of Yasuko, resisting, straining every muscle to free herself, yet joyfully welcoming her husband's return. Heartened, she sprang to her feet. The student also got up.

He saw Yuichi and attempted to squeeze past him and escape, but he was caught by the wrist. Yuichi pulled him out into the front yard. He hit him squarely in the jaw with his fist. The student fell flat on his back in the shrubbery around the well. Yuichi struck him in the face again and again.

This, to Yasuko, was an incident she would never forget. That night Yuichi stayed home. She believed in his love completely. And no wonder. Yuichi had protected Yasuko because he loved her. Yuichi guarded peace and order because he loved his home.

This strong-bodied, reliable husband did not talk to his mother about what he had done. Why, she did not know, but there was something embarrassing to him about the secret reasons for displaying his strength. There were two reasons. First, that student was beautiful. Second – and to Yuichi this was the most difficult reason to assert – that student had offended him by revealing at close quarters the painful truth of how much *he desired woman*.

It so happened that Yasuko did not menstruate during October.

11

Family Ritual: Tea with Rice

On the tenth of November, when his classes were done, Yuichi took the suburban car and met his wife at one of the stations. Because they had a visit to make, he had worn a suit to school.

Through the introduction of his mother's attending physician, they were going to the home of a famous gynaecologist, a man in the early autumn of his years, head of the gynaecology department, who went to the University Hospital four days a week. On Wednesdays and Fridays he was at home, where he had a fully equipped examination room.

Yuichi hesitated for a long time over whether he would do any good by coming along. Her mother should have been the one to accompany her. Yasuko, however, wheedled him into coming, and he didn't see how he could refuse.

Cars were parked in front of the doctor's quietly elegant Western-style home. In the dim living room, by the fireplace, they waited their turn.

It had been a frosty morning. The afternoon was particularly cold. The fireplace had been lit. The air smelled faintly of the white bearskin on the hearth. On a table a large cloisonné vase overflowed with yellow chrysanthemums. The room was quite dark, and the flames of the fire came warmly off the dark-green surface of the vase.

Four people were seated in the living room when they entered: a middle-aged lady accompanied by her servant and a young woman with her mother. The middle-aged lady's hair looked as if she had just come from the beauty parlour, and she held her face as if she was afraid to disturb her heavy makeup. This face encased in white powder looked as if cracks would open up on the skin if she so much as smiled. Her little eyes peered from behind a wall of powder. Her 'lacquer' kimmo spattered with blue shells, her sash, her jacket, her huge diamond ring were all slightly suggestive of a costume in accord with the current notion of what was extravagant. She had a copy of *Life* open in her lap. Ostentatiously she brought her eyes close to the small type of the captions and moved her lips as she read. She had a habit of flicking away nonexistent stray hairs as if she were brushing cobwebs. In the chair behind her waited her maid, who when addressed by her mistress would answer, 'Yes,' with a look as if her life depended on it.

The members of the other party glanced at these two every once in a while as if they despised them. The daughter was wearing a large purple arrow-feather pattern, the mother, a striped crepe in a waterfall design. The girl – one could not tell whether she was married – frequently exposed a white arm, poised a fist like the paw of a young fox, tilted her head to the side, and glanced at her tiny gold watch.

Yasuko saw and heard nothing. Though she strained her eyes to look at the gas flame in the fireplace, it cannot be said she saw it. For several days she had seemed not to be concerned with anything but this headache and nausea, a slight fever and dizziness, and a peculiar throbbing sensation that had suddenly seized her. Engrossed in this welter of symptoms, her expression seemed artless and earnest, like a rabbit with its nose buried in its feed trough.

When the two earlier patients had left, and Yasuko's turn had come, she pleaded with Yuichi to accompany her to the examination room. They passed down the hallway heavy with disinfectant. A cold breeze drifting in from the hall made Yasuko shiver.

'Come in,' called a calm professorial voice from within.

The doctor had the look of a figure in a portrait as he sat in his chair leaning towards the door. With a hand white and dehydrated from being dipped in disinfectant, bony and abstract, as it were, he indicated where his visitors might sit down. Yuichi gave the name of their mutual friend and introduced himself.

Shining in a row on the table like a dentist's tools were forceps used in curettage. The first thing that struck the eye on entering, however, was the examination table, its form designed with a special cruelty. It was an abnormal, unnatural form. The bed was higher than usual, with the lower half raised. On each side, swinging up diagonally right and left, leather stirrups had been fitted. Yuichi thought of the acrobatic figures of the young lady and the affected middle-aged woman which had just before occupied that machine. That odd bed took the form of destiny, one might say. Why? Because in the presence of that shape, the diamond ring, the perfume, the kimono splattered with shiny blue shells, the purple arrow-feather pattern were useless, powerless to resist it. Yuichi shuddered, thinking of Yasuko being fitted to the cold obscenity that unfeeling, implacable iron contrivance was charged with. He thought that he himself was like that bed. Yasuko deliberately kept her eyes from the bed and sat down.

Yuichi offered a word now and then as she described her symptoms. The doctor signalled to him with his eyes. Yuichi left Yasuko in the examination room and returned to the reception room. It was empty. He sat down in an easy chair. He was not comfortable. He sat down in a wooden armchair. He was still not comfortable. He could not rid his mind of the idea of Yasuko lying on her back on the table.

He leaned his elbow on the mantelpiece. Then he took from his inside pocket two letters that had come to him this morning and that he had previously read at school. One was from Kyoko. The other was from Mrs Kaburagi. It happened that both letters, with roughly the same contents, were delivered at the same time. He read them a second time.

Since that rainy day, Yuichi had met Kyoko three times and Mrs Kaburagi twice. On the most recent occasion he had seen them both at the same time. Of course, neither of the women knew the other would be there. It was all Shunsuké's idea.

Yuichi reread Kyoko's letter first. The lines overflowed with an indignation that gave a mannish strength to the handwriting.

'You are teasing me,' Kyoko wrote. 'I have managed to keep myself from believing that you were deceiving me. When you returned my shoes, you gave me two rare handkerchiefs. I was very happy and have had them washed over and over and always carry one in my handbag. Nevertheless, when I saw

Mrs Kaburagi again the other day, that person was using one of the same handkerchiefs. She and I recognized this immediately, but we said nothing. Women are quick to notice what other members of their sex own. Besides, handkerchiefs are bought a half dozen or a dozen at a time. Did you give her four and me two? Or did you give her two and some other unknown person two?

'Regardless, I am not thinking about the business of the handkerchiefs particularly now. What I am going to say is very difficult to express, but since the other day when you, Mrs Kaburagi and I, the three of us, happened accidentally to come together (the second time I had run into Mrs Kaburagi since the day whenever it was, I bought my shoes – an amazing coincidence!), I have been tortured by something to the extent that I can't even eat.

'When I met you at that time I should have been at the Foreign Office reception, and we were in the dining room at the Fugu restaurant, you lit my cigarette. When you took your lighter out of your pocket, an earring dropped on the tatami. "Hm, is that your wife's earring?" I said immediately. You said "Uh-huh," and put it back in your pocket without opening your mouth. I soon came to regret the carelessness and the haste with which I commented on that discovery. Why? Because I was very much aware that my tone was filled with jealousy.

'Thus, when I saw Mrs Kaburagi the second time, how shocked I was when I saw that person with the same earring hanging from her ear! After that I didn't open my mouth again, no matter what people may have thought, which must have put you out.

'I suffered terribly before I made up my mind to send this letter. If it had been a glove or a compact, it wouldn't have been so bad, but for one earring to get into a gentleman's pocket is a serious thing, as far as I can see. I am a woman who has come to be praised for not letting annoying things get on her nerves, and I don't know why I am suffering so much as I am in this instance. Won't you please do something right away to dispel my childish doubts? Even if not out of love, out of friendship at least, will you please not overlook the pain of this woman carried away by terrible doubt? It is in this hope that I have written. As soon as you get this letter, won't you call me? Until you call me, I shall stay home every day, pleading a headache.'

Mrs Kaburagi's letter went as follows:

'That practical joke of the other day was in bad taste. I did some quick figuring. If you gave me four handkerchiefs, and you gave Kyoko four, that leaves four. I would like to think you gave them to your wife, but I'm not sure about you.

'I was sad, however, to see that the affair of the handkerchiefs took all the joy out of Kyoko. She's a sweet girl, isn't she? Her dream that she is the only person in the world loved by Yuichi was broken.

'Thank you for the expensive gift you gave me the other day. It's a little old-fashioned, but that agate is a lovely stone. Thanks to it, everybody praises the earring and goes from that to praising the shape of my ear. If you gave it to me in return for the suit, you're pretty old-fashioned, too. All a man like you has to do to make a woman happy is simply take what she gives him.

'The tailors will finish the suit in two or three days, won't they? Please show it to me the first day you put it on. And let me pick out a necktie, too.

'P.S. Since the other day, for no reason at all, I have developed some self-confidence where Kyoko is concerned. Why? It may be annoying to you, but I foresee that I am going to win this *shogi* game I'm playing.'

*

'When I compare these two letters, I understand,' Yuichi said to himself. 'Kyoko, who seems to have no confidence, is confident: Mrs Kaburagi, who seems so confident, has none. Kyoko does not hide her misgivings, but it's plain as day that Mrs Kaburagi is hiding hers. It's just as Shunsuké said. Kyoko is gradually becoming more confident that Mrs Kaburagi and I are having an affair. Mrs Kaburagi is gradually becoming more confident that Kyoko and I are having an affair. Each is afraid that she will be the one whose body won't be touched.'

The only woman's body this marble youth would touch with

his hand now had inserted in it two dried-up, cool, lysol-scented fingers of a man, like the fingers of a gardener thrust into the soil while transplating a flower. The other dried-up hand was measuring the mass of internal organs externally. The root of life, as big as a goose egg, was touching the warm earth inside. Next, the doctor, as if he were picking up a shovel to dig in a luxurious flowerbed, took a uterine mirror from the hand of the nurse.

The examination was over. The doctor rinsed his hands and turned to his patient the face wearing the smile of human dedication. 'Congratulations,' he said.

Dubious, Yasuko was silent. The head of the gynaecology department had the nurse call Yuichi. He came in. The doctor said it again: 'Congratulations. Your wife is two months pregnant. She conceived in the very first days of your marriage. The mother's body is healthy; everything is normal. So don't worry. But even if she doesn't want to eat, she will have to. If she doesn't eat, she's apt to get constipated, and if she gets constipated, toxins will accumulate and that's not good. So I want her to have every day a shot of vitamin B_1 in a grape-sugar base. Don't worry about morning sickness. Get as muck rest as possible...' After that he winked at Yuichi, adding, 'That business doesn't hurt at all. At any rate, congratulations,' the doctor went on, comparing the two with his eyes. 'You're a model couple, as the eugenicists would see it. Eugenics is the only branch of study that has hope for the future of mankind. I shall be delighted to see your child.'

Yasuko was calm. It was a curious calm. Like an innocent husband, Yuichi looked at the area of his wife's womb bewilderedly. A strange vision made his body quiver. His wife was holding a mirror in the region of her abdomen; from that mirror, he felt, his own face was looking fixedly out at him.

It wasn't a mirror. It happened that the western sun was coming through the window, falling on her deep-red skirt and reflecting from it; that was all. Yuichi's fear was like the fear of a husband who had made his wife sick.

'Congratulations!' On the way back, he fancied he heard that greeting again and again. Up to now it had been repeated countless times. After this it would be repeated countless times.

He felt as if he was hearing the hollow sound of it like a litany. It would be better to say that what was ringing in his ears was not a congratulatory message but a droning of curses.

Even without desire a child is born. In the illegitimate child, born only from desire, there appears a paradoxical beauty; but in the child born from lack of desire, how unlucky must the features be! In artificial insemination, the sperm is that of a heterosexual man. Eugenics, the idea of social improvement that disregards desire – Yuichi hated the chairman of the gynaecology department's beautiful white hair showered with experience. The humble healthy attitude Yuichi had towards society was based on the fact that his special society had no sense of reality.

The couple shrank from the wind that gathered in the westering sun and walked with coat collars turned up, leaning towards each other. Yasuko linked her arm in Yuichi's; the warmth of their arms mingled through layers of clothing. What was it that was now keeping their hearts apart? The heart has no body; it has no way of linking arms. Yuichi and Yasuko feared the moment when their nameless accusations would be shouted out. In womanish haste, Yasuko rebelled against this mutual taboo.

'Well, should I be happy?'

Yuichi could not bear to look directly at his wife's face when she said that. All he had to do, he knew, was shout loudly and cheerfully, without looking at Yasuko: 'Of course! Congratulations!' A figure happened to be approaching them, however, and he lapsed into silence.

There were very few pedestrians on the suburban street. On the pebbly white roadbed the jutting and sinking shadows of the rooftops continued as far as the black-and-white grade crossing, mounting off at an angle. Towards them came a Spitz led by a boy in a sweater. Half the boy's white face glowed red from the rays of the setting sun, but as he came nearer it was plain that purplish-red fire scars covered that cheek. The boy averted his face in passing, but Yuichi thought of the colour of the fire in the distance and the fire sirens which so many times appeared before him in moments of desire. The scandalous sentiment of eugenics occurred to him once more. Finally, he said: 'Yes, be happy. Congratulations.'

Yasuko was disheartened by the echo of unmistakable protest in her husband's words.

*

Yuichi's behaviour was buried in obscurity. It was buried like the behaviour of a magnificent philanthropist. However, the thin smile of self satisfaction of the anonymously charitable philanthropist did not hover about his mouth.

In his youthfulness, he was pained by the lack of an outlet for his energies in daytime society. Was there anything more boring than becoming a paragon of morals and manners without expending any effort? Through the unbearable pain of being able to remain chaste without effort he learned how to hate women as well as morality. The men and women joined by affection that he once looked upon with eyes of envy he now saw with the darkly piercing eye of jealousy. He was sometimes amazed at the depth of reticence he had been driven into. About his night-time behaviour, he kept the marble silence of an immovable statue, but like a real statue, he was imprisoned in his form.

Yasuko's pregnancy filled life in the Minami household with activity, thanks to a sudden visit and a dinner made joyful by the Segawa family. That same night his mother remarked about the restlessness he showed by his desire to go out: 'What more can you wish for?' she said. 'You have a beautiful, sweet bride, and tonight we're going to celebrate the conception of your first child.' Yuichi answered somewhat cheerfully that he had everything he wanted, which made his good-tempered mother feel that her son was being sarcastic.

'What's causing it? Before he got married he never went out, so that his mother worried about it. Since he got married on the other hand, he's always walking off, having a good time. No, it's not your doing, Yasuko. It's surely so many bad friends he's made. Look how his friends never come around here.' Keeping Yasuko's family in mind, she half-blamed, half-defended her son before his wife.

Needless to say, the happiness of her son took most of the attention of his outspoken mother. When we plot the happiness of another, we unconsciously impute to the other person what is in another form the dream in which our own happiness is fulfilled. Thus by not thinking of our own happiness we make it possible for ourselves to become egotistic. She thought Yasuko was to blame for the life of dissipation Yuichi led immediately after his marriage. With the news of Yasuko's pregnancy all her doubts were cleared away. 'From now on, he'll quiet down,' she said, even to Yasuko. 'That child is becoming a father.'

Her kidneys had mended somewhat, but now various cares caused her again to wish for death. Now, however, the fatal illness refused to come. What tortured her was not Yasuko's unhappiness so much as – thanks to her maternal egoism – the unhappiness of her son. But the fear that this marriage based on impulses of duty was to Yuichi a forced marriage was the deepest root of the mother's anxiety and remorse.

She decided that before some catastrophe occurred in the household she must act as peacemaker. She therefore gently instructed the bride not to let them hear at home about Yuichi's philandering and attempted simply to skirt the subject with her son.

'Now if there's anything bothering you that you can't tell anybody about, any sexual problem, please tell me and we'll see. It's all right; I won't tell Yasuko. I foresee that if we keep on as we are something terrible is going to happen.'

These words, spoken before the news of Yasuko's pregnancy, made his mother look like a sorceress in Yuichi's eyes. Every household is surely pregnant with some misfortune. The fair wind that propels the sailing ship along the sea lanes is basically the same as the terrible gale that leads it to destruction. The home and the family are propelled by neutralized misfortune as by a favourable wind. In the corner of so many famous family portraits, the hand of misfortune is sharply outlined, like a signature.

In this way my family perhaps enters the class of healthy families, Yuichi thought, when he was in an optimistic mood.

As usual, the management of the Minami fortunes was placed in the hands of Yuichi. His mother, who never in her wildest dreams suspected that Shunsuké had presented them with 500,000 yen, was continually ashamed of the marriage portion given by the Segawa family. How could she know that not a sen of their own 350,000 yen had been touched! Oddly enough, Yuichi had a good head for business. He had a high school friend who worked in a bank. The 200,000 yen of Shunsuké's money that Yuichi invested with him for under-the-table loans was bringing in 12,000 yen a month interest. At present there was nothing dangerous about investments of this kind.

A school friend of Yasuko's had become a mother at a young age the year before, but she lost the child, Yasuko was informed, because of polio. Yuichi's joy when he heard about this made Yasuko's steps heavy when she went to pay her condolences. She felt that the beautiful but dark eyes of her husband had a hint of raillery in them, as if to say, 'See! See!'

How often another's misfortune is our good fortune! The alterations from time to time and moment to moment in ardent love show this formula in its purest form, yet even so in Yasuko's passionate head there was the suspicion that nothing consoled her husband so much as misfortune. Yuichi's thinking about fortune was quite unsystematic. He did not believe in what is called lasting happiness; in his heart, it seemed, he secretly feared it. When he saw something supposed to be lasting, terror gripped him.

One day they went shopping in Yasuko's father's department store, and Yasuko stopped for a fairly long time at the baby-carriage section on the fourth floor. Bored, Yuichi prodded his wife by applying a slightly urgent pressure to her arm, which she obstinately disregarded. He pretended not to see the look of anger that Yasuko flashed at him. In the bus on the way home she cooed incessantly at the infant who leaned towards her affectionately from the next seat. There was nothing pretty about this poor, dirty, slobbering child.

'Children are cute, aren't they?' Yasuko said to Yuichi, inclining her head coquettishly closer to him as the mother got off.

'What's the rush? It won't be born until summer.'

Yasuko fell silent again. Tears hung in her eyes. Any husband, even one quite unlike Yuichi, would have found it natural to tease her about this early manifestation of mother love. Surely this way of showing her feeling was devoid of naturalness. Not only that, there was a certain boastfulness in it, with, in fact, a note of reproach in the boastfulness.

One evening she was seized by a terrible headache and took to her bed; Yuichi stayed home with her. She felt nauseous and her heart was palpitating. While they waited for the doctor, Kiyo applied cold compresses to cool the patient's abdomen. Yuichi's mother came in to calm her son, saying, 'Don't worry. When I was carrying you, my morning sickness was awful. Maybe I just like odd things, but when we opened a bottle of wine, I suddenly wanted to eat the cork. It seemed like a mushroom.'

It was nearly ten o'clock when the doctor finished his rounds and Yuichi was left alone with Yasuko in the sickroom. The blood reviving in her pallid cheeks made her look fresher than usual, and her white forearms, extended languidly from the quilt, were charming in the shadowy lamplight.

'It's hard, but when I realize that I'm suffering for our child, it's nothing,' she said, lifting her hand to Yuichi's forehead and playing with a lock of hair. Yuichi let her do it. A cruel tenderness was born unexpectedly in him, and his lips were suddenly held against Yasuko's still-feverish lips. In a tone that would make any woman confess whether she wished to or not, he asked: 'You really want this child, don't you? Yet, admit it; it's a little early for maternal affection. If there's something you want to tell me, go ahead.'

Yasuko's tired, pain-filled eyes overflowed with tears as if they had been waiting long for this opportunity. Nothing moves a man like a woman's self-indulgent tears, accompanied by certain sentimentally evoked confessions: 'If we have a baby –' Yasuko said, hesitantly at first, 'if we have a baby, I don't think you'll leave me.'

It was at this time that Yuichi arrived at the idea of an abortion.

*

144

The public stared in wonder at the rejuvenation of Shunsuké and the return of his old dandyish habits of dress. At heart the works of Shunsuké's old age had a freshness about them. But it was not the freshness appearing in the evening years of an outstanding artist, but an overripe freshness as of something malignant that keeps growing and never matures. In the strict sense of the word, he could not be rejuvenated. If he were it would be the death of him. He possessed absolutely no powers related to life, and his total lack of aesthetic sense was perhaps the reason for his habit of dress. Harmony between the aesthetics of artistic creation and taste in daily life is commonly called for in our country. This nonsense to which Shunsuké had lent himself made the public, unaware of the influence of the morals of Rudon's, just a little suspicious of the old man's sanity.

Moreover, in Shunsuké's life a nameless, evanescent aura had come into being. From his speech and conduct that had formerly been far from humorous, a false lightness – to be exact, a light-headedness – seemed to show itself. The self-induced pains of rejuvenation were greeted with joy by his readers. His works were in steady demand. Word about the strange novelty of his psychological condition spurred the sales. Not even the keenest critic, or even the friend most blessed with insight, was able to discern the real cause of Shunsuké's transformation. The cause was simple. Shunsuké had come into possession of an idea.

On that summer day when he saw the youth appear in the foam on the beach, for the first time in his life an idea had come to dwell in his mind. To cure diseases of life he would impart the steely health of death. This was what, in artistic productions, Shunsuké had always dreamed of as the ideal manifestation.

In artistic works, there is a twofold possibility of existence, he believed. Just as an ancient lotus seed will flower again when dug up and replanted, the work of art that is said to possess everlasting life can live again in the hearts of all times, all countries. When one touches an ancient work – of space art, or time art – his life is captured by the space of the time of the work and abandons the rest of its existence. He lives another life. However, the internal time which he expends in this other life has already been measured, already settled upon. That is what we call form.

It is, however, unusual that form is lacking in human experience and in influence on human life. To clothe formless experience with form and offer, as it were, human life in a ready-made suit of clothes is what the work of art attempts to do, the naturalistic school believes. Shunsuké did not agree. Form was the inborn destiny of art. One had to believe that the human experience within a work and a real-life human experience are different in dimension, depending on whether form is present or not. Within real-life human experience, however, there is something that is very close to what is experienced in a work. What is it? It is the impression accorded by death. We cannot experience death, but we sometimes experience the impression of it. We experience the idea of death in a death in the family, in the death of a loved one. In sum, death is the unique form of life.

Doesn't the drive of the book that makes us so strongly conscious of life impel us because it is the drive of death? Shunsuké's Eastern vision sometimes leaned towards death. In the Orient, death is many times more vivid than life. The artistic work, as Shunsuké saw it, was a kind of refined death. It had a peculiar power to permit life to touch and experience death in advance.

Internal existence is life; objective existence is nothing but death or nothingness. These two forms of existence bring the work of art terribly close to natural beauty. He was convinced that a work of art, like nature, absolutely must not have soul. Much less thought! Through lack of soul, soul is verified; through the absence of thought, thought is verified; through the lack of life, life is verified. This indeed is the paradoxical mission of the work of art. In turn it is the mission-making characteristic of beauty.

Therefore is not creativity nothing more than the imitation of the creative powers of nature? For this question Shunsuké had a bitter reply in readiness.

Nature is a living thing; it is not a created thing. Creativity is that action that exists in order to make nature doubt its own birth. For creativity is, in the final analysis a method of nature. That was his answer.

That's right. Shunsuké was method personified. What Shunsuké asked of Yuichi was that he be permitted to take the beautiful young man's natural youth and make it into a work of art; to take the various weaknesses of youth and to make them something stronger, like death; to take the various powers by which he influenced his environment and make them into destructive powers like the power of nature – inorganic powers, devoid of anything human.

Yuichi's existence, like a work in process of creation, never left the thoughts of the writer. It had got so that a day that went by when he didn't hear that clear, youthful voice, if only over the phone, was an unhappy cloudy day. Yuichi's voice, filled with clarity and golden grace, was like a brilliant ray filtering through the clouds. It poured into the desolate soil of his genius. It brightened the configurations of those stones, that overgrown vegetation. It made it a slightly less unbearable place to reside in.

Using Rudon's as a means of getting in touch with Yuichi from time to time, Shunsuké pretended, as at first, to be one of the denizens of that street. He became conversant in the patois; he learned all the subtleties of the wink. A small unexpected romance pleased him. One melancholy-featured young man confessed to being in love with him. His twisted tendency among twisted tendencies led him to feel affection only for men who were sixty or older.

Shunsuké got into the habit of appearing with young homosexuals in various teahouses and Western restaurants here and there. He became aware of the subtle shift in years from adolescence to maturity, with momentary changes in colour like the evening sky. Maturity was the sunset of beauty. From eighteen to twenty-five years the beauty of him who is loved subtly alters its form. The first glow of sunset, when every cloud in the sky takes on the colour of sweet fresh fruit, symbolizes the colour of the cheeks of the boy between eighteen and twenty, the soft nape of his neck, the fresh blueness of his shaved collar line and his lips like a girl's. When the sunset glow reaches its peak and the clouds blaze many-coloured and the sky goes mad with an expression of joy, one thinks of the blossom time of youth, from twenty to twenty-three. Then his look is somewhat fierce, his cheeks are taut, his mouth is gradually making plain the will of the man. At the same time, in the colour still glowing shyly in his cheek, and in the soft streamlining of his brows, traces of the evanescent moment of a boy's beauty can be seen. Finally, the time when the burnt-out clouds take on a grave complexion and the setting sun tosses its remaining beams like hair is comparable to age twenty-four or twenty-five when, though his eyes are replete with pure gleams, in his cheeks are seen a beauty transcending the severity of its stern masculine will.

It must be said in all honesty that Shunsuké, while noting the various charms of the boys who consorted with him, was not sexually excited by any of them. He wondered if Yuichi, surrounded by women whom he did not love, might feel this way too. Whenever he thought of Yuichi alone, the old man's heart palpitated somewhat, although without sexual overtones. When Yuichi was not there, he would bring up his name, whereupon memories of joy and sadness flitted across the eyes of the boys. When he asked about it he found that Yuichi had had relations with each of them but had broken with them after two or three encounters.

A telephone call came from Yuichi. He asked if he might visit the next day. Thanks to that call, Shunsuké's first neuralgia attack of the winter, which was troubling him at the time, was relieved.

The next day was a mild Indian summer day, and Shunsuké found a sunny spot on the veranda off the living room and read a little while out of *Childe Harold*. Byron always amused him. While he was thus occupied, four or five callers came by. Then the maidservant announced Yuichi's arrival. With a sour look like that of an attorney taking up an unpleasant case, Sunsuké apologized to his guests. Not one of them went so far as to imagine that the new 'very important' guest being conducted to the second-floor study was still a mere student, not even singled out for his brains.

In the study there was a sofa that served also as a window seat, with five cushions painted in Ryukyu style in a continuous pattern. On the knickknack shelves lining the three sides of the bay window, a collection of old ceramics was haphazardly assembled. In one compartment stood a truly beautiful totem doll of ancient craftsmanship. The collection had no visible order or discipline, being made up altogether of gifts.

Yuichi sat in the bay window wearing the new suit given him by Mrs Kaburagi, and the early winter sun coming through the windows like steaming water made the black-lacquered waves of his hair glisten. He saw no seasonal flowers in the room – not a sign of life anywhere. There was only a black marble mantel clock gloomily keeping time. Yuichi reached for the old leather-bound foreign book on the table at hand. It was a volume of Pater's *Miscellaneous Studies*, published by Macmillan. Here and there in the 'Apollo of Picardy' were Shunsuké's underlinings. Beside it were the two volumes of the *Ojoyoshu* – the *Texts on Death* – and an oversize edition of Aubrey Beardsley prints.

When Shunsuké looked at Yuichi standing to greet him in front of the bay window, he almost shuddered. He felt that his heart was undoubtedly in love with this beautiful youth. Might his performance at Rudon's have deceived him (just as Yuichi's acting led him at times to feel he was in love with a woman) and forced him into some improbable delusion?

Somewhat dazzled, he blinked. There was something abrupt about what he then imparted to Yuichi, as he sank down beside him. He said that his neuralgia had been bothering him, but perhaps because of the change in the weather it caused no pain today. It was as if he had a barometer hanging at his right knee. He could tell in the morning whether it was going to snow.

Yuichi found it difficult to continue the conversation, so Shunsuké complimented him on his suit. When he heard who had given it to him, he said, 'Well, that woman blackmailed me for three hundred thousand yen. If you got her to give you a suit, my books are coming remarkably into balance. Next time, give her a kiss for good measure.'

This remark, coming from Shunsuké's habit of never missing an opportunity to spit upon mankind, was always good medicine for Yuichi, who for a long time had feared mankind.

'Now, what was your business?'

'It's about Yasuko.'

'Yes, you told me she's pregnant.'

'Yes, and –' The youth hesitated. 'I wanted to get your advice.'

'And you want an abortion, don't you?' This straightforward question made Yuichi's eyes open wide. 'But why, after all? I spoke to a psychiatrist who told me that tendencies like yours are not felt to be hereditary. You have nothing to fear on that score.'

Yuichi was silent. He hadn't even told himself his real reasons for considering an abortion. If his wife really wanted a child, perhaps he would not have hit upon this stratagem. There was no doubt that his present motivation was the fear that she wanted something more. From this fear Yuichi wished to free himself. To accomplish that, he must first free his wife. Pregnancy and maternity were binding. They denied liberation. The youth said, half in anger: 'That's not so; that's not the reason.'

'Then why?' Shunsuké's question was calm, as if spoken by a physician.

'For Yasuko's happiness, I felt that was the best.'

'What are you saying?' The old man threw his head back and laughed. 'For Yasuko's happiness? For a woman's happiness? You, who do not love women, take into account a woman's happiness?'

'That's the reason. That's why we must have an abortion ... if we do, the bond between us will be gone. If Yasuko wants a divorce, she'll always be able to divorce me. That will bring her happiness in the end.'

'Is your feeling based on human kindness? On benevolence? Or on egoism? On weakness of will? I'm amazed. I never thought I'd hear such trite sentiments from you.'

The old man was ugly in his anger. His hands trembled more violently than usual. He rubbed his palms together uneasily. As he did so, they made a dry, gritty sound. He nervously riffled through the pages of the *Texts on Death*, which he had been holding all the time, and closed the volume.

'You've forgotten what I said. This is what I told you. You

must think of a woman as inanimate matter. Never acknowledge that a woman has a soul. That's what made me lose out. I refuse to believe you're going to make the same mistake I made. You, who do not love women! You should have been ready for that when you got married. A woman's happiness? Nonsense! You feel sorry for her? Nonsense! How can you feel sorry for a bundle of sticks? By looking at her as a bundle of sticks you managed to get married, didn't you? Listen to me, Yuchan –'

This spiritual father looked earnestly at his beautiful son. His old eyes were faded. When they attempted to look fixedly at something, anguished wrinkles stood out beneath them. 'You must not fear life. You must make up your mind that pain and unhappiness will never come to you. Never to take on responsibility or duty is the moral code of beauty. Beauty has no time to assume responsibility for each and every unforeseen effect of its powers. Beauty has no time to think of happiness or things of that sort. Particularly not the happiness of other people. For that reason, however, beauty has the power to make suffering, even dying men happy.'

'I now understand,' said Yuichi, 'why you are against an abortion. That way you think Yasuko won't suffer enough, don't you? In order to get her into a predicament where she cannot divorce me even if she wants to, the best way, you think, is for her to have a child. I think Yasuko has suffered enough now. She is my wife. I'll return you the five hundred thousand yen.'

'Again you're contradicting yourself. What do you mean by saying "Yasuko is my wife; I must take pains to see that she can divorce me with ease"? You are afraid to see Yasuko suffering at your side all your life.'

'How about my suffering? I am suffering now. I am certainly not happy.'

'Forget about what makes you feel guilty, what makes you feel pain and remorse. Yuchan, open your eyes! You are absolutely innocent. You didn't act out of desire. Guilt is the seasoning of desire. You only tasted the seasoning and now you make a sour face. Why do you want to divorce Yasuko?'

'I'd like to be free. To tell the truth, I myself don't know why I am acting as you say I do. When I see myself as a person without a will I feel desolate.'

This tritely innocent statement gushed out and gradually rose to a shout. He continued: 'I want to become something. I want a *real existence*!'

Shunsuké listened intently. He felt he was hearing the first wail from one of his artistic productions. Yuichi went on, sadly: 'I'm tired of secrecy.'

*

This was the first time Shunsuké's works had been given a tongue. The terrible voice of this youth made Shunsuké feel as if a groan of the awful labour expended in the construction of a bell had become the diapason of a well-wrought masterpiece. At the same time, Yuichi's childish fretfulness made him smile. It was no longer the voice of his creation.

'I am not at all happy to be called beautiful. I would be much happier to have everybody call me that nice, interesting fellow Yuchan.'

'But' – Shunsuké's tone had become somewhat placid – 'it looks as if it is the destiny of you fellows not to be able to attain a real existence. In place of that, within the limitations of art, your fellowship can become a terrifically heroic antagonist to reality. The men of your street seem to be vested with the mission of representation when they are born. At least that's the way I see it. The action called representation straddles reality and pricks it to a halt; it is action that stops the root of reality's breath. Through this process, representation always becomes the heir of reality. This joker, reality, is moved by those whom it moves and is controlled by those whom it controls. For instance, those who are directly in charge of reality, who push reality and control reality, are the masses, you know. When it comes to representation, though, that is hard to push. Nothing on earth can force it to act. The person in charge of it is the artist. Only representation can give reality to reality; realism does not exist in reality but in representation.

'Compared with representation, reality is tremendously abstract. In the real world, mankind, men, women, lovers, the home, and so on live higgledy-piggledy and that is all. The world of representation, on the contrary, presents humanity, manhood, womanhood, lovers that are worthy of being lovers, homes that have been made homelike, and the like. Representation seizes the nucleus of reality, but it is not carried away by reality. Representation reflects its image in the surface of the water like a dragonfly; it skims that surface. Before one knows, it has laid eggs on the water. Those larvae are brought up in the water in preparation for the day they will fly about in the sky. They become conversant with the secrets of the water, but they hold the world of the water in contempt.

'This, indeed, is the mission of your fellowship. Once you told me of your annoyance over the principle of majority rule. Right now, I don't believe in your annoyance. What is so original about men and women being in love? In modern society institutions based on the instinct of love are becoming increasingly rare. Customs and models have permeated even the first impulses. What models, do you think? Shallow, artistic models. Many young men and women are stupidly convinced that only the artistic love is the true love, and their own loves are only clumsy copies.

'The other day I saw a romantic ballet performed by a dancer who I am told is a man of that street. As the lover, expressing in marvellous detail the emotions of a man in love, he was incomparable. The one he loved, however, was not the beautiful ballerina before our eyes. It was the boy apprentice who played an insignificant part and appeared only briefly on the stage. What intoxicated the audience so in his performance was the complete artificiality of it, for the reason that he did not desire the beautiful ballerina who was playing his lover on the stage. But for the young men and women among the unsuspecting audience, the love he portrayed was capable of becoming what can be called a model of this world's love.'

This long-winded peroration by Shunsuké made Yuichi feel infinitely disappointed. It had not alleviated his great human problem. The matter he felt to be so important seemed on his way homeward to have been disregarded as of small consequence.

At any rate, Yasuko wanted a baby. His mother was eager

for a grandchild. Yasuko's family's attitude was quite what one would expect. Even Shunsuké wanted it! Although Yuichi felt that an abortion was of utmost importance for Yasuko's happiness, he knew that securing her consent would be extremely difficult. No matter how terrible the morning sickness became, her demeanour would become increasingly obdurate.

Yuichi felt dizzy watching his friends and enemies dance frenziedly towards unhappiness. He went so far as to compare his unhappiness with that of the prophet who has divined the future, and he fell into despair. That evening he went to Rudon's, sat there alone, and drank heavily. Exaggerating his own loneliness, he resorted to cruelty and went off to spend the night with a boy completely devoid of charm. Play-acting at drunken roistering, he poured whisky down the boy's back. The boy tried to make a joke of it, laughing agreeably in a forced way, peering servilely at his tormentor. This depressed Yuichi. There was a rather big hole in the boy's sock. That caused an even greater deeper depression in Yuichi.

Dead drunk, he went to sleep without touching the boy. In the middle of the night he was shocked awake by the sound of his own voice. In his dream he had killed Shunsuké. In the darkness Yuichi peered in terror at his gleaming hand, wet with cold perspiration.

12

Gay Party

In pain and anguish, Yuichi's irresolution crawled slowly to Christmas without change. The time for the abortion had passed. One day, again filled with despair, he kissed Mrs Kaburagi for the first time. That kiss made her feel ten years younger.

'Where are you going to spend Christmas?' she asked.

'I'm afraid I must play the dutiful husband and spend Christmas Eve at least with my wife.'

'Goodness, my husband hasn't spent Christmas Eve with me once! This year we're stepping out separately again, I suppose.'

Having kissed her, Yuichi was amazed by her prudishness. The usual woman on such an occasion would have set out quite intolerably to play the part of the lover, but Mrs Kaburagi held her passion in check. It was an escape from the irregularity of her daily existence. Yuichi was all the more terrified by the thought that he was loved by a simple, sober side of her that no man knew.

Yuichi had quite different plans for Christmas. He had been invited to a 'Gei Pa-ti' that was to be given in a house in the hills of Oiso. 'Gei' is the American equivalent for homosexual.

The house in Oiso was a mansion that the property tax had not brought to a forced sale, but it had at least deprived the owner of funds for its maintenance. Jackie, who had influence there for many years, managed to rent it. It was owned by the family of the head of a paper company, which, after the master died, rented a small house in Tokyo and lived modestly. When they occasionally visited the mansion they had rented out, which was three times as big as their house, with a garden ten times the size of the one where they lived now, they were mystified by the constant bustle of guests there.

155

From trains departing from Oiso Station or passing through, the lights could be seen burning in the guest rooms at night. People coming from there to visit them in Tokyo would say that the lights burning redly in the old house made them think of old times. 'I can't understand the high life they live there at all,' a widow remarked suspiciously. 'Once I dropped in and found them making amazing preparations for a banquet.' No one could guess what went on inside the house, which looked out at the Oiso Sea across an expansive lawn.

Jackie's youth had been truly splendid – so splendid that only Yuichi seemed worthy of nomination as Jackie the Second. The times, however, were different. Jackie (despite this name, he was Japanese, and quite respectable) with his beauty as capital made a grand tour of Europe more luxurious than the Mitsui or Mitsubishi officials of that time could ever attain. He and his English patron, however, separated after a few years.

When he returned to Japan, Jackie lived for a short time in the Kansai area. His patron at that time was an Indian millionaire. At the same time, however, this woman-hating youth was the object of the attentions of three ladies of Ashiya society. The kind of service Yuichi paid to Yasuko he paid to each of these three guardians in turn.

The Indian was afflicted with a chest ailment. Jackie treated this sentimental big man heartlessly. While his young lover was whooping it up downstairs as usual, with hordes of his fellows, the Indian lay in a rattan sleeping chair in the sun room on the second floor, with his blanket pulled to his chin, reading the Bible and weeping.

During the war Jackie was a clerk in the Secretariat of the French Embassy. He was thought to be a spy. The elusive quality of his private life was mistaken for official conduct.

Promptly after the war Jackie got his hands on the Oiso mansion. He brought in the foreigner who was in love with him and proceeded to display his talent for management. He was still beautiful. Just as women have no beards, he displayed no sign of years. Moreover, the gay society's phallic worship – and this was their only religion – did not spare Jackie honour and adulation for the tireless way he lived.

156

That evening, Yuichi was at Rudon's. He felt rather tired. His cheeks, paler than usual, gave a strangely apprehensive air to his serene, clean profile. 'Yuchan has a beautifully cloudy eye today,' said Eichan. Like the eye of a first mate tired of gazing at the sea, he thought.

Yuichi naturally kept his marriage secret. This concealment was the source of exceedingly jealous rumours. Looking out the window at the street with its bustle of the dying year, he thought about his uneasiness of the past four days. As when he was first married, Yuichi once more dreaded the night. For with her pregnancy Yasuko demanded incessant, unfailing love; punctilious, nurselike devotion. And so Yuichi could not help thinking as he had before: I am an unpaid prostitute. I am cheap. I am a devoted toy, he reviled himself. If Yasuko wants to buy a man's soul so cheaply, she'd better learn to take a little unhappiness. Just the same, I'm like a self-seeking maid – I'm not even faithful to myself, am I?

In truth Yuichi's body lying beside his wife was much cheaper than Yuichi's body beside a boy he loved, but this perversion of values made what seemed to the world a perfectly matched beautiful young couple into an ice-cold harlotry, a relationship of unpaid prostitution. With this quiet, slow-working virus hidden from men's eyes incessantly eating away at Yuichi, who could guarantee that, even outside his little 'let's play house' circle, his doll-like, man-and-wife circle, he was not also being devoured?

For instance, until this time he had been faithful to his ideals in gay society. He never made sexual commitments except with boys who were younger than he and who appealed to him. This faithfulness was, of course, a reaction to his infidelity towards the marriage bed. From the beginning Yuichi had come to this society in faithfulness to himself. In general, however, his weakness and the mysterious will of Shunsuké were forcing him to be faithless to himself. Shunsuké said it was the fate of beauty as well as of art.

Yuichi's looks had turned the head of eight or nine of the ten foreigners who saw him. Disliking foreigners, he had rejected them all. One, for instance, had broken a two-storey pane of glass in Rudon's in a fit of anger. Another, in a fit of depression, had for no discernible reason, slashed the wrists of the boy staying with him. The crowd who specialized in living off foreigners respected Yuichi highly for his attitude. They had a masochistic love and respect for a mode of living that without harming them could lash out against their own subsistence. Why? Because no day goes by that we do not dream of a safe rebellion against our livelihood.

Nevertheless, Yuichi strove out of his inherent gentleness to refuse without wounding the other parties. When he looked at those pitiful beings who wanted him when he did not want them, Yuichi could not help viewing them with the same eyes he turned on his pathetic wife. The impulses of compassion and sympathy condoned a mood of acceptance not unmixed with disdain for these men, and in this mood of acceptance, oddly, an easy, worry-free coquetry flowered. It was a completely relaxed, aged coquetry like the kind seen in the gentle maternal instincts of old women visiting orphanages.

A limousine threaded through the congestion of the street and stopped in front of Rudon's. A second limousine followed it and stopped. The Oasis Kimichan did a single proud pirouette and greeted the three foreigners with his proudest, most amorous look. There were ten men in the group going to Jackie's party, including the foreigners and Yuichi.

When the three foreigners saw Yuichi, a gleam of anticipation and impatience came into their eyes. Who was going to share a bed with him tonight at Jackie's?

The ten men were loaded into two cars. Rudy handed a gift for Jackie through the window. It was a bottle of champagne decked with holly.

*

Oiso was less than two hours' drive away. The cars ran bumper to bumper on the Keihin Number 2 National Highway and the old Tokaido Road to Ofuna. The boys were having a merry time. One calculating boy had an empty Boston bag in his lap in which he planned to carry back all the loot he could get. Yuichi did not sit next to a foreigner. The blond young man next to the driver stared covetously in the rear-view mirror, in which he could watch Yuichi's face.

158

The sky was alight – a blue-porcelain night sky where countless stars twinkled, like snowflakes frozen before they could fall. The car was warm, thanks to the heater. Yuichi heard from his talkative seat mate, with whom he had once been intimate, a story about the golden-haired man next to the driver. After he had been in Japan a time, he shouted in the climax of sexual pleasure, *'Tengoku! Tengoku!'* – Paradise – which he had heard somewhere, and made his partner break up with laughter. This not unlikely story shook Yuichi with laughter – and just then it happened that his eye met the eye in the rear-view mirror. That blue eye winked, and the thin lips came closer to the surface of the glass and kissed it. Yuichi was amazed – the cloudy print of his lips on the mirror surface was tinged with red.

It was nine o'clock when they arrived. There were already three limousines in the circular drive. Human figures were moving busily in the windows from which came the sound of music. The wind was very cold, and the boys, stepping out, bent their newly shaven pale blue napes.

Jackie greeted his guests at the entrance. He sank his face in the bouquet of winter roses that Yuichi handed him and shook hands stylishly with the foreigners with his right hand, which bore a cat's-eye ring. He was quite drunk, so he greeted everyone, including the boy who sold pickles in the daytime in his family's store, with a *'Meri-Kurisumasu tsu yu.'* For a moment the boys felt as if they were abroad. In fact, many boys like them had been abroad, accompanied by their lovers. The stories that appear under the newspaper headlines, 'Public Spirit Far from Home/Houseboy Studies Abroad,' generally have this meaning.

The salon that gave off the entranceway was about twenty mats in size and was lighted only by a Christmas tree in the centre, adorned with tiny incandescent candles. A long-playing record sounded from a loudspeaker hung somewhere in the tree. About twenty guests were already dancing in the salon.

In truth, this evening the pure child was born from an immaculate mother's womb. The men dancing here were celebrating the nativity like 'the Righteous Man', Joseph. In short, they celebrated their freedom from responsibility for the infant born this night.

Men dancing together – this uncommon joke. As they danced, the rebellious smiles beaming from their faces said: 'We aren't doing this because we are forced to; we are only playing a simple joke.' While they danced, they laughed – a spirit-destroying laugh. In the usual dance hall, the men and women blithely dancing exhibit the freedom of the impulses they express. But when these men danced, arms intertwined, there was a feeling that they were forced by the impulse into a dark bondage. Why is it that men must, in spite of themselves, assume a posture to show they love each other? What is it but that this kind of love, confused by the impulse, may perhaps not be consummated if the dark taste of destiny is not present?

The popular piece became a fast rumba. Their dancing became frenzied, lewd. Under the pretext that 'It is the music above all, that is driving us,' one couple joined their lips and, until they fell, whirled about endlessly. Eichan, who had come earlier, winked at Yuichi from the arms of a fat little foreigner. The boy was half-laughing and half-knitting his brows. While they were dancing, the fat dancer kept biting the boy's earlobe. His moustache, traced with eyebrow pencil, was smudging the boy's face.

There Yuichi beheld the conclusion of the fate that had been first recorded for him. He saw precisely, in concrete form, the complete truth of that fate. Eichan's lips and teeth were as beautiful as never. His smudged face was indescribably endearing. But from his beauty all abstractness had disappeared. His slim hips twisted under a hairy hand. Yuichi averted his eyes impassively.

On the sofa and on the divan that ringed the fireplace, drunks and lovers were stretched out, uttering languid noises and giggles of delight. About seven or eight men were in close embrace, rubbing against various parts of each other's bodies. Two were joined at the shoulders, giving their backs to the caresses of another. Another man had his leg locked over that of the man beside him; at the same time his left hand was deep in the pit of the stomach of the man at his left. Like the evening haze, the sound of low, sweetly murmured caresses wafted. A dignified gentleman on the rug beneath their feet, solid gold cufflinks protruding from his sleeves, had removed the sock from a boy's foot – the boy was meanwhile being squeezed by three men on the divan – and was holding the foot to his lips. When the sole of his foot was kissed, the boy suddenly emitted a giggle of delight, and the impetus of his body being shoved backward affected those behind him. The others, however, seemed hardly to move at all. Like creatures native to the depths of the sea, they settled sluggishly.

Jackie came to Yuichi's side and gave him a cocktail.

'It's a swinging party; I can't say how happy I am about it,' he said. Even in his choice of words, there was the trace of youth. 'Oh, Yuchan, tonight somebody's coming who really wants to meet you. He's an old friend, so don't be too cruel to him. He has the Prince Genji name of Pope.' Saying this, he looked towards the entrance, and his eyes lit up.

'Oh, here he is!'

An affected-looking individual appeared in the dark doorway. One hand fumbling with the buttons on his overcoat showed white in the gloom. In mechanical gait that said, 'Screw one loose; then take a step,' he approached Jackie and Yuichi. A dancing couple passed close by; he made a wry face and averted his glance.

'Alias Mr Pope – Yuichi.'

In response to Jackie's introduction, Pope held out a white hand to Yuichi.

'Cheers!'

Yuichi looked hard at that face bathed in unpleasant light. It was Count Kaburagi.

13

Courtesy

Pope, the name by which Nobutaka Kaburagi had come to be called by men ignorant of its origin, was a *nom de guerre* he had taken from Alexander Pope, whose poetry he enjoyed. Kaburagi was an old friend of Jackie's. They had met ten years ago or more in the Oriental Hotel in Kobe, where they stayed together two or three times.

Yuichi had had much practice in the intricacies of meeting people unexpectedly at parties like this without being at all surprised. This society had broken up the discipline of the society outside; it had scrambled the alphabet of the outside and then rearranged it strangely – like CXMQA, for instance – changing the order and changing the grouping and demonstrating the virtuosity of the magician.

Count Kaburagi's metamorphosis, however, had caught Yuichi completely by surprise. For a moment he found it difficult to take the hand that Pope held out to him. Kaburagi's amazement was even greater. As a drunk stares fixedly at something, so he stared at Yuichi, saying: 'It's you! It's you!'

Then he looked at Jackie again and said, 'Me, of all people – for the first time in all these years this fellow has succeeded in conning me. In the first place, he's a very young married man. I first met him at the speaker's table at his wedding reception. To think that Yuichi is the famous Yuchan!'

'Yuchan has a wife!' said Jackie, evincing surprise in the manner of a foreigner. 'That's the first I've heard of it.'

Thus one of Yuichi's secrets was quickly out. It wouldn't take ten days, certainly, for news to leak out to the fellowship. Soon, he feared, all his secrets, in both his worlds, withheld from each other till now, would be violated one by one.

In search for a means of escaping these fears, he now turned to the task of regarding the former Count Kaburagi as 'Pope'.

That restless, craving look, he now understood, was caused by the desperate urge continually to seek out beautiful fellows. That disgusting something that hung about Kaburagi's features, like a stain in a garment that refuses to come out; that nameless, unpleasant mixture of effeminacy and impudence; that absurd, forced, squeezed voice; that ever so carefully planned naturalness: all were the seal of the fellowship and its compensatory endeavours. All the fragmentary impressions remaining in Yuichi's memory thus suddenly formed themselves along a single thread, a definite pattern. Of the two methods peculiar to this society – analysis and synthesis – he had worked the latter out completely. Just as a wanted man might alter his looks by surgery, Nobutaka Kaburagi had learned to conceal under his public face a portrait that he did not want seen. The nobility, especially, excel at concealment. A penchant for hiding vice comes before a penchant for committing vicious acts. It may therefore be said that Nobutaka Kaburagi had discovered the joy of being a nobleman.

He nudged Yuichi's back. Jackie led them to a sofa.

Five boys in white made their way through the crowd, bearing glasses of wine and plates of canapés. All five were Jackie's lovers. It was uncanny. Each was in some way like Jackie. They all looked like brothers. One had Jackie's eyes; another one had his nose. One had his lips; another looked like Jackie from behind. The last had inherited his forehead. Put together, they formed a matchless likeness of Jackie in his younger days.

His portrait hung above the mantel, adorned by the gift flowers and holly leaves and a pair of candles. It was bordered by a splendid gold frame and, due to dingy pigments, exhibited a highly sensual olive-coloured nude figure. It was the spring of Jackie's nineteenth year. Using him as a model, an Englishman who worshipped Jackie had painted this. It was a young Bacchus holding high a glass of champagne and smiling mischievously. On his brow he bore ivy; on his bare neck a tie was loosely draped. His left arm lithely supported the golden weight of the drunken boat of his body on the table on which he was half-sitting. His hand, like an oar, pressed back the waves made by the light pressure of his hips against the white tablecloth.

Just then the record changed to a samba. The dancers withdrew to the sides; a light went on behind the wine-coloured brocade curtain over the doorway to the stairs. The curtain shook energetically. Suddenly a half-naked boy appeared, dressed as a Spanish dancer. He was a small, narrow-hipped, charming boy of eighteen or so, wearing a scarlet turban; a gold-embroidered scarlet brassière covered his breast.

He danced. His limpid sexuality differed from the dark, indecisive hesitancy of a woman. It held a litheness rich with precise lines and glints that captured the hearts of the audience. Dancing, the boy threw back his head. When he brought it forward again he gave a clear look of desire in Yuichi's direction. Yuichi responded by closing one eye. A silent pact had been sealed.

Kaburagi did not miss the wink. Since he had earlier come to recognize Yuichi for what he was, his heart was filled with Yuichi. Pope was concerned about public opinion, so he never showed his face in the places in the Ginza district. Recently he had heard the name Yuchan everywhere, but imagined it meant no more than that an extraordinary person had taken his place among the garden-variety of beautiful boys. Half out of curiosity he had asked Jackie to introduce him. It turned out to be Yuichi.

Nobutaka Kaburagi was a master of seduction. Until today, in his forty-third year, he had been intimate with about a thousand boys. What was it that attracted him? It cannot be said that it was beauty that excited him and drove him to debauchery. Rather, it was fear – trembling fear – that held him captive. In the pleasures of that street, everywhere a kind of sweet corruption followed one. As Saikaku said so eloquently: 'Making love to boys is like the sleep of a wolf under a flower whose petals are falling.' That is the charm of it. Nobutaka searched constantly for new thrills. Only new things excited him. He had no sense that would have permitted him to compare the charms of the individual before him now with the charms of the individual he had just loved. Like a ray of light, passion illuminated one time, one space. Now Nobutaka felt like a suicide lured to the precipice. A fresh rent in the continuous exterior of our fixed lives was beckoning him, who had so little resistance.

Watch out this time, his heart soliloquized. Until just now I had seen Yuichi as nothing more than a young husband infatuated with my wife, a runaway colt galloping in the dawn down the normal paths of life. I looked at his beauty but kept calm. I never thought I could recklessly drag that runaway down my own little lane. When I then suddenly perceived Yuichi in this little lane, my heart was troubled. He's dangerous as lightning! I remember that long ago when I saw a young fellow just entering this street the same lightning lit my heart up brightly. I fell head over heels in love. I know the signs when it is going to happen. Since then twenty years have gone by, and the lightning has not struck again with the same force until today. Compared with this the lightning I felt for the other thousand was a child's sparkler. With the first throb, the first thrill, the issue was decided. Somehow I must get to sleep with this youth right away.

Even though he was in love, he excelled in techniques of observation and his glance had the power of making things transparent. In his words the power of mental telepathy lay concealed. From the moment he saw Yuichi, Nobutaka perceived the intellectual poison corroding this beautiful young person. Ah, already this youth has been rendered weak by his own beauty. His weakness is his beauty. He has recognized the power of his beauty, and the prints of the leaves are still on his back. That's what I'll aim at.

Nobutaka stood up and approached the terrace where Jackie was sobering up. As he did so, the blond foreigner who had come over with Yuichi asked Yuichi to dance. Another foreigner made the same request at almost the same moment.

Nobutaka motioned to Jackie, who then came in. The cold air struck Nobutaka's neck.

Jackie took his old friend to the bar on the mezzanine that looked out to the sea. In a corner, a bar had been set up where there were no windows, and there a faithful waiter whom Jackie had discovered in the Ginza was working with rolled-up sleeves as bartender. On the distant point at the left the flashing light was visible. The branches of the bare trees in the garden embraced the seascape and the starry sky. Caught between the cold air and the heat, the windows had been wiped and clouded over again. Playfully, the two men ordered a woman's cocktail, an angel's tip, and drank.

'Well? Terrific, eh?'

'A pretty boy. I've never seen anything quite like him.'

'The foreigners are all amazed by him. And not one of them has had him. He seems to dislike foreigners particularly. He's had about ten or twenty fellows, but they're all younger than he.'

'The tougher they are, the more exciting they are. The boys nowadays are pushovers.'

'Well, go ahead and see. At any rate, the veterans have done all they can, but now they're all played out. Now's the time for Pope to show his hand.'

'What I want to know is...' said the former count, transferring his cocktail to the palm of his left hand and staring fixedly at it. Whenever he looked at something, he put on an air of being observed. In short, he continually played the dual role of actor and audience. 'How shall I say it? I wonder if the kid has ever given himself to someone he doesn't desire. Whether, how shall I say it, he has given himself completely to his own beauty. If there is ever so little of love and desire for one's lover in the affair, then it can by no means be called giving onself purely to one's own beauty. From what you say he doesn't seem to have had such an experience, despite his good looks.'

'That's what I hear; although if he's married he must be sleeping with his wife mostly out of a sense of duty.'

Nobutaka dropped his eyes. He groped for the implications hidden in his old friend's words. When Kaburagi thought about something, he always acted as if people were staring hard at him, studying the tailoring of his ideas. The tipsy Jackie urged him to try what he had in mind. If by ten o'clock the next morning Nobutaka was successful, Jackie wagered, he would win the magnificent ring on his finger. Against it Pope wagered the early Muromachi *makie*-lacquered writing box in

166

the Kaburagi family storehouse. The beauty of that high-relief *makie* work had set Jackie pining incurably to possess it when he had first seen it in the Kaburagi home.

From the mezzanine they descended again to the ballroom. Before anyone knew it, Yuichi had started dancing with the one who had performed earlier. The boy had already changed to a suit. At his throat a lovely bow tie was knotted. Nobutaka knew his age. The homosexual's hell and the woman's hell are the same – namely, old age. Nobutaka knew for certain that he could never hope for the divine miracle that the beautiful youth would fall in love with him. The very impossibility of it brought his passion close to that of the idealist who knows from the beginning his ideals will never be realized. He who loves ideals hopes to be loved by ideals in turn.

In the middle of the number, Yuichi and the boy abruptly stopped dancing. The two disappeared from sight behind the wine-coloured curtain. With a sigh, Pope said, 'Well, they've gone to the second floor.'

On the floor above, there were three or four little rooms that could be used at any time, all furnished casually with sleeping alcoves and couches.

'You'll have to allow him one or two lovers, Pope. When you're young as he is, it doesn't make any difference.' Jackie said it in a comforting tone. He was looking over the shelves in the corner, deciding where to put the writing box he would get from Nobutaka.

Nobutaka was waiting. Even after Yuichi reappeared in an hour, his opportunity didn't come. Night was deepening. People were losing interest in dancing. Like alternately dying and reviving embers, however, several couples were continually exchanging partners and dancing on. Against the wall in a little chair, one of Jackie's favourites, his face innocent in slumber, was taking a nap. One of the foreigners winked at Jackie. Ever the generous host, he smiled and nodded. The foreigner grasped the sleeping boy very lightly. He carried him to a sofa on the other side of the curtain leading to the mezzanine. The boy's lips were slightly open as he slept. His eyes, hidden by long lashes, trembled as, out of curiosity, he stealthily looked at the breast of the husky person carrying him. He saw the golden hair of the man's chest protruding from a gap in his shirt and felt as if he were being embraced by a great hornet.

Nobutaka awaited his chance. The men there were mainly old acquaintances, and they had all sorts of things to talk about. Nobutaka, however, wanted Yuichi. All kinds of sweet and lewd imaginings tortured him. He was confident, moreover, that no expression of his would betray so much as a particle of his emotions.

Yuichi's eyes happened to fall on a new arrival. It was a boy who had arrived at two in the morning with four or five foreigners from Yokohama. From the collar of his two-tone coat hung a scarlet-and-black-striped muffler. When he laughed his teeth shone in strong, gleaming rows. His hair was cut square. It went well with his deep-cut full face. On his fingers, in which he clumsily held a cigarette, he wore a garish, initialed gold ring. In this wild boy there seemed to be something worthy of Yuichi's languid sexuality. If Yuichi could be called a superb sculpture, this boy would be a botched piece of work by comparison. Besides, to the extent that one would consider him an imitation, to that same extent one would have to admit he was much like Yuichi. Thanks to his extraordinary pride, Narcissus sometimes loves a bad mirror. A bad mirror saves one from jealousy, if nothing else.

The newcomers exchanged courtesies with those who had arrived before them. Yuichi and the boy sat together. Their young eyes sought each other. An understanding had already been formed.

When the two men attempted to rise from their places, hand in hand, however, one of the foreigners asked Yuichi to dance. Yuichi did not refuse. Nobutaka Kaburagi did not let the opportunity go by; he came up to the boy and asked him to dance. While they danced, he said, 'Have you forgotten me, Ryochan?'

'Could I forget you, Pope?'

'Have I ever asked you to do anything for nothing?'

'I'm indebted to you for your generosity. Everyone loves you for it.'

'How about tonight? Can you help me?'

'No reason why not, for you.'

'Right now.'

'Right now?' the boys eyes clouded. 'But, there's –'

'I'll give you twice as much as the last time.'

'Yes, but how about later? There's plenty of time before morning.'

'Later's no good; right now!'

'First come, first served.'

'But the first one doesn't have a cent to his name, does he?'

'For someone I love, I don't mind sacrificing my fortune.'

'Your whole fortune! You talk as if you were rich. All right, I'll lay out three times the money plus a thousand yen – ten thousand yen. I'll pay you afterwards.'

'Ten thousand yen?' The boy's eyes blinked. 'Was I that good last time?'

'Right.'

The boy raised his voice as he bluffed: 'You're drunk, aren't you, Pope? I find what you say too good to believe.'

'You don't value yourself highly enough, unfortunately. Have a little more pride. Here's four thousand down. The other six I'll give you later.'

The boy calculated. Four thousand yen ... if worst comes to worst, and the other six thousand yen goes sour, it's still not a bad deal, he told himself. How will I get around putting Yuichi off?

Yuichi was by the wall, smoking a cigarette while he waited for the boy to finish the dance. With the fingers of one hand, he drummed delicately on the wall. Nobutaka watched him out of the corner of his eye; he was struck by the fresh beauty of the body of this young man waiting for the signal to spring.

The dance had ended, Ryosuké came over towards Yuichi planning to make some excuse. Yuichi, who did not sense that, threw away his cigarette, turned his back to the other and went ahead. Ryosuké followed him; Nobutaka followed Ryosuké. While they climbed the stairs, Yuichi placed his hand lightly on the boy's shoulder. The boy's position was gradually becoming more difficult. As Yuichi opened the door of one of the rooms on the second floor, Nobutaka suddenly grasped the boy by the arm. Yuichi turned about in surprise. Nobutaka and the boy were silent; Yuichi's eyes coloured with youthful anger.

'What are you doing?'

'I'm first, am I not?'

'Rightfully, this boy is mine first.' Yuichi inclined his head and laughed a forced laugh. 'Quit the kidding.'

'If you think it's a joke, ask the boy and see whose claim he wants to honour first.'

Yuichi placed his hand on the boy's shoulder. The shoulder trembled. Attempting to compensate for the ugliness of the moment, the boy glared at Yuichi with eyes that were hooded with hostility, though he spoke gently: 'It's all right, isn't it? Later?'

Yuichi was about to strike the boy. Nobutaka intervened.

'Now, now; let's not have any rough stuff. We have lots of time to talk it over.'

Nobutaka put his arm around Yuichi's shoulders and led him into the room. When Ryochan attempted to enter behind them, Nobutaka slammed the door in his face. His remonstrations could be heard through the door. Nobutaka quickly latched it. He placed Yuichi on the divan by the window and lit a cigarette for both of them. Meanwhile, outside, the boy kept banging on the door. He gave it one more kick and then resignedly left.

The atmosphere of the room suited the occasion. On the wall there hung a picture of Endymion asleep in meadow grass and flowers and bathed in moonbeams. The electric space heater was turned on, and on the table was a bottle of cognac, a water pitcher, and a record player. On party nights the foreigner who occupied this room usually made it available to visitors.

Nobutaka turned on the record player, designed to play ten records in succession, then with deliberation poured two glasses of cognac. Yuichi suddenly got up, meaning to leave the room. Pope headed him off, fixing the youth with a deep, gentle stare. There was unusual power in his look. Yuichi, bound by a mysterious curiosity, sat down again.

'Relax. I don't give a hoot about that child. I gave him some money with the understanding he would back out on you. If I hadn't done that, I wouldn't have been able to talk to you at leisure. Since there's money involved, he'll wait for you.'

It must be said in all honesty that Yuichi's desire had swiftly abated since the time when he had wanted to strike the boy. He was far, however, from admitting this to Nobutaka. He sat silently, like a captured spy.

'I said I wanted to talk,' Pope went on. 'Not a particularly formal conversation – I just thought I'd like to have one heart-to-heart talk with you. You'll listen, won't you? I still re-member the day I first saw you at your wedding.'

It would be tiresome to go into all the long monologue that Nobutaka Kaburagi indulged in presently. It continued to the tune of ten dance records, both sides. Nobutaka knew well the telling effect of his own words. Before the caress of the hand comes the caress of words. He transformed himself into a mirror that reflected Yuichi. Behind that mirror he managed to conceal Nobutaka himself, his age, his desire, his complex-ity, and his ingenuity.

While Nobutaka's monologue droned on – without Yuichi's consent in the first place – Yuichi heard from time to time, in soothing tones: 'Are you tired of this?' or, 'If you're bored, tell me, and I'll stop,' or, 'Does this conversation annoy you?' all inserted like interludes. The first time the question came like a timorous entreaty; the second time it was hopelessly overbearing; the third time it was full of confidence, as if sure that Yuichi would smile and shake his head when the question came.

Yuichi wasn't bored. Far from it. Why? Because Nobutaka's monologue was about Yuichi and nothing else: 'Your eye-brows are so cold and clear. Your eyebrows are – how shall I put it – they exhibit pure youthful will.' When he ran out of comparisons, he stared silently for a time at Yuichi's brows. It was a hypnotic technique. 'Not only that, there is an exquisite harmony between those brows and these deep, sad eyes. The eyes show your fate. The eyebrows show your will. What lies between those two is struggle. It is the fight that must be fought by every youth. Your brows and your eyes are the eyes and brows of the most beautiful young officer on the battlefield. His name is youth.

'The only hat to match these eyebrows and those eyes is the Grecian helmet. How many times I have seen your beauty in dreams! How many times I have wished to speak to you! Nevertheless, when I meet you, the words stick in my throat like a boy's. I am convinced that of all the young men I have seen in the past thirty years you are the most beautiful. There are none to be compared with you. How can you take it into your head to love someone like Ryochan? Take a good look in a mirror. The beauty you discover in other men comes entirely from your own ignorance and self-delusion. The beauty you think you have found in other men is already possessed in its entirety by you; there is no more beauty anywhere to discover. When you "love" another man, you are only too ignorant about yourself – you who were born on the pinnacle of perfection.'

Nobutaka's face came slowly closer and closer to Yuichi. His high-flown words charmed the ears like slander. In fact, no ordinary flattery could compare with them.

'You don't need a name,' he continued. 'Indeed, beauty with a name doesn't count at all. Illusions of beauty that must have a name like Yuichi or Taro or Jiro won't fool me any more. You don't need a name to carry out your human function. You are a type. You are on the stage. Your stage name is "Young Man". There are no actors anywhere who can bear this title. All of them depend on a personality, a character, or a name. All they can portray to the best of their ability is Ichiro Young Man, John Young Man, Johannes Young Man. You, however, in your being are the animated universal name, "Young Man". You are the representative of the visible "Young Man" that has appeared in the myths, the histories, the societies, and the *Zeitgeist* of all the countries of the world. You personify all. If you did not exist, the youth of all the young men would suffer nothing less than a burial without ever being seen. In your brows the brows of millions of young men are prefigured. Your lips comprise the burgeoning design of millions of young lips. Your chest, your arms...' Nobutaka rubbed the youth's arms, encased in the sleeves of his winter suit. 'Your thighs, your palms...' He pressed his shoulder

172

harder against Yuichi's shoulder. He fixed the profile of the youth firmly in his gaze. Then he reached out one hand and turned off the lamp on the table.

'Sit still. Please, I beg you, don't move. What beauty! The night is breaking. The sky is growing white. Surely you feel that faint, random indication of dawn there on your cheek. This cheek, though, is still in night. Your consummate profile floats on the boundary between night and dawn. Sit still, I beg you.'

Nobutaka saw the youth's profile in miraculous relief in the pure hour that bounded day and night. This momentary carving had become an eternal thing. That profile brought external form into time, and by fixing one consummate beauty in time became itself an imperishable thing.

The window curtains had been open. The glass panes let in the whitening seascape. This little room offered an unobstructed view of the sea. The beacon blinked drowsily. Above the sea, muddy-white rays supported deep banks of clouds in the dawning-dark sky. The wintry stands of trees in rows in the garden, like flotsam washed up by the morning tide, vaguely mingled their branches.

Yuichi was overcome by a deep lassitude, a sudden sensation of sleepiness and intoxication. The portrait painter by Nobutaka's words stole out of the mirror and gradually bore down upon Yuichi. Yuichi's hair, pressing against the back of the sofa, seemed to become heavier and heavier. Desire mingled with desire; desire redoubled desire. This dreamlike sensation is not easy to explain. Spirit dozed above spirit. Without any help from desire, Yuichi's spirit was coupled with the spirit of another Yuichi which was already mingling with it. Yuichi's forehead touched Yuichi's forehead; beautiful eyebrows touched beautiful eyebrows. This dreamy youth's half-open lips were stopped by the beautiful lips of the self that he had dreamed up.

The first flicker of dawn came through the clouds. Nobutaka released Yuichi's cheeks, which he had been holding in both hands. His coat now lay on the chair at the side. His empty hands quickly released his suspenders from his shoulders.

Again he took Yuichi's face in his hands. His smug lips again pressed Yuichi's lips.

The next morning at ten o'clock, Jackie sadly handed his treasured cat's-eye ring to Nobutaka.

14

Alone and Independent

The year changed. Yuichi turned twenty-three, according to the calendar. Yasuko turned twenty.

The new year was celebrated by the Minami household in the family circle. It was essentially a season for festivity. First, there was Yasuko's pregnancy. Second, Yuichi's mother, unexpectedly in good health, had lived to greet the new year. There was, however, something darkly foreboding about the occasion. The seed, clearly, had been planted by Yuichi.

His frequent overnight absences and, worse, his increasing dereliction of connubial duty, Yasuko at times could, on reflection, ascribe to her own possessiveness, but just the same they tortured her. From what was said in the homes of her friends or her relatives, many a wife returned to her family when her husband stayed out only one night. Yuichi, furthermore, seemed to have lost somewhere the gentleness of spirit that was his nature, and though he stayed away overnight repeatedly without notice, he paid no heed to his mother's advice or the appeals of Yasuko. He was becoming more and more silent; his white teeth were seldom shown.

It would not do, however, to imagine that Yuichi's pride was a Byronic isolation. It was not an act of contemplation; his pride was a veritable necessity, springing from his way of life. He was no different from the incompetent captain who silently affects a scowl as he watches the destruction of the ship in which he is sailing. At the same time, the speed of this shipwreck was too orderly; the culprit, Yuichi, was not entirely to blame – it was a case that must be considered as nothing more than the simple action of self-disintegration.

After the holidays, Yuichi suddenly announced that he was becoming private secretary to the chairman of the board of a nameless company. Neither his mother nor Yasuko took him seriously until he mentioned that the chairman and his wife were coming to visit. This threw his mother into a panic. Yuichi had mischievously kept silent the name of the chairman, so when his mother saw none other than the Kaburagis standing in the doorway that day, she was doubly surprised.

That morning a light snow had fallen, and the afternoon was cloudy and extremely cold. The former count sat with his legs crossed in front of the living-room gas heater, hands held up before it, as if he were about to engage it in conversation. His wife was ebullient. The couple had never gotten along so well. When a funny story was told they both looked at each other and laughed.

Yasuko heard the lady's somewhat shrill laughter when she was in the hall on her way to greet the guests in the living room. Her intuitions had told her long ago that this woman was among those in love with Yuichi, but unnatural and uncanny insights engendered by her pregnancy, if nothing else, told her that the person driving Yuichi to exhaustion was neither Mrs Kaburagi nor Kyoko. It was without doubt someone she had not yet seen. Whenever she tried to imagine the woman Yuichi was hiding, Yasuko felt, aside from jealousy, a mysterious fear. So when Mrs Kaburagi's high-pitched laughter struck her ears, she felt not the least jealousy; in fact, her composure was hardly disturbed.

Worn out with anxiety, Yasuko had reached a point where she was inured to the habitude of pain and became like a shrewd small animal, its ears up and alert. Although she was aware that Yuichi's future depended on the good offices of her parents, Yasuko had not said a word to them about her difficulties. Yuichi's mother was filled with admiration at this demonstration of a forbearance beyond her years. The admirable courage of this so-young wife gave her the status of the old-fashioned model of womanly virtue, yet it must be said that Yasuko at some time had come to love the melancholy that Yuichi kept concealed behind his façade of pride.

Surely there are many who would doubt that such magnanimity could be acquired by a young wife of twenty or so. As time went by, however, she had come to realize her husband's unhappiness and at the same time was struck with the notion that she would be committing a crime against him if she allowed herself to admit her inability to cure it. In the conclusion that her husband's dissipation gave him no pleasure, in the conclusion that it was nothing but a manifestation of his indefinable suffering – in these maternal conclusions there was a misapprehension born of a pretence at adult sentimentality. It was close to moral torture, this childish fancy, this refusal, on grounds of unsuitability, to attach the word 'pleasure' to Yuichi's suffering. She felt, however, that if she were a man philandering in the manner of the run of the world's youths, then that man she would be would enjoy informing his wife about it.

Something incomprehensible is eating at him, she thought. Surely he's not plotting a revolution or anything. If he loved someone else and was untrue to me, that deep despair would not be playing about his features all the time. Yuchan does not love anything at all; I know this from wifely instinct.

Yasuko was partly right. She was not able to say that Yuichi loved boys.

The family chatted busily in the living room; the convenient cordiality of the Kaburagis had an unexpected effect on Yuichi and his wife. They laughed and talked quite like a couple who had nothing to hide from each other.

By mistake Yuichi drank Yasuko's cup of tea. Everyone was lost in a dream of conversation, and the blunder seemed not worth noticing. In fact, Yuichi had drunk it without immediately realizing it himself. Only Yasuko saw it and nudged his leg. Silently she pointed to his teacup on the table and smiled. In reply, he scratched his head boyishly.

This pantomime did not escape the alert eyes of Mrs Kaburagi. Her cheerfulness on this day centred about the happy anticipation that Yuichi was to become her husband's private secretary; it had its source further back in the tender appreciation she felt towards her husband for having some days before showed an interest in bringing this auspicious plan into reality. When Yuichi became the private secretary, how frequently she would be able to see his face! Her husband certainly had some calculation in mind when he entered into her plan, but she managed not to think about that.

When Mrs Kaburagi saw this smiling intimacy between Yasuko and Yuichi, even though it was insignificant and barely discernible, the hopelessness of her own love flashed upon her. The two were young and beautiful; even the problem of Kyoko seemed to her Yuichi's one little escapade when she looked at this loving young couple. And her own position, gifted with fewer alluring qualities than Kyoko possessed, she had not a bit of courage to contemplate.

Her appearance here in close though forced company with her husband had for Mrs Kaburagi another, quite different, design. She thought it would make Yuichi jealous. This notion, of course, had its fanciful elements, but she wished to get back at him for the pain he had caused her by his appearance with Kyoko, while at the same time she feared out of love for him that if she appeared somewhere before him with a young man in tow she would somehow wound Yuichi's pride.

She noticed a loose thread on her husband's shoulder and removed it. Nobutaka stared and said: 'What are you doing?' When he realized what she was doing, he was shocked. His wife was not a woman who did such things.

In his company, the Utsubo Far East Marine Products, Nobutaka had used an old-time steward as his private secretary. This useful old man had called him 'My lord', never 'Mr Chairman'. Two months ago he had died of a cerebral haemorrhage. A new private secretary was needed. When Nobutaka's wife suggested Yuichi for the job, he replied vaguely, 'Fine; it's only a light part-time job.' He judged from her look of indifference that she was concerned indeed.

Unexpectedly, however, this overture served neatly to disguise Nobutaka's own proposal a month later. When, soon after New Year, he himself got the idea of making Yuichi his private secretary, he gave his wife credit for the scheme and, affecting her own practical way of talking, added his own praises of Yuichi's business acumen.

'That young man is just the sort that job needs,' he said. 'The other day I met Mr Kuwahara at the Otomo Bank; he's a graduate of Yuichi's college. Far East Marine Products managed to get an illegal loan through Mr Kuwahara, but anyway he had a lot to say in praise of Yuichi. It's quite a thing for a man his age to be involved as he is with difficult property management.'

'Then let's hire him as private secretary,' suggested his wife. 'In case he hesitates, let's go to visit his mother, whom we haven't seen in a long time, and go to work on it together.'

Nobutaka had forgotten his long-standing habit of fluttering lightly as a butterfly around matters of the heart. He had not been able to live without Yuichi since the night at Jackie's party. Since then Yuichi had complied with his demands on two occasions, but in general he gave no sign that he loved Nobutaka. Nobutaka, though, thought more and more about him. Yuichi did not like to sleep away from home, and so the two had secretly gone to a hotel in the suburbs. The elaborate precautions astonished Yuichi. In order to meet him, Nobutaka would make a reservation for one or two days for himself, Yuichi would happen to call 'on business', and would leave late at night. Nobutaka would needlessly stay on afterwards.

After Yuichi left, however, this middle-aged nobleman would be struck by mindless passion. He would pace the narrow room dressed only in his robe. Finally he would fall down on the rug and roll about. In a small voice he would call out Yuichi's name hundreds of times. He would drink the wine Yuichi had left; he would light the cigarette butts Yuichi had left behind. He would beg Yuichi to leave his cakes in the plate half-eaten, with his tooth marks plain to see in the remnants.

Yuichi's mother was ready to believe that Nobutaka Kaburagi's suggestion that her son be permitted to study the world was the very remedy needed to cure the boy's dissolute ways. He was, after all, a student. It was not well to forget about the career he was to assume after he graduated.

'There is the matter of Father Segawa's department store,' she said, addressing Yuichi in tones designed for Nobutaka to hear. 'Your father-in-law wishes to help you get an education. Before we can take this offer seriously we must confer with him.'

He looked into his mother's eyes, which had weakened with the years. This old person is making sure of the future! This old lady who might, for all we know, drop dead tomorrow!

The one who, on the other hand, doesn't find a thing sure about tomorrow is youth, thought Yuichi. In general, old people believe in the future through force of habit, but young people don't have years of habit behind them. That's the only difference between them.

Yuichi lifted his beautiful brows. He set forth strong yet childish arguments: 'It's all right. After all, they didn't adopt me.'·

Yasuko looked at Yuichi's profile as he spoke these words. She wondered if he was being cruel to her because of his wounded pride. It was time for her to speak on his behalf.

'I can tell my father anything. You do exactly as you please.'

Yuichi then set forth what he and Nobutaka had agreed on earlier, how he might help out without interfering with his studies. His mother earnestly pleaded with Nobutaka in the matter of Yuichi's development. These pleas were far too earnest, and would certainly have sounded strange to a bystander. Nobutaka, it seemed, was going to work a miraculous education upon this precious prodigal son.

The talk had just about ended. Nobutaka Kaburagi invited everyone out to dinner. The mother declined at first, but gave in when she was told she would be taken and brought back by car. She got up to get ready. It was evening, and snow was falling again, so she put on a flannel stomach band and slipped a pocket heater inside it to protect her kidneys.

The five of them went out in Nobutaka's hired car to a restaurant in the Ginza. After dinner Nobutaka suggested they go to a dance hall. Even Yuichi's mother was willing to go; she wanted to see the worst. She even wanted to see a strip show, but this evening there was none.

She modestly admired the dancers' revealing costumes; 'How pretty! Really becoming. That blue diagonal line is absolutely charming.'

Yuichi felt a freedom in his whole body that he could not easily explain. He suddenly realized he had forgotten Shunsuké's existence. He made up his mind that he would not tell Shunsuké about this new private-secretary arrangement nor about his relationship with Nobutaka. This small resolution cheered him. It made him ask Mrs Kaburagi to dance. When she complied he asked: 'What makes you so happy?' Then he added, looking deep in the woman's eyes: 'Don't you even know?'

In that moment Mrs Kaburagi's happiness barely left her free to breathe.

15

Blue Sunday

On a Sunday long before spring, at eleven in the morning,
Yuichi and Nobutaka Kaburagi, who had spent the night together, parted at the ticket gate of the Kanda Station.

The night before they had had a little quarrel. Nobutaka had
reserved a hotel room without consulting Yuichi, and Yuichi
had angrily made him cancel it. Nobutaka strove to mollify
him, and in the end they went to a Kanda neighbourhood hotel
and took whatever room was available. They hesitated at staying at any of the usual assignation houses.

This was a miserable night. Since the regular rooms were
taken, they were given a tasteless ten-mat room that was sometimes used for parties. There was no heat, and it was cold as a
temple sanctuary. It was a run-down, ice-cold room in the
middle of a concrete building. The two sat by a hibachi containing embers dim as fireflies and an ash-tray filled with stale
butts, their overcoats hanging from their shoulders as if they
intended to stay here without seeing each other's misery. They
idly watched the fat legs of the unceremonious maid who came
in kicking the dust and made up the bed.

'My, you awful men. Don't look at me, like that!' the maid
said. Her hair was reddish and sparse.

The hotel was called the Tourist Hoteru. If a guest opened
the window, he had a view of the toilet and the dressing room
in back of the dance hall next door. The windows appeared red
and blue by the neon light. The night wind came sneaking
through the cracks about the window of their room, congealed
the air and fluttered the torn wallpaper. The sodden voices of
two drunken women and a man in the next room sounded as if
they were coming out of a drainpipe; they droned on till three
in the morning. Dawn came early through their window,
which had no storm shutter. There wasn't even a waste basket.

The only place to discard paper was on top of the six-foot-high room partition separating the main room from its foyer. It was piled high with rubbish.

It was a cloudy morning, promising snow. Since ten o'clock a guitar could be heard strumming. Driven by the cold, Yuichi walked rapidly as he left the hotel. Nobutaka followed him, breathing hard.

'Mr Chairman' – when the youth addressed him thus it was more by way of contempt than respect – 'I'm going home; if I don't there'll be trouble.'

'But didn't you say we were going to be together all day today?'

Yuichi looked abstractedly out of his beautiful eyes and said, coldly: 'If you don't stop always wanting your own way, we're not going to stay together very long.'

When Pope spent the night with Yuichi, he could not get enough of looking at the beloved sleeping form. He hardly slept a wink. His colour was not good that morning. Also, his cheeks were rather swollen. The blue-black face nodded reluctantly.

When Nobutaka's taxi drove off, Yuichi was left alone in the grimy throng. To go home all he had to do was go through the ticket gate. Instead he tore up the ticket he had purchased, turned about, and strode along a row of restaurants that stood adjacent to each other behind the station. The drinking places were silent, bearing 'Closed Today' signs. At an inconspicuous door among them, Yuichi rapped. A voice sounded from inside.

'It's me,' Yuichi said.

'Ah, Yuchan,' the voice said; the frosted-glass door slid open.

In the narrow shop there were four or five men in a circle hunched over a gas stove. All turned and greeted Yuichi. There was, however, no note of surprise in their eyes. Yuichi was already one of them.

The proprietor was a man of about forty, gaunt as wire. Around his neck he wore a chequered muffler. Beneath the coat he wore like a cloak, his pyjama trousers could be seen. The employees were three young chattering men, each in a garish ski sweater. One customer was present – an old man in a Japanese overcoat.

'Ooh, it's cold. What a chilly day! And the sun shining like that.' With these words all looked towards the frosted-glass door through which the weak sun angled dispiritedly.

'Yuchan are you going skiing?' said one young fellow.

'No, I'm not,' he replied.

When Yuichi came in the door he was aware that these men had assembled here because they had no place to go on a Sunday. A homosexual's Sunday is pitiful. On that day, all day, no territory is theirs. The daytime world, they feel, takes over completely.

Go to the theatre, go to a coffeehouse, go to the zoo, go to an amusement park, go to town, go out to the suburbs even; everywhere the principle of majority rule is lording about in pride. Old couples, middle-aged couples, young couples, lovers, families, children, children, children, children, children and, to top it off, those blasted baby carriages – all of these things in procession, a cheering, advancing tide. It was easy for Yuichi, too, to imitate them and go out walking with Yasuko. But above his head, somewhere in the shining sky, was God's eye, seeing through all sham.

Yuichi thought: The only way I can be myself on a bright Sunday is to lock myself up in a smoked-glass jail like this.

The men gathered here were already sick of each other's company. Exercising care not to look at each other, they would do nothing but cling to the topics of long years past. The gossip about a Hollywood star, the report that a certain high dignitary was one of their kind, talk about one's own amours, even more lewd funny stories from broad daylight – these were the topics.

Yuichi had no wish to be here. But he didn't want to be anywhere else. We human beings sometimes steer off in a direction in which we hope to find something a little bit better. With the satisfaction of that moment is combined a joy – 'This is a little bit better' – that revives the impossible wild hopes we hold in our heart of hearts. For that reason, indeed, Yuichi had just given Nobutaka the slip so that he could be somewhere like this.

If he went home, Yasuko's lamb's eyes would fasten upon his, as if in a refrain: 'I love you, I love you.' Her morning sickness ended when January was over. Only a sharp pain in her breasts remained. With these sensitive, easily hurt, purple antennae, Yasuko reminded him of an insect maintaining contact with the outside world. That sharp pain in the breasts that without difficulty felt out all the doings ten miles around filled Yuichi with indefinable fear.

Now, whenever Yasuko went downstairs rapidly, a sudden faint pulsation reached her breasts and she felt twinges of sharp pain. If her slip so much as touched her breasts, they hurt. One night when Yuichi tried to embrace her, she pleaded pain and pushed him away. This rejection was in truth unexpected even for Yasuko. It must have been that instinct had induced a subtle vengeance within her.

Yuichi's fear of Yasuko had gradually evolved into a complicated, paradoxical thing. Seen as a mere woman, his wife was much younger than Mrs Kaburagi and Kyoko, and doubtless had much more sex appeal. Objectively considered, Yuichi's fickleness was irrational. When Yasuko seemed too sure of herself, he became uncomfortable and sometimes deliberately and awkwardly hinted that he was having an affair with another woman. When Yasuko heard that, a smile that said 'How ridiculous!' started at the corners of her mouth. Her composure deeply wounded Yuichi's self-respect. At such times Yuichi was threatened by the fear and the unprotected feeling that if anyone knew he could not love women, Yasuko above all would be that person.

With that, in strange cruelty, he evolved a selfish theory. If Yasuko came face to face with the truth that her husband did not love women altogether, and believed that she had been hoodwinked from the start, there was nothing he could do. However, there were many husbands around who were able to love anyone but their wives. In those cases the circumstance in which the wives were then not being loved was evidence working against the truth that at some time earlier they had been loved. It was essential that Yasuko learn that he could not love her – for the love of Yasuko. To achieve it, Yuichi must now indulge in a little more debauchery. He must act proud of his refusal to sleep with his wife, and he must do it without fear, if he could.

At the same time, there was no doubt that Yuichi loved Yasuko. The young wife beside him usually fell asleep after her husband did, but on nights when she was unusually tired and the sound of her breathing came to him, Yuichi could relax and look at her beautiful sleeping face. At such times happiness in possessing such a lovely creature flooded his breast. It was a commendable possessiveness, accompanied by no wish to harm. He thought it strange that in this world he could never, under any circumstances, be forgiven.

'What are you thinking about, Yuchan?' one of the employees asked. All three employees here had already had relations with Yuichi.

'He's probably thinking about last night's sex,' remarked the oldest of the three, a man wearing a Japanese overcoat. He looked towards the door again. 'He's late – my sex. We're not of an age, though, to give each other a hard time.'

They all laughed, but Yuichi shivered. This man of sixty-plus had a lover of sixty-plus.

Yuichi wanted to get away. If he went home, Yasuko might greet him with joy. If he called Kyoko on the phone, she would come flying anywhere. If he went to the Kaburagi home, an almost painful smile of pleasure would flood over Mrs Kaburagi's face. If he met Nobutaka again today, all day – just to give Yuichi joy he would stand on his head in the middle of the Ginza. If he called Shunsuké – that's right, he hadn't met this old man in a long time – his aged voice would rise in eagerness in the telephone receiver. Nevertheless, Yuichi could not help thinking that he had a certain virtuous duty to stay here, cut off from all else.

'To become myself' – is that all? That beautiful thing that should be – is that all? Not fooling myself – but isn't the self that fools me myself? Where is the basis of truth? Is it in the moment when Yuichi for the sake of his outward beauty, for the sake of the self that exists merely to be seen by people, forfeits everything that is his own? Or is it in the moments like this – isolated from everything, giving up nothing? In the moment he loves boys, he is close to the last. Right. He himself is a thing like the sea. The sea's exact depth is the depth of the sea at what time? Had his identity sunk to its lowest tide there in the dawn at that gay party? Or at a time like this lazy high tide, asking for nothing, when anything is too much?

Again he was seized by the wish to see Shunsuké. He wished to go now and tell that trusting old man the most barefaced lies; it no longer satisfied him to withhold only the story of Nobutaka.

*

Shunsuké had spent the whole morning of this day reading. He read the *Sokonshu* and the *Tale of Shotetsu*. The authors, collectively called Shotetsu, were medieval priests who, tradition has it, were reincarnations of Teika Fujiwara. Of all the vast literature of the Middle Ages and the works that have attained world renown, Shunsuké found to his taste only two or three poets, two or three works. Scenic poems, from which mankind is completely absent, like that about the peaceful garden of the recluse of the Eifuku Gate, or the extraordinary tale of virtue about the prince who took on himself the guilt of the retainer Chuta and was beheaded by his own father – the fairy tale called 'The Broken Inkstone' – once nourished Shunsuké's poetic instincts.

In the *Tale of Shotetsu*, Section 23 says that if someone asks where Mount Yoshino is, a person should answer that when one writes poems about cherry blossoms he recalls Mount Yoshino; if about maple leaves, the River Tatsuta; that's all. Whether it's in Isé or Hyuga, one doesn't know. The information as to where it may be is useless to remember. Even though one makes no effort to remember, however, the fact keeps being remembered of itself that Yoshino was in Yamato. That's what it says.

When put into words, youth is a thing like that, the old man thought. For cherry blossoms, Yoshino; for maple leaves, Tasuta – other than that can there be any definition of youth? The artist spends the half of his life after his youth is over searching for the meaning of youth. He explores the native lands of youth. What does that amount to? Cognition has already ruptured the sensual harmony existing between cherry

blossoms and Yoshino. Yoshino has lost its universal meaning.
It has become a point on a map – or a period in past time:
Yoshino, in Yamato, nothing more.

While absorbed in these random reflections, no doubt Shunsuké without realizing it began to think about Yuichi. He read the tersely beautiful poem by Shotetsu:

> In that moment when
> the crowd on the riverbank
> sees the boat come in,
> and every heart among them
> beats with the same emotion.

Shunsuké imagined that moment when the hearts of the crowd waiting for the boat to come in to the shore purely blended and crystallized, and he felt a strange palpitation.

He expected four or five guests this Sunday. He had these guests in because he wished to demonstrate to himself that this amiability unsuited to his years was mixed with considerable contempt, but he also did it so that he could confirm the continuing youthfulness of his emotions. His complete works were coming off the press, in ever new editions. The disciples who were making revisions for him were coming in for conferences. And what did that amount to? What good did it do to edit slightly something that was one great error from beginning to end?

Shunsuké wanted to take a trip. He found this piling up of blue Sundays hard to endure. Yuichi's long silence had made him quite miserable. He thought he might take a trip alone to Kyoto. This very lyrical sadness, the frustrating sadness of having his writings interrupted by Yuichi's silence, this groan over things unfinished, as it must be called, was something Shunsuké had completely forgotten since his days of literary apprenticeship over forty years earlier. This groan was a harking back to the most awkward part of youth, the most unpleasant, least valuable part. That was a fatalistic incompleteness going far beyond the usual interruption, a ridiculous incompleteness filled with humiliation. Every time one reached out one's hand, all the branches and fruit would be carried high in the wind; no fruit ever reached the mouth of Tantalus. In this

188

incompleteness his thirst was never assuaged. In that period, one day – that was now over thirty years in the past – the artist in Shunsuké was born. The disease of incompleteness left him. In its place, perfection came to threaten. Perfectionism became his chronic complaint. It was an illness that showed no wound. It was an illness with no affected part. It was an illness without bacteria, fever, accelerating pulse, headache or twitches. It was an illness like death, above all.

He knew that nothing would cure this disease except death —unless his work died before his body did. The natural death of creativity paid a visit. He became moody. He was, to the same degree, cheerful. As he no longer turned out books, his forehead became carved with artistic wrinkles. His neuralgia seized his knee in romantic twinges. His stomach periodically knew artistic cramps. Then his hair began to change to the white hair of the artist.

Since he met Yuichi, the work he had dreamed about had to be crammed with a perfection cured of the disease of perfectionism, a health of death cured of the sickness of life. It had to be the recovery from everything: from youth, from old age, from art, from life, from venerableness, from world knowledge, from madness. Through decay, victory over decay; through artistic death, victory over death; through perfection, victory over perfection. All these things the old man dreamed of through Yuichi.

At that time, suddenly, that strange illness of his youth returned; incompleteness and outright failure caught Shunsuké while he worked.

What was this? He hesitated to give it a name. The horror of giving it a name made him hesitate. In truth, was it not a peculiar quality of love?

Yuichi's face never left Shunsuké's heart day or night. In his torture, he reviled him; by all the mean names he knew he cursed this false youth in his heart. Only then was he at ease in the knowledge that he clearly detested this young scoundrel. With the same mouth he had used to sing praises of Yuichi's complete absence of intellect, he now ridiculed him for his lack of intellect. Yuichi's inexperience; his annoying lady-killer pose; his self-centredness; his intolerable self-love; his outbursts of sincerity; his capricious naïveté; those tears; all the rubbish of his character: Shunsuké took them up and tried to laugh at them, but whenever he realized that he in his own youth had not a single one of them, he sank into abysmal jealousy.

The character of the youth called Yuichi that he had once grasped was now a will-o'-the-wisp. He realized that he had until now not known one thing about the youth. Yes, he didn't know a thing. To begin with, where was the evidence that he did not love women? Where was the evidence that he loved boys? Had Shunsuké been on the spot so much as one time? But, then, after all, what did it matter? Wasn't Yuichi supposed to have no actual existence? If he was real, his meaningless changeability would be tricking Shunsuké's eyes. How could something so unreal put it over on the artist?

Nevertheless Yuichi was gradually – above all through this silence – at least as far as Shunsuké was concerned, attaining the state Yuichi himself had so dearly wished for, in other words, the 'real existence'. He now appeared before Shunsuké's eyes in his uncertain, untrue, yet real, beautiful form. In the middle of the night, Shunsuké started to ponder: Somewhere in this great city, now, whom is Yuichi embracing? Yasuko? Kyoko? Mrs Kaburagi? Or some nameless boy? He did not go back to sleep. On the day after such nights he would go to Rudon's. Yuichi, however, would not appear. It went against Shunsuké's grain to meet Yuichi accidentally at Rudon's. It would be particularly horrible to receive a distant nod from this lone youth who had slipped his traces.

This Sunday was especially hard to take. He looked out of the window of his study at the withered, tufty lawn of the garden. There was a hint of snow. The colour of the dry grass seemed faintly bright with warmth; it made him think a weak sun was shining. He strained his eyes. The sun wasn't coming through anywhere. He closed his *Tale of Shotetsu* and put it aside. What was he looking for? Sunlight? Snow? He rubbed his shrivelled hands as if they were cold. He looked down at the lawn again. As he did so a wisp of sunlight bled into the front of that gloomy garden.

He went down to the garden.

A lone surviving Corbicula moth was fluttering about on the lawn. He stepped on it with his garden *geta*. When he sat down in a chair in a corner of the garden he took off one *geta* and looked at the bottom of it. A scaly dust mixed with frost shone there. Shunsuké felt refreshed.

A human shape appeared in the dark veranda: 'Master, your scarf, your scarf!'

The old maidservant was calling inconsiderately in a loud voice. Over her arm fluttered a grey scarf. She put on garden *geta* and started to come down into the garden when she heard the telephone ringing in the dark house. She turned her back and lunged off in that direction. To Shunsuké, that intermittent, sharp ring sounded like an auditory hallucination. The pulse raced in his breast. This vision that had betrayed him so many times, would it be Yuichi on the phone this time?

*

They met at Rudon's. After getting off the trolley from Kanda Station at Yurakucho, Yuichi lithely threaded the Sunday throng. Everywhere men and women were strolling together. Not one of those men was as beautiful as Yuichi. The women all stole looks at him. Bold women turned their heads. In that moment women in their hearts forgot the existence of the man beside them. At times when he perceived this, Yuichi revelled in the abstract joy of his hatred of women.

In the daytime Rudon's was like the usual tea room, even its clientele. The youth sat down in his usual chair in the back. He took off his scarf and overcoat and held his hands out towards the gas heater.

'Yuchan, you haven't been here for a while. Who are you meeting today?' asked Rudy.

'Grandpa,' Yuichi replied. Shunsuké had not yet arrived. In a chair across the way a woman with a face like a fox, her hands folded in their soiled deerskin gloves, talked chummily with a man.

Yuichi was anticipating Shunsuké's arrival. He felt like a middle school student who had mischievously concealed something in the teacher's desk and was now waiting impatiently for the teacher to come in and start the class.

After about ten minutes, Shunsuké arrived. He wore a black chesterfield with velvet collar and carried a pigskin suitcase. Silently he came and sat down before Yuichi. The old man's eyes seemed to enfold him in their shining stare. Yuichi perceived in his eyes an indescribable stupidity. Reason enough. Shunsuké's heart, incapable of learning from experience, was again planning some foolishness.

The steam from their coffee gave countenance to their silence. They clumsily started to speak at the same time, and their words clashed. This time, oddly enough, Shunsuké was the shy one.

'It's been a long time,' said Yuichi. 'I've been busy for so long with my exams, and there's been trouble at home. Besides –'

'That's all right. That's all right.' Shunsuké quickly forgave everything.

In the short time he had not seen Yuichi, the youth had changed. His words, every one of them, were pregnant with adult secrets. All the many wounds he used to lay out before Shunsuké without reserve were now firmly wrapped in antiseptic bandages. Yuichi looked like a youth without a care.

Let him lie, Shunsuké thought. He seems to have graduated from the age of confession. Just the same the sincerity of his age is stamped on his brow. It is a sincerity appropriate to an age which prefers lies to confession. He asked aloud; 'How's Mrs Kaburagi?'

'I'm right at her side,' said Yuichi, thinking Shunsuké must have heard of his becoming private secretary. 'She couldn't live without having me near her to be nice to her. After a while she talked her husband into setting me up as his private secretary. Now we can meet at worst every three days.'

'That woman has gotten patient, hasn't she? She didn't used to be one who would worm herself in like that, did she?'

Yuichi contradicted him, his voice rising from nervousness: 'Just the same, that's what she is now.'

'You're defending her! You haven't fallen in love with her, have you?'

Yuichi almost laughed at how widely Shunsuké had missed the mark.

Outside of that, however, the two had nothing to talk about. They were very much like two lovers who came to meet each other thinking of all the things they would say when they got together, and when they met had forgotten them all.

Shunsuké had to turn to his primary proposal: 'I'm going to Kyoto this evening.'

'Is that right?' Yuichi eyed his suitcase without a flicker of interest.

'How about it? Would you like to go with me?'

'Tonight?' The youth's eyes widened.

'When you called me, I decided to leave right away, tonight. Look, I have two sleeping-car tickets; one's yours.'

'But, I –'

'Call home and tell them; it'll be all right. Let me talk to them and make the excuses for you. We'll be staying at the Rakuyo Hotel, in front of the station. Call Mrs Kaburagi, too; she can fix things up with the count. She trusts me, at least. Stay with me this evening until it's time to go. We'll go anywhere you like.'

'But my job –'

'It pays to let jobs go once in a while.'

'But my exams –'

'I'll buy you books you need for your exams. In two or three days' travelling you'd be lucky to read one. All right, Yuchan? Your face looks tired. Travel is the best medicine. In Kyoto you won't have a care in the world.'

Yuichi again felt himself powerless before this strange force. He thought a moment and consented. In truth, although he did not know it, a hurried departure on a trip was just what his heart had been crying for. If this opportunity hadn't come along, this blue Sunday would surely have driven him to take off for somewhere.

Shunsuké took care of the two telephone calls. Passion drove him to more than ordinary powers. There were still eight hours until the night train departed. He thought of the guests who were being kept waiting and, for Yuichi's edification alone, used up the time at the movies, the dance hall, and restaurants. Yuichi paid no attention to his aged patron; Shunsuké was happy enough. After they had managed to sample

193

the town's ordinary pleasures, they walked the streets with happy, mild intoxication. Yuichi carried Shunsuké's bag. Shunsuké walked with the long strides of a young man, his breathing animated. Both were drunk on the freedom of having nowhere to go back to that night.

'Today, I didn't want to go back home, no matter what,' said Yuichi.

'There are days like that – when you're young. There are days when everybody seems to be living a rat's life, and on those days you hate living like a rat more then ever.'

'On days like that, what can you do?'

'You can at least gnaw the time up as would a rat. When you do that you make a little hole. Even though you still can't escape you can at least stick your nose out.'

They watched for a new cab, stopped it, and directed it to the station.

16

Flight in Formation

In the afternoon of the day they arrived in Kyoto, Shunsuké
hired a cab and introduced Yuichi to the Daigo Temple. When
the car passed the wintry fields of the Yamashina Valley, some
convicts from the prison in that area were repairing the roads.
It was like unrolling the scroll of a dark tale of the Middle
Ages; the convicts stood clearly visible outside the window,
and two or three of them craned their necks to peer inside the
car. Their work clothes were dark blue, reminiscent of the
northern sea.

'Poor fellows,' said the young man, usually moved only by
the pleasures of human existence.

'I don't feel a thing,' said the old man. 'When you get to be
my age, you'll become like that, I expect – immune even to the
fear of having that happen to your imagination. Not only that,
fame has an odd effect. Countless people I don't recall ever
having seen before storm up looking as if I owe them something. In short, I am in the dilemma of being expected to have
countless emotional responses. If I don't have even one emotion on call, I find myself branded as a mere brute. Sympathy
towards sadness, altruism towards indigence, gladness for good
fortune, understanding towards love – in my emotional bank,
as it were, I must always have ready gold for countless convertible notes current in society. If I don't, faith in the bank
falls. Since I've brought faith down as much as it can go, I'm
content.'

The cab went through the Sammon of the Daigo Temple
and stopped in front of the gate of the Samboin. In the square
front garden with its famous weeping cherry trees, winter
reigned, ordering all into square shapes – winter given over to
maintenance. This feeling deepened greatly as they mounted to
the entrance with the two characters, Ranho, for the red and

the blue phoenix, written large on a single leaf screen, and as they were shown to chairs in the sunny projection of the garden pavilion. The garden was so packed with artificial winter, so controlled, so abstracted, so composed, so carefully planned, that there was no space for real winter to enter. Standing by each and every rock, the graceful form of winter made itself felt. The island in the centre was decorated with shapely pines; the little waterfall in the south-eastern part of the garden was frozen. The artificial mountain fastness covering the southern side was mostly evergreens, and thanks to that, even in this season, the impression was far from weak that the garden view extended endlessly through groves of trees.

While they waited until the abbot came, Yuichi bathed once more in the privilege of hearing Shunsuké's lectures. As he saw it, the gardens of Kyoto's various temples were the most direct statement of aesthetic Japanese thinking. The craftsmanship of this garden, the view from the moon-viewing platform of the Katsura Detached Palace – the most representative example – as well as the copying shown in the glen of the mountains in the background of the Katsura's Shokatei: in the extreme artificiality of their skilful copying of nature, they attempted to betray nature. Between nature and the work of art, there is a secret rebellion brewing. The revolt of the work of art against nature is like the intellectual defilement of a woman who gives her body away. These famous old gardens are fastened by the cord of a passion for the invisibly faithless female known as the work of art They are men who have forgotten their basic warlike mission. We look at them and see alliances of never-ending despair, marital lives filled with fatigue.

The abbot appeared then. He expressed regret that he and Shunsuké saw so little of each other. Then he ushered the two into another room. At Shunsuké's insistence, he showed them a document that was kept hidden in the most esoteric precincts of the temple. The old writer wanted to show it to Yuichi.

In the back of the book the date was given as the first year of Genkyo (1321). It was a secret book of the time of the Emperor Godaigo. They rolled the scroll out on the tatami lit by the winter sun. Its name was the *Copybook on the Catamite*.

Yuichi couldn't read the foreword, but Shunsuké put on his glasses and read it flawlessly:

About the time the Ninna temple was established, it seems, there was in that place a priest well respected in the world. As he grew older he became distinguished for his knowledge of the three laws, his virtues, and his experience, but he could not refrain from certain practices. Among the many boys serving there, was one whom he loved dearly, with whom he slept. When a man grows old, no matter how high or low his birth, his body will continue to do what he wishes. Though the priest's desires mounted, his body was like a scene of the moon sinking into the earth, or the dying fall of an arrow shot over a mountain. The unhappy boy wrote letters every night to Chuta, the son of his governess, and with him did . . .

The homosexual pictures that were shown following this simple, frank foreword were filled with a pleasant, artless sensuality. As Yuichi studied excitedly every scene, Shunsuké's mind was drawn to the name of the son, Chuta, the very name of the retainer in 'The Broken Inkstone'. The innocent prince had taken the blame of the family retainer on himself. The strength of character that led him to keep silent even until death led one to imagine some kind of pact in the terse, simple description. As a result was not just the sound of the name Chuta – one given to the person fulfilling that particular function – enough to bring a dark smile to the faces of the men of that age?

This scholarly problem did not leave Shunsuké's mind as they rode back in the cab. When they ran into Mr and Mrs Kaburagi in the hotel lobby, all his leisurely contemplations went out the window.

'Are you surprised?' said Mrs Kaburagi, holding out her hand from her mink jacket. Nobutaka, looking strangely composed, got up from the chair behind her. For a moment, the older people behaved quite awkwardly. Only Yuichi was relaxed, keenly aware of his extraordinary youthful power.

For a moment Shunsuké could not grasp what the Kaburagis were up to. He put on the formal scowl he assumed when he had his mind fixed on something else. The professional discernment of the novelist led him, however, to ponder the first impression the couple had given him: This is the first time I've ever seen this pair so close. It makes you feel they've got their heads together in some plot.

In fact, the Kaburagis had been pretty close lately. Perhaps from contrition over the fact that each was using the other to gain something from Yuichi, or perhaps from gratitude, the couple were treating each other with much more consideration than ever before. Theirs was a marvellous meeting of minds. This calm and collected couple would face each other across the *kotatsu* and read newspapers and magazines far into the night. Should there be a sound in the direction of the ceiling, they would look up at the same time; their eyes would meet, and they would smile.

'You're pretty jumpy lately.'

'So are you.'

After that they would sit for a time, unable to control the inexplicable surgings in their hearts.

Another unbelievable change was Mrs Kaburagi's transformation into a housewife. She stayed home so that when Yuichi had to come to the house on company business she could feast him on cakes of her own making. She was even knitting him a pair of socks.

To Nobutaka, his wife's knitting was an utter absurdity. Fascinated by it, he bought a great quantity of imported wool and, knowing that she would sooner or later use it to make Yuichi a sweater, he played the part of the doting husband and held the skeins while his wife rolled the yarn. The calm satisfaction he felt in this task was incomparable.

Although Mrs Kaburagi's love was thus becoming so obvious, when it occurred to her that she had as yet received not a single reward from it, she remained serene. There was something unnatural about this relationship between her and her husband, but she felt that even though her love had not been consummated her husband was not looking down on her because of it.

At first Nobutaka had been offended by his wife's stolid composure. He had felt that she and Yuichi were probably intimate. After a time he realized that these fears were imaginary. Her unwonted action in hiding this love from her husband – something she did intuitively for no other reason than

198

that it was true love – sprang from the sister of Nobutaka's emotion, which had to be carefully hidden because of its forbidding aspects. Nobutaka was sometimes perilously tempted by it to talk about Yuichi with his wife. Yet when she praised Yuichi's beauty too highly, he would be struck again by anxiety over what Yuichi was up to each day, and he would end up maligning Yuichi like a normal husband jealous of his wife's lover. When they heard of his going off on a trip, they were brought even closer together.

'Let's go to Kyoto right after the two of them,' Nobutaka said. Oddly enough, his wife had felt that he would say such a thing. Early the next morning they departed.

Thus the Kaburagis ran into Shunsuké and Yuichi in the lobby of the Rakuyo Hotel.

Yuichi saw a servile look gleaming in Nobutaka's eyes. Thanks to this first impression, Nobutaka's reprimand had no authority.

'What kind of private secretary are you? Who ever heard of a company where the private secretary goes off and the chairman of the board and his wife have to pursue him? Better watch out!' Nobutaka abruptly shifted his gaze to Shunsuké and with an inoffensive smile, full of social banter, he added: 'Mr Hinoki must really be captivating!'

Mrs Kaburagi and Shunsuké each defended Yuichi, but he made no apology, and simply cast a cool glance towards Nobutaka, filling that poor man with anger and chagrin that left him speechless.

It was time for supper. Nobutaka wanted to go out to eat, but everyone was tired and did not relish traipsing about the frigid street; so they went to the restaurant on the sixth floor and huddled around a single table. Mrs Kaburagi's stylish chequered suit, of fabric designed for men, fitted her well, and the slight fatigue of the trip made her somehow extremely attractive. Her colour, however, was rather poor. Her skin had the whiteness of a gardenia. Happiness is the feeling of being slightly drunk, slightly ill. Nobutaka knew that was what gave his wife's face its lyrical shading.

Yuichi could not help being aware that these three mature adults could blithely veer from the beaten path of common sense on his account, and in doing so act completely in disregard of him. There was Shunsuké, for instance, who had abruptly carried him off on a journey away from his job. There were the Kaburagis, who had followed them to Kyoto as if it happened every day. Each attempted to palliate his own conduct by pushing it off on another. Nobutaka, for instance, offered the pretext that he had come only to please his wife. The reasons each gave for coming would be shown up in all their unnaturalness if examined coldly. At this dining table it was hard not to feel that each of the four was supporting one of the corners of a single fragile spider's web.

They drank Cointreau and got a little high. Yuichi was repelled by Nobutaka's pose as the man of magnanimity and good will. He was repelled by the childish vanity with which Kaburagi advertised over and over to Shunsuké his deference to his wife – how he had made Yuichi private secretary at his wife's behest, and how he had taken this trip also on her account.

In Shunsuké's eyes, however, this wild avowal seemed plausible. It was entirely plausible to him that a frigid marriage might have been rejuvenated by the wiles of a wayward wife.

Mrs Kaburagi had been pleased by the call Yuichi had made the night before. She believed that the cause of his compulsive flight to Kyoto was not so much to get away from her as to get away from Nobutaka. Somehow I can't get hold of what this young man is thinking. That's why he always seems so refreshing. Whenever I look at his eyes they are so beautiful. How youthful his smile!

On different soil, she found that gazing at Yuichi had new charm. Her poetic spirit was firmly struck by this tiny bit of inspiration. Oddly, it gave her more of a lift to look at Yuichi in her husband's presence. Lately she hadn't been particularly titillated by talking to him alone. At such times she had only become ill at ease and irritated.

This hotel was used exclusively by foreign buyers and therefore had comfortable central heating. They sat by the window and talked while looking down at the lighted activity of Kyoto Station across the way. Shunsuké behaved as if he didn't see Mrs Kaburagi, who had noticed that Yuichi's cigarette case was empty and took a pack out of her bag and slipped it into his pocket.

'My dear wife, it doesn't pay to bribe my secretary.' Nobutaka watched his wife's every move and wished to make that public. His ostentatiousness about it seemed ridiculous to Shunsuké.

'I think trips for no reason at all are a good idea,' said Mrs Kaburagi. 'Where shall we all go tomorrow?'

Shunsuké looked at her hard as she spoke. She was beautiful, but quite deficient in appeal.

He had loved her and been blackmailed for it by her husband, but what he loved her for was her lack of spirituality. Now, however, in contrast to that earlier time, she had entirely forgotten about her own beauty. Shunsuké watched her smoking. She lit a cigarette, took two or three puffs from it and laid it in the ash-tray. Then, forgetting the cigarette she had started smoking, she took out a fresh one and lit it. Yuichi held out his lighter and lighted each of them.

This woman is as clumsy as an ugly old maid, Shunsuké thought. His revenge was already complete.

By all rights they should all have gone to bed early, tired as they were from travelling. A little thing happened, though, that served to bring them all wide awake. It was caused by Nobutaka, who was suspicious about what was going on between Yuichi and Shunsuké. He suggested that this evening, they divide up so that he and Shunsuké shared one room, while Yuichi and his wife shared the other.

Nobutaka's effrontery in proposing this cynical scheme reminded Shunsuké of the man's past trickery. He did it out of the innocence that belonged to his unscrupulous, noble person and out of his ability to be brutally insensitive to another's feelings. It was courtly cruelty at its worst. The Kaburagi family was very high in the nobility.

'I haven't talked to you in a long time and would enjoy it,' Nobutaka said. 'I would hate to go to sleep at once. You're accustomed to staying up pretty late, I suppose, sir. The bar is going to close right away, so how about it? Let's have some drinks brought to our room and sit awhile.' He looked at his wife. 'You and Mr Minami look sleepy. Don't fret; go on to bed. It's all right if Minami sleeps in my room. I'll just go to Mr Hinoki's room and talk for a while. I might even ask him if I can stay over in his room, so don't worry about me, and sleep well.'

Yuichi naturally demurred. Shunsuké was simply shocked. The youth enlisted Shunsuké's aid with his eyes. This filled the keen-sighted Nobutaka with jealousy.

As for Mrs Kaburagi, she was accustomed to treatment of this sort from her husband. This time, however, the problem was different. The man was her dearly beloved Yuichi. She almost voiced her resentment of her husband's rudeness, but the temptation that she might secure what she wished all day, every day, placed anger out of the question.

She was tortured by the hope that Yuichi would not hold her in contempt. The power of that lofty emotion had led her to this point, but now for the first time she had the opportunity of separating herself from it. If she did not, she might not be able by her own efforts alone to devise a second opportunity. This inward battle only raged for a few seconds in time, but the unwillingness and yet the joy in the feeling which accompanied her decision seemed like the result of a battle that took years. She turned to the youth she loved and smiled as gently as a whore.

In Yuichi's eyes, however, Mrs Kaburagi had never looked so gentle and so maternal as now. He listened while she said: 'All right, you old men enjoy yourselves. If I have another day without enough sleep, I'll get bags under my eyes. Those who can't possibly get any more wrinkles can sit up all night, or whatever they like.'

She looked at Yuichi and said: 'Yuchan, don't you think it's time to go to sleep?'

'Yes.'

Yuichi immediately made a great show of being overcome by sleepiness. Mrs Kaburagi was fascinated by the crudeness of the performance.

This went on with a naturalness that filled Shunsuké with dismay, but he found no opening by which to thwart them. He just couldn't figure out what Nobutaka had in mind. The tone of these proceedings seemed to be entirely concerned with arranging something between Yuichi and Mrs Kaburagi. He could not fathom what made Nobutaka countenance this.

Shunsuké also did not know how Yuichi felt about it, so his ready wit was hindered. There in the soft chairs by the bar he racked his brains for something harmless to say to Nobutaka. At last he said: 'Mr Kaburagi, do you happen to know the meaning of the name Chuta?'

As he brought this out he recalled the content of the mystic book and said nothing more. This topic could cause trouble for Yuichi.

'Chuta?' Nobutaka asked sleepily. 'Is that a man's name?' He had drunk more than he could hold and was already far gone: 'Chuta? Chuta? Oh, that's my alias.'

The reply made Shunsuké's eyes open wide.

After a time the four got up and took the elevator down to the third floor.

The two rooms were three rooms apart. Yuichi and Mrs Kaburagi went into the one farther back, 315. They said nothing. She got up and locked the door.

Yuichi took off his jacket, which only increased his embarrassment. He walked about the room like an animal pacing a cage. He opened the empty drawers one by one. Mrs. Kaburagi asked him if he wanted to bathe. He told her to go first.

While she was in the tub, someone knocked at the door. Yuichi opened it, and Shunsuké entered.

'May I use your bath? Ours is out of order.'

'Surely.'

Shunsuké took Yuichi by the arm and said: 'Are you interested in this at all?'

'I can't stand it.'

The liquid voice of Mrs Kaburagi came from the bathroom clear and hollow as it echoed from the ceiling: 'Yuchan? Would you like to get in with me?'

'Oh?'

'I left the door open.'

Shunsuké pushed past Yuichi and turned the doorknob. He passed through the dressing room and opened the inner door a crack. Mrs Kaburagi's face went white.

'At your age?' she said, lightly touching the surface of the water.

'A long time ago your husband came into our bedroom in just this way, ' Shunsuké said.

17

One's Heart's Desire

Mrs Kaburagi was not a woman to be overly shaken by happenings. Rising from the soap bubbles in the bathtub, she stood erect. She looked at Shunsuké without wavering. 'If you wish to come in, please do.'

That naked body, deterred by not a trace of shyness, treated the old man standing there as if he were little more than a stone by the roadside. The wet breasts glowed, for all the world unmoved. Shunsuké's eyes were assaulted for a moment by the beauty of the body that had filled out and ripened with the years, but then, coming back to himself, he thought of the dumb humiliation he himself was experiencing, and all his desire to look further fled. The naked woman was serene; the old man before whom she stood exposed was the one to blush in embarrassment. For a moment Shunsuké felt as if he understood Yuichi's pain.

'I just don't seem to have the capacity for revenge. My potency for revenge, too, is gone.'

After this blinding confrontation, Shunsuké silently drew back and closed the bathroom door. Yuichi, of course, had not entered. Shunsuké found himself alone in the little dressing room with the light out. He closed his eyes and saw a bright vision – a vision evoked by the sound of hot water.

Shunsuké was tired of standing, yet too embarrassed to return to Yuichi. He sank into a squat, grumbling in reasonless discontent. Mrs Kaburagi gave no sign of getting out of her bath.

After a time Shunsuké heard her rising from the water. The door opened roughly. A wet hand turned on the light in the dressing room. Mrs Kaburagi looked at Shunsuké, who had risen suddenly from the doglike crouch he had assumed. She said with no surprise in her voice: 'Are you still there?' She was wearing a slip. Shunsuké helped her like a lackey.

When the two came out into the room, Yuichi was quietly smoking a cigarette and looking out of the window into the night. He turned to ask: 'Have you finished with your bath, sir?'

'Yes, he has,' said Mrs Kaburagi, answering for him.

'You were pretty fast!'

'You go now,' she said brusquely. 'We'll be in the other room.'

Yuichi went to take his turn in the bath, and Mrs Kaburagi hurried Shunsuké to his own room, where Nobutaka was waiting.

'You didn't have to act so short with Yuichi,' Shunsuké said in the hall.

'You two had it all worked out, didn't you?' she replied. She did not realize that he had come to Yuichi's rescue.

Kaburagi had passed the time playing solitaire. Seeing his wife enter, he said, absolutely without feeling: 'You're back, eh?'

The three played poker listlessly. Yuichi came back from his bath. His skin, refreshed from the bath, glowed with youthful loveliness. His cheeks were flushed like a boy's. He smiled at Mrs Kaburagi. Teased by his innocent grin, the corners of her mouth arched. She nudged her husband, who stood up.

'It's your turn to bathe. We'll sleep over in that room. Mr Hinoki and Yuchan will stay here.'

Perhaps because this announcement sounded so decisive, Nobutaka did not demur. Good nights were exchanged all around. Mrs Kaburagi went two or three steps and then turned and, as if to apologize for her earlier brusqueness, squeezed Yuichi's hand tenderly. Her rejection, she felt, had taught him enough of a lesson.

Thus, in the end, only Shunsuké had made a bad draw: only he had not taken a bath.

He and Yuichi got into their beds and turned off the lights.

In a somewhat jesting tone, Yuichi spoke in the darkness: 'Thanks for what you did.'

Shunsuké turned over contentedly. A recollection of friendship in his youth, a memory of his dormitory life in high school, came back to him. It had been a time when Shunsuké was writing poetry. His vices had managed to go no further.

Regret was in his voice as he spoke in the darkness: 'Yuchan, I have lost the power to avenge myself. Only you can get revenge against that woman.'

The voice, filled with the tension of youth came back from the dark: 'She certainly got short-tempered fast, didn't she?'

'Never mind. Her eyes flatly contradict her coldness. It's really a good opportunity. All you have to do is give her a jumbled childish explanation and she'll sweeten up. She'll be dreaming about you more than ever. Tell her this: "Even though that old man introduced us, he became fiendishly jealous when we got attached to each other. The bathroom incident was caused by his jealousy entirely!" Tell her that, and everything will fit together.'

'All right.'

The extreme docility in his voice made Shunsuké feel that the arrogant Yuichi he had met after so long had changed since yesterday to the Yuichi of old. He decided to use the momentum he had gained and said: 'How's Kyoko doing lately, do you know?'

'No.'

'Lazy! My, you're a peck of trouble. Kyoko has gone right off and found herself another lover. I hear she tells everybody she meets that she's forgotten Yuchan exists. It's gotten so bad, there are rumours she's separating from her husband so she can go off with this fellow.'

Shunsuké stopped talking, alert to the effect his words would have. The effect was pronounced. Yuichi's conceit was pierced. The blood ran.

His murmured response after a moment, however, couched words that did not come from a young man's heart: 'Fine, if that makes her happy.'

As he said these words, the youth, in honesty to himself, could not help recalling his manly vow when he met Kyoko in the door of the shoe store: 'All right. I'll really make that woman unhappy.'

This paradox of a knight was repenting for neglecting the

mission in which he was to lay down his life for the unhappiness of womankind. Another anxiety, half superstition, nagged at him. Whenever a woman treated him coldly he could not help wondering if she had discovered his distaste for her sex.

Shunsuké detected a cold ferocity in Yuichi's voice, and he breathed easier. Then he casually said: 'As far as I have observed, though, the only thing wrong with her is that she can't forget you. Several things make me believe that. So when you get back to Tokyo, why don't you call Kyoko up? It certainly won't lower you in her estimation.'

Yuichi did not reply. Shunsuké felt the youth would certainly call Kyoko when he returned to Tokyo.

The two were silent. Yuichi seemed to have dropped off to sleep. Shunsuké did not know quite how best to show the fullness of his heart, and turned over again. The bed creaked; the warmth was exactly right; all was right with the world. He had come to realize how mad it would be to make a trial of what had occurred to him in a daring moment: 'I shall let Yuichi know that I love him.' Was anything more required between them?

Someone knocked at the door. After two or three raps, Shunsuké called: 'Who is it?'

'Kaburagi.'

'Come in.'

Shunsuké and Yuichi turned on the lights at their pillows. Nobutaka entered, in a white shirt and dark-brown trousers. With forced cheerfulness he said: 'I'm sorry to disturb you, but I left my cigarette case behind.'

Shunsuké sat up. He told Nobutaka where the room light was. Nobutaka switched it on. The plain hotel room, with its two beds, a night table, a vanity, two or three chairs, and other furnishings sprang into light. Nobutaka crossed the room with the ostentatious gait of a juggler.

He picked up a tortoise-shell cigarette case from the table, opened it, and arranged its contents. Then he went to the mirror, and pulled down one lower eyelid as if to see whether his eye was bloodshot.

'There. Excuse me. Good night.'

He turned off the light and departed.

'Was that cigarette case on the table all the time?' asked Shunsuké

'I didn't notice,' Yuichi said.

*

Back from Kyoto, Yuichi felt his heart riven with unhappiness whenever he thought of Kyoko. As Shunsuké had calculated, the proud youth called her up. She hemmed and hawed sulkily for a time, wondering whether she could and whether she couldn't, but when Yuichi was about to hang up she hurriedly told him where and when she would meet him.

Examinations were near at hand. Yuichi was cramming in the economics, but when he compared his present work with his performance in last year's exam, he was amazed at his inability to absorb it. He had lost the pure rapturous joy he used to get when he plunged feverishly into differential calculus. This young man, learned in the techniques of being half in touch with reality and half in contempt of it, under the influence of Shunsuké preferred to find in all thought only pretence and in all life only the spell of custom that devoured it. The miseries he saw in the adult world since he had come to know Shunsuké were entirely unexpected. The men with position, fame, and money – the three-in-one on the marquee of the masculine world – of course did not wish to lose them; but it staggered the imagination to see how at times they seemed to despise them. Shunsuké's behaviour amazed Yuichi at first. He trampled on his own reputation as if he were a pagan treading on a tablet designed to detect Christians: without a care, or, worse, with a burst of sadistic laughter in the pleasure of it, the joy of it.

On the appointed day, Yuichi arrived fifteen minutes late at the store where Kyoko was waiting. Kyoko was standing on the sidewalk in front of the store, fidgeting. She pinched Yuichi's arm hard and complained about his lack of consideration. Her quite ordinary charm, it must be said, served somewhat to dampen Yuichi's enthusiasm.

It was a fair day in early spring, though cold. Even in the bustle of the street a certain limpid quality could be felt. The air was for all the world like transparent quartz against the skin. Under his navy-blue coat Yuichi wore his student uniform, so his high neckband and white collar stood out above his muffler. Kyoko looked at the neckband that formed a line with his shoulders as he walked beside her. She saw the white collar neat upon the soft shaven skin and caught the scent of early spring. Her dark-green overcoat was pinched in at the waist. Inside her turned-up collar a salmon-coloured scarf protected her throat. Where it touched her neck, traces of flesh-coloured powder clung. Her cold, red little mouth was amiable.

This giddy woman had not said one word of complaint about Yuichi's silence, and he was held captive by the uncomfortable sense that something was missing, like a boy whose mother is silent when he expected to be scolded. In spite of all the months and days that had gone by since their last rendezvous, she possessed no sense of rupture – evidence that her passion passed along a fixed, safe track, as from the beginning. Be it as it may, the light-hearted appearance of a woman like Kyoko served the purposes of concealment and self-control. It was always her way, actually, to be taken in by a frivolous exterior.

They went to a near-by street corner, where a new Renault was parked. A man sitting in the driver's seat smoking a cigarette indolently opened the door from the inside. When Yuichi paused, Kyoko invited him to get in and slid in beside him. She introduced them swiftly: 'Cousin Keichan – Mr Namiki.'

Namiki, who seemed about thirty, turned in the driver's seat and nodded. Yuichi was suddenly cloaked in the guise of a cousin, and without a by-your-leave his name had been changed, but Kyoko's game, he knew, had not started here. Intuitively he perceived that Namiki was Kyoko's rumoured lover. His own position comforted him considerably. He almost forgot to be jealous.

Yuichi did not ask where they were going, so Kyoko slipped her arm under his and quietly took his gloved fingers in hers. Then she spoke softly in his ear: 'Don't be angry. We're going to Yokohama today to buy some dress material for me; on the way back we'll stop somewhere and eat. There's nothing to get upset about. Namiki, though, is mad because I wouldn't sit in the front seat. I'm going to break it off with him. I brought you along on this trip as a demonstration.'

'You're demonstrating against me, too, I suppose.'

'Silly. I'm the one who should have suspicions about you. Are you keeping busy in your work as private secretary?'

Kyoko and Yuichi whispered together throughout the thirty-minutes journey along the Keihin National Highway to Yokohama. Namiki said not a word. Indeed, Yuichi played well the part of the ardent rival for the love of a lady.

Today Kyoko seemed like a woman whose giddiness would always prevent her from falling in love. She chatted about useless things; she left out the essentials. The only saving merit of this shallowness was that she failed to convince Yuichi of all the happiness that was hers. The world is in error when it refers to unconscious concealment of this kind, practised by an unsophisticated woman, as coquetry. With Kyoko flightiness was like a fever; only in the midst of her ravings could the truth be heard. Among the coquettes of the metropolis, there were many who had become coquettes out of shyness. Kyoko was one of them.

Since she had last seen Yuichi, Kyoko had slipped back into frivolous thoughtlessness. Her shallowness was limitless; her life was absolutely rudderless. Her friends loved to come by and watch the life she led, but no one had the wit to notice that her frantic activity at this time was like the frivolity of men dancing barefoot on red-hot iron. She didn't think about anything. She couldn't read a novel all the way through, but after reading one third would skip to the last page. There was something disorganized about the things she said. When she sat down, she would soon cross her legs. Even then, her leg would tremble as if she were bored. When she happened to write a letter, the ink would stick to her finger or her dress.

Since Kyoko did not know what love was, she mistook it for boredom. She passed the months and days she did not see Yuichi wondering why she was so bored. As ink stuck to her dress or her fingers, ennui clung to her everywhere.

They passed Tsurumi and when the sea became visible between the yellow warehouses of a refrigeration plant, Kyoko squealed like a child: 'Oh, the ocean!' An old steam engine in the harbour passed between the warehouses pulling freight cars and blocked the sea from view. By the time the men looked again, there was nothing to exclaim about. The port sky in early spring was smirched by soot and smoke and a forest of masts.

Kyoko was sure that the two men riding with her were in love with her – it was her unshakable conviction. Or was it only an illusion?

Yuichi, observing the passion of a woman with the feelings of a stone, his body incapable of responding to her, had become involved in the paradoxical process of thinking that since he could not make any woman who loved him happy, the only thing he could do for Kyoko, the only spiritual gift he could give her, was to make her unhappy. As a result, he felt not the slightest moral compunction about the purposeless revenge he held in store for Kyoko.

The three got out of the car in front of a little store that sold women's dress material, on a corner of Yokohama's Chinatown. Here, imported goods could be bought cheaply, so Kyoko had come to select her spring fabrics. She draped stuffs she liked over her shoulder one after the other and went to look in the mirror. After that she came over to Namiki and Yuichi and asked: 'How does it look?' The two offered not very useful comments. They teased her by saying things like: 'If you go out of here with that red material over your shoulder, you'll drive the bulls wild.'

Kyoko looked over twenty fabrics, but she didn't like any and left without buying a thing. They went to the second floor of the Bankaro, a restaurant serving Peking specialities, and the three ordered an early dinner. While they talked, Kyoko asked for the plate in front of Yuichi: 'Cousin Yuchan, would you be so kind as to –?' He could not help seeing the expression of Namiki's face as she unexpectedly said these words.

That flashily dressed youth twisted the corners of his mouth slightly; a smile of mature cynicism passed over his dark face. Then he looked from Kyoko to Yuichi and skilfully changed the subject. He spoke about a football game concerning Yuichi's college, when he had participated during his college days.

It was clear that he was aware of Kyoko's lie about Yuichi –

or Keichan – and had been aware of her ruse from the beginning. Moreover, he had simply forgiven the two of them. Kyoko's expression at that time was something laughable. Not only that, there was the tension in the words: 'Cousin Yuchan, would you be so kind as to ...?' It betrayed the fact that the slip had been deliberate. The earnestness of her expression, so like that of a woman scorned, was almost pitiful.

Nobody in this world loves Kyoko, Yuichi thought. Then the cold heart of this youth who could not love women justified the fact that no one loved this woman – justified also his own lack of feeling for her as well as his desire to make her miserable. In addition, he couldn't help regretting that she was already unhappy without his help.

After dancing at the Cliffside Dance Hall by the harbour, they took the same seats they had before and drove back on the Keihin National Highway to Tokyo. Kyoko made another trite remark. 'Don't be angry about today. Mr Namiki is really only a friend.'

Yuichi was silent. Kyoko was sad; she felt he still didn't believe her.

18

Sightseer's Misfortune

Yuichi's exams were over. It was already spring by the calendar. On an afternoon when the gusty wind sent the dust dancing and the street seemed to be wrapped in yellow mist, Yuichi dropped by at the Kaburagi home on the way home from school, as Nobutaka had directed him to do on the previous day.

To get to the Kaburagi home, he had to leave the train at a station not far from the college. It was not really out of his way. Today Mrs Kaburagi was to go to the office of an important foreign 'friend' to pick up some licensing documents required in a new venture by her husband's corporation. It had been arranged that when she came home Yuichi, who would be waiting there, would take them to her husband's office. The documents were readily available thanks to the exertions of Mrs Kaburagi. Only the hour when she would pick them up was not clear, so Yuichi had to wait until she arrived home.

When he got there, Mrs Kaburagi was still home. Her appointment was for three p.m. It was still only one o'clock.

The Kaburagi home was in the steward's house of the old family mansion, which had survived the fires. There were many nobles of the highest rank who did not have a traditional mansion in Tokyo. The father of the present Kaburagi household had made a fortune in electrical enterprises during the Meiji era. He bought one of the lesser mansions of a *daimyo* and moved into it, something quite exceptional. After the war, Nobutaka disposed of this in order to pay his estate tax. He evicted the man who had succeeded to the steward's house and settled him in a rented dwelling. Then he planted a new hedge as a barrier between himself and the alienated main house, and set up a gate at the end of a little lane that turned off the street.

An inn was opened in the main house. The Kaburagis had to get used to party music every once in a while. Through the gate that Nobutaka long ago passed under when brought home from school by the family tutor – to whom he had entrusted the heavy knapsack he had carried – now limousines passed, carrying geisha from long distances away, circling the drive, depositing their fair passengers at the impressive porch entrance. The carvings that Nobutaka had made in the pillars of his study room were gone. The map of Treasure Island that he had hidden under one of the stones in the garden thirty years ago and forgotten had undoubtedly rotted away, though it had been drawn in coloured pencil on veneer.

The steward's house had seven rooms. Only the room above the western entranceway was over eight mats in size. That western room served both as Nobutaka's den and guest room. From the windows of the room, one could look squarely into what had been the serving room in the second floor rear of the main house; but that serving room had been made into a guest room, and a blind installed in the windows facing Nobutaka's den.

One day while they were renovating the main house he watched them tearing out the serving shelf. In the old days when they held functions in the grand hall on the second floor, the shining black serving shelf had seen much activity. Gold-lacquered bowls stood in rows; maids came and went busily, trailing kimonos. The sound of that shelf being destroyed came to him like the echoes of countless eventful banquets. It was a sound of some deeply buried memory being uprooted.

Nobutaka, who had not so much as an atom of sentimentality, slid down in his chair, put his feet on the desk, and cheered: 'Rip it apart! And again!' Every inch of that mansion had tortured him in his youth. Upon the secret that he loved men that moral mansion always rested with an unbearable weight. He did not know how many times he had wished for the death of his father and mother and the destruction of the house by fire, but it now struck Nobutaka's fancy to see the mansion undergo the blasphemous alteration of having drunken geisha sing popular songs in the hall in which his father used to sit with a glum look, rather than have it burned in an air raid.

After they moved into the steward's house, the couple renovated the whole house in Western style. In the alcove they put up bookcases; they took out the sliding partitions and hung thick damask curtains. They moved all the Western furnishings out of the main house and placed the rococo chairs and tables on rugs spread over the tatami floors. With these changes, the Kaburagi home came to look like a consulate in the Edo era or the apartment of a foreigner's concubine.

When Yuichi arrived, Mrs Kaburagi was wearing slacks and a lemon-coloured sweater, over which she had draped a black cardigan. She was sitting beside the stove in the sitting room, which was raised a few steps. With her red-nailed fingertips she cut a deck of Viennese cards. The queen bore the letter D; the jack, B.

The maidservant announced Yuichi's arrival. Mrs Kaburagi's fingers went numb; the cards stuck together as if they had paste between them. Lately she was not able to stand up to greet Yuichi when he came. When he came in she would turn her back. When he went around and stood in front of her, she would finally have the strength to lift her eyes. Yuichi would meet her unwilling, sleepily raised eyes. The youth always had to hold himself back from asking if she was ill.

'My appointment is for three o'clock. There's still plenty of time. Have you eaten?' she asked. Yuichi said he had.

There was a short silence. The glassed door to the veranda rattled annoyingly in the wind. The dust accumulated on all the mullions was visible from within. Even the sunlight streaking across the veranda seemed dust-laden.

'I hate to go out on a day like this. When I get back I know I'll have to wash my hair.' She suddenly ran her fingers through Yuichi's hair.

'My, that dust! That's what you get for putting on too much pomade.'

The fault-finding that entered into her words as she said this confused Yuichi. Every time she looked at Yuichi she wanted to flee; she felt almost no joy in meeting him. She could not

216

imagine what it was that kept them apart, what it was that kept them from coming together. Chastity? Don't make me laugh! The lady's purity? Make room between the jokes to allow for laughter! Then Yuichi's purity? He already had a wife.

No matter how hard she tried, with all her womanly faculties, Mrs Kaburagi could not come to grips with the cruel truths in the situation. She certainly did not love Yuichi so completely because he was beautiful. It was because he did not love her, nothing more.

Men whom Mrs Kaburagi had gotten rid of within a week had at least loved her with body or soul, if not both. With all their various and sundry endowments, they were alike in at least this respect. But in Yuichi, this lover in the abstract, she could not find anywhere a quality she had seen before. She could do nothing but grope in the dark. When she thought she had cornered him, he turned out to be over there; when she thought she was far away, he was close. She was like one tracking down echoes, like one trying to take in hand the image of the moon reflected in the water.

It was not that there never were times when circumstances conspired suddenly to make her think Yuichi loved her. There were times when her heart filled with happiness, she knew well that what she was looking for was not happiness, or anything like it.

Even the horrendous farce of that night in the Rakuyo Hotel was rather easier for her to explain by the theory that Yuichi had taken part at Shunsuké's instigation than the theory that, as he explained it, Shunsuké had done it all out of jealousy. Her heart, intimidated by happiness, began to lean towards loving only evil portents. Whenever she met Yuichi, she prayed that his eyes would reflect loathing, hatred, or superiority; but instead she was cast down to see in those eyes a clarity that knew no cloud.

Pregnant with dust, the wind deposited its burdens on the strange little garden consisting only of rocks and pines and cycads, and rattled the glass door. Mrs Kaburagi looked fixedly through the vibrating glass, her eyes feverish.

'The sky is yellow, isn't it?' said Yuichi.

'I can't stand the wind in early spring,' she said, her voice a little high. 'Nothing is clear.'

The desserts she had prepared for Yuichi were brought in by the maid. It helped her somewhat to watch Yuichi's childlike consumption of the hot plum pudding. The familiarity of that young little bird eating the bait from her hand! The joyful pain of having that hard little bill peck her palm! How good it would be if what he was eating like that were the flesh of her thigh!

'Delicious,' Yuichi said. He knew that open guilelessness helped his charm. To ingratiate himself with her, he took up both her hands and started to kiss them, an act that could only be interpreted as an expression of gratitude for the dessert.

She crinkled her eyes; she made a terrible face; her body stiffened and trembled. She said: 'No. No. It hurts me. No.'

If the Mrs Kaburagi of a decade earlier had seen the kind of game she was now playing, surely she would have laughed her habitual dry, high-pitched laugh. She had never dreamed that just one kiss could provide so much nourishment for emotion, that it could be filled with such deadly poison, that she could wish almost instinctively to avoid it. To make matters worse, this cold lover was observing the earnest expression of the face of this impure woman desperately fighting off a casual kiss as if he were watching through a glass barrier the ridiculously agonized expression of a woman drowning in a tank.

Yuichi was not, however, displeased to see before him such clear evidence of his power. He was rather jealous of the drunken fear the woman was experiencing. This Narcissus was unhappy that Mrs Kaburagi, unlike her clever husband, would not allow him to intoxicate himself with his own beauty.

'Why,' Yuichi fidgeted, 'why won't she let me lose myself as I would like to? Is she going to leave me in this cloying loneliness forever?'

Mrs Kaburagi moved to a distant chair and closed her eyes. The front of her lemon-coloured sweater rolled in waves. The continuous rattling of the glass door seemed to shrivel the skin of her temples. Yuichi felt she had suddenly aged by three or four years.

In this dreamlike state, Mrs Kaburagi did not know how she was going to get through this short tryst of one hour. Something had to happen. A great earthquake or explosion, some catastrophe had to come and blow them to smithereens. If not that, during this painful assignation she would welcome having her body turned to stone by slow, ineluctable torture.

Suddenly Yuichi cocked his head to one side. He had the expression of a young animal concentrating on a distant sound.

'What's wrong?' Mrs Kaburagi said. Yuichi did nót answer. 'What do you hear?'

'Wait a minute. I just thought I heard something.'

'Aren't you awful! You're just doing that because you're bored.'

'There, I heard it again. It's a fire-engine siren. Things will burn well today.'

'You're right – they sound as if they're coming down the road by the gate. I wonder where.'

The two looked at the sky. All they saw was the second storey of the main house, now an inn, towering on the other side of the hedge of the little garden.

The siren approached with a clamour. In the wind the sound of the wildly beaten alarm bell rose and suddenly retreated. Again there was only the rattling of the glass door.

Mrs Kaburagi got up to change her clothes. Yuichi idly went to the stove that was only faintly warm and stirred the coals with a poker. It sounded as if he were stirring bones. The coal was all but consumed.

Yuichi opened the door. He bathed his face in the wind.

My, this is good, he thought. This wind doesn't give you any time to think.

Mrs Kaburagi appeared; she had taken off her slacks and put on a skirt. In the dimness of the hall only the freshness of her lipstick was visible. She saw Yuichi sticking his head out into the wind but said nothing. Her last-minute primping, her way of holding up her spring coat in one hand and of signalling simply that she was going out, made her look as if she had lived with this youth for a year. This phony wifely affectation seemed to Yuichi to be an insinuation of some kind.

He walked as far as the gate with her. There was another little garden gate along the path that led from the entranceway to the street outside. On either side stood a hedge the height of a man. The hedge was covered with dust. Its greenness had no strength.

On the other side of the garden gate, the sound of Mrs Kaburagi's high-heeled shoes along the paving stones halted. Yuichi, wearing a pair of the sandals that were kept in the entranceway, followed her, but was stopped by the closed gate. Thinking she was playfully holding it closed, he pushed against it. She resolutely pressed the bodice of her lemon sweater against the woven bamboo in the gate and held it closed with all her strength. There was a hostile earnestness in her effort. The youth drew back.

'What's wrong?' he asked.

'It's all right. This is far enough. If you come with me any farther, I won't be able to go.'

She walked parallel to the hedge and stood on the other side. The hedge hid the lower half of her from sight. Her hair – she wore no hat – waving in the wind, clung to the edges of the leaves of the tight-clipped hedge. She wore a gorgeous watch that looked like a little gold snake around her wrist. Her white hand moved and loosened it.

Yuichi stood in front of Mrs Kaburagi with the hedge between them. He was taller than she. He placed his arms lightly on the top of the hedge, then bent his face towards it and looked at her. His face was hidden except for his eyes. The wind again came down the dusty little path. It mussed Mrs Kaburagi's hair and blew it around her face. Yuichi lowered his head to shield his eyes.

This is the way it is, Mrs Kaburagi thought. Even in this short period when our eyes try to meet, something comes between us. The wind let up. The two searched each other's eyes. Mrs Kaburagi no longer knew what emotion she wished to read in Yuichi's eyes. I love something I do not understand in the slightest, something dark, she thought – clear, limpid darkness. As for Yuichi, he was uneasy to think that everything he couldn't fathom hung on the slight emotional displays of such moments, that other people would not stop finding in him something that went beyond what his consciousness was able to detect. That truth revolved again and enriched his consciousness – it was almost as if he were thinking about someone else.

Finally, Mrs Kaburagi burst out laughing. It was a forced laugh, a laugh of parting.

This separation, even if it ended with her return in two hours, was like a rehearsal for a complete break, Yuichi thought. He was reminded of the many solemn rehearsals for military inspections and graduation ceremonies in his middle school days. The representative of the class would carry an empty lacquered tray – containing no diploma – and back away respectfully from the principal's chair.

After Mrs Kaburagi left, he went back to the vicinity of the stove and picked up an American fashion magazine. Presently a telephone call came from Nobutaka. Yuichi told him his wife had departed. Nobutaka decided to give the conversation a personal turn; he broke into his ridiculous cat-petting tone: 'Who was the young man I saw you walking with in the Ginza the other day?' He always asked wheedling questions like this on the phone. Yuichi would sulk if he put them to his face.

Yuichi answered: 'It was just a friend. He asked me to come with him to look at some suit materials, so I did.'

'Do you walk with "just friends" with your pinkies hooked together?'

'You don't seem to have any business to talk about. I'm hanging up.'

'Wait a minute. Yuchan, I shouldn't have said that. When I heard your voice, I couldn't resist. I'm coming to see you right now by car. Don't go anywhere until I get there. Well? Answer me.'

'All right. I'm waiting – Mr Chairman.'

Nobutaka arrived thirty minutes later.

In the car, Nobutaka realized that in all he could remember of Yuichi in the past several months there was never a false note. Whatever the luxury or the splendour, he met it all without surprise. What is more, he never seemed to be guilty of the flimsy expedient of deliberately warning himself not to be surprised. He wanted nothing, and so one wished to give him all,

221

but one never found he was any the more affectionate in his gratitude. Even if one took him among nobles and monks, the hoi-polloi, the good breeding of this beautiful youth and his complete freedom from pretence made people take him at the highest value. In addition to all that, he was spiritually cruel. This was the reason Nobutaka's dreams were built to a height greatly beyond necessity.

Nobutaka was a master of concealment. He had succeeded in seeing his wife every day without ever being caught red-handed. He gave himself up to the joy of savouring his own slyness. But he was becoming extremely deficient in prudence.

Without so much as removing his overcoat, Nobutaka proceeded up to his wife's sitting room, where Yuichi waited. The maid saw that he had not taken off his coat; she stood behind him in confusion, wondering what she was supposed to do. 'And what are you gawking at?' he said testily.

'Your coat, sir,' she said hesitantly.

He tore the coat off and flung it into her arms. Then he said to her loudly: 'Go down there, and if I want anything I'll call.'

He tapped the youth's elbow, led him to the concealment of the curtains and kissed him. Whenever he came in contact with the roundness of Yuichi's lower lip, he went mad. The gold buttons on the chest of Yuichi's uniform collided with Nobutaka's tie clasp with a sound like gnashing teeth.

'Let's go upstairs,' said Nobutaka.

Yuichi pulled away, looked him in the face and giggled: 'My, you do like it, don't you?'

Five minutes later, the two of them were in Nobutaka's den, 'conferring'.

It must be said it was no accident that Mrs Kaburagi got home earlier than planned. In her hurry to get back to Yuichi, she looked for a cab and found one right away. When she got to the office her business was rapidly transacted. Then, too, that 'friendly' foreigner offered to drive her home. His car sped. When he dropped her off at their gate, she invited him in, but the foreigner was pressed for time, and promising to come another time, drove off.

Moved by a sudden impulse – not at all an extraordinary

222

thing with her – she entered from the garden and ascended to the sitting room from the veranda. She thought she would surprise Yuichi, who should have been there.

The maid met her and told her that the count and Yuichi were having a conference in the second-floor den. She decided that she would like to see Yuichi taking part in a serious conference. She wanted to see Yuichi involved in something while unaware that she was looking.

Out of a surplus of love, she wished to peep for a moment at the beloved image of Yuichi in a situation without her, her participation suppressed – to see in the eternal form his image assumed when she was not there the vision of happiness her appearance for one moment would have destroyed.

Keeping the sound of her footsteps quiet, she ascended the staircase and stood by her husband's den. The door had been closed, but the latch had not hooked. So there was a crack of an inch or two in the door. She stood against the door and peered into the room.

Thus Mrs Kaburagi saw what she was bound to see.

When Nobutaka and Yuichi came down, Mrs Kaburagi was nowhere to be found. The documents had been placed on the table. An ash tray served as a paperweight. In the ash tray a cigarette, barely smoked, lipstick clinging to it, had been stumped out. The maid said only that her mistress had come home and seemed to have gone out after a short time.

The two awaited her return, but when she did not arrive, they went to town to have a good time. Yuichi got home about ten o'clock.

Three days went by. Mrs Kaburagi had still not returned.

19

My Helpmate

Yuichi was embarrassed about visiting the Kaburagi home. Nobutaka had to call and leave word many times before he finally complied one evening.

When, some days earlier, Nobutaka Kaburagi and Yuichi had come downstairs and failed to find Mrs Kaburagi, Nobutaka was not greatly concerned. When a day passed and she had not returned, he began to worry. This was no ordinary absence. There was no doubt that she was concealing her whereabouts. What was more, there could be only one reason why she had disappeared.

On this evening the Nobutaka whom Yuichi saw was a different person. He was haggard; he needed a shave – a state Yuichi had never seen him in before. The cheeks that always had such good colour were baggy and had lost their glow.

'Hasn't she come back yet?' Yuichi said. He sat down on the arm of the sofa in the den and tapped the end of a cigarette against the back of his hand.

'That's the way it looks. We were seen.'

This laughable solemnity was so unlike the usual Nobutaka that Yuichi agreed with him purely out of cruelty: 'I suppose so.'

'That's the way it looks. I can't think of anything else.'

Actually, Yuichi had noticed that the latch was not in place, and had realized immediately what might have happened. His extreme embarrassment had come to be diluted after a few days by a sense of liberation. At the same time he fell into the coldly heroic state of feeling neither embarrassment for himself nor sympathy for Mrs Kaburagi.

This was why Nobutaka seemed ridiculous in Yuichi's eyes. He suffered pain and lost weight only because he had been 'seen'.

'Have you notified the Missing Persons Bureau?'

'I don't like to do that. It isn't that I don't have some idea.'

Yuichi observed that Nobutaka's eyes were misty, and he marvelled. Then Nobutaka said: 'I hope she hasn't done anything regrettable.'

These words, incongruously sentimental as they were, pierced Yuichi's heart. There had never been one word to indicate so clearly the spiritual harmony between this strange couple. Only a heart forced to feel tremendous understanding of the love that his wife felt for Yuichi would be capable of such minute powers of the imagination. That same heart would have been wounded in the same degree by his wife's spiritual unchastity. In the consciousness that none other than his own wife was in love with the person he himself loved, Nobutaka became a cuckold twice over; what is more, he tasted the pain of using his wife's passion to whip up his own. The wounds of his heart Yuichi now saw for the first time.

This is how necessary Mrs Kaburagi has been to Count Kaburagi, Yuichi thought. Perhaps it was beyond the youth's powers of understanding. However, through these considerations, Yuichi momentarily arrived for the first time at a supremely tender feeling towards Nobutaka. Did the count see this ever so tender look in the eyes of the one he loved?

Nobutaka looked down. He was worn out, his confidence gone; his corpulent body, in a flashy dressing gown, was slumped in a chair. He held his downturned cheeks in both hands. His hair, generously oiled and too abundant for his years, made the baggy skin of his unshaven face seem grimy. He avoided the youth's gaze. Yuichi, however, studied the wrinkles across his neck. Suddenly he remembered the faces of the fellows he had seen in the street car that first night in the park.

From that moment of gentleness, Yuichi returned to a more appropriate cruel coldness. I shall become more and more cruel to this man. That's what must happen, he thought.

The count forgot the existence of the cold lover in front of him. He thought earnestly of the missing helpmate he could not forget and of the long years they had lived together and sinned together, and he wept. Left behind as they were, he and

Yuichi shared the same sense of isolation. They were like two castaways on a raft; for many minutes they exchanged not a word.

Yuichi whistled. Nobutaka lifted his head, like a dog that has been called. But he saw only the teasing smile of a youth.

Yuichi poured cognac into a glass. Holding the glass, he went to the window, opened the curtain. There was a banquet going on, with many guests, at the main house this evening. The light from the great hall showered down on the evergreen trees and on *kobushi* flowers in the inn garden. The sound of singing, so out of place in this residential quarter, was faintly audible. It was a very warm evening. The wind had died down; the sky had cleared. Yuichi felt an inexplicable freedom throughout his body – a freedom like that of the traveller who in his wanderings at last feels refreshed in body and soul, his breathing easier than ever before. He felt the wish to drink a toast to this freedom: 'To disorder, banzai!'

*

The youth blamed his lack of concern over Mrs Kaburagi's disappearance on the coldness of his disposition, but this was not necessarily true. Perhaps something intuitive helped him to rationalize his uneasiness.

Mrs Kaburagi's Karasuma family also had noble antecedents. When, about the fourteenth century, Nobui Kaburagi was connected with the Northern court, Tadachika Karasuma was connected with the Southern court. Nobui handled tactics and intrigue as superlatively as a magician; Tadachika had a flair for politics, which he handled passionately with an air of simple-minded magnanimity. The two families represented more or less the yang and yin of statecraft. Nobui was the true heir of the politics of the Monarchic Age, an adherent of political aesthetic in the worst sense of the term. In that time when *tanka* poetry and politics were closely intertwined he moved into the realm of statecraft all the defects of the lovers of art, all aesthetic subtleties, pragmatism, the doctrine of passionless calculation, the mystique of weakness, deception through display, humbug, moral insensitivity, and the like. Nobutaka

Kaburagi's spiritual refusal to fear degradation, his brave refusal to fear base actions, was chiefly the gift of this ancestor.

On the other hand, Tadachika Karasuma's utilitarian idealism was always troubled by self-contradiction. He perceived clearly that only through passionately refusing to look at oneself directly does one have power enough to realize oneself. His idealistic political theory depended more on fooling himself than on fooling others. Later on Tadachika committed suicide.

At this time, a relative of Nobutaka who was also his wife's great-aunt, a noble, ancient lady, was the Superior of an old nunnery in Shishigatani in Kyoto. This old lady's lineage contained the historical point of fusion of the opposing Kaburagi and Karasuma essences. The successive generations of her Komatsu family were made up of a top-rank priest who stayed out of politics, an author of a diary with literary value, an authority on ancient court and military practices and usages – in short, in every generation, men who took up positions as critics and revisionists in opposition to new customs. Now, however, after the death of this old Superior, her line would be no more.

Nobutaka Kaburagi, surmising that his wife had fled thither, dispatched a telegram there on the day after her disappearance. On the evening that Yuichi granted him a visit, there was still no answer to that telegram. The gist of the reply, wired two or three days later, was as follows: 'Your wife has not come here. However, since we have some idea about it, when we know more we shall inform you.' Such were the cryptic words.

About the same time, however, a bulky letter from Mrs Kaburagi, bearing the return address of that nunnery, was delivered to Yuichi. He hefted the letter in his hand. It seemed to whisper in its weight: 'Here I am.'

The letter said that the plain view of such a frightful scene had weakened her hold on life. That scene, so disgusting to look at, not only made her tremble with fear and humiliation, it also made her feel that she had absolutely no power to intervene in human affairs. She was already accustomed to an unconventional way of life. She had lightly skipped across its chasms, but this time she had finally looked into one. Her legs

227

were numb; she could not walk. Mrs Kaburagi was contemplating suicide.

She started off towards the suburbs of Kyoto, where it was still early for cherry blossoms, and took a long walk alone. She enjoyed seeing the great bamboo groves rustling in the wind of the early spring.

How vain, how vexatious, these bamboos in their greatness! she thought. And then, what stillness!

The greatest manifestation of her unhappiness lay in her conviction that if she was going to die, she should not think too much about being dead. When people do this, they escape death. For suicide, whether a lofty thing or lowly, is rather a suicide of thought itself; in general a suicide in which the subject does not think too much does not exist.

If it happened that she couldn't die – her thoughts took the opposite tack – it would be because the very thing that once drove her to death was now coming to look like the only thing that would keep her alive. What charmed her now much more fiercely than Yuichi's beauty was the ugliness of his action. As a result she had calmly reached the view that there was no greater meeting of minds than in the absolute, incontrovertible humiliation that lay in the identity of their feelings when she saw him and he was seen by her.

Was the ugliness of that action his weak point? No. One must not think that a woman like Mrs Kaburagi loved weakness. It was nothing more than the most extreme challenge to her sensibilities that his power could exert upon her. Thus she did not realize that what at first seemed a matter for her sentiments was, after various stern ordeals, becoming a problem of her will. There is not so much as a scintilla of gentleness in my love, she reflected, incongruously. As her steeled sensibilities saw him, the more monstrous Yuichi seemed, the more reason she had to love him.

When he read the next passage, Yuichi smiled a bitter smile. How naïve! While making me out to be beautiful, and she with her heart pure, now she tries to compete with me at being dirty, he thought to himself.

Nowhere so much as in this interminable, whorish confession had Mrs Kaburagi's passion ever come so close to being maternal. In trying to equal Yuichi's sins, Mrs Kaburagi laid bare all of her own sins. In order to mount to the height of Yuichi's immorality, she laboriously piled upon her own immorality. She produced evidence to show that she and he were blood relatives. She was like a mother gladly taking guilt on herself in order to protect her son. She laid her own misconduct bare. In her disregard of the effect her confession would have on the youth, moreover, she practically attained the egoism of maternity. Did she divine that this resolute baring of her soul, by rendering her completely unlovable, would provide the only means by which she could be loved? Frequently a mother-in-law is driven to be cruel to her daughter-in-law by a certain frantic impulse to make herself less lovable in the eyes of a son who already does not love her.

Before the war Mrs Kaburagi was only another commonplace lady of the nobility, a little promiscuous, but far purer than people thought. When her husband met Jackie and immersed himself quietly in the affairs of that street, and began neglecting his functions as a husband, she accepted a state of affairs that seemed not at all different from that of the normal couple. The war rescued them from boredom. They could take pride in the fact that they had had no children to bind them hand and foot.

It became clear at this time that her husband not only recognized her waywardness but indeed incited it. Nevertheless, she found no joy in the two or three casual affairs she experienced. She tasted no new emotion. She came to consider herself as indifferent, and as she did so her husband's insupportable attitude towards her became a source of annoyance. He interrogated her about it, point by point, and realized that the indifference he had nurtured in her over a long period of time was not wavering ever so slightly, and he rejoiced. There was no certificate of chastity like this stony indifference.

At that time there was always a group of silly admirers around her. There were middle-aged gentlemen, businessmen types, artist types, younger-generation types – how ridiculous that phrase sounds! – like the types of women in a whorehouse. They were representative of the idle life at the height of the war, a life that knew no tomorrow.

One day in summer a telegram came to the Shiga Heights Hotel, bringing one of her coterie his draft call. On the night before he departed, Mrs Kaburagi yielded this youth something she had not yielded to the others. Not because she loved him. At this time she knew this young man needed not a particular woman but an unknown woman, woman in general. She had the confidence to play the part of that woman. In that respect she differed from ordinary women.

The youth had to leave in the morning, on the first bus. They rose in the dawn. The youth was amazed at the sight of this woman busily packing his bags. I've never seen her act so much like a housewife, he thought. In one night, that's how I changed her. That's the feeling you get from conquest.

One should not take too seriously a man's feelings on the day he is being inducted. Beguiled by sentimentality and pathos, confident that whatever he did would be dismissed as harmless, he felt that any stupidity would be forgiven him. Youths who find themselves in this position are more complacent than middle-aged men.

Room service came in with the coffee. Mrs Kaburagi averted her gaze when she saw the utterly prodigal tip the young man gave.

Then the youth said to her, 'Oh, I forgot, ma'am, to ask for a picture.'

'What picture?'

'Yours, dear.'

'Why?'

'To take to the front with me.'

Mrs Kaburagi burst out laughing, in laughter that knew no control. While she laughed, she opened the french doors. The dawn fog whirled into the room.

The soldier-to-be turned up the collar of his pyjamas and sneezed.

'It's cold. Close the door.'

The tone of command in which he concealed his resentment upset Mrs Kaburagi. 'Well, if that makes you cold – soldiers never have it that good!' she said. She made him put on his clothes and rushed him to the door. He didn't get the picture.

In fact, the tearful youth didn't even get the good-bye kiss he requested from this so suddenly ill-tempered lady.

'Well, I can write you, can't I?' the youth, nervous about the other well-wishers, whispered in her ear as they were about to part. She smiled in silence.

When the bus melted away into the fog, Mrs Kaburagi, her shoes soaked through, followed a little path to the boat dock of Maruike Pond. One rotted boat was half-filled with water. There was about this place, too, the lonely neglect of a summer resort in wartime. In the fog, the reeds looked like the ghosts of reeds. In one place the fog, lighted faintly by the rays of morning, seemed to be a reflection of the surface of the water floating in the air.

To give one's body when one does not love, Mrs Kaburagi thought, picking at the hair that had become twisted at her temples as she slept. What comes so easy to a man, why is it so difficult for a woman? Why is it only prostitutes are permitted to know about it?

Oddly, she realized now that the vexation and the laughing disdain that had suddenly welled up in her for that young man were caused by his extravagant tip to the waitress. I gave my body – free. I had a little spirit left; I had my pride, she rationalized. If he had paid for my body with that money, I would certainly have been able to see him off with a freer spirit. Just like a whore at the front lines, I would have thrown open my body and my soul to a man's last desires, with a free spirit, filled with conviction.

She heard a faint sound at her ear. The mosquitoes that had been resting their wings at the tips of the reeds through the night buzzed by her head. There was something strange about the existence of mosquitoes here on the plateau. They were, however, light blue and delicate-seeming; it was hard to believe they would suck one's blood. Soon a cloud of mosquitoes ascended softly into the morning fog. Mrs Kaburagi realized that her white sandals were half-filled with water.

In that time by the lakeside, the thoughts that flickered through her mind clung to her wartime existence. To be forced to think that a simple gift was mutual love was surely to commit an inevitable sacrilege against the pure act of giving. Every time she committed that offence she tasted the humiliation of it. War was a blighted gift. War was one blood-smeared sentimentality, a squandering of love – in short, a squandering of watchwords.

From the bottom of her heart, she paid the whole noisy business a laugh of ridicule. Her flashy dress showed no concern for what people thought. Her character degenerated ever further. She went so far as to be seen kissing a blacklisted foreigner in the hallway of the Imperial Hotel, was questioned by the Military Police, and ended by getting her name in the newspapers. Anonymous letters never stopped coming to the Kaburagi family mailbox. The bulk of them were threats. Some called the countess a traitor; one of them, for instance, politely suggested that she commit suicide.

Count Kaburagi's guilt was not heavy. He was only a laggard. The time when Jackie was interrogated on suspicion of espionage was many times more upsetting to the count than the occasion of his wife's investigation, but even this affair ended without any real ill effect on him. When he heard just a rumour of air raids, he fled with his wife to Karuizawa. There he made connections with an old admirer of his father's, now the commander of the Nagano District Defence Forces, who was so good as to deliver them once each month an abundance of army rations.

When the war ended, the count looked forward to limitless freedom. Moral disorder, to be inhaled easily as morning air! He was drunk with indiscipline. Now, however, economic troubles and the tightness of money stole the freedom from his hands.

During the war Nobutaka had been elevated for no good reason to the chairmanship of the Federation of Marine Products Industries Associations. As one of the perquisites of his office he set up a small company selling bags made of moray leather, which fell outside the leather controls of the time. That was the Far East Marine Products Corporation. The moray has an eel's body with no scales, and is yellowish brown in colour with horizontal stripes. These strange fish, which grow to five feet in length, live among the reefs of near-by waters. When men come near them they stare with languid eyes and open wide their jaws, lined with sharp teeth. Guided by members of the Association, Nobutaka went one day to visit the seaside caves where the moray live in great numbers. For a long time he watched them from a little boat rocking in the waves. One of the creatures, slithering among the rocks, opened his mouth wide and menacingly at the count. This strange fish caught Nobutaka's fancy.

After the war, controls were suddenly lifted. Far East Marine Products business declined. The company altered its articles of incorporation and diversified to Hokkaido kelp, herring, Sanriku abalone, and other marine products. At the same time, it specialized in products that were used as Chinese foodstuffs and sold them to Chinese merchants in Japan as well as to smugglers in the China trade. Then assessment of the estate tax forced the sale of the Kaburagi mansion. Far East Marine Products, too, was low on funds.

At this time, a man named Nozaki, who said that Nobutaka's father had helped him long ago, appeared from nowhere and advanced him funds. Except that he was a former follower of Michiru Toyama in China and that Nobutaka's father had put him up in his home during his student days, this man's lineage and history were obscure. Some said that while the Chinese Revolution was going on, this man had gathered some former Japanese artillerymen and plunged into the revolution. He contracted for a certain amount per direct hit. Others said that after the war he loaded false-bottom suitcases with opium, smuggled them into Shanghai, and sold them through his followers.

Nozaki appointed himself president. Nobutaka was installed as chairman of the board, and was given 100,000 yen a month to keep far away from the management of the business. From that time Far East Marine Products assumed a vague, amorphous character. Then Nobutaka took lessons from Nozaki in buying up dollars. Nozaki entered into agreements with the Army of Occupation on behalf of heating companies and packing companies. He lined his own purse with the commissions. Sometimes, in order to cheat on the bid price, he played two clients against each other, all the while skilfully making use of the organization of Far East Marine Products and the name of

Nobutaka. At one time, when the families of the Army of Occupation were departing in great numbers, Nozaki's efforts to secure a contract in favour of a certain packing company were balked by the veto of the colonel in authority. He decided to fall back on the social talents of the Kaburagis and invited the colonel and his wife to dinner. Nozaki and the Kaburagis went to meet them. The colonel's wife did not appear.

It was on the next day that Nozaki visited the Kaburagi home on what he said was a private matter and asked for Mrs Kaburagi's help. She told him she needed till the next day to make up her mind. 'After I speak to my husband, I'll give you our answer,' she said. The thunderstruck Nozaki leaped to a common-sense interpretation. The forwardnes of his request had angered her. Still, she smiled.

'Don't give me that kind of answer. If it's no, say no. If you're angry, I apologize. Let's forget the whole thing.'

'I'll talk to my husband. Our house is different from others, you see. My husband will say yes, I'm certain.'

'Ha!'

'Just leave it to me. Of course, instead,' Mrs Kaburagi said in a businesslike and thus disrespectful tone, '– instead of that, if I throw in with you, and the contract is signed, how about giving me twenty per cent of the commission you get?'

Nozaki's eyes became round. He looked at her with confidence. Then, in Tokyo dialect that lacked a certain nuance and showed that the speaker had worked long elsewhere he said: 'Right; you're on.'

That evening, in a tone she might have used while reading from a primer, Mrs Kaburagi straightforwardly reported to Nobutaka that day's business discussion. He listened with eyes half closed. Then he glanced at his wife and mumbled something. This inscrutable pusillanimity on his part angered her. He looked delightedly at his wife's provoked face and said: 'Are you getting angry because I'm not stopping you?'

'What are you talking about now?'

Mrs Kaburagi knew very well that her husband would not interfere with her plan. And it was not true that she hoped somewhere in her heart that he would be upset with what she was doing and oppose it. The reason she was angry was only her husband's abject supineness.

Whether he stood in her way or did not stand in her way amounted to the same thing. Her own mind was made up. It was just that at this time she wished, with a humility that surprised her, to confirm the strange tie that kept her from breaking away from a husband in name only, the indefinable tie she felt inside herself. Nobutaka, who had trained himself to affect an indolent sensibility when he was in front of his wife, had overlooked this quite noble feature of hers. Never to believe in misery – in that characteristic nobility lies.

Nobutaka Kaburagi was frightened. His wife reminded him of an explosive about to go off. He took the trouble to stand up and put his hand on her shoulders.

'I apologize. Do as you wish. It's all right.'

From that time, Mrs Kaburagi despised him.

Two days later she drove to Hakoné with the colonel. The contract was sealed.

Perhaps because she had been caught in a trap unconsciously set by Nobutaka, contempt somehow set Mrs Kaburagi up as her husband's partner in crime. The two would now always work hand in glove. In order to catch unsuspecting pigeons they set the snares of their blackmail arrangements. Shunsuké Hinoki was one of their victims.

Men in high places in the Army of Occupation who had dealings with Nozaki one by one became Mrs Kaburagi's lovers. Replacements came from time to time. New faces were taken in quickly. Nozaki came to respect her more and more. . . .

'Since I met thee, however,' Mrs Kaburagi wrote, 'my world has changed completely. I thought my muscles were entirely voluntary, but I seem to have the involuntary ones everyone else does. Thou wert a wall – to barbarian armies a fortress thousands of miles long. Thou wert a lover who would never love me. For that reason, I adored thee; I still adore thee as then.

'When I say this, I should say that besides thee I have another Great Wall – Kaburagi. When I saw *that*, I understood for the first time. That is certainly why I have not been able to leave him until now. But Kaburagi is different from thee. He is not beautiful.

'Since I met thee, I have given up all my mock harlotries. That Nozaki and Kaburagi have coaxed and wheedled, striving to get me to alter my decision, thou canst well imagine. Just the same, until the other day, I got by without listening to them. Since Kaburagi's value depended on me, Nozaki held up his monthly salary. Kaburagi pleaded with me. At last I gave in, vowing that this would be the last time, and I played the harlot again. If I say that I was a prophet, thou wilt laugh, I suppose. When I came back with the document I had garnered on that day, I happened to see *that*.

'I got together just a few jewels and left for Kyoto. I will sell those jewels in order to live for the present, and will find myself a respectable job. Fortunately, my great-aunt has told me I can stay here as long as I like.

'Without me, perhaps Kaburagi will lose his job. No man can live on the pittance he gets from that sewing school.

'For several nights in a row I have dreamed of thee. I would really like to see thee. For the time being, though, I had better not.

'I don't mean to say do this please or that please when thou readest this letter. I won't say now go on loving Kaburagi, and I won't say throw Kaburagi over and love me. I want thee to be free; thou must be free. How could I wish to make thee mine? It would be like wishing to own the blue sky. The only thing I can say is that I adore thee. If ever thou shouldst come to Kyoto, be sure to come to Shishigatani. The temple is just north of the tomb of the Emperor Reizei.'

Yuichi finished reading the letter. The mocking smile was gone from the corner of his mouth. Quite unexpectedly, he was moved.

He had received the letter when he came home at three in the afternoon. After he read it, he reread the important passages. The blood rose to his face. His hand shook involuntarily from time to time.

First and foremost – and most unfortunately – he was moved by his own sensitivity. He was moved by the realization of how little volition there was in his feelings. His heart had

236

jumped like that of a sick man who has recovered from a serious illness: 'I am sensitive!'

He pressed his beautiful, burning face against the letter. In this mad paroxysm, he found ecstasy. Drunker than if he had drunk saké, he was drunk on intoxication. At the same time he began to feel that within him an emotion that he had not yet discovered was forming. He was like a philosopher who, before writing a treatise, happily smokes a cigarette; he took pleasure in deliberately putting off the discovery of this emotion.

On his desk sat the clock left by his father, clutched by its bronze lion. He strained to hear the interplay of his heartbeats and the sound of the clockwork. He had an unfortunate habit of looking at the clock whenever he encountered a new feeling. He would wonder how long it would last, and no matter how joyful a sensation it was, when it passed before five minutes had gone by, he would feel strangely relieved.

His eyes closed in terror. Mrs Kaburagi's face hovered before him. It was a truly clear vision, every line etched: the eyes, the nose, the lips – every feature was distinct. Was he not still the same Yuichi who, in the train with Yasuko on the way to their honeymoon, had been so reluctant to sketch her face in his mind as she sat by him? The clarity of his recollection was mostly caused by the desire awakening within him. Mrs Kaburagi's face as he recalled it was truly beautiful. He felt as if he had never in his life seen such a beautiful woman.

His eyes opened wide. The late afternoon sun was shining on the camellia tree in full bloom in the garden. The blossoms of the eightfold camellia gleamed. To that emotion that he had deliberately discovered so late, Yuichi, in full control of his senses, gave a name. As if thinking it was not enough, he whispered it: 'I love her. That at least is sure.'

Certain emotions turn false as soon as one articulates them, Yuichi had learned from bitter experience. He was subjecting his new emotion to the acid test.

'I love her. I can't believe that is not true. With all my power, I cannot deny this emotion. *I am in love with a woman.*'

He did not try to analyse his emotions. He was raptly confusing imagination with desire, memory with hope. His joy had gone mad. He was going to take his 'penchant for analysis', his 'consciousness', his 'fixed idea', his 'destiny', his 'innate understanding of truth', put them all together, curse them and bury them. Of course, these are what we commonly refer to as the symptons of the disease of modernity.

Was it an accident that in the midst of this tempest of emotions Yuichi should have remembered the name of Shunsuké?

'That's it; I must see Mr Hinoki right away. That old man is just the person for me to confess the joy of my love to. Why? Because if I make this confession to him so abruptly he will sympathize with my joy, and at the same time the old fellow will have the terrible revenge he has been plotting so diabolically.'

He hurried into the hall to the telephone. On the way he met Yasuko, coming from the kitchen.

'What's the hurry? You certainly look happy,' she said.

'How can you tell?' said Yuichi in the best of spirits, with a cruel magnanimity he had never displayed till now. He loved Mrs Kaburagi and did not love Yasuko! His emotions could not possibly be more natural or more honest.

Shunsuké was at home. They agreed to meet at Rudon's.

*

He waited for the streetcar, hands in his coat pockets like a cutpurse watching, awaiting his chance, kicking the stones, stamping his feet. He whistled shrilly but cheerfully at a bicycle rider who whizzed by.

The slow pace and the sideward motion of the old-fashioned trolley was well suited to this visionary passenger. Yuichi leaned by a window; thus he could look out at the rows of houses darkening in early spring and dream.

He felt his imagination spinning swiftly, like a top. If a top does not keep spinning, though, it will fall. And can one reach out one's hand and whip up its flagging revolutions as it spins? When the power that propelled it spent itself, that was the end, was it not? Thus he had misgivings about having only one reason for his joy.

Now that I think about it, I have loved Mrs Kaburagi from

238

the beginning, surely, he thought. If so, why did I avoid her there in the Rakuyo Hotel? That reflection was enough to send cold shivers down his spine. Of course, fear, cowardice itself, was to blame, Yuichi rationalized. He had fled from Mrs Kaburagi in the Rakuyo Hotel all because of cowardice.

Shunsuké had not yet arrived at Rudon's.

Yuichi had never waited for Shunsuké with such impatience. Again and again he felt for the letter in his inside pocket. When he touched it, it had the effect of a charm; he felt that when Shunsuké arrived his passion would not have abated at all.

There was something majestic in the way in which Shunsuké pushed open the door of Rudon's this evening; perhaps Yuichi's impatience had something to do with it. He was wearing an Inverness, over a kimono. Even that was a variation from the flashiness he had been affecting recently. Yuichi was surprised to see him exchange bows with boys at the tables here and there before he took the chair beside him. There was not a boy among those present this evening who had not been entertained by Shunsuké.

'Well, it has been a long time.' Shunsuké thrust out his hand with youthful vigour. Yuichi kept himself in check, and Shunsuké calmly started the conversation: 'I hear Mrs Kaburagi has left home.'

'Then you know?'

'Kaburagi's been foaming at the mouth; he came over, and we had a heart-to-heart talk. He seems to consider me a mystic finder of lost persons.'

'Did Mr Kaburagi –' Yuichi began, and then smiled a dissimulating smile. It was a smile of pure craft, like that of a boy playing a practical joke; it ran counter to his chief concern. 'Did he tell you the reason?'

'He was keeping mum; he didn't say. But it must have been because his wife saw you and him in a love scene.'

'Exactly!' said Yuichi, dumbfounded.

'As I look at things, that had to happen.' In his self-satisfaction, Shunsuké broke into a fit of coughing, Yuichi rubbed his back and did what he could to help him.

When the coughing stopped, Shunsuké turned his ruddy

face and brimming eyes towards Yuichi again and asked:
'Well – what's up?'

Without a word, Yuichi handed him the letter.

Shunsuké put on his glasses and swiftly counted the sheets.
'Fifteen pages,' he said, almost angrily. Then he settled himself
noisily in his chair as the Inverness and the kimono beneath it
rubbed against each other, and began to read.

Although it was not his own letter, Yuichi felt as if he sat
before a professor during the examination of his paper. He had
lost his confidence, doubt gnawed at him. The sooner this
period of penance was over the better he would like it. Yuichi
observed that the passages that he had read with so much
emotion brought no change of expression in Shunsuké's face.
Yuichi felt more and more uneasy about the correctness of his
feeling.

'A nice letter.' Shunsuké took off his glasses and idly toyed
with them. 'It is certainly true that women don't have any
brains, yet this is good evidence that at certain times and in
certain circumstances they have something that will serve in
place of brains. In short, spite.'

'I didn't bring you here, sir, to hear your criticisms.'

'I didn't criticize it! I couldn't criticize anything so marvellously contrived. Do you criticize a marvellous bald head? A
marvellous case of appendicitis? A marvellous Nerima rad-
ish?'

'But I was moved,' the youth said, pleading.

'You were moved? That surprises me. When you write a
New Year's card you try to move the other fellow somewhat.
If, however, by some error something has moved you, and that
something was in a letter, that is in the worst form possible.'

'You're wrong. I understood. I understood that I love Mrs
Kaburagi.'

Shunsuké began to laugh – a long sticky laugh from which
he didn't seem able to extricate himself. The men at the near-by
tables turned to watch as he struggled. He drank water,
choked, and went on laughing. The peals of laughter, it
seemed, would never stop coming.

20

Calamity to Jane is Calamity to John

In Shunsuké's idiotic laughter, there was no ridicule, not even good humour, not the slightest hint of feeling. It was an outright guffaw. It might be called the only act of which the old novelist was now capable. It was different from a coughing spasm or neuralgia; this explosive laughter was not forced.

Perhaps Yuichi, listening, considered him mad; but Shunsuké Hinoki felt that, thanks to this laughter, he now had within him a sense of kinship with the world.

Laugh it off! Laugh and pass it by! Thus, for the first time, the world stood before him. Jealousy and hatred, his traditional responses, even with the aid of Yuichi's vicarious anguish, had only served to spur him on to create works of art. Such was the power of this laugh that it held within it a kind of connection between his existence and the world, an ability through which he could see with his own eyes the blue sky on the other side of the globe.

Long ago he had taken a trip to Kutsukaké and encountered an eruption of the Asama volcano. Late at night, the glass in the windows rattled thinly and woke him from a light slumber into which he had fallen, frazzled by work. A series of explosions was occurring at thirty-second intervals. He got up and looked towards the crater. There was no sound there to speak of. A faint rumble came from the mountaintop, and after it a scarlet burst of flame. It was like the ocean surf, Shunsuké thought. The dancing spray of flame collapsed softly; but then half of it revivified into a circle of fire, half of it played about in the sky in the form of dark red smoke. It was like watching the lasting rays of sunset.

This volcanic laughter in Rudon's had in it a faint, distant rumbling. Shunsuké, however, felt that an emotion that came to him only rarely was hidden symbolically within his volcanic laughter.

This emotional link, which had kept him going several times during his humiliating youth, was a feeling of sympathy for the world. It visited him only at rare instances late at night, as now, or when he was about to descend from a high peak, alone in the dawn. At such times he felt himself to be an artist. His soul regarded the feeling as one of the extra emoluments of his office, a comic respite that gave him faith in the immeasurable height of his soul's station. It was an emotion as delicious as the taste of fresh air. As mountain climbers are shocked by their own gigantic shadows, so he was shocked by this gigantic emotion granted him by his soul.

What could he have called this emotion? Shunsuké didn't call it anything; he merely laughed. Certainly, respect was missing from that laugh – even respect for himself.

So in those moments when his laughter tied him to the world, that connecting bond of sympathy brought his heart close to the supreme love, that superlatively perfidious thing we call love of man.

At last Shunsuké stopped laughing. He took a handkerchief from his pocket and wiped away his tears. His aged lower lids folded in tear-soaked wrinkles.

'You felt! You love!' he said, exaggerating. 'That's outright nonsense! This thing called feeling, like a beautiful wife, is something that goes wrong easily. For that reason it can only excite men who don't amount to very much.

'Don't be angry, Yuchan. I didn't say you were a man who didn't amount to much. It's just that, unfortunately, you have been yearning for emotion. Into the utter purity of your heart the thirst for emotion has happened to enter. It's simply a case of illness. Just as boys who arrive at adolescence fall in love with love, you were moved by being moved; that's all. When you're recovered from this fixed idea, your emotion will vanish like the mist, surely. You, too, must already know that – that outside of sexual feeling there is no feeling. No matter what the notion or the conception, if it has nothing of sex in it, it cannot make man feel. Men, moved by the secret elements of thought, like coxcombs spread the word that they have been moved by thought itself. It would be better if we stopped using vague words like "emotion".

'I know I'm being picky, but I'll try to analyse your testimony. First, you testified, "I felt". Then you testified, "I love Mrs Kaburagi". What do these two things have to do with each other? Briefly, you know very well that there is no such thing as emotion that is unconnected with sexual attraction. So you immediately added the word "Love" as a postscript. In doing so, you used the word "love" as a synonym for animal desire. Perhaps you have no objection to that point. Mrs Kaburagi's gone off to Kyoto. As far as animal passion is concerned you can be completely at ease. And so for the first time you have allowed yourself to love a woman. Isn't that right?'

Yuichi did not submit to this claptrap the way he had formerly. His deep, sad eyes watched closely Shunsuké's excited movements. He had learned to strip each word bare, seeking out ways to test them.

'Just the same, how?' the youth said. 'When you speak of animal desire, you are talking about something much colder than what people mean when they speak of reason. The emotion I felt when I read that letter was much warmer than the animal desire you refer to. Is it true that all feeling in this world other than sexual desire is a lie? If so, is not sexual desire also a lie? If only the deficient state in which one desires another is the real thing, all the states of momentary fulfilment are illusions. I certainly can't see that. It is an existence like that of a beggar who, in order that people will later throw more alms into his receptacle, always hides his alms before the receptacle is full. It seems awfully mean to me.

'I sometimes think I would like to involve myself wholeheartedly in something. If it is done on behalf of some lie, that's all right. If it has no object, fine. In high school, I did a great deal of high jumping and diving. It was great to throw my body into the air. "Now, now, now, I have stopped dead in the air!" I told myself. The green of the field, the green of the pool water – they were always around me. Now, I have nothing green around me. If what I want to do is being done on behalf of a lie, good. For instance, is the action of a man who enlists in the service and distinguishes himself less distinguished because he did it out of self-deception?'

'My goodness, you're getting highfalutin, aren't you? You used to be in agony because you found it hard to believe in the existence of your own emotions; there wasn't a thing I could do with you. So I showed you the joy of being without feeling. Now you want to be unhappy again, eh? As your beauty is perfect so must your unhappiness be. I have never said it outright before, but the power that you have to make women and men unhappy one after the other is not derived only from the power of your beauty; it also comes from your gift of being more unhappy than anybody.'

'You're right. At last you've said it, sir. With that, sir, your instruction has become quite ordinary. All you've taught me is that I must see my own unhappiness and live with it, and that there is no way by which I can escape it. Tell me truly, sir, has there never been one time when you have felt something?'

'Other than sexual desire, no.'

The youth went on with a half-bantering smile: 'Well, what about the first time I saw you, on the shore last summer?'

Shunsuké marvelled. He recalled the fierce sunlight of summer: the deep blue of that sea, a single eddy of water, the sea breeze striking his ears. Then he recalled the Greek vision that moved him so keenly, the vision of a bronze sculpture of the Peloponnesus school.

Was there no sexual desire in that? If not, then a presentiment of sex? At that time Shunsuké, who had passed his life far away from thought, for the first time came to embrace thought. Was that thinking really filled with sexual desire? Until today his undying misgivings had revolved around that question. Yuichi's words had caught Shunsuké off guard.

The music from Rudon's record player stopped just then. The place was quiet; the proprietor had gone off somewhere. Only the horns of passing automobiles echoed noisily in the room. Neon signs were coming on in town; an ordinary night was commencing.

For no reason at all Shunsuké thought of a scene from a novel he had written long ago:

244

He loitered a while and looked at the cryptomeria tree. It was a tall tree; its age, too, was very great. There was a rift in one corner of the cloudy heavens, and through it one shaft of sunlight came down like a waterfall and lit up the tree. It lit it up but it could not by any means penetrate inside the cryptomeria. In vain it reached the periphery of the tree, falling on the moss-covered earth. He was oddly conscious of the will of the tree he was raising, its will to rise to heaven all the while stubbornly holding off the penetrating light. It was as if he had been given the mission of communicating to heaven the exact image of that life's dark will.

He was reminded of a passage from Mrs Kaburagi's letter that he had just read: 'Thou wert a wall – to barbarian armies a fortress ten thousand miles long. Thou wert a lover who would never love me. Therefore I adored thee, I still adore thee, even now.'

Shunsuké looked at the rows of white teeth, like that long fortress, between Yuichi's slightly parted lips.

Do I not feel sexual desire for this beautiful youth? he thought to himself with a cold shiver. If not, there would be no reason for my feeling this heart-rending emotion. It is as if before I was aware I started feeling desire. It's impossible! I love the flesh of this young man.

The old man shook his head slightly. Without doubt his thinking had become filled with sexual desire. His thinking gained power for the first time. Shunsuké had forgotten that he was dead – he loved!

Shunsuké's heart suddenly became humble. In his eyes the arrogant flame flickered out. He shrugged his Inverness-clad shoulders as if he were folding his wings. Once again he stared longingly at Yuichi's streamlined brows. Youth pervaded the air around him.

If I love this youth sexually, he thought, and if this impossible discovery is possible at my age, I cannot say that Yuichi cannot love Mrs Kaburagi sexually. How do you like that?

'Perhaps you do love Mrs Kaburagi, for all I know. When I listen to your voice, I somehow get that impression.' Shunsuké did not realize how bitter was the feeling in his words. The thoughts he was expressing affected him as if he were stripping the skin off his body. He was jealous!

As a teacher, Shunsuké was a little too honest. Thus he said what he did. Those who teach young men are completely aware of their youth and know that what the teacher says will be taken as if he had the opposite end in mind. Sure enough, Yuichi, having been spoken to thus directly, took the opposite tack. Without help from anyone, he somehow had the courage to look directly within himself.

No, that isn't so, he thought. I can't love Mrs Kaburagi, that's sure. For all I know I was in love with a second me, a beautiful young man with a beauty beyond possibility in this world, whom Mrs Kaburagi loves so much. That letter certainly had power enough. Anybody receiving a letter like that would have difficulty in thinking of himself as the subject of it. I am not Narcissus, he rationalized proudly. If I were in love with myself I might without difficulty see myself and the subject of that letter as the same thing. But I am in love with myself. That is why I fell in love with Yuchan.

Because of these reflections, Yuichi felt a somewhat confused affection for Shunsuké. The reason was that, in this moment, both Yuichi and Shunsuké loved the same person. You like me; I like me; let's be friends – this is the axiom of egoistic affection. At the same time it is the one and only manifestation of mutual love.

'No, that cannot be. I understand now. I do not love Mrs Kaburagi,' Yuchan said.

Shunsuké's countenance overflowed with joy.

*

That thing called love is very much like a fever, even with the long period of incubation. During the incubation period the various sensations of malaise await the onset of the illness, when for the first time the symptoms are plain. As a result, the person coming down with a disease believes that the underlying causes of all the problems of the world are explicable in terms of fever. War occurs: 'That's the fever,' he says with a gasp. A philosopher suffers to resolve the pains of the world: 'That's the fever,' he says, suffering under his high temperature.

When Shunsuké Hinoki recognized that he desired Yuichi, he knew the cause of his sentimental pining, of the jealousy that pierced him from time to time, of the life which came to be worth living when there was the possibility that Yuichi would phone, of the mysterious pain of frustration, of the pain of Yuichi's long silence that led him to plan the trip to Kyoto, of the joy of that trip to Kyoto. This was, however, an ominous discovery. If it was love, he thought, in the light of his past experience failure was inevitable. There was no hope. He must wait for his opportunity; he must hide his feelings as much as he could. These were the things this old man, so very deficient in confidence, told himself.

Free of the fixed idea that had held him fast, Yuichi discovered again his happy confessor in Shunsuké. His conscience was slightly troubled, and he said: 'A little while ago, you seemed to know about me and Mr Kaburagi, sir, I didn't want to tell you about that. How long have you known it? And how did you find out?'

'Since the time he came looking for his cigarette case in the hotel in Kyoto.'

'But that time –'

'That's all right. That's all right. I'm not interested in hearing about it. It would be wiser to think about what to do about this letter. Here's the way you'd better think about it. No matter whether she explains it a million times, if she really had any respect for you she would have committed suicide for your sake. You have to pay her back for that slight. Don't answer her. If you become a plain ordinary third party, you'll help them revert to what they were before.'

'What about Mr Kaburagi?'

'Show him this letter,' said Shunsuké, trying to make this disgusting part of the conversation brief. 'Then you'd better let him know you're breaking things off. The count will be put out, and when he has nowhere else to turn he'll go to Kyoto, probably. That way Mrs Kaburagi's pain will be complete, too.'

'I was just thinking that's what I should do,' said Yuichi,

finding his urge to do mischief stimulated. 'But there's one little problem. Kaburagi is having financial trouble, and if I throw him over –'

'Oh, are you concerned about something like that?' Shunsuké said, looking with pleasure at this youth over whom he seemed to be regaining his power. Then he went on, happily and strongly: 'If it were true that you let him do as he pleased with you because of his money, that's another matter, but if that's not true, it's no concern of yours whether he has money or not. At any rate, you'll probably not get any salary from now on.'

'To tell you the truth I barely got last month's salary the other day.'

'See what I mean? Just the same, you're not sweet on Kaburagi, are you?'

'Cut it out!' He almost shouted it; his pride had been wounded. 'I only let him have my body.'

This reply, so lacking in psychological clarity, suddenly oppressed Shunsuké. He thought of the 500,000 yen he had given Yuichi, and at the same time of the youth's docility in the matter. It frightened him to think that, while they had this financial arrangement, Yuichi might not find it hard to let him have his body. Again Yuichi was a riddle.

Not only that: when he thought over the scheme he had just laid out and recalled Yuichi's agreement with it, Shunsuké was uncomfortable. Some parts of the scheme were superfluous. There was the superfluity provided by Shunsuké's self-interest, which he permitted himself for the first time: I'm carrying on like a jealous woman.... He enjoyed reflections like this that made him seem even more disagreeable.

At this moment an elegant gentleman entered Rudon's.

He was about fifty, clean-shaven, with rimless glasses, and had a mole beside his nose. He had a square, arrogant, handsome face, like a German's. He kept his chin pulled in tight; the gleam in his eye was frigid. The sharp cleft under his nose accentuated the impression of coldness. His entire face was so formed that it did not need to look down very much. It took into account the laws of perspective; the wilful forehead stood ruggedly in the background. There was only one fault; and

248

that was the slight facial neuralgia on the lower right side. When he stood just inside the restaurant and looked around him, a tic ran like lightning from his eye to his jawbone. When that moment passed, his entire face immediately looked as if nothing had happened.

His eyes met Shunsuké's. As he did so an ever so slight shadow of bewilderment passed over him. He could not act as if they did not know each other. He smiled in a friendly fashion and said, 'Oh, it's you, sir.' His human goodness came out on his face. It was something he showed only to his most intimate friends.

Shunsuké indicated the chair beside him. The man sat down. He talked with Shunsuké; but once he became conscious of Yuichi, his eyes somehow never left the youth's face. Yuichi was not a little amazed by that face, and cheek on which the lightning ran every ten or twenty seconds. Shunsuké realized he should introduce them.

'This is Mr Kawada, president of Kawada Motors, an old friend. This is my nephew, Yuichi Minami.'

Yaichiro Kawada was born in Satsuma, in Kyushu, and was the eldest son of the Yaichiro Kawada who started Japan's first domestic auto industry. He was not a credit to his father as a child and wanted to be a novelist. He entered the preparatory course of K— University and took Shunsuké's course in French literature. Shunsuké was asked to read his early flights in fiction. He did not seem to have any talent, and was discouraged. His father took advantage of this opportunity and sent him to Princeton University, in America, to major in economics. After he graduated he was sent to Germany for practical instruction in the motor industry. When he came home Yaichiro was completely changed. He had become a practical man.

He remained in obscurity until after the war, when his father was purged. Then he became president of the firm. After his father died he demonstrated ability that surpassed the old man's. When the construction of large-size automobiles was prohibited, he changed over to the construction of small cars and concentrated on exports to Asian countries. He also organized a subsidiary in Yokosuka, through his own initiative took up the repair of jeeps, and reaped tremendous profits. After he became president, a certain incident served to rekindle his old association with Shunsuké. He was the organizer of Shunsuké's lavish sixty-first birthday party.

This chance meeting in Rudon's was nothing less than an unspoken confession. The two men never touched on the self-evident subject. Kawada asked Shunsuké to dinner. After he invited him, he took out his notebook, flipped his glasses up on his forehead and looked for gaps in his calendar. It was for all the world like searching a tremendous dictionary for the place where a forgotten flower lay pressed.

At last he found it: 'Next Friday at nine. That's all. The meeting set for that day has been postponed. I hope you can make it.' Still, this busy man had had the time to leave his automobile at a corner a block away to come stealthily to Rudon's. Shunsuké accepted. Kawada added an unexpected request: 'How about the Kurohané, in Imai Cho? They have Takajo cuisine. Of course, your nephew is invited. Is that all right?'

'Yeah,' Shunsuké grunted ambiguously.

'I'll make reservations for three people. I'll call you again so you won't forget.' He looked at his watch as if pressed for time. 'Oh, excuse me. I'd like to stay here and talk, but I can't. I'll be looking forward to seeing you again.'

The big shot departed in leisurely enough fashion, but the impression he left on the two men quickly evaporated.

Shunsuké, out of sorts, said nothing. He felt as if in one short instant of time Yuichi had been reviled before his eyes. He talked about Kawada's career without being asked; then, with a rustle of his Inverness, he arose.

'Where are you going, sir?'

Shunsuké wanted to be alone. Besides, he had to be at a banquet of the Fellows of the Academy in an hour.

'I have a meeting. That's why I came out. Come to my house before five next Friday; Kawada will undoubtedly send a car over to my house for us.'

Yuichi realized that Shunsuké had extended his hand from the voluminous sleeve of the Inverness. That wasted hand with its prominent veins, extended from the shelter of the heavy

250

cloth, was filled with humiliation. If Yuichi were a little more ill-tempered, he could easily have overlooked that miserable hand. However, he took it. The hand trembled ever so slightly.

'Well, *sayonara*.'

'Thank you very much, sir, for today.'

'Thank me? Don't thank me for anything.'

When Shunsuké had departed, the youth called up Nobu-taka Kaburagi to find out whether he was free.

'What's that? You got a letter from her?' he asked with a rising inflection in his voice. 'No, don't come over. I'll meet you. Have you had supper yet?' He gave the name of a res-taurant.

*

While they waited for their food, Nobutaka read his wife's letter hungrily. When the soup came, he still had not finished. By then, the swollen bits of alphabet macaroni, impossible to decipher, had become sodden at the bottom of the bowl.

Nobutaka did not look at Yuichi. He looked in another direction and sucked at his soup. Yuichi looked with more than a little curiosity at this unfortunate man who wanted sympathy but had no one to turn to, thinking that surely, at the expense of good manners, he would spill the soup in his lap. His soup was soon gone, though, without spilling.

'Poor thing,' Nobutaka soliloquized, putting down his spoon. 'Poor thing ... no woman was ever so unfortunate.'

There was a reason that Nobutaka's way of exaggerating his feelings should now have an exasperating effect on Yuichi. It was Yuichi's moral concern for Mrs Kaburagi.

Nobutaka said over and over: 'That poor woman. That poor woman.' Then, using his wife as a pretext, he tried indirectly to excite sympathy for himself. But Yuichi's expression never altered, and Nobutaka at last lost patience and said: 'I was the bad one all the time. Nobody is to blame.'

'Is that so?'

'Yuchan, how can you be so cruel? Yes, be cold to me. But my wife, who was not to blame –'

'I wasn't to blame either.'

The count carefully picked the small bones from the fish on

251

his plate and placed them on the edge of his dish. He said nothing. After a time he said, almost weeping: 'You're right. I'm finished.'

This was more than Yuichi could stand. This hard-shelled, middle-aged homosexual was amazingly deficient in candour. The unseemly behaviour which he now displayed was ten times worse than candid unseemliness. He was trying to make it look noble.

Yuichi looked around him at the other diners. A very prim young American couple ate their supper facing each other. They said little. They smiled almost not at all. The woman gave a little sneeze and hurriedly covered her mouth and said. 'Excuse me.' Elsewhere a group of Japanese, related to one another, who seemed to have come from a memorial service, sat at a big round table. They were exchanging slander about the deceased and laughing loudly. The voice of a woman of about fifty – evidently the widow – dressed in blue–grey mourning clothes and wearing rings on every finger, spoke shrilly: 'My husband bought me seven diamond rings altogether. I sold four of them without his knowing it and substituted glass stones. When the war came, along with the jewellery-donation drive, I lied and said I had donated the four I sold. I kept the three genuine ones as my share. Here they are.' She spread out her hand so they all were visible. 'My husband congratulated me for not reporting them all to the government! "Your dishonesty amazes me!" he said.'

'Ha, ha! The only one who didn't know was your husband.'

The table where Yuichi and Nobutaka sat seemed cut off from the rest. The metal furnishings – flower vase, knives, and spoons – glittered coldly. Yuichi suspected that the distaste he felt for Nobutaka probably originated from the fact that they were members of the special fraternity.

'Will you go to Kyoto for me?' Nobutaka said abruptly.

'Why?'

'Why? You're the only one who can bring her back.'

'Are you using me?'

'Using you?' A pained smile lifted Pope's proud lips. 'Don't be so distant, Yuchan.'

252

'It won't work. Even if I went, your wife would never come back to Tokyo.'

'How can you say that?'

'Because I know your wife.'

'This amazes me. I've been married to her for twenty years.'

'I haven't known her for even half a year, but I fancy I know your wife well.'

'You're setting yourself up as a rival in love, eh?'

'Yes. Maybe.'

'You don't say, Yuchan –'

'Don't worry. I can't stand women. But you, sir, have you decided lately to be a husband to this woman?'

'Yuchan,' he said, in a horrible, sticky voice, 'let's not quarrel. Please!'

After that the two ate in silence. Yuichi had miscalculated somewhat. He was acting like an attending surgeon scolding his patient in order to encourage him; before he broached the subject of separation, he wished to destroy the other's affection for him. If he was kind enough to wish to do it with as little pain as possible, however, the cold treatment he had been using was certainly wrong. He should have humoured Nobutaka in a kindly and cooperative spirit, even though he didn't mean it. For what Pope had fallen in love with was his spiritual cruelty. To the extent he showed that, he would stimulate Pope's imagination agreeably and deepen his illusions even more.

When they left the restaurant, Pope gently linked his arm in Yuichi's. Yuichi let him do it – out of disdain. The young lovers passing by were also walking arm-in-arm. He heard a youth who looked like a student murmur in a girl's ear: 'Look, there; they must be homosexuals.'

'Oh, how awful!'

Yuichi's face reddened in humiliation and anger. He pulled his arm away and put his hands in his pockets. Nobutaka suspected nothing. He was accustomed to treatment like this.

'Them! Them!' Yuichi ground his teeth. 'They who pay three hundred and fifty yen for a lunch hour together in a hotel bed, and have their great love affair in the sight of heaven. They who, if all goes well, build their rat's-nest love

253

nests. They who, sleepy-eyed, diligently multiply. They who go out on Sundays with all their children to clearance sales at the department stores. They who scheme out one or two stingy infidelities in their lifetimes. They who always show off their healthy homes, their healthy morality, their common sense, their self-satisfaction.'

Victory, however, is always on the side of the commonplace. Yuichi knew that all the scorn he could muster could not combat their natural scorn.

It was still too early to go to the nightclub to which Nobutaka had invited Yuichi in order to celebrate his wife's return from the dead. They went to a movie to kill time.

It was a film of the American West. Up in the yellow-brown mountains a rider is pursued by a band of villains. The hero takes a short cut and from a crevice in the rocks at the top of the mountain snipes at his pursuers. A villain who has been shot falls headlong down the slope. Yonder, at the horizon overgrown with cactus, the tragic clouds shine.... With mouths slightly open, the two men looked aghast at this world of undeniable action.

When they went out, the street at ten on that spring evening was cold. Nobutaka stopped a taxi and ordered it to Nihonbashi. Tonight they were celebrating the opening of a nightclub featuring service until four a.m. in the basement of a famous Nihonbashi stationery store.

The manager, in tuxedo, stood at the reception desk greeting the guests. What Yuichi found out when he got there was that Nobutaka, an old friend of the manager, had been invited this evening for a free party. This evening's celebration was to be on the house.

A number of so-called famous people came. Yuichi uneasily watched Nobutaka passing out his cards from Far East Marine Products. There were artists and literary men. It almost seemed as if Shunsuké's 'meeting' would be this one, but of course he was nowhere here. The music blared constantly; many couples danced. Hostesses who had been rounded up for the opening wore their latest-style hired dresses buoyantly. Their evening gowns were certainly unsuited to the interior decoration of a mountain hut.

254

'Let's drink until morning,' the beautiful woman dancing with Yuichi said. 'Are you that man's private secretary? Let's give him the slip. Come sleep at my house and get up at noon. I'll fry you some eggs. Since you're just a boy, though, you like scrambled eggs better, don't you?'

'Me? I like an omelet.'

'Omelet? Oh, you're cute.' The drunken woman kissed him.

They went to their seats. Nobutaka was waiting with two gin fizzes. He said, 'Let's make a toast.'

'To what?'

'To the health of Mrs Kaburagi.'

The curiosity of the women was piqued by this toast so full of hidden meaning. Yuichi looked at the lemon floating with the crushed ice in his glass. Around that circumference of lemon a hair, seemingly a woman's, was twined. He closed his eyes and drank it down, as if it were a hair belonging to Mrs Kaburagi.

It was one o'clock when Nobutaka Kaburagi and Yuichi left. Nobutaka started for a cab. Yuichi unconcernedly walked off. He's sulking, thought the man who loved him. He must have known we would sleep together after all this. If not, he wouldn't have come this far. My wife isn't here, so he can stay at my house with impunity.

Yuichi did not turn around; he walked quickly towards the Nihonbashi intersection. Nobutaka followed behind him, breathing painfully: 'Where are you going?'

'I'm going home.'

'Don't be stubborn.'

'I have a family.'

A cab arrived. Nobutaka opened the door. He took Yuichi by the arm. The youth was stronger than he. He pulled his arm away and said, 'You go on home alone.' The two stood glaring at each other for a time. Nobutaka gave up and closed the door in the face of the grumbling driver.

'Let's walk a little and talk. While we're walking we'll sober up.'

'I have something to say, too.'

Nobutaka's breast palpitated uneasily. They walked for a

time on the deserted sidewalk, the sound of their shoes echoing.

On the trolley street, cruising cabs slipped back and forth. One step into the alleys, however, the firm steadfast calm of the city's centre reigned. After a time they walked in back of the N— Bank. There the round street lamps shone bright. The bank structure towered darkly in a collection of tall strong ridges. Except for the night watchman, the residents of this section were all gone. Only piles of stones in the disciplined ranks remained. The windows were shut, dark behind iron bars. In the cloudy sky, distant thunder sounded. Lightning faintly lit a surface of the round pillars of the bank next door.

'What did you want to say?'

'I think we should break up.'

Nobutaka did not answer. For a time only the sound of their footsteps echoed in the broad expanse of the street.

'Why so sudden?'

'The time has come.'

'Aren't you being selfish?'

'I'm being objective.'

The childishness of that word 'objective' made Nobutaka laugh.

'I can't leave you.'

'Suit yourself; but I'm not going to sleep with you any more.'

'But, Yuchan, since I met you, philanderer though I have been, I haven't once been untrue to you. I lived for you alone. The hives that appear on your chest on cold nights, your voice, your profile in the dawn at the gay party, the smell of your pomade: if these things were gone ...'

The youth muttered in his heart: 'Then buy the same pomade and smell it to your heart's content. How's that?' He found the pressure of Nobutaka's shoulder against his distasteful.

They suddenly realized that the river was just in front of them. Several boats tied up along the pier were incessantly emitting heavy, squeaky sounds. Headlight beams of the automobiles on the bridge across the way crisscrossed and threw out great shadows.

They turned back, walking again. Nobutaka talked constantly and excitedly. He stubbed his toe against something that went rolling off with a faint, dry noise. It was a branch of an imitation cherry tree used as decoration for a department-store sale. The dirty paper cherry tree rustled with the sound of waste paper.

'Do we really have to part? Do you mean it? Yuchan, is our friendship really at an end?'

'Friendship? That's odd. If we were friends, we wouldn't have had to sleep together, would we? We'll be able to meet as friends from now on, if that's what we are.'

Nobutaka said nothing.

'Well, you don't like that.'

'Yuchan, please, don't leave me alone.' They entered a dark alley. 'I'll do anything you like. Anything. If you ask me to kiss your shoes, I'll do it.'

'Stop the theatrics, won't you?'

'I'm not acting, I mean it. I'm not acting.'

Possibly a man like Nobutaka is only himself on the occasions when he is involved in a big act. In front of a candy store, its iron grating pulled down over its display window, he knelt down on the sidewalk. He embraced Yuichi's leg and kissed his shoe. The smell of shoe polish threw him into ecstasy. He even kissed the toes of the shoes, which had become dusty. He unbuttoned the youth's coat and attempted to kiss his trousers, so Yuichi bent over and with all his power tore himself free from Pope's arms, which were clinging to his calves like a trap.

Terror took possession of Yuichi. He started running.

Nobutaka did not follow. He got up and brushed off the dust. He took out a white handkerchief. He wiped his lips. The handkerchief was smudged with shoe polish. Nobutaka was already the Nobutaka he had always been. He walked off in his affected, turn-a-screw-walk, turn-a-screw-walk gait.

On one street corner he could see the far-off shape of Yuichi stopping a taxi. The cab moved off. Count Kaburagi wanted to walk until the night brightened. His heart called not Yuichi but the name of his wife. She was his partner, his partner in crime and also his partner in calamity, in disappointment, and in grief. Nobutaka thought he would go to Kyoto alone.

21

Chuta in Old Age

Now spring suddenly became itself. It rained often, but between the rains it was very warm. There was one unusually cold day; for about an hour snow flurried.

The day approached when Kawada would take Shunsuké and Yuichi to dine in the Takajo style; meanwhile the Hinoki ménage, consisting of a maid and a houseboy, found Shunsuké's ill temper hard to bear. It wasn't only the maid and the houseboy. When the admirer-turned-chef was called one evening to cook for Shunsuké's guests, he was treated to a surprise. Usually Shunsuké would praise the skill of his cooking in friendly fashion. He would never forget to have a drink with him and thank him for his pains. The man was amazed this time, therefore, when Shunsuké, without a kind word of comment, went up to his second-floor study and shut himself in.

Kaburagi came over to announce that he was going to Kyoto and to leave a keepsake for Yuichi. Shunsuké accorded him a lukewarm reception and sent him packing.

Shunsuké thought so many times of phoning Kawada to call off the date. But he could not – why, Shunsuké himself could not explain.

Yuichi's words, 'I only let him have my body,' nagged him.

The night before, Shunsuké worked very late. He had stretched out on the little bed in the corner of his study. The night was far gone. When he bent his knees and tried to sleep, they suddenly became acutely painful. His right knee had required medication lately because of frequent seizures of neuralgia. He still used the analgesic Pavinal, morphine in powdered form, which he washed down with water from the bottle on his night table. Although the pain stopped, he remained wakeful.

He arose and went to his desk again. He relighted the gas heater which he had earlier turned off. The desk is a mysterious piece of furniture. Once a writer faces it, he is mysteriously seized by it and held fast. After that it is only with great effort that he can tear himself away.

Shunsuké's creative powers were returning to life, like the reviving flowers. He had written two or three fragmentary books brimming with a mysterious energy. They were recrudescences of the time of the Taiheiki, novels filled with arabesques like the display of decapitated heads, or the burning of monasteries, or the revelation of the child of the Hannya Temple, or the love affair of the Great Priest of the Shiga Daitoku Temple and the Great Imperial Concubine of Kyogoku. They also turned to the ancient world of the Kagura songs, and touched upon the heartbreak of the man who must relinquish the boy wearing the hairlock of childhood. The long occasional piece named 'Even a Spring Day', patterned after the 'Ionian melancholy' of ancient Greece, had behind it also the paradoxical influence of an actual society like that of the 'plague-infested meads' of Empedocles.

Shunsuké put down his brush. He had been attacked by wild, unhappy imaginings. Why do I look on with arms folded? Why? the old man thought. Am I acting the craven part of Chuta at my age? Why don't I call up and cancel it? Now that I think of it, it's because Yuichi himself consented. Not only that, he and Kaburagi have already broken up. In short, I am upset that Yuichi belongs to nobody. If so, why don't I...? Oh, it's not right that I should. It would never be right. It would not be right for me who can't even look directly at myself in a mirror. Besides, a work of art is by no means the property of its creator.

Now and then the crowing of roosters was audible. Hearing those bursting voices was like glimpsing the redness inside the roosters' mouths. Dogs, too, barked fiercely from place to place. They were like a band of thieves, each tied up separate from the others, all gnashing their teeth at the ignominy of their bonds and exchanging shouts with one another.

Shunsuké sat down on the sofa that served as a window seat and smoked a cigarette. The collection of old ceramics and the totem doll stirred no emotion in him as they stood around the window in the dawn. He looked at the pitch-black garden trees and the purple sky. When he looked down, he noticed that a rattan lounge chair the old maidservant had forgotten was lying in the middle of the lawn at an angle. Morning was born from the yellowish-brown rectangle above this ageing rattan. He was very tired. The lounge chair in the garden gradually brightening in the morning mist taunted him. It was like a long rest floating in the distance, a long layoff forced upon him by death. His cigarette was burning to its end. He defied the cold air, opened the window, and threw out the cigarette. It did not reach the rattan chair but fell into a Kamiyo cryptomeria and came to rest in its foliage. A point of fire burned an apricot colour for a while. He went downstairs to his bedroom and slept.

*

In the evening, Yuichi arrived early and Shunsuké immediately told him the story of Nobutaka Kaburagi's visit several days before.

After Nobutaka had arranged to sell his house to the inn that occupied the main house, to be used by them as an annex, he had immediately set out for Kyoto. Yuichi was somewhat disappointed that Nobutaka had not said much about him. He had said that the corporation had fallen into bad straits, and he was going to work for the Forestry Bureau of something in Kyoto. Shunsuké gave Yuichi the keepsake from Nobutaka. It was the cat's-eye ring Nobutaka had received from Jackie on the night when Yuichi first became his.

'Well,' Shunsuké said, with a mechanical cheerfulness brought on by lack of sleep. 'This is your party tonight. If you had seen Kawada's look the other day, you would know that I am not the guest of honour, but really you are. Even so, it was fun the other day, wasn't it? Our relationship must have been cause for some wondrous suspicions.'

'Let's keep it that way, shall we?'

'Somehow lately I am like a puppet and you are the puppet master.'

'Just the same I took care of Mr and Mrs Kaburagi just as you told me to.'

'By some blessed chance.'

Kawada's car arrived. The two waited for a time at the Kurohané, and before long Kawada joined them. He was very relaxed from the moment he sat down on a cushion. Gone was the awkwardness of the other day. When we meet men of differing occupations, we like to affect ease like this. Kawada's old student-teacher relationship with Shunsuké helped: he was trying to exaggerate for Shunsuké the way in which the air of the boorish man of affairs had replaced the literary sensitivity of his youth. Thus he deliberately made mistakes in the French classics he had learned long ago. He confused Racine's *Phèdre* and *Britannicus* and sought a ruling by Shunsuké.

He told a story of the *Phèdre* he had seen at the Comédie Française. He recalled the pure beauty of that youth, closer to the woman-disdaining Hippolytus of ancient Greek tradition than the elegant Hippolyte of traditional French drama. He seemed to be uttering a long, tedious, self-centred statement of opinions in order to demonstrate his complete lack of literary sensibility.

At the end he looked at Yuichi and remarked: 'It would be a pity if you don't take a trip abroad while you're young.' Who in the world was there to help him do it? Kawada had been calling Yuichi 'Nephew San' constantly, going by the statement Shunsuké had made the other day.

In the Takajo fashion a metal grill is placed over burning charcoal before each person. Each guest is covered with an apron from the neck down and cooks his meat himself. Shunsuké, his face flaming from the effects of wine and with a ridiculous apron tied to his neck, looked indescribably silly. He compared Kawada's and Yuichi's faces. He could not figure out what on earth had led him to accept the invitation and bring Yuichi here when he had full knowledge what was going to happen. It was quite painful for him to compare himself with the aged high priest in the book he had seen in the Daigo Temple. He felt perhaps that he preferred the role of Chuta, the intermediary.

Beautiful things always intimidate me, Shunsuké thought. More than that, sometimes they drag me down. How can that be? Is it a superstition that beauty elevates mankind?

Kawada spoke to Yuichi about his choice of a profession. Yuichi half-humorously said that once he started depending on his in-laws he would probably not be able to hold his head up in their presence for the rest of his life.

'Do you have a wife?' asked Kawada, surprised.

'Don't worry, Kawada, old fellow,' the old novelist put in, before he realized what he was saying. 'Don't worry. This young man is Hippolyte.' The meaning of this slightly clumsy metaphor was quickly understood by Kawada.

'Fine. Hippolyte, that's good. I'd like to do what I can in the matter of finding employment for you.'

Their dinner progressed pleasantly. Even Shunsuké was cheerful. He felt a strange pride at seeing the desire mounting in Kawada's eyes as he looked at Yuichi.

Kawada sent the waitresses away. He wanted to talk of something in the past that he had never told anyone about. He had looked forward to the opportunity of telling this to Shunsuké. It seems he had maintained his bachelorhood up until this time only by heroic effort. He had even had to take desperate measures when he was in Berlin. When it was nearly time to return home, he had deliberately lavished money on a low-class prostitute and, holding his nose, had moved in with her. He then sent a letter off to his parents for permission to marry. The elder Yaichiro Kawada had some business to do in Germany and stopped by to have a look at his son's intended wife. He was shocked when he saw her.

The son pleaded that if he was not permitted to marry her he would die, and displayed the revolver in his inside pocket to show he meant it. The woman acted as one would have expected her to. The elder Yaichiro Kawada was a man of dispatch. He gave this pure-hearted German 'lotus in the mud' money to help her bear her lot, and by way of controlling his son, took him back to Japan on the *Chichibu Maru*. On the ship's deck, he never left his son's side. His anxious eyes were always fixed on the region of his son's belt, ready to grab it if the boy tried to jump overboard.

When he got back to Japan, the son would listen to no marriage proposal. He could not forget his German Cornelia. On his desk there was always a picture of her. When it came to work he became a practical, hard German taskmaster; when it came to living, he acted the part of a pure German dreamer. He persisted in this conduct and remained single.

Kawada tasted to the less the pleasure of pretending to be what he himself despised. Romanticism and the habit of dreaming were among the utterly stupid things he had discovered in Germany. Just as a traveller buys by impulse, he out of his great wisdom bought and donned the flimsy hat and mask needed for his fancy ball. Chaste emotions and certainty of the superiority of the inner world in the style of Novalis, and out of reaction to them a dry-as-dust practical life and a misanthropic will: these he maintained effortlessly until the time when these attitudes were no longer suited to him. He lived ostensibly by an idea he felt would never affect him. Perhaps Kawada's facial twitch had come from this constant internal betrayal. When there was talk of his marriage, he put on a show of misery that he had enacted so many times before. Everyone found it easy to believe at such times that his eyes were fixed on the vision of Cornelia.

'I looked over there. Exactly in the direction of the lintel,' he said, indicating with the hand that held his saké cup. 'There. Don't my eyes look just as if they're fixed on a memory?'

'Your glasses are shining. Unfortunately we can't see your eyes,' Shunsuké said. Kawada took off his glasses and rolled his eyes upwards. Shunsuké and Yuichi laughed at him.

Cornelia was in truth a double memory. First, Kawada, playing the part in the memory, fooled Cornelia. After that, he became the person he himself had been in Cornelia's memory and fooled others. So that he might create the legend about himself, Cornelia absolutely had to exist. The woman who existed by not being loved – consciousness of her was a phantasmagoric image in his heart. If he did not establish the reasons for his lifelong bondage to that image, it would disappear. She became the generic term for all the diversity of which his life had been capable, the incarnation of the negative power that would carry his real life through its course. Now Kawada himself could not believe that she was mean and ugly;

he saw her as nothing less than an extraordinarily beautiful woman. When his father died, he resolutely burned his vulgar pictures of Cornelia.

This story moved Yuichi. If it is wrong to say moved, let us say intoxicated: 'Cornelia really exists!' Let it needlessly be added that the youth was thinking of Mrs Kaburagi, who through absence had acquired a beauty unknown in the world.

*

It was nine o'clock. Yaichiro Kawada untied his bib and glanced at his watch. Shunsuké felt himself shiver faintly.

One should not think that Shunsuké had descended to the level of this worldly creature. His abysmal feeling of impotence had its source in Yuichi.

'Well,' Kawada said, 'this evening I'm going to Kamakura for the night. I'm going to stay at the Kofuen.'

Yuichi felt that the die had been cast before his eyes. The roundabout formality of soliciting a man is quite different from that of approaching a woman. All the limitless twists and turns of the hypocritical joys of heterosexuality are closed to homosexuals. If Kawada desired Yuichi's body this evening, politeness required that he ask for it. This Narcissus looked at the middle-aged man and the old man, neither of whom held for him so much as an infinitesimal amount of charm. They had completely forgotten their worldliness and were making a fuss over him alone. They were not concerned in the slightest about his mind. Only his body was of supreme concern, and he felt something different from the thrill of sensuality a woman would feel under these circumstances. It was as if his body had become independent of himself, and he himself was a second person admiring that independent body. His soul, while trampling upon and vilifying his first body, clung to that admired body and attempted to achieve a tenuous balance. He was finding a pleasure rare in the world!

'I always speak my mind, and I hope you'll forgive me if I say something that may trouble you, but Yuichi is not really your nephew, is he?'

'Really? No, not a real nephew. But, after all, even though there might be such a thing as a real friend, I'm not sure that there is such a thing as a real nephew.' This was Shunsuké's novelist's way of giving a straight answer.

'And if I may ask another question, are you and Yuichi only friends? Or –'

'You're wondering if we're lovers, aren't you? I'm not of the age for love.'

The two men almost simultaneously looked over at the beautiful eyelashes of the youth sitting cross-legged beside them, holding a folded bib in his hand and looking away from them, calmly smoking. A roguish beauty had come to dwell upon Yuichi.

'That's all I wanted to ask, and I feel better,' Kawada said, deliberately not looking at Yuichi. As he said these words a tic ran down his cheek like a jagged underscoring drawn by a soft, broad-pointed pencil. 'Well, I hate to break up the party, but we have talked about a lot of things, and I've really enjoyed it. From now on I'd like very much to have a secret meeting with the same people at least once a month. I'll look around to see if I can find a better place. When it comes to the mob that congregates at Rudon's, they're not really worth talking to, and I never have any opportunities to chat like this. At the bars of that kind in Berlin, now, first-class nobility, industrialists, poets, novelists, and actors used to appear.' It was typical that he should list them in that order. In short, in this unconscious grouping, he obviously displayed the German *Bürger* thinking which he had convinced himself was all a pretence.

In the darkness before the gate of the restaurant two automobiles were parked on the not very wide, sloping street. One was Kawada's Cadillac 62. The other was a hired cab.

The night wind was still cold, the sky cloudy. In this section there were a good many houses that had been built after the fire bombings, and there was a strangely brand-new board fence built in continuation of a stone wall with a ruined corner repaired with zinc-covered boards. The colour of the fresh white lumber was livid, almost lurid under the faint gleam of the street lights.

Only Shunsuké hesitated, putting on his gloves. In front of this old man solemnly pulling on his leather gloves, Kawada covertly touched Yuichi's finger with his bare hand and toyed

265

with it. Then the time came when it had to be decided which of the three would be left alone in one of the cars. Kawada said good night and in a perfectly natural way put his hand on Yuichi's shoulder and led him to his own car. Shunsuké dared not follow. He still had hope, however. When Yuichi, propelled by Kawada, had one shoe on the running board of the Cadillac, he turned and said in a cheerful voice: 'Oh, sir, I'm going along with Mr Kawada; would you be so kind as to call my wife?'

'Tell her he is staying over at your house,' said Kawada.

The hostess who was seeing them off said: 'My, the awful problems men do have.'

And thus Shunsuké became the single passenger in the cab.

That was only a matter of a few seconds. Although the inevitability of this developing course of events was clear, watching it one could not escape the impression that it had resolved itself quite suddenly. Of what Yuichi was thinking, with what feelings he had followed Kawada, Shunsuké knew nothing. For all he knew, Yuichi, with the attitude of a child, simply wanted to take the drive to Kamakura. The only thing clear was that he, Shunsuké, had again been ousted.

The car passed through the deteriorating shopping section of the old city. He felt the rows of street lights slipping by at the edges of his vision. When he thought so intently about Yuichi, he was pushed down to the realm of beauty alone. Perhaps deeper. There, behaviour became lost; everything became resolved into spirit, into nothing but shadows, nothing but metaphors. He was spirit itself – namely, a metaphor of the body. When would he be able to arise from this metaphor? Not only that, should he be content with his destiny? Should he puncture the conviction that held that since he was of this world he must die? At any rate, the heart of this aged Chuta almost reached the point of anguish.

22

The Seducer

When he got home, Shunsuké immediately dashed off a letter
to Yuichi. The passion that had gone with writing in the old
French diary revived, and the brush with which he wrote the
letter dripped oaths, gushed hatred. Naturally he was incapable
of directing that animus towards Yuichi. Shunsuké took the
anger of the present and used it to inflate all the more his
unyielding resentment against the vagina.

As he cooled down a little in the process of writing, he
recognized that his tedious, emotional letter was not very per-
suasive. It was not a love letter. It was an order. He rewrote it,
slipped it in an envelope, and ran his tongue along the glued
flap. The hard Western paper cut his lip. He stood in front of
the mirror, pressed a handkerchief against the cut, and mumbled: 'Yuichi will do as I say. He will do just what it says in
the letter. That much is clear. The orders in the letter will not
go against his desires. The parts of it that he doesn't like will
still be under my control.'

He walked about the room in the deep night. If he stood still
for a moment he could not keep from seeing Yuichi's form in
that Kamakura inn. He closed his eyes and crouched before
the three-way mirror. In the mirror, which he could not see,
flashed a vision of a naked Yuichi lying supine on a white
sheet, his lovely, strong head and shoulders fallen away from
the pillow and slumped down on the tatami. His throat, held
back as it was, appeared faintly white, perhaps because of the
moonlight falling upon it. The old author lifted his bloodshot
eyes and looked at the mirror. The sleeping form of Endymion
had vanished.

*

Yuichi's spring vacation was over. The last year of his student life was about to begin. His class was the last under the old system.

On the edge of the thick wood that ringed the college pond, numerous grassy hummocks formed a rolling landscape towards the sports field. The green of the grass was still pale. Though the sky was clear, the wind was cold. At such times as the lunch hour, however, students could be seen here and roundabout on the lawn. The season when lunch could be eaten out of doors had arrived.

They lay sprawled about at their ease, careless of how they looked, sat cross-legged, chewed on fine, bright-green wicks of grass they picked, and watched the athletes busily moving about the field. One of the athletes pranced near. When his shadow, small at noon, stood for a solitary moment on the sand, he seemed bewildered, embarrassed, deserted, ready to turn to the supreme naked body in the sky and shout: 'Hey! Hurry back, please! Hurry back and dominate me! I'm dying of embarrassment! Soon! Now!' The athlete jumped back upon his shadow. His heels adhered to the darker heels beneath them. The sun shone abroad; there were no clouds.

Yuichi, wearing a suit, sat on the grass. A literature student engrossed in Greek language studies told him the plot of Euripides' *Hippolytus* in reply to his questions.

'Hippolytus came to a tragic end. He was chaste, stainlessly pure and innocent, and he died under a curse, believing in his own innocence. Hippolytus' ambitions, however, were really quite small; his wishes were something that could be granted to anyone.'

The young pedant in spectacles recited a speech of Hippolytus in Greek. When Yuichi asked what it meant, he translated: ' "I would like to conquer all the men of Greece in the games and become the champion. However, I would not mind taking second place in the city if I could live happily with virtuous friends. Indeed, there lies the true happiness. And since, thus, freedom from danger will give me joy greater than that of a king..." '

His hopes were something that could be granted to anyone, were they? Perhaps not, Yuichi thought. Beyond that, how-

268

ever, his thoughts did not go. As for Shunsuké, here's how he would think: this ever so small wish of Hippolytus could never be granted. Thus his wish was the symbol of pure human desire, a brilliant, resplendent thing.

Yuichi thought about the contents of the letter he had received from Shunsuké. The letter had its charm. It was an order to act, no matter how artificial the action. Moreover – and this took for granted faith in Shunsuké – such action had a safety valve in complete, cynical blasphemy. None of his plans were tedious, that much could be said for him.

'Of course; now I remember,' the young man said to himself. 'I remember my telling him once that I wanted to give myself to something, even something false – even something purposeless. He must have remembered that and cooked up this plan. Mr Hinoki is a bit of a scoundrel.' He smiled. At that very moment left-wing students were parading in twos and threes at the edge of the grassy elevation. It occurred to him that they, too, were moved by the same impulse as he.

It was one o'clock. The bell in the clock tower sounded. The students got to their feet. They brushed away the dirt and the grass stems that clung to their uniforms. Yuichi's coat, too, held the light dust of spring, dried grass, and lawn clippings. The friend who brushed him was struck again with admiration at the tailoring of the coat he wore so casually.

His friends went to their classrooms. Yuichi, who had a date with Kyoko, left them and walked alone in the direction of the main gate. There he was surprised to see Jackie, dressed like a student, getting off the trolley along with four or five others. This so astonished him that he failed to get aboard.

They shook hands. Yuichi said nothing as he looked Jackie full in the face. To an onlooker, surely these two would have seemed to be nothing more than two carefree classmates. Under the bright noontime sun, Jackie was hiding at least twenty years of time, age, and experience.

After a while Jackie, laughing loudly at Yuichi's amazement, led him into the shade of the trees along the street, to the side of the school fence festooned with political posters of all shapes and colours. There he explained in detail the reasons for his disguise. He could pick out a youth of his persuasion at a glance, but as a result his palate had become jaded with adventures of that sort. For the same seductive purposes, however, he had come to wish that he could fool another completely – one who would be much more at ease if his lover were a classmate. There would be mutual esteem, an absence of inhibition, and a pleasant aftertaste. Jackie had a student uniform copied for him, and with great deliberation came hunting from Oiso to this harem of young men.

Jackie looked quite content with Yuichi's loud praise of his youthfulness. He asked in a somewhat hurt tone why Yuichi did not come to enjoy himself at Oiso. He braced himself against a tree with one hand, crossed his legs gracefully, and with a look that said 'I don't care,' drummed with his fingers on the posters on the fence. 'Huh, they've been making the same statements for twenty years,' the ageless youth muttered.

The trolley came. Yuichi left Jackie and rode away.

*

Kyoko was to meet Yuichi in the clubhouse of the international tennis club in the Imperial Palace grounds. She played tennis until noon. She changed her clothes. She ate. She chatted with her tennis companions. After they left, she remained alone in a tennis chair.

The scent of her Black Satin perfume mingled with faint perspiration rose from her flushed cheeks like a vague anxiety undermining her sweet after-exercise fatigue in the dry, windless air of high noon. She wondered if she had put on too much. She took a hand mirror out of her navy-blue handbag and looked in it. The mirror couldn't reflect the smell of perfume, but it satisfied her and she put it away.

She didn't wear light-coloured coats in spring; the navy-blue coat she had chosen so deliberately was spread over the white chair. It protected her tender back from the rough frame of the chair. Her bag and shoes were of the same blue; her suit and gloves were salmon pink, her favourite shade.

It would be well to say that Kyoko Hodaka did not love Yuichi in the slightest. Her frivolous heart was exceedingly pliant. In the lightness of her feelings there was an elegance

270

that fell short of any standard of purity. Once in the depth of her heart a fairly sincere yearning for self-deception had suddenly flared up and then gone out, without any awareness on her part. Kyoko had one resolve, one self-imposed, indispensable, easily fulfilled duty: never to keep watch over her own heart. 'I haven't seen him for a month and a half,' she said. 'That seems like a day. In that time I haven't thought of that man once.'

One and a half months! What in the world did Kyoko do with herself? Countless dances. Countless movies. Tennis. Shopping. All kinds of Foreign Office parties she had to attend with her husband. The beauty parlour. Drives. A fantastic number of useless arguments about various loves and infidelities. Countless notions and whims encountered in the course of keeping house.

The oil landscape painting, for instance, that graced the wall of the stairway landing had been moved during that time to the wall of the entranceway. Then it was taken to the guest room. Then she changed her mind and hung it again on the landing where it had been originally. She rearranged the kitchen and found fifty-three empty bottles. She sold them to the junkman and with the money, supplemented by some of her pocket money, bought a table lamp made from a curaçao bottle. She soon decided she didn't like that and gave it to a friend, receiving in exchange a bottle of Cointreau. Then the shepherd dog she was raising got distemper. He frothed at the mouth, trembled in all four legs, and without making a sound died with what looked like a smile on his face. Kyoko cried for three hours; the next day she had forgotten it.

Her life was filled with immeasurable amounts of stylish rubbish. It had been like that since her girlhood, when she was infected with a bug for collecting safety pins, and filled lacquer boxes with safety pins large and small. The same kind of fever that is referred to in poor women as being 'the fever of their existence' motivated the life of Kyoko. But if hers was an earnest existence, it was marked by an earnestness which did not in the least stand in the way of her frivolousness. An earnest existence that knows no distress is apt to have trouble finding an outlet.

271

Like a butterfly that flits into a room and flutters madly about when it can find no open windows, Kyoko, too, lived her restless inner life. Not even the zaniest butterfly, however, is apt to believe that the room into which it has flown is its own. Sometimes, indeed, exhausted butterflies collide with forests on painted landscapes and fall unconscious.

No one saw clearly the state of the stupefaction into which Kyoko, like that butterfly, would sometimes fall – a wide-eyed, confused absence of mind. Her husband would think to himself only: It's started again. Her friends and her cousins would think nothing more than: She's in love again – for a half day, no more.

*

The phone rang in the club. It was the guard at the front gate asking if he could give a man named Minami an entrance pass. Before long Kyoko saw Yuichi walking through the pine trees on the other side of the opening in the great stone wall.

In all her punctilious self-respect, she was content that the youth had come on time to this deliberately conceived, out-of-the-way meeting place. It gave her ample pretext to forgive him for his neglect of her. However, she didn't venture to rise; she bowed to him while holding five brightly painted fingernails before her smiling face.

'It's only been a short time since I've seen you, but somehow you've changed,' she said, partly as an excuse for looking him full in the face.

'How?'

'Hm-m. Something a little as if a wild animal has developed.'

Yuichi laughed uproariously on hearing this. Kyoko saw in his laughing mouth the white teeth of a carnivorous beast. Formerly Yuichi had mystified her more; he had seemed more docile, yet lacking in conviction. Now, as he had come striding directly out of the maple shade and into the sunlight, with his hair glistening, and as he had stopped after about twenty paces and looked this way, he had seemed like a lone young lion seething with fresh energy, his eyes gleaming with youthful mistrust.

272

His beautiful eyes looked at Kyoko directly; they did not waver. Their gaze was incomparably gentle, and at the same time they rudely, tersely, told of his desire.

In the short time I haven't seen him he's come a long way, Kyoko thought. It must be the tutelage of Mrs Kaburagi. But now that things have gone sour between him and Mrs Kaburagi, and he's stopped working as her husband's private secretary while she's gone off to Kyoto, I am going to reap the harvest of it all.

They couldn't hear the horns of the cars beyond the moat across the stone wall. All they could hear was the sound of tennis balls and rackets repeatedly striking each other. There were only happy voices and shouts and quick laughter with laboured breath. These evaporated into the air and struck the ear only infrequently – languid, opaque sounds, seemingly covered with dust.

'Do you have anything to do today, Yuchan?'

'No, I'm free all day.'

'Was there anything? With me that is?'

'Not really. I just wanted to see you.'

'Aren't you sweet.'

The two conferred and came up with the quite predictable plan of going to a movie, then to dinner, then dancing. Before that they would take a little walk, even though it was the long way round, leaving the Imperial Palace at the Hirakawa gate. The path went by the side of the Equestrian Club under the old second circle and crossed a bridge behind the stables. Then it ascended to the third circle where the library was, and arrived at the Hirakawa gate.

When they started walking and were struck by the gentle wind, Kyoko felt a certain feverishness in her cheeks. She worried for a moment that she was becoming ill. Really, though, it was the spring.

The beautiful profile of the youth walking beside her filled Kyoko with pride. His arm every once in a while brushed lightly against hers. The fact that her escort was beautiful was to her the most direct and objective authentication of the fact that together they made a beautiful couple. The reason Kyoko liked Yuichi was that he gave her an overwhelming sense of safety and security in her own beauty. With every step she took, a line of salmon pink could be glimpsed within the unbuttoned freedom of her elegant, blue, princess-style coat, like a bright vein of cinnabar.

Between the offices of the Equestrian Club and the stables, the broad plaza had dried out. In one place dust danced faintly; then it died away as the breeze dropped. The two started to cross towards this visionary whirlwind, when they were met by the noise of a procession carrying flags diagonally across the plaza. It was a procession made up entirely of old people from the country. It was a group of gold-star relatives of men who had died in the Second World War, invited to a visit at the Imperial Palace.

It was a slow-moving procession. Many of its members wore *getas* and honest old-fashioned clothes, with old soft felt hats on their heads. Bent old women, their necks thrust forward, seemed as if they would lose the bath towels each wore rolled into a ball protruding from an otherwise bare bosom. Even though it was spring, from the collars of some, edges of raw cotton padding stuck out; the glow of that countrified silkiness outlined the wrinkles in their sunburned necks. All one could hear was the sound of tired *getas* and *zori* grinding against the earth and of false teeth clacking with each stride. With all their fatigue and their pious joy the pilgrims were scarcely able to speak a word.

Kyoko and Yuichi had much trouble passing them. Everyone in the procession of old people looked towards the two of them. Even people who were looking down sensed that something was up and raised their eyes to look at the couple, with a gaze that did not waver.

It was a look without the slightest shade of criticism, and at the same time, of supreme openness. This multitude of eyes like black stones stared cunningly and fixedly out of the wrinkles, and the gummy secretions, and the tears, and the white cataracts, and the dirty veins. Yuichi involuntarily hastened his pace, but Kyoko was unperturbed. She simply and accurately read the truth. Surely it was her beauty alone that struck them.

The procession of pilgrims passed, slowly undulating in the direction of the Imperial Household Agency.

They went along the side of the stables and entered a dark, shaded path. They locked arms. Before their eyes there was a slight rise, with an earthen bridge built in conformity with the uphill slope. Ramparts surrounded the hill area. Near the summit there was a single cherry tree in the very centre of a group of pines.

A one-horse carriage reserved for court use came down the hill and scuttled past the two pedestrians. The horse's mane fluttered in the wind; the sixteen-petalled gold chrysanthemum passed resplendently before their eyes. The two climbed the hill. From the plateau of the old third circle they could look for the first time at the panorama of the city on the other side of the stone wall.

With what freshness did the whole city come together to strike the eye! The slippery comings and goings of the shining autos – what animated life they bore! The businesslike afternoon prosperity of Noshikicho across the moat! The revolutions of the countless anemometers on the meteorological station! With what loving exertion they lent their ears to the many winds passing through the sky, offering them such charms! How indefatigably they spun about!

The two went out through the Hirakawa gate. They had not walked enough yet; so they strolled along the edge of the moat for a time. As they did so, there in the very middle of this aimless afternoon walk, in the very middle of the auto horns and the earth-shaking rumble of trucks, Kyoko came to savour something close to a real sense of what life is.

*

In the Yuichi of that day there was certainly that 'real sense', strange though the phrase is. It was almost as if he were convinced that he was impersonating the man he most wished to be. This consciousness of beauty, this endowment with substance, as it were, was to Kyoko particularly essential. Until now this beautiful youth had seemed to comprise only bits and pieces of sexuality. His sharp brows, his deep set eyes, the marvellous ridge of his nose, his artless lips, had always brought Kyoko joy, but after the simple enumeration of these parts, there had been the feeling that the most important thing was missing.

'You certainly don't look like a married man!' Kyoko opened her innocently incredulous eyes as she burst out with this.

'Yes, somehow I feel like a bachelor.' They looked at each other and laughed at this rejoinder.

Kyoko never touched upon the subject of Mrs Kaburagi, and Yuichi too made it a point never to broach the subject of Namiki, who had gone to Yokohama with them. This courtesy helped them to get on well together, and the reflection in Kyoko's mind that he had been jilted by Mrs Kaburagi just as she had been thrown over by Namiki served only to make her feel closer to the youth.

At the risk of being prolix, however, it must be said that Kyoko no longer loved Yuichi in the slightest. There was in this meeting with him only an undiscriminating joy, a delight. She drifted. Her truly light heart drifted like a plant seed carried by the wind, tufted with white thistledown. A seducer doesn't always go after a woman he loves. A woman like this, weighed down by nothing spiritual, standing on tiptoe within herself, as much a dreamer as she was a realist, was the ripest bait for the seducer.

On this point Mrs Kaburagi and Kyoko were diametric opposites. Kyoko had the ability to ignore any kind of irrationality, to close her eyes to any kind of absurdity, while never forgetting her conviction that the party in question was in love with her. Observing how gentle was Yuichi's attitude towards her, and how he never flirted with another woman – in fact she was the only one he seemed never to tire of looking at – Kyoko's reaction was very much what one would expect. She was happy.

*

They had dinner at the M— Club near Sukiyabashi.

This club, which had been raided by the police recently because of big-time gambling, was the gathering place for broken-down expatriate Americans and Jews. Through the Second

276

World War, the occupation, and the Korean War, this group, accustomed to scalping for profit, hid under their brand-new suits (along with sundry tattoos of roses and anchors and nude women and hearts and black panthers and capital letters on both arms and chest) the mysterious smells of the countless ports of the various countries of Asia. Somewhere deep in their – at first glance – gentle blue eyes, the memory of opium transactions gleamed, and the lingering view of some harbour somewhere, filled with myriad shouts and a profusion of masts – Pusan, Mokpo, Dairen, Tientsin, Tsingtao, Shanghai, Keelung, Amoy, Hong Kong, Macao, Hanoi, Haiphong, Manila, Singapore.

Even after they had returned to their home country, the entry 'Far East hand' remained, a single, mysterious, dark line in black ink in their personal histories. For the rest of their lives they could not escape the tiny, ugly aura of glory that hovers over men who have thrust their hands into exotic soil in search of gold dust.

The decor of this night club was entirely Chinese; Kyoko regretted that she had not come in her Chinese dress. Of Japanese guests there were only a few Shimbashi geisha who had been brought here by foreigners. The rest were all Westerners. On Kyoko's and Yuichi's table a three-inch candle burned in a frosted-glass cylinder on which a little green dragon had been painted. In the pandemonium around it, the flame burned with an uncanny quietness.

The two ate, drank, and danced. They were after all young enough. Drunk with the feeling of closeness engendered by this youthfulness, Kyoko forgot her husband. Even if she didn't have this special provocation, it would have been no problem for her to forget him. When she decided to close her eyes and forget him, she could do it even though he was there in front of her.

For Yuichi, however, this was the first time that he had ever joyfully played the part of one in love. This was the first time he had ever seen himself press against a woman in such masculine fashion. Usually such behaviour brought about an adverse reaction in Kyoko and cooled her ardour, but this time she happened to think that he was faithfully responding to her

277

own mood of exhilaration. When I stop liking a man, he always gets excited about me, she thought to herself, without the slightest rancour.

The blood-red sloe gin fizz she had imbibed imparted a drunken glide to Kyoko's dancing. She leaned against Yuichi, her body lighter than a feather, feeling as if her feet barely touched the floor as she danced. The basement dance floor was surrounded by tables on three sides. Facing it in the darkness was an orchestra stand with a scarlet drapery hung behind it. The musicians played 'Slow Poke', which was very popular. They played 'Blue Tango' and 'Taboo'. Yuichi, who had taken third prize in that contest some time ago, danced well; his breast pressed steadfastly against Kyoko's small, soft, padded bosom. As for Kyoko, she looked across Yuichi's shoulder at the darkened faces of the people at the tables and at the sprinkling of heads of golden hair brightened at the edges by dim halos. At tables here and there she saw the wavering little dragons, green, yellow, red, blue, on the frosted-glass candle shades.

'You had a big dragon on your Chinese dress that time, didn't you?' Yuichi said.

It was a coincidence that could have been born only from emotions so close that they were almost identical. Kyoko was seized with the desire to keep this tiny secret to herself, so she did not confess that she, too, had been thinking about the dragon, and answered: 'Yes, it was in a pattern of white satin; you remember it well. Do you remember how we danced five dances in a row?'

'M-m-m, I was fascinated by your face with its little smile. After that, when I saw women smile and compared theirs with yours, they never satisfied me.'

This flattery touched Kyoko deeply. She remembered how as a child she had been continually and severely criticized by her outspoken cousin for showing her gums when she smiled. After that, she spent ten years in practice before a mirror, and learned never to let her gums show. Now Kyoko showed extraordinary confidence in the light, wavy motion of her smile.

A woman who is complimented feels, spiritually, something

familiar to prostitutes. Yuichi fell in with the easy-going behaviour of the foreigners and took the opportunity to allow his
smiling lips to brush against Kyoko's lips.

Kyoko, though a giddy creature, was not a wanton. The
dance, the wine, and the influence of this expatriate-style club
were not equal to the task of making her romantic. She became
only a trifle too tender, and a little too tearfully sympathetic.

In the bottom of her heart she believed that the plight of all
men in the world was an unfortunate one. It was a religious
prejudice with her. The only thing she had managed to see in
Yuichi was his common everyday youthfulness. But since
what we call beauty is basically so far removed from originality, surely there was nothing original to be found in this beautiful youth! Trembling in sympathy, Kyoko felt like shedding
conventional tears at the loneliness of men, at the animal
hungers and thirsts of men, at all the shackles of desire that
make man seem so tragic.

This overwhelming emotion subsided, however, when they
got back to their seats. They said little. Seeming to be searching
for something to say, perhaps for an excuse to touch Kyoko's
hand, Yuichi took notice of her unusual wrist watch and asked
if he might look at it. The tiny dial was difficult to read in the
gloom even if one looked very closely. Kyoko took it off and
handed it to him. Yuichi then told her stories about various
Swiss watch companies, with a knowledge whose extent surprised her.

'What time is it now?' she asked.

Yuichi looked at the two watches and said: 'Ten minutes to
ten; yours says a quarter to ten,' and handed her watch back.
They would have to wait more than two hours for the floor
show.

'Let's go somewhere else, shall we?'

'Let's,' she said, looking at her watch again. Her husband
was playing mah-jongg and wouldn't be back before midnight.
It would be all right if she returned about then.

Kyoko stood up. As she did so, a slight wavering showed her
intoxication. Yuichi noticed it and took her arm. Kyoko felt as
if she were walking on deep sand.

*

In the car Kyoko felt quite foolishly generous and brought her lips very close to Yuichi's. In response, his lips displayed a joyous, brutal power. The light of the tall neon signs coming through the window on to her face cradled in her arms flowed into the corners of her eyes. There was in all the rapidity of that flow a current that did not move. The youth realized that it was tears. She realized it, too, at about the same time, when she felt the cold flow on her temple. Yuichi touched it with his lips and with his lips drank a woman's tears.

Kyoko's teeth shone dimly white in the unlighted interior of the car; she called Yuichi's name over and over in an almost inaudible voice. Then she closed her eyes. Her faintly moving lips burned in anticipation of being held again suddenly by that brutal power; then the anticipation became reality. The second kiss, however, had in it the ease of something long settled. It was not exactly what Kyoko had anticipated; it gave her time to act as if she had regained her composure. The woman sat up and gently detached herself from Yuichi's arms.

Kyoko sat on the edge of the seat and, throwing back her head, looked in the mirror she held aloft in one hand. Her eyes were slightly red and wet, her hair somewhat mussed.

While she put her face in order she said: 'If we keep this up, I don't know what's going to happen. That's enough of that.'

She stole a look at the stiff nape of the neck turned towards her by the middle-aged driver. Her conventionally virtuous heart saw in the back of that ancient blue suit the symbol of all society turning its back.

At the night club in Tsukiji, owned by a foreigner, Kyoko repeated, in words that were becoming habitual: 'I have to go soon.' This club was, in contrast to the last Chinese-style place, entirely of modern American construction. Kyoko kept suggesting they go, and kept on drinking.

She went on thinking about one thing after another. As she thought about each, she forgot what she was thinking about. As she grew gay and danced, she felt as if she had roller skates attached to the soles of her shoes. There in Yuichi's arms, it hurt her to breathe. The quickened pulse of her intoxication communicated itself to Yuichi.

She looked at the American couples and soldiers as they danced. Then she suddenly pulled her head back and looked hard at Yuichi. She insistently asked him whether she was drunk. She was very much relieved when he told her she was not. If she was sober, she could still walk home to Akasaka, she thought.

They went back to their seats. She felt quite composed. Then she was struck by vague doubts. She looked with dissatisfaction at Yuichi, who had not embraced her so tightly as she had wished. As she looked at him a dark joy burst its bonds inside her and came welling up.

This heart of hers, still certain that she was not in love with this beautiful youth, was fully aware. However, she realized that she had never felt this same deep sense of surrender with any other man. The compelling beat of the bass drum in the Western music drove her into a state of rapture.

This feeling of receptiveness – that one must call almost a natural impulse – brought her heart close to a kind of universality. That feeling, like evening coming over the moor, with long shadows thrust out by thick undergrowth, hill and valley bathed each in its own shadows – that feeling of wishing to be wrapped in ecstasy and twilight – transfigured Kyoko. She thought she saw this young, manly head, moving against a pale backlighting, merging with a shadow spread out like a pool above her. Her inner feelings overflowed outward; inwardness impinged upon things outside. Beset by the height of drunkenness, she shivered.

She believed, however, that she would sleep this evening in the bosom of her husband.

'This is living!' her giddy heart exulted. 'This is really living! What thrills and what release! What a dangerous dream of adventure! What fulfilment for the imagination! Tonight in the taste of my husband's kisses I shall be reminded of the lips of this youth! What safe and at the same time supremely adulterous joy! I can stop there. That far I'm in control. As for anything else, the best way. . . .'

Kyoko called one of the waiters in scarlet uniform with gold buttons and asked him what time the floor show would start. Midnight, he told her.

'We won't be able to see the show here. I'll have to leave at eleven thirty. We still have forty minutes.'

At her urging, Yuichi danced with her again. The music stopped, and they went back to their table. The American band leader grasped the microphone with tremendous fingers, on one of which golden hair and a ring with a beryl glittered, and introduced himself in English. The foreigners laughed and applauded.

The musicians broke into a fast rumba. The lights went off. Lights glowed on the dressing room door. Then the catlike forms of the rumba dancers, a man and a woman, glided out of the half-open door.

Their silk costumes fluttered in great pleats. Countless tiny, embroidered, round metal scales shimmered, green, gold, and orange. The hips of the man and woman, shining in silk, were like lizards in the grass. They drew together. Then they separated.

Kyoko rested her elbows on the tablecloth, held her throbbing temples with painted fingernails that seemed as if they would penetrate into her head, and watched. The pain caused by the fingernails was as pleasant as peppermint.

Suddenly she looked at her watch.

'We'll have to be getting –' She became concerned and held the watch to her ear. 'What happened? The show started an hour early or something.'

She was distinctly alarmed. She bent over and looked at the wrist watch on Yuichi's left hand resting on the table.

'That's strange. Same time.'

Kyoko watched the dancers again. She stared at the male dancer, whose mouth was shaped in a sneer. She was trying with all her might to think of something. The music and the tapping of feet, however, interfered. She stood up, not knowing why. She staggered as she walked holding on to tables. Yuichi stood up and went with her. She stopped one of the waiters and asked him: 'What time is it?'

'Ten after twelve, ma'am.'

Kyoko brought her face up close to Yuichi's and said: 'You set the watches back, didn't you?'

A mischievous smile floated at the corners of Yuichi's mouth: 'Uh-huh.'

Kyoko was not angry: 'I can still make it. I must go.'

Yuichi's face became more serious: 'Must you?'

'Yes, I'm going.'

At the checkroom she said, 'My, I'm really tired today. I played tennis, walked, danced ...'

Holding up her hair in back, Kyoko slipped into the coat Yuichi was holding. Once she had the coat on she tossed her hair again broadly and gently. Her agate earrings, of the same colour as her clothing, waved wildly.

Kyoko pulled herself together. In the cab with Yuichi she took the initiative and gave the driver the location of her house in Akasaka. While the cab was on its way, she recalled the streetwalkers spreading their nets to catch foreigners at the door of the club. She thought about it confusedly.

Oh, my. That awful green suit! That painted brunette! That flat nose! To make matters worse, honest women can't smoke cigarettes as if they enjoy them like that. How good those cigarettes seemed to be!

The cab came closer to Akasaka. 'Turn left there, please. That's right. Straight ahead,' she said.

At that point, Yuichi, who had been silent, pinioned her arms forcefully and, burying his face in her hair, kissed the back of her neck. Kyoko could smell again the scent of the same pomade that had perfumed her dreams so many times.

'Now, at a time like this, I wish I could smoke,' she said to herself. 'That would be really stylish.'

Kyoko's eyes were open. She looked at the lights outside the window; she looked at the cloudy night sky. Suddenly she had the strange power to see everything as worthless. Another day was ending without incident. Only capricious, dispirited memories – lackadaisical, intermittent, and perhaps based on nothing other than weakness of imagination – would be left. Only the daily routine of life, assuming some strange, blood-curdling shape, would be left. Her fingertips rubbed against the young man's fresh-shaven nape. In the roughness and warmth of his skin there was a startling sensation.

Kyoko closed her eyes. The shaking of the cab made one fancy that the wretched road ran endlessly over a succession of ruts.

She opened her eyes and whispered in Yuichi's ear with an all-surpassing gentleness: 'All right, you win. We passed my house long ago.'

Yuichi's eyes gleamed with joy. 'To Yanagibashi,' he said quickly to the driver. Kyoko heard the squeal of the wheels making a U-turn. It might best be called a regretfully joyful squeal.

*

This imprudent decision had tired Kyoko considerably. Her fatigue and her drunkenness spun together about her. She had to struggle to keep from falling asleep. She used Yuichi's shoulder as a pillow and, out of the necessity of forcing herself to feel charming, she imagined she was a linnet or some such small bird closing her eyes.

At the entrance of an *avec* hotel bearing the name 'Kichijo', she said: 'How do you know about such places as this, darling?'

As she said it, she felt a numbness in her legs. She walked down the halls through which the maid conducted them with her face hidden against Yuichi's back. They went along an endlessly long zigzag hall and up a staircase that suddenly towered around a corner. The cold of the night hallways against stockinged feet made her head ring. She could barely stand. She wished they would get to the room where she could crumple into a sitting posture.

When they got to the room, Yuichi said: 'We can see the Sumida River. That building over there is a beer company warehouse.'

Kyoko didn't dare to look at the riverscape. She wanted only that everything be done with as quickly as possible.

*

Kyoko Hodaka woke up in complete darkness.

She could see nothing. The storm shutters had been drawn over the windows. Not a crack of light filtered through anywhere. Her bare bosom was cold, making her think the weather was getting colder. She groped about and drew together the collar of her well-starched hotel nightrobe. She reached her hand down. She was wearing nothing under the robe. She could not recall when last she had taken off every stitch. She could not recall when she had put on this stiff robe.

That was it! This room adjoined the room with the river view. She had surely come in here before Yuichi and undressed herself. Yuichi at that time had been on the other side of the partition. After a time, all the lights had been extinguished in the other room. Yuichi came from the dark room into the darker room. Kyoko kept her eyes closed tight. Then everything began marvellously and ended in dreams. Everything ended with indisputable perfection.

What happened after the lights in the room went out – and Yuichi's image – filled Kyoko's thoughts as she lay with her eyes closed. Even now she did not have the courage to touch the real Yuichi. His form was the incarnation of joy. In it were indescribably blended greenness and wisdom, youth and mastery, love and scorn, piety and sacrilege. Even now not the slightest resentment or guilt sufficed to dull Kyoko's joy; even her slight hangover could not alter it. After a time, her hand searched for Yuichi's hand.

Her hand touched that hand. It was cold. The bones protruded. It was dry like tree bark. The veins were hollow bulges and pulsed faintly. Kyoko shuddered and released the hand.

He coughed suddenly in the darkness. It was a long, gloom-enshrouded cough. It was a painful cough, dragging a tangled, muddy tail. It was a cough like death. Kyoko was touched by that cold dry arm and almost screamed. She felt as if she were sleeping with a skeleton.

She got up and felt about for the lamp that should have been by the pillows. Her fingers slipped fruitlessly about on the cold tatami. There was a lamp with a Japanese-lantern shade far from the pillows in one corner. She lit the lamp and discovered, resting on the pillow next to her vacant one, the face of an old man.

Shunsuké's cough, dragging tail and all, had stopped. He raised his eyes as if dazzled. He said: 'Shut it off, won't you?

It's too bright.' As he finished speaking, he closed his eyes again and turned his face away from the light.

Kyoko couldn't figure it all out; she stood up. She passed in back of Shunsuké's pillow and searched out her clothes in the garment box. Until the woman had put on her clothes, the old man lay silent, cunningly feigning sleep.

When she showed signs of leaving, he said: 'Are you going?'

The woman said nothing and started out.

'Wait, huh?'

Shunsuké got up.

He started to throw his padded dressing gown over his shoulders to stop the woman. Kyoko stopped, but showed every intention of leaving immediately.

'Wait, please. It's too late to go now.'

'I'm going. I'll scream if you stop me.'

'Go ahead. You don't have the courage to scream.'

Kyoko asked with her voice shaking: 'Where is Yuchan?'

'He went home long ago. He's now probably sleeping snug as a bug beside his wife.'

'Why have you done this? What have I done? What do you have against me? What do you hope to achieve? Have I done anything you hate me for?'

Shunsuké did not answer. He turned on the light in the room with the view of the river. Kyoko sat down as if struck by that ray of light.

'You don't blame Yuichi at all, do you?'

'How do I know? I don't even know what's going on.'

Kyoko stretched out and burst into tears. Shunsuké let her cry. It was impossible to explain all, even if Shunsuké understood everything. Kyoko did not deserve this much humiliation.

He waited for the woman to compose herself and then said: 'For a long time I was in love with you, but you turned me down and laughed at me. Even you must admit that I could not have brought this about by ordinary means.'

'Why did Yuchan do this?'

'He likes you in his own unique way.'

'You two were in cahoots, weren't you?'

'Not at all. I wrote the synopsis. Yuichi just lent a hand.'

'Oh, how ugly –'

'What's ugly? You wanted something beautiful and you got it. I wanted something beautiful, too, and I got it; that's all. Isn't that right? We're in the same line. When you talk about things being ugly, you're falling into self-contradiction.'

'I don't know whether I'm going to die or have you arrested.'

'Terrific! If you can give out with words like those, we've made a lot of progress in one night. But please try to be more frank. The humilation and the ugliness you're thinking about are all imaginary. For surely we've seen something beautiful. It's certain that we have, the two of us, seen something of the quality of a rainbow.'

'Why isn't Yuchan here?'

'Yuichi isn't here. He was here until a while ago, but he's not here any more. There's nothing mysterious about that. We have been left together, no one else.'

Kyoko shuddered. This approach to existence was beyond her powers of comprehension. Shunsuké went on unconcernedly.

'It's over, and we are left behind. Even though Yuichi went to bed with you, the result is six of one and half a dozen of another.'

'This is the first time in my life I have ever seen people so despicable as you two.'

'Now come, come. Why do you say "you two"? Yuichi is innocent. Today, for this one day, three people have done what they desire, that's all. Yuichi loved you in his fashion; you loved him in your fashion; I loved you in my fashion, that's all. Everybody loves in his own fashion; there's no other way, is there?'

'I can't figure out what Yuichi has in mind. That fellow is a spook!'

'You're a spook. After all, you loved a spook. But Yuichi doesn't hold the slightest particle of ill will towards you.'

'How could he do such a horrible thing to a person he didn't hold any ill will towards?'

'Briefly, he knew full well you had done nothing to deserve this. Between a man bearing no ill will and a guiltless woman –

who have not a thing to share with each other – if there is anything that might tie them together, it is ill will from the outside, guilt brought in from the outside, that's all. In all the old tales that's the very way it happens. As you know, I am a novelist.' Seized with the outright ridiculousness of it, he started to laugh by himself but then stopped.

'Yuichi and I weren't in cahoots or anything. That's a figment of your imagination. We simply had no connection. Yuichi and I – well –' He smiled slowly. 'We're just friends. If you must hate someone, hate me, to your heart's content.'

'But –' Kyoko twisted her body modestly as she cried: 'I don't have any room for hate; right now I'm just horrified.'

The whistle of a freight train crossing the near-by iron bridge reverberated in the night. It was an endless, monotonous, stumbling repetition. After a time, from the other side of the bridge it had just crossed, the train flashed a long whistle and then was silent.

Truthfully, the one who really saw the 'ugliness' was not Kyoko but Shunsuké. Even in the moment the woman raised her moan of pleasure, he did not forget his own ugliness.

Shunsuké Hinoki had known many times this awful moment in which the existence of something unloved intrudes upon an existence that is loved. Woman subjugated – that is a superstition created by novels! Woman can never be subjugated. Never! Just as there are occasions in which men out of their reverence for women attempt to humiliate them, there are occasions in which women as a manifestation of supreme contempt give their bodies to men. Mrs Kaburagi, of course, as well as every one of his three wives, had never once been conquered. Kyoko, anaesthetized into giving her body to a vision of Yuichi, was no different – incontrovertibly. If one needs reasons, there is only one. It was because Shunsuké himself was convinced that no one could love him.

These were strange intimacies. Shunsuké tortured Kyoko. He ruled now by a terrible power. But it added up to nothing more than the machinations of a person who was not loved. The conduct of Shunsuké, who from the beginning had had no hope, was marked by not the slightest mercy, by nothing of what society calls humanity.

Kyoko was silent. She was sitting straight up, without making a sound. To this flighty female, such a long period of silence was something that had never occurred before. Once she had learned this quietness, perhaps it would become the way she naturally comported herself. Shunsuké, too, kept his mouth closed. They seemed to believe they could go on here until dawn without saying a word. When night came to an end she would take the little tools out of her bag, make herself up, and return to her husband's house. It would be a long time, though, until the river whitened; the two people suspected this night would go on for ever.

23

Days of Ripening

Her husband's busy life, with its unknown motives, went on. When she thought he was at school, he would return home in the middle of the night; when she thought he was staying home, he would suddenly go out. Even though Yuichi was pursuing the daily existence of a 'ne'er-do-well', as his mother called him, Yasuko's life was now truly serene, one might say almost happy. There were reasons for her peace. She was oblivious to everything but what was going on inside her.

The comings and goings of spring excited in her not the slightest concern. Things outside her had no power. The sensation of little legs kicking within her, the sensation of nourishing tiny violence – it was all a continuing drunkenness that had started with her and would end with her. The so-called external world was possessed by her inner world; she embraced the world inside herself. The external world was simply superfluous.

When she imagined the small shiny ankles, and the small shiny soles covered with clean tiny wrinkles, thrust out of the deep night and kicking the darkness, she felt that her own existence had become nothing but the warm, blood-smeared, nourishing darkness itself. The feeling that she was being consumed, the feeling that her insides were being deeply violated, the feeling she was ill – above all, the feeling she was being deeply ravished: whatever the immoral desires or the indulgent sensations, they were ostentatiously pardoned there. Yasuko wore a smile of her very own, sent as from afar. Sometimes she laughed a transparent laugh; sometimes she did not laugh at all. Her smile was quite like a blind man's smile, a smile barely alight on the face of a person straining his ears for a distant sound that only he could hear.

If for just one day the child inside her did not move, her

anxiety was more than she could stand. Surely it was dead! It pleased her sweet mother-in-law considerably to be told of these childish fears and to be importuned into detailed consultations.

'It figures; Yuichi, too, is a boy who doesn't let his feelings come to the surface,' she said to her daughter-in-law, with a comforting look on her face. 'That must be why he goes out drinking. This baby coming must have him all mixed up, what with the joy of it and the anxiety of it.'

'No, I don't think so,' said Yasuko with conviction. For this self-sufficient spirit, comfort was unnecessary. 'Instead of that, what bothers me most is not knowing yet whether the child I'm carrying is a girl or a boy. What if I've pretty much decided that it's a boy, and am thinking of a child the image of Yuchan; what will I do if a girl just like me is born?'

'Oh, my! I'm hoping for a girl. I've had my fill of boys. Nothing is that hard to raise.'

Thus the two got along swimmingly. When Yasuko had things to do that would have taken her out of the house in all her embarrassing physical unshapeliness, her mother-in-law gladly went instead. But when this woman with her kidney ailment presented herself, escorted by Kiyo, the maid, few met her without rounding their eyes in surprise.

On one such day Yasuko, left home to mind the house, went into the garden for exercise. She walked around the backyard flower bed, only about four hundred yards in area, which was mostly kept up by the hard work of Kiyo. She held a pair of scissors, planning to cut some flowers for the living room.

Azaleas rimmed the garden, blooming at their best. Seasonal flowers – pansy, sweet pea, nasturtium, Rodger's bronze leaf, and hornwort – romantic flowers all, were blooming. She wondered which to cut. Actually, she wasn't very much concerned about the flowers. The luxury of choice, the ease of acquiring whichever she selected, the beauty of them all – what did it matter? She hesitated, clicking the scissors. The blades were a little rusty, and they resisted in her fingers with a slightly gritty sound.

Suddenly it occurred to her that she was thinking of Yuichi, a reflection that threw doubt into her mind about her maternal instincts. But was this not, after all, Yuichi? This lovely creature shut up inside her, that expressed such outright self-indulgencies, that however much violence it dealt would not be expelled until the appointed time – was it not, after all, he? Fearful that she might become discouraged when she saw the baby, she went so far as to think that this confining pregnancy might go on for years and she would not care.

Unconsciously she cut the stem of the light purple Rodger's bronze leaf in front of her. Left in her hand was a single blossom on a stem about the length of her finger. 'Now why did I cut such a short one?' she asked herself.

'Pure heart! Pure heart!' The words sounded empty and awkward. Yasuko was acutely aware in her mind's eye as to how greatly she had matured. What in the world is a purity that is close to a desire for vengeance? Hasn't it always given me pleasure to look into my husband's eyes with my special look of purity and then wait for his expression of guilt and embarrassment? All the various pleasures she anticipated her husband would not give her – and for that reason even the concealment of the purity of her heart – these things she wished to think of as her 'love'.

That serene hairline, however, those lovely eyes, the delicacy of the elaborate tracery between her mouth and nose, were almost noble, owing to a slightly anaemic skin colour. The loose garment she had specially made to hide the shape of the lower half of her body fitted remarkably well in its classic pleats. Her lips were dry in the wind, and she moistened them frequently with her tongue. The charm of her lips was thus enhanced considerably.

Yuichi, returning home from school, came up the path in back of the house and happened to approach by way of the garden gate. The gate usually set the bell ringing wildly when it was opened. Before the bell rang, however, he had held the gate with his hand and slipped into the garden. He stood in the shadow of the row of pasania trees and watched his wife. He did it purely and innocently out of mischief.

'From here, now,' he said sadly in his heart, 'from here, now, I can really love my wife. Distance gives me freedom. When I cannot reach her, when I can simply look at her, how beautiful Yasuko is. The pleats in her dress, her hair, her look – how pure it all is. If only I could keep this distance!'

At that moment, however, Yasuko saw the brown leather brief case peeping behind a trunk in the shade. She called Yuichi's name. It was a shout like that uttered by a person about to drown. He stepped into the open and she hurried in his direction. Her skirt caught on the low, bent bamboo palings of the flower garden. She stumbled and fell on the slippery earth.

Yuichi closed his eyes as a nameless fear struck him. He ran to his wife and helped her up. Her skirt had been muddied by the red earth, no more; she did not have a scratch.

Yasuko breathed heavily.

'You'll be all right, won't you?' Yuichi said fearfully. Having said this, he recognized that the fear he felt when Yasuko fell was related to a certain wish, and he shuddered.

As he spoke, Yasuko went white. Until he helped her up her mind was engrossed with Yuichi. She had not thought of the child.

Yuichi put Yasuko to bed and phoned the doctor. When his mother returned shortly with Kiyo and saw the doctor, she was, oddly enough, not concerned. As she listened to Yuichi's story, she told him that during her own pregnancy she had fallen downstairs two or three steps and nothing had happened.

'Are you really not worried?' Yuichi could not keep from asking.

'I suppose it's natural that you'd be worried,' his mother said with a smile.

Yuichi flinched, as if she had seen through his dire wish.

'The body of a woman,' his mother said, as if she were lecturing, 'is, for all its seeming fragility, surprisingly strong. When she took that little tumble, the baby in her belly probably felt it was going down a slide and enjoyed it. A man, on the other hand, is brittle. No one thought your father's health would break down as it did.'

The doctor left, saying that Yasuko was probably all right but they would have to wait for developments, but Yuichi did not leave his wife's side. When a phone call came from

Kawada, Yuichi told Kiyo to say he was not home. Yasuko's eyes overflowed with gratitude; the youth could not help feeling satisfaction that he had come to grips with something serious.

The next day the foetus again kicked his mother's insides vigorously, almost arrogantly. The whole family was greatly relieved. Yasuko did not doubt that such proud strength of foot belonged to a boy baby.

Yuichi could no longer keep his deep-felt joy to himself. He told Kawada of the episode. On the haughty face of the listening businessman in the early stages of decrepitude, jealousy swam.

24

Dialogue

Two months went by. It was the rainy season. Shunsuké, on his way to a meeting in Kamakura, went up to the Yokosuka Line platform in Tokyo Station and discovered Yuichi standing with both hands thrust into his raincoat pockets, a perplexed look on his face.

With Yuichi were two rakishly dressed boys. One, in a blue shirt, held Yuichi's arm. The other, in a red shirt with sleeves rolled up, faced Yuichi with his arms folded. Shunsuké stepped behind them and listened to their conversation from the concealment of a pillar.

'Yuchan, if you're not going to break up with this guy, kill me right here.'

'Stop that plain nonsense,' the boy in the blue shirt interjected. 'Yuichi and I are never going to break up. You, as far as Yuichi is concerned, are just a little cupcake he ate. And that's what you look like, a cheap little, sweet little, icky little cupcake.'

'Cut it out or I'll kill you.'

Yuichi pulled his arm from Blue Shirt's grasp. Then he said in an older, more composed tone: 'Won't you cut it out? Later on I'll listen to all you've got to say. It doesn't look right in a place like this.' He turned to Blue Shirt and added: 'You're acting too much like a wife!'

Blue Shirt lost his temper: 'All right, come on outside. I want to talk to you.'

The red-shirted boy smiled, showing his beautiful white teeth: 'You nut, you. You are outside. See? Everybody's going by with hats and shoes on.'

Things were getting out of hand, so Shunsuké circled about and approached so that Yuichi faced him. The look with which they met was quite natural. Yuichi bowed with a smile

295

that indicated he had been rescued. It had been a long time since Shunsuké had seen on his face such a beautiful smile full of brotherly affection.

Shunsuké was dressed in well-tailored tweeds; he wore a natty brown checkered handkerchief in his breast pocket. When the ceremonious and highly theatrical greetings between him and Yuichi began, the two boys watched with blank looks. One of them said, with all the charm he could inject into his glance, 'Well, Yuchan, I'll be seeing you.' The other turned his back without saying a word. Both of them disappeared. The yellowish Yokosuka Line train thundered in beside the platform.

'You make dangerous associations, don't you?' Shunsuké said, going towards the train.

'You're one of my associations, aren't you, sir?' Yuichi replied.

'But he was talking about killing or something.'

'So you heard. Those guys always talk that way. You can't get up a fight between cowards. Besides, those two snapping and snarling fellows are having an affair.'

'Affair?'

'When I'm not around, they sleep with each other.'

The two seated themselves facing each other in the second-class coach. The train picked up speed. Neither inquired about the other's destination. They looked wordlessly out of the window for a time. The landscape along the railroad touched Yuichi's heart.

They passed wet, ill-humoured blocks of grey buildings which were followed by cloudy, black factory landscapes. Across a swamp and a wasted, narrow meadow stood a glass-walled factory. Several panes of glass were broken; in the dark, sooty, hollow interior, naked light bulbs could be seen scattered about, weakly shining in the daylight. Then they passed an old wooden elementary school, built on fairly high ground. The U-shaped building looked in their direction out of lifeless windows. In the rain-soaked, vacant schoolyard stood a set of Swedish wall bars with the whitewash peeling. Then endless billboards – Takara Ale, Lion Toothpaste, Plastics, Morinaga Caramels.

It had grown warm, so the youth took off his coat. His new

suit, his shirt, his necktie, his tie pin, his handkerchief, even his
wrist watch were the utmost in luxury. They were combined
with inconspicuous harmony. Not only these, but also the new
Dunhill lighter he took from his pocket, as well as his cigarette
case, were elegantly attractive. Altogether they reflected
Kawada's taste, Shunsuké thought.

'Where are you going to meet Mr Kawada?' Shunsuké
asked sarcastically. The youth suddenly shifted his attention
from the lighter flame which he was applying to his cigarette
and stared at the old man. The tiny blue flame didn't flare up;
it hung spectrally in mid-air.

'How do you know?'

'I'm a novelist.'

'You surprised me. He's waiting for me at the Kofuen, in
Kamakura.'

'Is that right? I've got a meeting in Kamakura, too.'

The two were silent a while. Yuichi became conscious that
something distinctly red was cutting unexpectedly across the
dark field of vision. He looked and saw that they were passing
by the framework of an iron bridge being repainted. The
undercoat was red.

Suddenly Shunsuké said: 'Do you love Kawada, or what?'

Yuichi lifted his shoulders high: 'You're joking.'

'Why are you going to meet someone you don't love?'

'Aren't you the one, sir, who encouraged me to marry a
woman I didn't love?'

'A woman and a man are two different things.'

'Ha! They're the same thing. They're both horny, and
they're both a bore.'

'Kofuen – that's a fine, luxurious inn, but –'

'But?'

'In the old days, son, the big businessmen used to take geisha
there from Shimbashi and Akasaka.'

The youth, seemingly hurt, was silent.

Shunsuké did not understand. He did not know how terribly
bored the youth always was; and what kept this Narcissus
from being bored even more was the fact that this world was
filled with nothing but mirrors; in the prison of the mirror this
beautiful captive could be held for the rest of his life. The

297

ageing Kawada at least knew how to transform himself into the mirror.

Yuchi said: 'I haven't seen you since then. How was Kyoko? You told me on the phone it went very well.' He smiled, but he did not recognize that his smile was a carbon copy of Shunsuké's. 'Everything turns out so well – Yasuko, Mrs Kaburagi, Kyoko. How about it? I'm always faithful to you.'

'If you're faithful why are you never home to me?' Shunsuké said, with an indignation he could not suppress. He did his best to keep his complaint offhand: 'In two months I've talked to you on the phone just two or three times, haven't I? On top of that, whenever I suggest we meet, you hem and haw.'

'I felt if you had some business with me, you'd write me a letter.'

'I almost never write letters.'

Two or three stations had gone by. On the wet platform where there was no roof stood the lone sign bearing the name of the station. In the dark congestion on the platform under the roof were the great numbers of blank faces and the great numbers of umbrellas; the workmen clothed in wet blue serge looked up towards the windows of the train from the tracks below – somehow these ordinary scenes deepened the silence of the two men inside.

Soon Yuichi, drawing his body away, repeated: 'How was Kyoko?'

'Kyoko? How must I say it? I didn't have the slightest feeling that I'd got what I wanted. When, there in the darkness, I took your place and got into that woman's bed, and when that drunken woman, with her eyes still closed, called me Yuchan, I really felt a sense of rejuvenation moving within me. It was just a short time, but I took on the guise of your youth. That's all. When Kyoko woke up, she never let out another peep until morning. Since then I haven't heard anything from her. As far as I can see, that woman is apt to go downhill after this affair. In a way, I feel sorry for her. She's not a woman who needed something like that done to her.'

Yuichi felt no twinge of conscience whatsoever. It was an

action without object, without impulse from which regret could come. In his memory his action was pristinely pure. That action, governed by neither desire nor grudge; that action, possessed of not a scintilla of malice – it ruled over a fixed period of time which would not come again. It went from one pure point to another pure point.

Perhaps at no other time was there a time that Yuichi fulfilled so completely his role as a product of Shunsuké's art, freed of all moral considerations. Kyoko was thus not really taken in by him. The aged man lying beside her when she awakened was the same character as the beautiful young presence that had been at her side since the daylight hours.

For the visions, the fascinations, provoked by the work he had himself created, the author naturally had no responsibility. Yuichi represented the exterior of the work – the body, the dreaminess, the unfeeling coldness of intoxicating wine. Shunsuké represented the interior of the work – the moody planing, the formless desire, the fulfilled lust of the action called creation. That combined character, however, participating in the same work, was reflected in the eyes of the woman as nothing less than two different men.

There aren't many memories so completely miraculous as that one, thought the youth, as he turned his eyes to gaze at the scene outside the window, wrapped in fine rain. Though I was infinitely removed from the meaning of the action, I was close to the superlatively pure form of the action. I did not move, yet I cornered the prey. I did not covet the object, yet the object turned into the form that I coveted. I did not shoot, yet the rare prize was wounded by my missile and felled.

Thus at that time, from day to dark, pristinely pure, without flaw, I was spared the moral duties imposed by events of the past that nagged at me. If that evening I wished to devote myself to the pure desire of carrying a woman to bed, that was fine.

That memory, however, is unpleasant to me, thought Shunsuké. Even in that moment I could not believe that my interior beauty was consonant with Yuichi's exterior beauty. Socrates' prayer to the various gods of the place on that summer morning when he lay under the plane tree on the bank of the Ilissus

River, chatting with the beautiful boy Phaedrus until the day cooled, seems to me the highest teaching on earth: 'Pan, first, and all the gods that dwell in this place, grant that I may become fair within, and that such outward things as I have may be at peace with the spirit within me.'

The Greeks had the rare power to look at internal beauty as if it were hewn from marble. Spirit was badly corrupted in later times, exalted through the action of lustless love, and smirched through the action of lustless loathing. Beautiful young Alcibiades, drawn by the internal, love-lust wisdom of Socrates, was so aroused by the prospect of being passionately loved by that man as ugly as Silenus that he crept in with him and slept under the same mantle. When I read the beautiful words of Alcibiades in 'The Drinking Party' dialogue, they almost bowled me over: 'It would be embarrassing to tell men of intelligence that I did not give my body to someone like you – even more embarrassing than to admit to the uncultured multitude that I had surrendered to you. Much more!'

He lifted his eyes. Yuichi was not looking his way. The young man was immersed in something very small and inconsequential. In the rain-soaked backyard of a lone little house by the tracks, a housewife was squatting, assiduously starting a fire in a charcoal burner. The busy motion of her white fan and the tiny red draught vent were visible. What is life? Perhaps it is a riddle that does not have to be solved, Yuichi thought.

'Does Mrs Kaburagi write you?' Shunsuké said, abruptly again.

'Once a week, great long ones,' said Yuichi, smiling faintly. 'The letters of husband and wife always come in the same envelope. The husband writes one page, at most two. They're both astonishingly free, telling me they love me and things like that. In the wife's letter the other day, there was this masterpiece of a line: "The memory of you makes us happy with each other."'

'An odd couple, aren't they?'

'Married couples are all odd,' Yuichi said, childishly.

'Mr Kaburagi seems to be bearing his job in the Forestry Bureau, eh?'

'His wife just started as an automobile broker. That way they'll get along somehow.'

'Is that right? That girl will do it very well, too. And by the way, Yasuko is due this month, isn't she?'

'Yes.'

'You're going to be a father. That's funny.'

Yuichi did not smile. He was looking at the tightly shut warehouses of a shipping agency along the canal. He saw the rain-soaked jetty and the new wood colour of two or three boats tied to it. The name of the company in white letters on a rusty warehouse door imparted a vague feeling of expectation to this unmoving waterfront. Was that something coming out of the distant seascape in this direction, disturbing the sad reflection of the warehouses in the stagnant water?

'Are you scared?' The bantering tone intruded upon the youth's proud complacency.

'No, I'm not scared.'

'You're scared.'

'What am I scared of?'

'Plenty. If you're not scared, stand by Yasuko during the delivery. That will show you what your fear consists of. But you can't. Because, as everybody knows, you love your wife.'

'What are you trying to tell me, sir?'

'A year ago you got married, as I told you to. You now must gather the fruits of the fear you conquered back then. The oath you swore when you were married, the one about self-deception – are you keeping that now? Can you really torture Yasuko without torturing yourself? Aren't you confusing Yasuko's pain with that you have felt and seen in yourself all the time? Are you suffering under the delusion that that is married love?'

'You know everything, don't you? Have you forgotten that some time ago you were so good as to discuss an abortion with me?'

'Have I forgotten it? I was dead set against it.'

'Right. So I did what you told me to do.'

The train drew into Ofuna. The two saw the nape of the neck of the tall, downward-looking statue of Kwannon between the mountains facing the station. It dominated the smoky green of the trees as it stood out against the slate-coloured sky. The station was deserted.

When the train started, Shunsuké spoke rapidly, as if he wished to get everything said in the short time it would take to get to Kamakura, two stations away.

'You don't think you would like to make sure of your innocence with your own eyes? You don't think you would like to make sure with your own eyes that your uneasiness, your fear, and your pain, whatever it is, are without basis? I don't think you can do it. If you could, perhaps a new life would have to begin for you, and that would be too tough.'

The youth laughed nasally: 'New life, you say?' He carefully lifted the sharp creases in his trousers with one hand and crossed his legs.

'How would I go about seeing with my own eyes?'

'Just stay beside Yasuko during her delivery.'

'How stupid!'

'It's too difficult for you.'

Shunsuké had struck upon Yuichi's repugnance. He stared intently, as if at prey wounded by an arrow. Around the youth's lips a mock-sardonic, bewildered, unhappy smile of chagrin momentarily drifted.

Whereas other people are embarrassed about their joy, in this marriage the repugnance was embarrassing. Shunsuké was always delighted to look at the young couple and find ever that relationship, ever the unloved existence of Yasuko.

But Yuichi had to come face to face with that repugnance. Was not that very repugnance what he thought he had been savouring until this time? In Yasuko, in Count Kaburagi, in Mrs Kaburagi, in Kyoko, in Kawada?

Still, within the preceptorial kindness with which he pressed this delicious repugnance upon Yuichi, Shunsuké hid his never-to-be-requited love. Something had come to an end. At the same time, something had to begin.

Perhaps Yuichi would be cured of his repugnance. Shunsuké, too . . .

'At any rate, I'll do as I please. Nobody is going to give me orders.'

'Fine. That's fine.'

302

The train approached Kamakura Station. When he got off the train Yuichi would go to where Kawada was. Shunsuké was struck by conflicting emotions. However, his words belied his feelings as he said coldly: 'Just the same, you can't do it.'

25

Turnabout

Shunsuké's words rankled long in Yuichi's heart. The more he tried to forget them, the more obstinately those words confronted him.

The spring rains had not let up at all, and the time for Yasuko's delivery was late. It was now four days after the expected date. She had made excellent early progress, but now the last stages of her pregnancy were showing symptoms that caused concern.

Her blood pressure was over 150; a slight oedema was visible in her legs. High blood pressure and oedema in pregnancy are common prodromal symptoms of toxicity. In the afternoon of June thirtieth, the first labour pains started. In the middle of the night on July first, they came every fifteen minutes. Her blood pressure reached 190. To make matters worse, the doctor feared that the severe headache she complained of might be a symptom of eclampsia.

The attending chairman of the gynaecology department had had Yasuko admitted to the hospital of his own college several days earlier, but though the labour pains had been going on for two days, the delivery was not progressing, it seemed. They searched for the cause and discovered that the angle of Yasuko's pubic bone was smaller than normal. Thus a forceps delivery was decided upon, to be performed by the chairman of the gynaecology department himself.

July second was one of those harbingers of midsummer that come once in a while during the rainy season. Early in the morning, Yasuko's mother came by in a car to pick Yuichi up in accordance with his wish to be at the hospital on the day of the delivery. The two mothers greeted each other ceremoniously. Yuichi's mother wanted to go along too, but she had decided not to, she explained, because in her illness she would be a bother to the others. Yasuko's mother was fat, healthy, and middle-aged. Even after they got into the car, she continued with her usual heavy-handed teasing of Yuichi.

'According to Yasuko, you're an ideal husband, but just the same I'm not blind. If I were young I wouldn't leave you alone whether you had a wife or not. How they must make a fuss about you! But let me ask one thing. Please be clever in your deception of Yasuko. Where there is clumsy deception there is no true affection. Since of course I can keep my mouth shut, tell the truth only to me. Has anything interesting happened lately?'

'It won't work. You can't trap me that way.'

Supposing he did tell the truth to this woman who was like a cow basking in the sun. A terrible vision of the reaction he would excite suddenly flashed through his mind. At that moment, however, the youth was astonished to feel the woman's hand reach out to touch the hair that fell over his forehead.

'Oh! I thought your hair was getting white. It was only shining.'

'Really!'

'It surprised me, too.'

Yuichi saw that the sun was glaring outside. In some corner of this morning street Yasuko was still suffering from labour pains. As he thought of her, those pains appeared graphically before his eyes. He felt as if he could gauge the weight of them in the palm of his hand.

'She'll be all right, won't she?' the son-in-law said. As if in disdain of his uneasiness, his mother-in-law answered: 'She'll be all right.' She knew that the best way to calm a young, inexperienced husband was to show confidence and optimism in these matters that were entirely of womanly concern.

When the car stopped at a crossroads they heard the sound of a siren. Pell-mell down the sooty, grey street came a bright-red fire engine, shimmering like a picture in a child's story-book. The truck was almost prancing, its wheels touching the ground lightly. It seemed to make the neighbourhood rumble as it hurtled past. Yuichi and Yasuko's mother watched it graze the car in which they were riding and then looked out of the car window to see where the fire was.

'Stupid, isn't it? A fire at this time,' said Yasuko's mother. In all this bright sunlight she would not have been able to see a fire even if it were burning right beside her. There was, however, certainly a fire somewhere.

*

As Yuichi came into the sickroom and wiped the perspiration from Yasuko's suffering brow, he found it strange that he should be coming here so soon before the impending delivery. Something like a joy that courted danger lured him and forced him on. Since there was nowhere he could go to be spared thinking about Yasuko's pain, a desire to be close to her pain held him to her side. The Yuichi who ordinarily hated to go home came to Yasuko's pillow as if returning home.

The room was very warm. The sliding door to the balcony was standing open. White curtains shielded the rays of the sun, but the curtains were seldom touched by a breeze. The rain and cold had continued until yesterday, so no fans had been installed; but as soon as the mother walked into the room she grasped the problem and phoned to have a fan sent from her home. The nurses were busy elsewhere. Yuichi and Yasuko were alone. The young husband wiped the perspiration from her forehead. Yasuko gave a deep sigh and opened her eyes. She relaxed her tight, sweaty grip on Yuichi's hand.

'I feel better now. I feel fine now. It will be all right for ten minutes or so.'

She looked around her as if noticing things for the first time: 'My, it's hot!'

Yuichi was frightened by Yasuko's relief. In her relieved expression he recalled a fragment of the daily life he feared most. The young wife asked her husband for a mirror. She combed her hair, in disarray from the pain. In her pale, swollen face, with no make-up, there was an ugliness in which she herself could not divine the sublime qualities of pain.

'I'm a mess. Please excuse me,' she said pathetically, in a voice that would not have been heard in one not ill. 'In a jiffy I'll be pretty again.'

Yuichi looked directly down on that face like a child's, prostrated by pain. How was it to be explained, he wondered? This unsightliness and pain was immersing him in human emotion here in close proximity to his wife. When his wife was untroubled and beautiful in a way that it was natural to love, however, he was oddly driven away from human feeling and reminded only of her soul, which he could not love. How could that be explained? But Yuichi's error lay in his stubborn refusal to believe that within his present tenderness was mingled the tenderness of a common, ordinary husband.

Yasuko's mother came back with the nurse. Yuichi left his wife in the hands of the two women and went out on the balcony. The third-floor balcony overlooked the courtyard. His eyes were met by the multitude of hospital windows across the courtyard and the glass wall of the stairwell. He could see the white uniform of a nurse descending the stairway. Upon the glass of the stairs bold parallel lines were etched. The morning sun coming from the opposite direction cut diagonally across those parallel lines.

In the fierce glare, Yuichi smelled the odour of disinfectant and recalled Shunsuké's words: 'Don't you think you would like to make sure of your innocence with your own eyes?'

That old man's words always have a poisonous power over me. From an absolutely despised object, I shall see my own child born, he told me. He divined that I shall be able to do it. There was in his cruel sweet goading a triumphant self-confidence.

He rested his hand on the iron railing of the balcony. As he did so, the tepid feel of the rusty iron warmed by the heat of the sun suddenly reminded him of his honeymoon, when he had whipped the railing of the hotel balcony with his necktie.

In Yuichi's heart an unnamable impulse arose. The repugnance that Shunsuké had built up inside him, which called up with it a vivid pain, placed the youth under its spell. To resist it, or to retaliate against it, was just about the same thing as abandoning himself to it. It was difficult for him to distinguish between his passion for determining the source of the repugnance and a desire, motivated by appetite and lust for the flesh, to seek out the fountainhead of pleasure. When he thought about it, Yuichi's heart palpitated.

The door to Yasuko's room slid open.

Preceded by the white-suited chairman of the gynaecology department, two nurses came into the room pushing a wheeled stretcher. At that moment the labour pains attacked Yasuko again. She called the name of her husband as if she were calling someone far away. He ran over and took her hand.

The chairman of the gynaecology department smiled a sweet smile. Then he said: 'Just be patient a little while longer. Just a little while.'

There was something about his beautiful white hair that led people to trust him at first glance. Yuichi conceived a violent antipathy towards that white hair, that venerability, all the good intentions of that open-and-above-board great physician. All anxieties, all concerns about this pregnancy, about this delivery fraught with more or less unusual difficulties, about the child to be born, fell away from Yuichi. The only thing he thought of was his wish to see *that*.

The suffering Yasuko kept her eyes closed even while they moved her to the mobile stretcher. The perspiration ran in torrents on her forehead. Her supple hand sought for Yuichi's in the air. As the youth's hand grasped hers, her bloodless lips turned towards his bent head.

'Stay with me. If you don't stay by my side, I won't be able to go through with it.'

Was there ever so moving, so naked a confession? It was almost as if his wife had read the wish within the innermost depths of his mind and was struck by the wild fancy that she could help him. Even the bystanders perceived an extraordinary intensity in the emotions he displayed on seeing this selfless devotion in his wife.

'What's that?' the doctor said.

'My wife asked me to go with her all the way.'

The doctor grasped the arm of this demure, inexperienced husband. In a low, yet powerful voice he said: 'We have young wives who say things like that once in a while. Don't take her seriously. If you do, both your wife and you will regret it surely.'

'But my wife said if I'm not there –'

'I understand the way your wife feels, but she has had during her pregnancy all the encouragement she needs just to become a mother. If you are present ... for you, her husband, to be present, would be a terrible mistake. Even though you feel this way now, you will certainly regret it later.'

'I shall never regret it.'

'But all the fathers I've seen would have nothing to do with this. I've never seen one like you.'

'Doctor, I implore you!'

The instincts of the actor were leading Yuichi at this time to portray the stubborn, unshakable distraction of a young husband who has lost all sense of judgement out of anxiety for his wife. The doctor nodded curtly. Yasuko's mother, listening to their conversation, was shocked. 'It's mad,' she said; 'please leave me out. And do stop! You'll surely regret it. Worst of all, do you have to be so mean as to leave me all alone in the waiting room?'

Yasuko did not let go of Yuichi's hand. He felt as if her hand were pulling him with a suddenly augmented power, but it was the two nurses pushing the stretcher. The nurse on duty in that room opened the door and ushered them out into the hall.

Yasuko's stretcher, with its entourage, took the elevator to the fourth floor. It moved quietly across the cool reflections of the corridor. As the wheels of the stretcher clicked slightly over the joints in the floor, Yasuko's soft white chin bounced flaccidly back and forth. The double doors of the delivery room swung open. Only Yasuko's mother remained outside as they swung shut. As they left her, Yasuko's mother said: 'Really, Yuichi, you'll be sorry. If it gets too horrible, please come out. I'll be sitting in a chair in the hall.'

The smile with which Yuichi replied to her was like that of a man going into danger. This gentle young man knew his own fears.

The stretcher was pushed to the side of another stretcher, fitted out with equipment. Yasuko was moved to it. When she had been moved, a curtain was drawn by a nurse between two posts that were fixed to opposite sides of the new stretcher.

This curtain, drawn above the chest of the woman in labour, shielded her eyes from the glare of the equipment and the cruel knives.

Yuichi grasped Yasuko's hand and stood above that curtain. There he could see the two halves of Yasuko – her upper half, and the lower half separated from her by a curtain she could not see over.

The windows faced south, and the breeze blew through softly. The necktie of the young husband, in shirtsleeves as he was, flapped and fluttered and clung to his shoulder. He stuffed the end of it into the breast pocket of his shirt. He carried out this action swiftly, as if interrupting a most engrossing enterprise. Nevertheless, all he was doing was helplessly holding the hand of his perspiring wife. Between this suffering body and this non-suffering body there was a distance across which no action taken by either could be linked.

'Just be patient a little longer. It will be done soon,' said the head nurse into Yasuko's ear again. Her eyes remained tight shut. Yuichi felt freer because of the fact that his wife could not see him.

The chairman of the gynaecology department appeared, his hands scrubbed, his sleeves rolled up, followed by two assistants. He did not so much as glance in Yuichi's direction. He signalled to the head nurse. Two nurses removed the lower half of the table on which Yasuko was lying. Her legs were stretched out in conformity with two strange hornlike projections sticking up in the air on each side of the bottom edge of the half table on which she lay.

The low curtain on top of her chest was designed to keep her from seeing the pitiless transformation of the lower half of her body into a thing, an object. Regardless, the pain of the top half of Yasuko had become a pure, spiritual pain that knew nothing about how she had been so transformed, that had nothing to do with the incident involving her lower half. The prehensile power with which she grasped Yuichi's hand was not a woman's power. It was the arrogant power of flourishing pain, capable of plucking out Yasuko's existence.

Yasuko groaned. In the swelter of the room between gusts of wind, the groans hovered like the sound of wings of count-

310

less flies. She tried continually to raise her abdomen and, frustrated, would drop back on the hard bed; her face, with eyes closed, moved from side to side in tiny tremors. Yuichi remembered. Last autumn, when he was with that passing student in the daytime in that inn in Takagicho, he had heard fire-engine sirens in his dream. Then he thought: In order that my guilt might become a pure thing immune to fire, must not my innocence first pass through the fire? My complete innocence where Yasuko is concerned ... Didn't I once ask to be born again for Yasuko's sake? And now?

He rested his eyes by looking at the scene outside the window. The summer sun burned down on the woods in the big park on the other side of the government railway line. The oval of the track was like a pool of radiance. No human shape was visible there.

Yasuko's hand tugged strongly again at the hand of her husband. It seemed to be calling his attention to something. He instantly noticed the radiant bright gleams from the scalpel a nurse had just handed to the doctor. Yasuko's lower body moved like the mouth of a person vomiting. On to the cloth applied to it, which looked like the canvas of a sail, oozed urine from the catheter and dripping mercurochrome.

That sailcloth, applied to a fissure painted red with mercurochrome, resounded as a fierce flow struck it. First local anaesthetic was applied; then the fissure was enlarged with scalpel and shears. Yasuko's complicated, crimson interior came clearly into the view of her young husband, who was drained of all cruelty. Looking here at the insides of his wife, the skin stripped from them, Yuichi was surprised that this flesh which he had felt to be so much irrelevant pottery was something he could no longer treat as inanimate.

'I must look. No matter what, I must look,' he told himself, attempting to control his nausea. 'That system of countless, gleaming, wet red jewels; those soft things under the skin, soaked in blood; those squirming things – a surgeon must soon grow accustomed to things like that: I should be able to become accustomed to being a surgeon. Since my wife's body is no more than pottery to me sexually, there is no reason that the inside of her body should be any more than that.'

All the honesty of his consciousness soon betrayed his bluff. The fearful contents of his wife's body turned inside out were more than pottery. It was as if his feeling for humanity compelled him, even more deeply than the sympathy he felt with his wife's pain, to see, as he confronted this wordless scarlet flesh and looked at the wet surface of it, his own inimitable self. Pain does not transcend the body. It is alone, the youth thought. But this naked, scarlet flesh was not alone. It was related to the red flesh that indubitably existed within Yuichi; even the consciousness of one who merely looked at it had to be instantly affected by it.

Yuichi saw another, purely gleaming, mirror-like, cruel machine being passed into the doctor's hand. It was a large scissors device, disjoined at the fulcrum. Where the blades should have been, there was a pair of large, curved spoons. One side was inserted deep inside Yasuko. After the other side was crossed over and inserted, the fulcrum was engaged for the first time. It was the forceps.

There at the utmost extremity of his wife's body, touching her hand, the young husband keenly perceived the gropings of that instrument, roughly invading with the intent of grasping something in its metal talons. He saw his wife's white front teeth biting her lower lip. In all this suffering, he recognized that her tender, tender faith in him never left her face, but he dared not kiss her. For the youth did not have the confidence demanded by even so natural an action as that gentle kiss.

In a morass of flesh, the forceps sought out the soft head of the infant and grasped it. Two nurses, one on each side, pressed against Yasuko's white abdomen.

Yuichi earnestly believed in his own innocence; perhaps it would be more appropriate to say that he prayed for it.

At this time, however, Yuichi's heart, pondering his wife's face at the pinnacle of suffering, and the burning colouration in that part of her that had been the source of his loathing, went through a process of transformation. Yuichi's beauty, that had been given over for the admiration of man and woman alike, that had seemed to have existence only to be seen, for the first time had it faculties restored and seemed now to exist only to see. Narcissus had forgotten his own face. His eyes had another object than the mirror. Looking at this awful ugliness had become the same as looking at himself.

Until now Yuichi had been incapable of feeling he existed unless he 'was seen' *in toto*. His consciousness of existing, in short, was a consciousness of being seen. The youth now revelled in a new sense of existence, an indubitable existence in which he was not looked at. In short, he himself was seeing.

How transparent, how airy, this existence in its true form! This Narcissus who had forgotten his face could even consider that his face did not exist. If, beside herself with pain, his wife had turned her face and opened her eyes, she would certainly have had no trouble seeing there the expression of one who lived in the same world as she.

Yuichi let go his wife's hand. He brought both his perspiring hands to his forehead, as if to touch this new self. He took out a handkerchief and wiped it. Then he saw his wife's hand, left behind there in the air, still clasping the impression of his hand, and, as if thrusting his hand into a mould of itself, he took her hand once more.

The amniotic fluid flowed out. The head of the baby, eyes closed, was already visible. The work going on around the lower half of Yasuko's body was of a kind with the back-breaking exertions of a ship's crew bucking a gale. It was a common enough power; human power was bringing forth life. Yuichi could see the muscles straining even in the wrinkles of the white coat of the chairman of the gynaecology department.

Released of its fetters, the child slipped forth. It was a white, faintly purple, half-dead lump of flesh. A murmuring kind of sound welled forth. Then that lump of flesh began to cry. With each cry it grew a little redder.

The umbilical cord was cut. The infant was cradled in a nurse's arms and shown to Yasuko.

'It's a girl!'

Yasuko did not seem to understand.

'It's a girl.' She heard and nodded faintly.

She lay silently with eyes open. Her eyes did not seem to see her husband or the child that had been brought forth. If she saw them, she did not smile. This impassive expression, properly an animal's expression, was one that human beings are rarely able to achieve. Compared with that expression, thought the man in Yuichi, all human expressions of tragicomic pathos were little more than masks.

26

Sobering Summer

They called the child Keiko; the family's joy was unbounded.
This was true despite the fact that a girl was not what Yasuko
had set her heart on. In the week after the delivery, there in
the hospital, Yasuko's heart was full enough, but from time to
time she immersed herself in the useless preoccupation with
why it was a girl and not a boy. Could she have been mistaken
in praying for a boy? she wondered. Could it have been only
an empty illusion from the first – her joy that she held captive
a beautiful child the very image of her husband? It was still
hard to tell which parent the baby favoured, but at present she
seemed to have more of her father's features.

Every day Keiko gained weight. A scale was placed beside
the mother's bed, and every day the rapidly recuperating
Yasuko would record the increased weight on her graph. At
first, Yasuko thought that the child she had brought into the
world was some kind of monstrous object that had not yet
attained human form, but after the first stablike pains of suck-
ling and the almost immoral delight that followed, she found
her love for this offspring with its strangely pouting face
something she could not drive from her heart. Besides, visitors
and those around her treated this shape that was not yet
humanly all one might desire as if it was perforce a human
being, plying it with words that it could not reasonably be expected to understand.

Yasuko attempted to compare the fearful physical pain she
had gone through two or three days earlier with the long
period of mental torture Yuichi had brought her. In the peace
of her heart, now that the first was over, strangely she found
hope in the thought that the pangs of the second would last
much longer and require much more time for convalescence.

First to note Yuichi's transformation was not Yasuko but

his mother. This meek, uncomplicated soul in all the simplicity of its nature perceived immediately the transformation of her son. As soon as she heard about the safe delivery, she left Kiyo to mind the house and set out for the hospital in a cab. She opened the door of the hospital room. Yuichi was standing by Yasuko's pillow; he ran over and embraced his mother.

'Be careful; you'll knock me down' – she struggled and struck a small fist against Yuichi's chest. 'Don't forget that I'm sick. Why, how red your eyes are! Have you been crying?'

'I'm pretty tired. It was pretty tense. I stayed through the delivery.'

'You stayed through?'

'That's right,' Yasuko's mother said. 'I tried to stop him, but he wouldn't listen. Yasuko for her part wouldn't let go of his hand.'

Yuichi's mother looked at Yasuko, the picture of motherhood. Yasuko was smiling weakly, but her face showed no sign of embarrassment. The mother looked at her son again. Her eyes said: 'What a strange child! Now that you have witnessed such a terrible thing, for the first time you and Yasuko look like a real couple. You wear the expression of people sharing a sweet secret.'

Yuichi feared his mother's intuitions of this kind more than anything. Yasuko did not fear them in the least. Now that her pain was over, she was amazed that she felt no embarrassment over having asked Yuichi to stand by her during the delivery. Perhaps Yasuko vaguely believed that only through something like that would she be able to make Yuichi believe the pain she was going through.

*

One might well say that, except for supplementary lectures on a few subjects, Yuichi's summer vacation started at the beginning of July. His routine, however, consisted of passing the day at the hospital and running around town in the evening. On evenings when he did not see Kawada, he gladly went back to his old habits, in company with those whom Shunsuké called his 'dangerous associations'.

316

At a number of bars for the initiated, as well as at Rudon's, Yuichi had become a familiar figure. One of them was ninety per cent foreign in patronage. Among the guests was a counter-intelligence man who liked to wear women's clothing. He wore a stole on his shoulders and sidled about flirting with the customers, he did not care who.

At the Elysée Bar, a number of male prostitutes greeted Yuichi. He returned their greetings and laughed to himself: 'Are these dangerous associations? Associations with such weak, effeminate fellows as these?'

The rains had been falling again since the day after Keiko's birth, Yuichi was in a bar at the end of a muddy lane. Most of the guests were already pretty drunk; they came and went, showing splashes on their trousers they did not bother to brush off. At times water flowed in a corner of the dirt floor. On the rough plaster wall a number of umbrellas dripped, deepening the flow.

Yuichi sat silently facing some nondescript hors d'oeuvres, a pitcher filled with saké that was not of the best, and a saké cup. The saké was barely contained by the thin lip of the cup. It trembled at the brim, a transparent, pale yellow. Yuichi looked at the cup. It was a cup into which no kind of vision could enter. It was, simply, a cup. Ergo, it was nothing else.

Four or five persons were present. Even now Yuichi never returned to one of the bars of the clan without getting involved in one or two adventures. Older men approached him, spinning sweet phrases. Younger boys flirted with him. Even this evening there was at Yuichi's side a pleasant youth of about his own age constantly pouring him saké. One could tell from the look in his eyes, as he studied Yuichi's profile from time to time, that he was in love with him.

The youth was good to look at. His smile was clean. What did that mean? It meant that he wished to be loved. It was not a wish based on any particular ignorance of himself. In order to make his worth known, he went on and on with stories about how he had been pursued by any number of men. It was more or less a bother, but such self-introductions are typical of the gay people. He wasn't carrying it to any point worth com-

plaining about. He dressed well. He was not badly formed. His
nails were nicely manicured. The line of the white undershirt
visible at his belt was tidy. But what did that mean?

Yuichi raised his dark glance to the pictures of boxers pasted
on the wall of the bar. Vice that had lost its glitter was a
hundred times more boring than virtue that had lost its glitter.
Perhaps the reason vice is called crime lies in this boredom
brought about by repetition, which does not permit one to steal
a second of self-satisfaction. Devils must be bored by nothing
else but the glut of eternally seeking out original evil deeds.

Yuichi knew all the developments. If he smiled in assent to
the youth, they would go on until late at night calmly drinking
together. When the bar closed up, they would go out. Feigning
drunkenness, they would stand in front of a hotel entrance. In
Japan, as a rule, there is nothing strange about men friends
spending the night in the same hotel room. They would turn
the key of a room on the second floor within earshot of the
whistle of the midnight freight train close by. A kiss instead of
a salutation, disrobing, the neon signs nullifying the effect of
the extinguished lamp, the double bed with its superannuated
spring squealing piteously, impatient hugs and kisses, the first
cold contact of the skin of their naked bodies after the sweat
had dried, the smell of flesh and pomade, endless groping for
satisfaction filled with impatience for the same bodies, little
screams belying masculine vanity, hands wet with hair oil ...
Then the pitiable facsimile of physical satisfaction, the evapor-
ation of all that perspiration, the groping under pillows for
cigarettes and matches, the faintly shining whites of eyes.
Then the endless conversation surging as over a broken dam,
and the descent to the childish play of nothing more than two
men friends with their desire for a time satisfied, tests of
strength in the dark night, stabs at wrestling, various other
inanities....

Suppose I go out with this youth, Yuichi thought, looking at
his saké cup. It will be nothing new; I know that the demands
of originality will be no more satisfied than before. Why is the
love of men so irresolute as this? And yet is not the very stuff
of homosexuality that simple state of pure friendship that
comes after the act? That lonely state of returning, lust

318

appeased, mutually to the state of being simply members of the same sex – had not their lust been granted for the very purpose of building to such a state? Those of this ilk love each other because they are men, they like to think, but is it not the cruel truth that by loving they recognize for the first time that they are men? Before loving, something extremely subtle inhabits the consciousness of these people. Their desire is closer to metaphysics than to sexuality. And what is that?

Nevertheless, everywhere he looked he found only the wish to get away. Saikaku's homosexual lovers had found no way out save the priesthood or love suicide.

'Are you leaving already?' said the youth to Yuichi, who had asked for his check.

'Yes.'

'From Kanda Station?'

'Kanda. Right.'

'Good, I'll walk to the station.'

They made their way out of the muddy hole and walked slowly through the jumbled alley of drinking places under the elevated tracks towards the station. It was ten p.m. Activity was at its height in the alley.

The rain started again. It was extremely muggy. Yuichi wore a white polo shirt; the youth wore a blue one and carried a brief case by the handle. The street was narrow; they got under a single umbrella. The youth suggested they get something cold to drink. Yuichi assented, and they went into a little tea shop in front of the station.

The youth talked happily – of his parents, of his cute little sister, of his family business in a fairly big shoe store in Higashinakano, of his father's hopes for him, of his own small bank account. Yuichi watched the youth's rather beautiful peasant's face and listened. This was a man indeed born for conventional happiness. His circumstances were just about perfect for the maintenance of such happiness. There was just one secret, guiltless defect, known to nobody. That flaw brought everything down. Ironically, it gave to the face of this conventional youth a kind of metaphysical shading he was not aware of. It made him look as if worn out by the exertions of higher metaphysical speculation. He was the kind of man who seemed certainly to have been brought up, were that defect not present, to become attached at the age of twenty to his first woman and thereafter to be filled with satisfaction like that of a man of forty, over which he would ruminate until the day he died.

Over their heads the fan whirled sluggishly. The ice in their iced coffee melted quickly. Yuichi ran out of cigarettes and was given none by the youth. He found it amusing to imagine what would happen if the two became lovers and lived together. Men friends refusing to clean up, the house untidied, a life spent doing nothing all day but loving and smoking – the ash-trays would certainly get full in a hurry!

The youth yawned – a great, dark, glossy spreading of his oral cavity, bordered by nicely even teeth.

'Excuse me. It's not that I'm tired. Just the same, I never stop thinking I'd like to get the dust of this company off my feet.' (This did not mean he wanted to break away from gay things; Yuichi understood it to mean that he wished to enter into a settled life quickly with a chosen companion.) 'I have a charm here. Let me show it to you.'

Forgetting that he was not wearing a jacket, he moved his hand towards his breast pocket and had to explain that he had put his treasure in a brief case when he decided not to put on a jacket. Beside his thigh his bulky brief case lay, the leather peeling off its sides. Its flustered owner opened the clasp too quickly; the bag turned upside down, its contents spilling to the floor with a clatter. The youth bent over excitedly and picked them up. Yuichi did not help him, but scrutinized the objects the youth picked up as they shone under the flourescent light. There was cream. There was lotion. There was pomade. There was a comb. There was eau de cologne. There was another bottle of cream of some kind. Looking forward to sleeping out, he had brought these things along for his morning toilet.

Yuichi could not help feeling repelled by these cosmetics carried about by a man who was not an actor. Unconscious of Yuichi's revulsion, the youth held the bottle of eau de cologne up to the light to see whether it was broken. When Yuichi saw that only about a third of the eau de cologne was left, his revulsion doubled.

The youth finished putting the fallen articles back into the bag. Then he looked at Yuichi, puzzled that he had not moved to help him. He remembered why he had picked up the bag and bent down again, his face red to the ears from stooping. From the compartment meant for small articles he took something tiny and yellow and waved it at the end of a red silk thread before Yuichi's eyes.

Yuichi took it in his hand and looked at it. It was a tiny straw sandal, plaited of yellow stuff, with a red strap.

'Is this your charm?'

'Yes, a fellow gave it to me.'

Yuichi looked at his watch, not hiding the fact. He said he had to go. They left the shop. At the Kanda Station the youth bought a ticket to Higashinakano, Yuichi one to S— Station. Their trains were on the same line. When the train approached S— and Yuichi was ready to get off, the youth, who supposed Yuichi had purchased the ticket to S— Station because of reticence about going to the same destination, was overcome with confusion. His hand gripped Yuichi's hand. Yuichi thought of the hand of his suffering wife and shook it off brusquely. The youth's pride was wounded. Wishing to take Yuichi's impolite behaviour as a joke, he forced a laugh.

'Are you really getting off here?'

'Yes.'

'All right, I'll go with you.'

They got off together at the quiet, night-enshrouded station. 'I'm going with you,' the youth insisted, exaggerating his drunkenness.

Yuichi became angry. He suddenly remembered a visit he must make.

'Where are you going to go when you leave me?'

'You don't know, do you?' said Yuichi coldly. 'I have a wife.'

The youth went white. He was unable to move. 'Then you've been stringing me along!'

He burst into tears as he stood there. Then he went over to a bench, sat down, clutched his brief case to his chest, and cried. Yuichi witnessed this comical end to matters and swiftly ran up the stairs to escape. He was not being followed, evidently. He left the station and almost flung himself into the rain. Before his eyes stretched the hospital buildings, reposing in silence.

I wanted to come here, he thought soberly. When I saw the contents of that man's bag fall on the floor, I suddenly wanted to come here.

By all rights, it was time he went to his home, where his mother was waiting alone. He couldn't stay over in the hospital. He felt, however, that if he didn't go to the hospital he wouldn't be able to sleep.

At the gate the watchmen were still awake, playing Japanese chess. Their dim, yellow lamp was visible from afar. From the admitting window a dark face looked out. Fortunately the guard remembered Yuichi, who had made a reputation for himself as the man who had stayed by his wife while she delivered her baby. Yuichi knew his excuse didn't make much sense, but he explained that he had left something valuable in his wife's room.

'She's probably asleep,' said the guard. The expression on this uxorious young man's face, however, touched his heart. Yuichi ascended the dim stairway to the third floor. The sound of his shoes reverberated harshly on the staircase.

Yasuko wasn't sleeping, but she heard the sound of the gauze-wrapped knob being turned as if it were a sound in her dream. She suddenly became frightened, sat up, and switched on the light on the stand. The human form standing out of range of the light was her husband. Before she could breathe a sigh of relief, a paroxysm of incredulous joy struck her breast. The manly white front of Yuichi's polo shirt moved before her.

The couple exchanged two or three casual words. Out of her native sagacity, Yasuko refrained from asking why he had come to see her so late at night. The young husband turned the lamp so that it shone towards Keiko's basinet. Small, pure, half-transparent nostrils solemnly drew breath in sleep. Yuichi was enraptured by the conventionality of his emotions. These emotions, which had until now lain dormant within him, at this moment found a safe and sure path before them and were capable of intoxicating him. Yuichi bade a gentle good-bye to his wife. He had every good reason to sleep well tonight.

*

On the morning after Yasuko returned home from the hospital, Yuichi got up and heard an apology from Kiyo. The mirror he had always used while tying his necktie had dropped and broken during housework. This small accident made him smile. It was perhaps a sign that the beautiful youth had been released from the legendary power of the mirror. He was reminded of the small, jet black, ornamented mirror stand at the inn at K— last summer when his ears were first assaulted by Shunsuké's praise of beauty and he entered so closely into that association with the all-seeing mirror. Before that, Yuichi, following the usual male predilection, had resolutely refrained from thinking of himself as beautiful. Now that the mirror was broken, would he not once more be governed by that taboo?

One evening they were having a going-away party for a foreigner at Jackie's house. Yuichi was invited through an intermediary. His presence would be important during the evening's festivities. Jackie would rise in the estimation of the many guests if Yuichi came. On hearing this, Yuichi vacillated, but he finally decided to accept.

Everything was the same as the gay party last Christmas. All the young men who had been invited were waiting at Rudon's. All wore aloha shirts, which were really very becoming to them. Eichan, the Oasis Kimichan, and others were among them just as the year before. The foreign contingent was different, making the gathering fine and fresh of feature. There were also new faces in the group. A young man named Kenchan was one; Katchan was another. The former was the son of the owner of a large eel shop in Asakusa. The father of the other was the manager of a branch bank, noted for reliability.

Everyone grumbled about the rainy mugginess as they sat waiting for the foreigner's car. They told silly stories over their cold drinks. Kimichan had an interesting story to tell. The former proprietor of a fruit store in Shinjuku had moved a barracks building after the war, and when he was preparing to have it made into a two-storey permanent building, he took

323

part, as the head of the firm, in a ground-breaking ceremony. With a smug face he offered the sacred tree to God. Then it became the special duty of a beautiful young employee to offer the sacred tree. The other people didn't know it, but this altogether ordinary ceremony was a secret wedding performed before the eyes of the populace. The two men, lovers for a long time, would set up housekeeping together the evening after the ground-breaking ceremony – the boss had secured a divorce from his wife a month before.

The young men in their colourful aloha shirts, arms bare, sat variously posed in the chairs of this habitual hangout. Their necks were all cleanly shaven, their hair gave off a strong perfume, their shoes all shone like new. One leaned his elbows far forward on the bar, crooned a popular hit, and kept throwing dice from a frayed leather dice cup; affecting grown-up weariness, he toyed with the black dice, which had red and green spots.

How worthy of attention their futures! A limited number of the boys who entered this world, hounded by lonely impulses or seized by guiltless temptations, would make the lucky toss that would bring them a prize of study abroad, unattainable in the ordinary course of events. The overwhelming majority, after a time, for the excesses of youth, would probably be cast with shocking suddenness into the lot of ugly age. Already in their youthful faces, addiction to curiosity and ceaseless craving for stimulation had left its traces. The gin drunk at seventeen, the taste of proffered foreign cigarettes, those dissipations that wore the mask of fearless innocence – dissipations of a kind that never left even the fruits of remorse – all the tips forced upon them by adults and the secret expenditures of them, the effortlessly instilled desire for indulgence, the awakening of the instinct for bodily adornment – theirs was a flaunted degradation, without concealment, no matter what form it took. Their youth was self-sufficient, and nowhere could they flee the innocence of their flesh. If one asked why, it was because their youth, which felt no sense of completeness, could gain no sense of having lost anything at all, though it is customary to feel a kind of completeness in the loss of innocence.

'Screwy Kimichan,' said Katchan.

'Bats Katchan,' said Kimichan.

'Usurer Eichan,' said Kenchan.

'Moron!' said Eichan.

This primitive repartee was like the frolicking of puppies in the glass-walled kennels of a pet shop.

It was very warm. The fan wafted a breeze like tepid water. All were already finding this evening's journey tedious, but the foreigners' two cars that came to pick them up just then – convertible sedans with the tops rolled back – revived their spirits considerably. Thanks to this, they were able to enjoy their conversation, sitting in the wind heavy with suspended rain during the two-hour trip to Oiso.

*

'Yuchan! Glad you could come!' Jackie embraced Yuichi with wholehearted friendly affection.

The host, clad in an aloha shirt with a sea, sail, shark, and palm-tree pattern, had instincts sharper than a woman's, and when he conducted Yuichi into the hall in which the sea breeze swirled, he immediately whispered in the youth's ear: 'Yuchan! Has something happened?'

'My wife had a baby.'

'Yours?'

'Mine.'

'Wonderful!'

Jackie laughed heartily. They clinked their glasses together and drank to Yuichi's daughter. There was, however, something in this action that brought home to them the distance between the two worlds they inhabited. As always, Jackie was a tenant of the mirror room, the domain of the men being looked at. He would perhaps dwell there until the day he died. If a child were born to him, it would probably have to live on the other side of the mirror, separated from its father. All human concerns, as he saw it, were devoid of urgency.

The orchestra struck up a popular song. The men danced, perspiring. Yuichi looked down out of the window and gaped. Here and there in the grassy garden were clumps of bushes and shrubbery. In each of the shadows thrown by them, there was a

325

shadow locked in embrace. In the shadows points of fire were spotted about. Now and then a match was struck, revealing clearly part of the prominent nose of some foreigner.

Yuichi saw in the shadow of an azalea on the garden's edge a T-shirt with horizontal stripes, of the kind worn by seamen, detach itself from another's body. The companion wore a plain yellow shirt. Two men, supple as cats, gave each other a light kiss and departed in different directions. After a time Yuichi noticed the one in the striped T-shirt leaning by one of the windows as if he had been there for quite a while. He had a small, fierce face, impassive eyes, a mouth like a pouting child's, and the complexion of Cape jasmine.

Jackie got up, went to his side, and asked him casually: 'Where did you go, Jack?'

'Ridgeman had a headache, so I went off to the drugstore to get him some pills.'

This young man, with his cruel white teeth, his lips so suited to the lie he was telling – deliberately and obviously a lie just to torture the other person – Yuichi recognized as Jackie's current lover. He had heard rumours about the youth and only needed to hear the alias to know him. Jackie heard his excuse and came back to Yuichi, holding in both hands a whisky glass filled with crushed ice.

He said in Yuichi's ear: 'Did you see what that liar was up to in the garden?'

Yuichi said nothing.

'You saw it, didn't you? Anywhere, even in my own backyard, he does things like that.'

Yuichi saw the pain on Jackie's brow.

'You're awfully big about it,' said Yuichi.

'Those who love are always magnanimous; those who are loved are the cruel ones. I, Yuchan, have been crueller than he to men who loved me.' With that he told boastful stories of how he, even at his age, was made much of by older foreigners.

'What makes a man cruel is the consciousness that he is loved. The cruelty of men who are not loved is not worth talking about. For instance, Yuchan, those men known as humanists just had to be ugly men.'

Yuichi had wished to treat the distress of Jackie with due

respect. Jackie, however, had anticipated him and was himself administering to his pain the white talcum powder of vanity. He ended by making a kind of incomplete obscure grotesquery of it. The two stood there for a time and talked of the recent affairs of Count Kaburagi, in Kyoto. Even now, it seemed, the count showed his face occasionally at one of the 'in' bars in the Shichijo-Naihama neighbourhood.

Jackie's portrait, as ever, was attended by a pair of candles. Above the mantel it projected its delicately olive-coloured nakedness. At the corners of the mouth of this young Bacchus with a necktie sloppily tied on his naked neck, there was an expression that seemed to speak of the imperishability of joy or the immutability of pleasure. The champagne glass he held in his right hand was never empty.

That evening Yuichi forgot Jackie's disappointment and, ignoring the enticing hands held out to him by the many foreign guests, went to bed with a boy who pleased him. The boy's eyes were round; his round cheeks – with beard not yet developed – were white as peeled fruit. After the act was over, Yuichi yearned to return home. It was one o'clock in the morning. One of the foreigners, who also had to be back in Tokyo that night, offered to drive Yuichi back in his car. Yuichi was very grateful for the offer.

Out of natural courtesy, he sat in the seat next to the foreigner, who was driving. The middle-aged, ruddy-complexioned foreigner was an American of German ancestry. He treated Yuichi politely and spoke of his home in Philadelphia. He explained the origin of the name, from a town of Asia Minor of the time of ancient Greece. The '*Phil*' was the Greek word *phileo*, meaning 'love'; '*adelphia*' was from *adelphos*, meaning 'brother'. 'In short, my home town is the country of brotherly love,' he said. Then, still speeding along on the deserted highway, he took one hand off the wheel and gripped Yuichi's hand.

He put his hand back on the wheel and suddenly swung it hard to the left. The car veered into a small, little-used road, then turned right and stopped under a grove of trees rustling in the night wind. The foreigner grasped Yuichi's hands. The two looked at each other for a time and struggled. It was the

327

foreigner's heavy arms covered with golden hair against the youth's arms, tight and smooth. The giant's strength was amazing; Yuichi was no match for him.

In the lampless interior of the car the two fell in a heap. Yuichi was the first to right himself. He reached out his hand to cover himself with the pale blue aloha shirt and the white under-shirt that had just been torn away from his body. Then the youth's bare shoulder was held in the power of the lips of the other, again overcome by passion. Avidly, giant canine teeth, accustomed to meat, sank voraciously into the glowing flesh of the shoulder. Yuichi yelled. Blood ran across the young man's breast.

He twisted his body and rose to his feet. The roof of the car, however, was low. Besides, the front glass at his back sloped downward. He could not stand upright. He pressed one hand against his wound. White with humiliation and his own helplessness, he stood in a half slouch, simply glaring at the man.

The foreigner's eyes recovered from their passion. He suddenly turned obsequious. Seeing the evidence of his behaviour, he was struck with horror. His whole body shook, and finally he cried. Even more stupidly, he kissed a little silver cross that hung from a chain on his chest. Then, still half-dressed, he leaned against the steering wheel and prayed. After that he begged Yuichi again and again to forgive him, explaining tearfully that his virtues and his upbringing were powerless against obsessions of this kind. There was a ridiculous self-righteousness in his entreaties. When he attacked Yuichi with overwhelming force, Yuichi's momentary physical weakness had brought a salutary change in the spiritual weakness of his adversary – or so he wished to say.

Yuishi hastened to adjust his shirt. The foreigner soon became conscious of his own nakedness and covered himself. It had taken him time to recognize his nakedness, just as it had taken him time to recognize his weakness.

Owing to this mad incident, it was morning before Yuichi got home.

The wound in his shoulder did not take long to heal. When Kawada saw the scar, he was filled with jealousy and schemed for a way that he too might be privileged to inflict such a wound without incurring Yuichi's wrath.

Yuichi was frightened by the difficulties of associating with Kawada, who made a sharp distinction between his social dignities and the joy he felt in the humiliations of love. His treatment threw the young man, not yet schooled in the realities of society, into confusion. Even though Kawada did not mind kissing the soles of the feet of the one he loved, he would not permit that person to touch his social position with so much as one finger. In this regard he was the exact opposite of Shunsuké.

The bitterness of understanding ... Yuichi had a happy natural gift for bearing the bewilderment with which understanding attacks youth. With Shunsuké's guidance he had come to all the ready-made understandings: the emptiness of wealth and fame and position; the hopeless ignorance and stupidity of mankind, particularly the worthless existence of women; and the way life's tedium gives substance to all its passions. The sensual urges that even in his boyhood years had discovered for him human life and all its ugliness had accustomed him to bearing any ugliness or vanity whatever as self-evident. Thanks to his calm innocence, therefore, his understanding was spared from bitterness. The horrors of the life that he had seen, the eye-popping sensations that some dark, deep pit of life was opening beneath his feet, were so many healthy preparatory exercises for his role as a spectator at Yasuko's delivery – nothing more than clean physical training for a track man under a clear, blue sky.

Now Yuichi's social ambitions were good-tempered and childish, what one would expect in a youth. His financial capacities were acknowledged. At the urging of Kawada, he was thinking of going into industry.

As Yuichi saw it, economics was an extremely human subject. To the extent that it was connected directly and deeply with human desire, the activity of its organization was strengthened. At one time, in the developing years of free enterprise economics, it exhibited autonomous faculties, thanks to a close connection with the desires – the self-interest – of the rapidly rising bourgeoisie. Today, however, it was in a period of decline, owing to the fact that its organization had been separated from desire and mechanized, thus bringing about the attenuation of desire. A new system of economics had to find new desire.

The greatest evil, certainly, lies only in reasonless desire, objectless desire. Why? Love with the object of propagating children, selfishness with the object of distributing profits, passion for a revolution of the working class with the object of attaining Communism are virtues in the various ruling societies.

Yuichi did not love a woman, and the woman bore Yuichi a child. At that time he saw the ugliness, not of Yasuko's will, but of objectless desire in life. The proletariat also, without realizing it, are probably born from desire of this kind. Yuichi's economic studies had thus brought him to a new concept of desire. He conceived the ambition to make himself over into that desire.

Yuichi's outlook on life was not, as one would expect in a young man, marked by impatience to resolve matters. When he looked at the contradictions and the ugliness of society, he had the strange urge to take their place. Confusing his instincts with the objectless desire of life, he wished for the various gifts of the industrialist. If Shunsuké had heard his wishes, he would have averted his eyes at the thought that Yuichi had become captive to common ambition. Ages ago, the beautiful Alcibiades, also accustomed to being loved, had become in the same way a hero of vanity. Yuichi began to think he would take advantage of Kawada's good offices.

*

It was summer. Between sleeping and crying, and crying and feeding at the breast, the child of not yet one month was not much to speak of. Her father, however, never tired of watching her monotonous routine. Carried away by curiosity, he tried to open forcibly her tiny, tight-closed fist in order to see the ball of lint she had accumulated there since her birth, for which he was reproved by her mother.

Yuichi's mother, too, out of the joy of seeing the thing she had hoped and dreamed of, quickly improved in health. Yasuko's various symptoms which had occasioned anxiety before her delivery left her without a mark. The happiness of the household grouped around Yuichi was almost perfect.

As early as the day before Yasuko left the hospital, on the day of the seventh-night observance of Keiko's naming, a ceremonial robe came from Yasuko's family. Of scarlet gauze crepe, it was embroidered in gold with the wood sorrel of the Minami crest. A yellowish-pink obi and a red brocade purse embroidered with the crest accompanied it. This was the harbinger of gifts. From friends and relatives everywhere came red silks and white silks. Baby sets came. Silver spoons engraved with the crest came. Thanks to these, Keiko would literally be brought up with a silver spoon in her mouth. Kyoto dolls came, in glass cases, along with baby clothes, Imperial palace dolls, baby blankets.

One day, a big deep-red baby carriage was delivered from the department store. Its truly luxurious construction astounded Yuichi's mother. 'Who, now, could have sent this? Why, it's someone I don't even know,' she said. Yuichi looked at the name of the sender. It was Yaichiro Kawada.

When Yuichi was called to the back door by his mother and saw it, he was suddenly struck by an unhappy memory. It was very much like the baby carriage in front of which Yasuko had stopped for so long on the fourth floor of her father's department store. This was the day they went there soon after she had been diagnosed as pregnant.

Because of this gift, he had to sketch for his wife and his mother the background of his association with Yaichiro Kawada, short of matters that would offend them. His mother only had to understand that Kawada was a student of Shunsuké's; she was satisfied again that her son was the kind of person to be loved by those in high places. And so, at the end of the first week of summer, when an invitation came from Kawada asking Yuichi to his cottage on the Hayama-Isshiki shore, his mother insisted on his going.

'Give him the best wishes of your wife and family, won't you?' she said, and out of her firm sense of duty entrusted her son with cakes as a gift to his host.

The cottage wasn't as big as its lawn, which was almost a quarter of an acre. When Yuichi got there at about three o'clock, he was surprised to see that the old man who faced Kawada on the glassed-in veranda was Shunsuké. Yuichi wiped away his perspiration as he smilingly approached the two men on the sea-breeze-laden veranda.

In public, Kawada restrained any emotion that might appear excessive. He spoke deliberately, and avoided looking at Yuichi's face. When Shunsuké joked about the box of cakes and the message Yuichi's mother had sent, the three men felt easier. Things were as they always had been.

Yuichi noticed a chessboard with kings, queens, minor pieces, and pawns.

Kawada asked if he wanted to play chess. Shunsuké had been learning the game from Kawada. Yuichi declined. With that Kawada suggested going outdoors while the wind was still good. Shunsuké had consented to go along to the Toshi-Abuzuru yacht basin when Yuichi arrived, after which they were to sail in Kawada's yacht.

Kawada looked youthful in a stylish plain yellow shirt. Even the aged Shunsuké wore a bow tie. Yuichi had taken off his sweat-soaked shirt and changed to a yellow aloha.

They went to the yacht basin. Kawada's Sea Horse Number 5 boat was named the *Hippolyte*. Kawada had not mentioned it earlier; the name was, of course, something he wanted to surprise his guests with. Shunsuké and Yuichi were charmed. There were also a boat named the *Gomennasai*, owned by an American, and also the *Nomo*, meaning 'Drink'.

There were many clouds, but the afternoon sun was quite strong. On the Zushi coast across the water, crowds of weekend visitors were visible.

Everywhere there were the signs of summer. The bright concrete slope of the yacht basin continued undeviatingly down into the water. The parts of it that were always in the sea were patchy with slippery moss filled with countless half-petrified shells and tiny air bubbles. Other than a few waves that swayed the masts of numerous anchored boats, ever so delicately spreading the shiny reflections of ripples against the hulls, the sea rolled from afar towards the breakwater, rippling the surface of the tiny harbour.

Yuichi threw everything he was wearing into the yacht and

332

stripped down to his swimming suit. He walked into the water up to his thighs and pushed the *Hippolyte* out. The mild breeze which he had not felt while he was on land struck him squarely and affectionately in the face as it came across the water.

The yacht went out of the harbour. Kawada, with Yuichi's help, lowered the heavy, zinc-plated, iron centreboard through the middle of the boat into the water. Kawada was a good yachtsman. When he was sailing, however, his facial neuralgia tugged at him more than usual and caused his guests the uneasy feeling that his tight-clenched pipe would fall from his mouth into the sea. The pipe didn't fall. The boat swung west and headed for Enoshima. At that time, in the western sky, there was a majestic cloudscape. A few rays pierced the clouds, as in an ancient painting. In the eyes of the highly imaginative Shunsuké, alienated from nature, the surface of the deep blue distance was filled with a vision of dead men lying in heaps.

'Yuichi has changed,' Shunsuké said.

Kawada answered: 'Not really. I wish it were true. He's one that I can't relax with unless I'm with him out here on the sea or some such place. A while ago, during the rainy season, I went to dinner with him at the Imperial Hotel. Afterwards we were drinking at the bar when a beautiful boy came in with a foreigner. He and Yuchan were dressed like identical twins. Their neckties, their suits ... after a while I looked carefully; even their socks were the same. Yuchan and that lovely boy exchanged quick glances, but it was clear they were deeply embarrassed ...

'Oh, Yuchan, the wind has changed! Spread that sheet over there, won't you? That's right ...

'But there was something even more embarrassing between me and that unknown foreigner. After we had taken one glance at each other, we could no longer remain indifferent to each other. Yuichi's clothes that day were not to my liking. He had wanted them, though, so I agreed to having them made – suit and necktie in American taste. It seemed sure that Yuichi had got together with that beautiful boy and they had arranged to go out together in similar clothes. It was a strange accident, an unfortunate one, that they should have bumped into each other accompanied by their patrons. It was a confession that they were intimate with each other. The beautiful boy was of light complexion, a marvellously turned-out youngster. The purity of his eyes and the charm of his smile gave a strikingly vivacious power to his beauty. I'm a terribly jealous person, as you know, and that whole evening afterwards I was in a rotten mood. After all, that foreigner and I had been two-timed right before our eyes!

'Yuchan, it seemed, knew that whatever he said would make him seem more guilty, so he sat there quiet as a stone. At first I was mad and heaped accusations on him, but in the end I had to admit defeat. It's always I who end up trying to cheer him.

'Always the same developments, always the same results. It sometimes bothers me at work, and when judgements that should be clear come out cloudy, I worry about how I must seem to others. Do you understand, sir? An industrialist like me, with a large organization, three factories, six thousand stockholders, five thousand employees, capable of producing six thousand trucks alone – if a man like me, able to influence all that activity, were in my private life under the influence of a woman, the world would find it easier to understand. But if they knew that I, such as I am, were influenced by a student of twenty-two or -three, the absurdity of that secret would give people the greatest laugh.

'We aren't embarrassed about immorality. We are afraid of being laughed at. That the president of an automobile company might be a homosexual is something earlier times might have tolerated, but nowadays it would be as funny as if a millionaire were addicted to shoplifting, or if a great beauty farted. When a man is funny up to a certain point, he may use the ridicule to make people love him. When he is ridiculous beyond that point, however, it is unforgivable for people to laugh at him.

'Do you know, sir, why the third president of the Krupp Steel Works committed suicide before the First World War? A love that turned all values upside down took over his sense of dignity and destroyed all the balance by which he had supported himself in society.'

This lengthy complaint coming from the mouth of Kawada had the air of a lecture of instructional discourse, and Shunsuké found it difficult even to chime in with words of assent. But then, whatever breaks there were in this story of ruin were filled by Kawada's seamanship as the yacht glided through the water.

Yuichi was spending most of his time stretched out on the prow, fixedly scanning the area towards which the boat headed. Though he was clearly aware that the words being spoken were meant for him, he kept his back turned to the middle-aged narrator and his aged listener. The sun's rays seemed to glisten off the shining skin of his back; still untanned, that marble young skin gave off the odour of summer greenery.

They approached Enoshima, and turned their backs to the view of Kamakura shining in the distance as Kawada swung the *Hippolyte* south. Although the conversation between the two men was entirely about Yuichi, he took no part in it.

'At any rate, Yuichi has changed,' said Shunsuké.

'I wouldn't say so. Why do you say that?'

'I don't know why. But he's changed. Frighteningly, as I see it.'

'He's a father now. But he's still a child. Basically, he hasn't changed a bit.'

'Let's not argue; you know Yuichi much better than I do,' said Shunsuké, carefully moving the camel-hair blanket he had brought along so that it shielded his neuralgic knee from the sea breeze. He adroitly changed the subject. 'As to what you were saying about the relationship between people's evil deeds and whether they're thought ridiculous, I'm very much interrested in the subject. At present, we have taken out of education the minute concern with immorality we used to feel had such tremendous importance. The metaphysics of immorality is dead; only the humour of it is left. It has become something funny. Isn't that right? The disease of ridicule throws the balance of life into confusion; but if only immorality would maintain its dignity, it would not destroy life's balance. There's something strange about this logic, isn't there? Is it not a reflection of the shallowness of modernity, that something lofty now is without power and something ridiculous has savage strength?'

'I don't particularly care to have immorality looked at as something dignified.'

'You think there are just common, ordinary vices, eh? A "golden mean" of them?' Shunsuké had slipped into his lecture platform tone of many decades earlier. 'In ancient Sparta the boys were not punished for the thefts they carried out so deftly as a way of developing the agility demanded on the battlefield. One boy stole a fox, but he bungled and was caught. He hid the fox under his clothing and denied the offence. The fox chewed right into the boy's middle. Nevertheless, he kept right on protesting and, without a cry of pain, died. You may think that what is great in this story is its demonstration that self-discipline is a greater virtue than theft. It shows that all is redeemed. But that is not so. He died because he was humiliated that through his exposure extraordinary vice was brought down to the level of ordinary crime. The morality of the Spartans had a sense of beauty in it that cannot be excluded from the models of ancient Greece. Subtle evil is more beautiful than coarse goodness, and is therefore moral.

'Ancient morality was simple and strong, and thus magnificence was always on the side of sublety, and humour always on the side of coarseness. Nowadays, however, morality has been separated from aesthetics. Thanks to cheap bourgeois principles, morality has taken sides with mediocrity and with the "golden mean". Beauty has taken on an exaggerated form, become old-fashioned, and it is either magnificent or a joke. These days it doesn't matter which; the two have the same meaning. However, as I said before, false modernism and false humanism have propagated the heresy of adorning human defects. Modern art has tended, since *Don Quixote*, towards the glorification of the ridiculous. Maybe you wouldn't mind having the homosexual proclivities of an automobile company president like you worshipped as ludicrous. In short, since it is funny, it is beautiful; therefore, if even you with your upbringing aren't able to resist, it society is even happier. You should be smashed; then you would be a real modern manifestation of one deserving respect.'

'Humanity. Humanity,' Kawada muttered. 'That is the only place we can hide, the only basis we have for vindication. Isn't that perversity itself – this need to drag in all humanity in order to prove that you yourself are human? If humanity is humanity, isn't it vastly more human to do as people usually do, to seek the help of something outside humanity – God, or physical or scientific truth? Perhaps all the humour lies in the fact that we go about setting ourselves up as human beings and defend our instincts as human. But the men of society who should listen to us are not at all interested in us as human beings.'

Shunsuké remarked with a little smile, 'I'm very much interested in them.'

'You're a very special case, sir.'

'Yes; I am, after all, the monkey known as an artist.'

There was a great splash near the bow. When they looked they saw that Yuichi, perhaps feeling left out, perhaps sick of the boring dialogue, had dived into the water and swum off. From the glassy troughs between the waves, the sinews of a smooth back and shapely arms appeared, glittering and coruscating.

The swimmer had not plunged in without a purpose. A hundred yards to the right of the yacht appeared Najima, whose strange shape had been visible even in the offing back at Abuzuru. Najima was a low, oblong island formed by a succession of bald rocks that barely protruded from the sea. There were no trees except a single, undergrown, twisted pine. Thus, what made the sight of the uninhabited island even more mysterious was a gigantic *torii*, towering above the water line at the centre of the highest rock and supported, since it was not yet complete, by great ropes stretched from the surrounding terrain.

Under the light filtering dazzlingly through the clouds, the *torii* and the ropes leading to it soared in a silhouette full of meaning. No workmen were visible; the shrine that should have been grouped with the *torii* – under construction, probably – was not visible. One could not determine, therefore, which way the *torii* faced. It stood aloof upon the sea, the figure of objectless adoration. Its form was black, but all around, the sea glittered in the western sun.

Yuichi caught hold of a rock and climbed on to the island.

He seemed to be impelled by childish curiosity to advance closer to the *torii*. He disappeared between the two rocks and then climbed another. When he got to the *torii*, the naked youth, the western sky ablaze at his back, presented the lines of a sculpture in marvellous silhouette. He rested one hand on the *torii* and, lifting the other hand high, waved to the pair on the yacht.

Kawada brought the *Hippolyte* as close to Najima as he could without striking some sunken reef, and waited for Yuichi to swim back.

Shunsuké pointed to the form of the young man at the side of the *torii* and said: 'Is that funny?'

'No.'

'What is it?'

'That's beautiful. It's frightening, but that can't be helped.'

'If so, Mr Kawada, where is the humour?'

Kawada slightly bowed his eternally unbending head and said: 'I must rescue myself from the ridiculous.'

When he heard this, Shunsuké laughed. It seemed as if his uncontrollable laughter had crossed the water and reached Yuichi's ears. The young man ran along the rocks and appeared to be setting out for a point on the shore close to the *Hippolyte* ...

The party sailed as far as the Morito coast, then followed the shoreline back to Abuzuru. Then they proceeded by car to the Kaihin Hotel in Zushi for supper. The hotel there was a small summer resort. Recently it had been released from government requisition. During that period, many of the vessels belonging to the yacht club members had been commandeered for excursions by the Americans at the hotel. This summer the beach in front of it had been thrown open to public use, clearing the air, some hoped, of long-standing grievances.

It was evening when they arrived at the hotel. In the grass-covered garden five or six tables with chairs were set out. The colourful beach umbrellas attached to the tables were folded like cypress trees. The turnout was still poor. A loudspeaker on an R—— Chewing Gum billboard was blaring a popular song. At intervals it would repeat an announcement about a lost child and cleverly work in a commercial pitch: 'We have a lost child! We have a lost child! He is about three years old and has the name Kenji in his sailor cap. Will those looking for this boy please report below the R—— Chewing Gum sign?'

When the three men finished eating, twilight had enshrouded the lawn tables. The patrons were suddenly gone; the loudspeaker was silent. All that remained was the sound of waves. Kawada left his seat. Between the old man and Yuichi there fell a silence that had become habitual now.

After a time Shunsuké spoke.

'You've changed.'

'Is that so?'

'You certainly have. It frightens me. I had a hunch it would happen. I had a hunch that sometime the day must come that the person you were would disappear. Because you are radium. You are a radioactive substance. Now that I think about it, I have feared it for a long time. Still, to a certain extent, you are the person you were before. So now, I think, we should part company.'

The word 'part' made the youth laugh. ' "Part", you say? You make it seem as if there was something between us up to now, sir.'

'Surely there has been something. Do you doubt it?'

'I only understand you in the vulgar sense.'

'There! That expression wouldn't have been used by the old you.'

'In that case, I'd better keep quiet.'

Yuichi was not aware of the long-standing perplexity and the deep deliberation that these casual words of the author expressed. Shunsuké exhaled deeply in the darkness.

There was indeed in Shunsuké Hinoki a profound perplexity about his own creation. This perplexity had its abysses, and it had its vistas. If he were a young man, he would soon have recovered from his perplexity. To him at his age, however, the value of that awakening was doubtful. Is not awakening an even deeper delusion? Where are we going? Why do we wish to wake up? Since humanity is an illusion, is not the supremely wise awakening the erection of well-disciplined, logical, artificial illusions in the midst of this greater, highly complicated,

339

uncontrollable illusion? The will not to awaken, the will not to recover, now maintained Shunsuké's health.

His love for Yuichi was part of that perplexity. He worried; he suffered. The well-known irony of the formal beauty of his work, the spiritual pain and confusion expended in disciplining his emotions, and yet the irony that only through that disciplining would a final, real confession of the pain and the confusion be attained – all these struggled in him now. By holding fast to the course he had planned at the beginning, he maintained the right and the initiative of confession. If love went so far as to take away his right of confession as the artist saw it, the love he had not confessed would not exist.

Yuichi's transformation, in Shunsuké's sharp eyes, had sketched out this dangerous possibility.

'It hurts, but at any rate...' Shunsuké's voice, hoarse with age, came from the darkness, 'even though it hurts me more than I can express, Yuchan, I think for the time being we'd better not see each other. Up till now you were the one to cavil about whether you would see me. You were the one who would not meet me. Now it is I saying we should not meet. If ever the necessity arises, however, if for some reason it becomes necessary to see me, then I will meet with you gladly. Now, I suppose you don't think that necessity will arise...'

'No.'

'That's what you think, but...'

Shunsuké's hand touched Yuichi's as it lay on the arm-rest. Though it was midsummer, Shunsuké's hand was extremely cold.

'At any rate, we won't meet again until then.'

'All right – if that's what you wish, sir.'

Fishing torches flickered in the offing. Conscious that they would probably not have the opportunity again for a time, they fell into their familiar, uncomfortable silence.

The yellow of Kawada's shirt appeared in the darkness, preceded by a boy in white with beer and glasses on a silver tray. Shunsuké tried to seem unconcerned. When Kawada revived the argument that had been going on earlier, Shunsuké responded with the air of a cynic. It seemed as if no one knew where this argument, with all its moot points, would end, but after a time the increasing cold drove the three into the hotel lobby.

That night Kawada and Yuichi planned to stay at the hotel. Kawada urged Shunsuké, too, to stay over in the separate room reserved for him, but he firmly declined. There was no alternative but to have the chauffeur drive Shunsuké back to Tokyo. In the car, the old author's knee throbbed painfully under the camel-hair blanket. The driver heard him cry out once and stopped the car in surprise. Shunsuké told him not to worry and to drive on. From an inner pocket he withdrew his favourite medicine, the morphine preparation Pavinal, and took some. The drug made him drowsy, but it relieved his spiritual pain. His mind, dwelling on nothing at all, engrossed itself in the meaningless process of counting the road lights. His anti-heroic heart recalled the strange story that Napoleon on the march never could keep himself from counting the windows along the road.

27

Intermezzo

Minoru Watanabe was seventeen. His eyes were gentle in his regular, fair, round face; his smile, complete with dimples, was beautiful. He was a sophomore in a certain new-system high school. One of the great bombings late in the war, on March tenth, had reduced to ashes the downtown grocery store that was his family home. His parents and his younger sister were burned to death. Only Minoru survived. He was brought to the home of relatives in Setagaya. The head of that family was a clerk in the Welfare Ministry, for whom it was not easy to assume the added expense of even the single small mouth of Minoru.

When Minoru was sixteen he secured, in answer to an advertisment, a job in a coffee shop. After school he would go there and cheerfully work the five or six hours until ten o'clock. Before examinations he was permitted to go home at seven. His pay was good; one had to admit that Minoru had found a good job.

Not only that, Minoru's boss became extremely interested in him. His name was Fukujiro Honda. He was a fortyish, woefully thin, quiet, upright man. His wife had left him five or six years earlier, and he still lived alone on the second floor above the shop. One day he called on Minoru's uncle in Setagaya and asked if he might adopt Minoru. The uncle did not have to think twice. The adoption proceedings were quickly completed; Minoru's surname became Honda.

Minoru still helped out in the shop once in a while, but that was only because he found it interesting. He lived his student life as he pleased; once in a while he would go with his foster father to dine, or to the theatre, or to the movies. Fukujiro liked the traditional theatre, but when he went out with Minoru he patiently watched the noisy comedies or the

342

westerns Minoru loved. He bought Minoru boy's clothes for winter and summer. He bought him skates. For Minoru, this life was something he had never known; his uncle's children, when they happened to visit him, envied him.

Meanwhile a change had come about in Minoru's character.

His smiling face did not change, but a love for solitude developed in him. For instance, when he went to a Pachinko pinball parlour, he preferred to go alone. Occasions when he should have been studying, he would go and stand in front of a Pachinko machine for hours on end. He didn't associate particularly with his school friends.

His still tender sensibilities were pervaded by unbearable fears and revulsions. Somewhat different from the average boys who faced degradation, he shivered at the visions of his future depravity. He burned with the fixed idea that, no matter what, he would come to no good. At night, when he saw the physiognomists sitting under their dim lights in the shadow of a bank or the like, he was filled with fright. Surely a future of bad luck, crime, and evil was visible on his forehead, he thought as he hurried by.

Minoru loved, however, his own clear, smiling face; his future seemed reflected in the pure white line of his teeth when he laughed. His eyes belied his depravity and were even beautiful in their purity. The form that sprang from mirrors at unexpected angles on street corners also showed a fine, boyish neck, neatly barbered. He felt then that he could be at ease so long as his external appearance did not alter, but that respite did not continue for long.

He tried saké, he immersed himself in detective stories, he also learned to smoke. The fragrant smoke coursing luxuriously through his lungs made him feel as if a still unformed, not yet known sense was reaching for expression out of the depths of him. On days when he was distraught by self-revulsion, he prayed that war would start again; he dreamed of the great city wrapped in conflagration. In the midst of that holocaust he felt he might meet his dead parents and sister again.

He loved the momentary excitements and at the same time the hopeless starry nights. He practically wore out a pair of shoes in three months, wandering from neighbourhood to neighbourhood at night.

He would return from school, eat supper, and change to flashy boyish sport clothes. He would not show his face in the coffee shop until the middle of the evening. His foster father was worried and secretly followed him, but his certainty that the boy went everywhere alone appeased any jealousy he might feel. Out of that relief and the sad knowledge that, separated by years as they were, he was not the person the boy would have fun with, he withheld his complaints and let him do as he pleased.

One day during the summer vacation, when the sky was filled with clouds and it was too cool to go to the beach, Minoru put on a red aloha shirt with a white palm tree design and set out with the pretext of a trip to the house in Setagaya. The red shirt went well with the boy's fair skin.

He thought he might enjoy the zoo. He got off the subway at Ueno Station and came out under the statue of Saigo-San. At that moment the sun broke from behind clouds. The high granite staircase gleamed.

He lit a cigarette on the way up the stairs. The flame of the match was hardly visible in the bright sunlight. Brimming with the joy of being alone, he almost flew up the rest of the stairs.

Few people were in Ueno Park. He bought a ticket with a coloured picture of a sleeping lion and walked through the gate. Minoru paid no heed to the arrows marking the circuit. He let his feet take him wherever they would. In the heat the odour of the animals seemed as deeply intimate as the smell of his own bedding.

The giraffe cage appeared before him. From the giraffe's contemplative face, along his neck and towards his back, the shadow of a cloud descended. The sun was hidden. The giraffe brushed away flies with his tail as he moved. He took each step as if it had staggered the imagination of the artisan who put his great skeleton together. Then Minoru saw the polar bear sweltering in the heat, madly plunging into the water and flopping back on his concrete perch, over and over.

344

He came to a certain path and found a place where he could look out across Shinobazu Pond.

Automobiles glittered by on the road around the edge of the pond. From the clock tower of Tokyo University in the west to the Ginza crossroads towards the south, here and there the uneven horizon reflected the summer sun. A building white as a matchbox shone like quartz. An advertising balloon for an Ueno department store hung languidly in the air, its roundness distorted by gas leakage. It hovered just above the dismal building of the department store itself.

Here was Tokyo. Here was a sentimental view of the metropolis. The myriad streets the youth had so diligently traversed all lay concealed within this panorama. Many nights of wandering were wiped away without a trace in this clear scene. Yet there was not a vestige of freedom from the inexplicable fears that haunted his dreams.

A street-car that wound around the edge of the pond from the direction of Shichikencho rumbled beneath his feet. Minoru went back again to look at the zoo.

The smell of the animals arose from the distance. The most smelly place was the hippopotamus house. The male hippo, Deca, and the female, Zabu, wallowed in the dirty water with only their snouts showing. To either side of them was the wet floor of the cage. Two rats went in and out of the cage, heading for the grain box when the keeper was away.

The elephant pulled hay a bunch at a time and stuffed it into his mouth. Before he had finished chewing one he would gather the next. Once in a while he would take too much, and then he would lift his pillar of a front leg and crush the rest to the floor.

The penguins looked like so many people at a cocktail party. Each of them looked in whatever direction he pleased, and now and then stuck a wing out away from his body and shook his backside.

The civet cats, two deep on their perch about a foot above a floor littered with the red chicken heads they fed on, gazed languidly in Minoru's direction.

Minoru found pleasure in seeing the pair of lions; now he

thought he might go home. The popsicle he had been sucking was almost gone. Then he realized that there was a small building near him that he had not yet seen. He went nearer and saw it was the small bird pavilion. The window panes, shaped like stylized chameleons, were broken in a few places.

There was no one in the bird pavilion but a man in a snow-white polo shirt, who had his back to Minoru.

Minoru chewed a slice of gum and looked at a bird whose white bill was bigger than its head. The interior of the building, less than forty yards square, resounded with strange, raucous cries, like the jungle birds in a Tarzan movie, Minoru thought. He looked about to see what bird owned it, and saw it was a parrot. Parrots and parakeets outnumbered the other birds in the small pavilion. The colouring of the wings of the red diamond parakeets was particularly beautiful. The white parrots had all turned their heads and with one wing around the feeding box were hammering away with their hard bills as if they were indeed hammers.

Minoru walked in front of the mynah bird cage. This bird, black of wing, only his face yellow, held his perch with dirty yellow legs. He opened his red bill and, as Minoru wondered what sound he would utter, said, 'Hello!'

Minoru answered with a smile. The youth in the white polo shirt near him smiled too and turned in Minoru's direction. Since Minoru's head came to about the youth's eyebrows, the youth had to look downward slightly. Their eyes met and held. Each was surprised by the beauty of the other. The movement of Minoru's gum-chewing ceased.

'Hello,' the mynah bird said again. 'Hello,' the youth said, mimicking. Minoru laughed.

The stranger withdrew his gaze from the cage and lit a cigarette. Not to be outdone, Minoru took a crumpled package of foreign cigarettes from his pocket, hurriedly spat out his chewing gum, and stuck a cigarette in his mouth. The youth lit a match and offered a light.

'Do you smoke, too?' the youth asked, surprised.

'Yeah. We're not allowed to at school, though.'

'What school?'

'N— Academy.'

'And I –' The youth named a famous private university. 'May I ask your name?'

'Minoru.'

'My first name will be enough, too: Yuichi.' The two left the bird pavilion and started walking.

'Your red aloha looks nice,' Yuichi said. Minoru flushed.

*

They talked of many things. Minoru was charmed by Yuichi's youth, his artless conversation, and his beauty. He conducted Yuichi to the animal cages that he had seen and Yuichi had not. In about ten minutes they had become like brothers.

This man is one of them, thought Minoru. But just the same how nice it is that so pretty a man should be one of them. I like this man's voice, his laughter, the movement of his body, his whole body, his smell, everything. I hope we can sleep together soon. With this man I would do anything, let him do anything. I think he'd like what I have for him. He put his hand in his pocket and deftly changed the position of something that was suddenly causing him pain. He felt better. He found a stick of chewing gum in his pocket, took it out, and popped it in his mouth.

'Have you seen the martens? Haven't you seen them yet?'

Minoru took Yuichi by the hand and led him towards the foul-smelling cages. They kept their hands linked together.

In front of the cage of the Tsushima marten hung a placard explaining, among other things, the habits of the animal: 'Early in the morning or at night he is active in the camellia groves sucking the nectar of the blossoms.' There were three of the little yellow animals. One of them stuck the comb of one of the red chicken heads in his mouth and looked warily at the visitors. The eyes of those watching met the eyes of the animal. The eyes outside were certainly looking at a marten, but it was not necessarily true that the marten was looking at human beings. Yuichi and Minoru, however, felt that they loved the eyes of a marten more than they loved human eyes.

The backs of their necks became very warm – the sun was already descending, but its rays were still fierce. Minoru looked behind him. There was nobody around. Thirty minutes after they had met, they kissed lightly and naturally. Now I am very happy, Minoru thought. This boy had been taught nothing but sexual happiness. The world was splendid; there was no one there – only dead silence.

The roar of the lion shook the air. Yuichi lifted his eyes and said: 'Oh! We're in for a shower.'

They noticed the gathering clouds. The sun was soon obscured. When they got to the subway station, the first drops were striking the pavement. They got into the train. 'Where are you going?' said Minoru, uneasily, as if he were being left behind. They got off at the station by the shrine. From there they went by street-car along a different road, which incidentally showed no trace of rain, to the inn in Takagicho where Yuichi had been taken some time ago by the student from his college.

*

Possessed by the sensual memories of that occasion, Minoru manufactured excuses that kept his foster father at a distance. Fukujiro had no way that he could fill this boy with visions.

He took good care of his relationships within the neighbourhood, and when there was a misfortune there, the devout Fukujiro would wrap up a votive offering and set out for the temple. Then he would sit for a long time silently before the Buddha, paying no attention to the other mourners. There was in his wasted frame, so devoid of charm, something that gave the impression of bad luck.

Somehow he could not surrender his place at the counter of the coffee shop to someone else. But it was not a wise policy in this student neighbourhood to have such an unsociable old codger at the cash register all day. Even his regular customers would have left him if they had seen him assiduously going over the day's receipts for a full hour every night after closing.

Meticulousness and niggardliness were the substance of Fukujiro's religious zeal. If the sliding doors were left slightly open, or even if the door pulls supposed to be on the left and the right somehow turned up in the middle, he had to get up right away and fix them. Fukujiro's uncle came from the country and ordered rice and eels for supper. Minoru was aghast to see Fukujiro exact the price of the meal from his uncle.

One could not compare young Yuichi's body with that of Fukujiro, who was nearly forty. Not only that, Yuichi was to Minoru a vision of the hero out of so many action movies and the daring youth of adventure stories. Everything that Minoru wished to be he saw embodied in Yuichi. Shunsuké had used Yuichi as the material of a work he dreamed of; but Minoru used countless old tales as the material of a dream of Yuichi.

Yuichi would turn his head sharply – in the boy's eyes he had turned his head in order to defend himself against the terrible onslaughts of young villains. Minoru fancied himself to be the boy companion sure to be accompanying such a hero. He was confident in the very depths of him in the courage of his master. He was a pure servant who felt that when he died it would be with his master. As a result, it was not love he manifested so much as sexual loyalty, the joy of imaginary renunciation and self-sacrifice. What he exhibited was perfectly natural boyish propensity to dream. In his dreams one night, Minoru saw Yuichi and himself on the battlefield. Yuichi was the beautiful young officer; Minoru was his beautiful boy orderly. The two were simultaneously struck in the chest by rifle bullets and died embracing, their lips locked in a kiss. Another time Yuichi was a young seaman; Minoru was a boy sailor. The two landed on an island in the torrid zone, and while they were there the ship, at the order of the crafty captain, set sail. There on the island the two castaways were attacked by savages. They warded off countless poison arrows fired from the bushes, using a great scallop shell for a shield.

Thus a night the two spent together was a fabulous night. Around them swirled the night of a gigantic, hostile world. Villains and bitter enemies and savages and assassins prayed for their misfortune. The eyes of adversaries who would shout for joy if they died were outside, peering through the dark window panes. Minoru was sad that he could not sleep with a pistol under his pillow. What would he do if some scoundrel had hidden himself in the wardrobe and was opening the door a crack and taking dead aim at the sleeping forms of the two with a revolver? He could not help feeling that Yuichi, sleeping undisturbed by these fancies, had courage beyond that of other men.

The unreasoning fear from which Minoru had longed to escape suddenly was transformed into a sweet, fabulous fear that made him feel only the joy of living under its influence. When he came upon articles in newspapers about opium smuggling and secret societies, he would read them avidly, thinking that each was an incident involving themselves.

Yuichi had been slightly infected by these proclivities in the boy. The stubborn bias against society that Yuichi once held – and still held – was in this dreamer something to encourage fantasies, romantic enmities, romanesque perils, plebeian defences against justice and nobility, the unyielding, reasonless prejudice of the rabble. When he saw this, Yuichi felt better. When he realized, moreover, the source of these inspirations – that it was he, Yuichi, nothing else – he was amazed at his own intangible power. 'Those guys' – the only term by which the boy referred to society – 'are after us, aren't they? We've got to watch out,' Minoru liked to say. 'Those guys would like to see us dead!'

'What do you mean? Those guys don't give a damn. They hold their noses and pass us by, that's all,' said his realistic protector, six years his senior. His opinion, however, did not convince Minoru.

'Cripes! Women, now' – Minoru spat towards a group of girl students going by. Then he threw out words of sexual vituperation that he had learned only recently, so that the girls could hear: 'Women, now, what are they? All they have tucked away between their legs is a smelly, dirty pocket, ain't that right? And all they've got stuffed in that pocket is rubbish.'

Yuichi, who of course was keeping his wife a secret, smiled at this remark.

The walks that he had formerly taken alone Minoru now took with Yuichi. Everywhere about the dark street corners imaginary assassins lurked. Without a sound, the assassins were treading close behind the two of them. Giving them the slip, or teasing them, or playing practical jokes on these non-existent adversaries was Minoru's favourite pastime.

'Look, Yuchan!' Minoru proposed a prank that would certainly result in their being followed. He took the wad of gum from his mouth and stuck it to the door handle of a foreigner's shiny car at the curb. This accomplished, he acted as if he didn't know a thing about it and hurried Yuichi away.

One evening Yuichi went with Minoru to the roof of the Ginza Hot Springs for beer. Having downed one, the boy proffered his glass for a second. The evening breeze on the roof was quite cool; their shirts, which had stuck to their backs with sweat, started billowing in the breeze like hoods. Red, yellow, and water-green lanterns swung above the dark dance floor as two or three couples took turns to the guitar music. Yuichi and Minoru, although they wished to dance, did not join them. It was difficult for men friends to dance together here. They looked on fixedly at the fun the others were having and, caught up in the activity, left their seats to lean against the railing. The gleam of the street enveloped the summer evening. In the south there was a dark shadow among the populated areas. They decided it must be the forest of the Hama Detached Palace Park. As they looked idly in the direction of that forest, Yuichi put his arm about Minoru's shoulders. From the midst of the forest a glow began to rise. Fireworks spread out from a great green ball, then with a noise like thunder turned yellow, then collapsed into pink parasol shapes, then shattered and went out, and all was silent.

'Pretty, isn't it, like that?' said Minoru. He paraphrased a passage he had read in a detective story: 'If you took everybody in the world and sent them up in fireworks and killed them – all the guys that cause trouble, one at a time, and made fireworks of them and killed them – there'd be only Yuichi and me left in the whole world!'

'Then who would have the children?'

'Who needs children? If we got married and had kids, the kids would grow up and make fools of us, or if not that, they'd become just like us, that's all.'

These words sent a shiver through Yuichi. He felt that divine intervention had made Yasuko's child a female. The youth grasped Minoru's shoulder gently. In this rebellious spirit that lay within Minoru's soft boyish cheek and his pure smile, Yuichi somehow usually found balm for his basically uneasy nature. As a result, their sympathies strengthened the sensual tie between them and in turn cultivated the most essential elements, as well as the most decent elements, of their friendship. The boy's imaginativeness pulled at the youth's doubts and pertinaciously set them in motion. Thus, even Yuichi was plunged into infantile dreams. One night, for instance, he kept himself awake earnestly imagining that he had set out on an expedition into the upper reaches of the Amazon.

When it was quite late they went to the boathouse on the shore across from the Tokyo Theatre, intending to take a boat ride. The boats were all moored at the dock, the light in the boathouse shack was extinguished, its Nanking lock tightly fastened. There was nothing to do but sit down on the boards of the dock and let their legs dangle over the water, and smoke. The Tokyo Theatre across the way was closed. The Shimbasi Playhouse, on the other side of the bridge at the right, was closed too. The water reflected hardly any light. No more remnants of the heat, it seemed, would rise from that dark, still surface.

Minoru thrust out his forehead: 'Look, I have prickly heat!' He showed Yuichi the faint red signs. This boy showed everything to his lover: his notebooks, his shirts, his books, his socks – whatever new thing he was wearing.

Suddenly Minoru burst out laughing. Yuichi looked at the dark path along the river near the Tokyo Theatre to see what was making him laugh. An old man in a bath garment had fallen off his bicycle and lay on the path beside it. He had landed on his hip, perhaps, and could not get up.

'A fine thing, riding a bike at his age. I wish he'd fallen in the river.'

His happy laughter and his cruel teeth, white and luminous in the darkness, were beautiful. Yuichi could not help thinking of the ways beyond imagination that Minoru was like himself.

'You must be living with a steady boy friend. How do you manage to stay out so late and get away with it?'

'I suppose his weak point is that he's in love with me. And he's become my foster father to boot. It's legal.'

There was something laughable in the word 'legal' coming from this boy's mouth. Minoru went on: 'You have a steady boy friend, too, I guess.'

'Yes, but only an old man.'

'I'll go kill that old man.'

'No use. He's one you can kill and he won't die.'

'Why, now, do young, pretty, gay fellows all have to be somebody's prisoner?'

'It's more convenient so.'

'They buy you clothes and give you all kinds of money. And you get attached to them, even though you hate them.' As he said this the boy spat a great white wad of saliva into the river.

Yuichi put his arm around Minoru's waist. Then he brought his lips close to the boy's cheek and kissed him.

'That's awful,' said Minoru, kissing him back unrestrainedly. 'You kiss me and I get an erection. Then I don't want to go home.'

After a time Minoru said: 'Ah, a cicada!' Through the stillness that followed after a trolley car had thundered over the bridge, the mincing, tangled voice of the night cicada threaded its way. There was not much foliage in the area. The cicada must have blundered out of a park somewhere. It flew low over the surface of the river, then headed for the lights of the bridge on the right, where tiger moths were flitting about.

Thus the night sky came irresistibly into their eyes. It was a splendid starry sky, returning its brilliance to the street glare unflinchingly. Yet Yuichi's nostrils were full of the stench of the river, close to whose surface their shoes dangled. He really liked this boy, but he could not help thinking that people talk of love as if they were ditch rats.

*

Fukujiro Honda had begun to entertain definite suspicions about Minoru. The heat was terrible. One night when sleep was difficult, he was reading a samurai adventure magazine under the mosquito netting, unhappily waiting for the tardy Minoru to come home. His head was filled with mad thoughts. At one o'clock in the morning, he heard the back door opening, then the sound of shoes being removed. Fukujiro turned off the light by his pillow.

The light went on in the adjoining room. Minoru seemed to be undressing. Then an interminable period of time passed by while Minoru, it seemed, sat naked at the window, smoking. Then smoke, glinting with lamplight, was visible rising above the room partitions.

Minoru had slipped naked into the mosquito netting in his room and was about to get into bed. His body was suddenly pinned by Fukujiro's body. He had a rope coiled in his hand, with which he bound Minoru's hands. Then he passed the rest of the long rope several times around Minoru's chest. All the while Minoru struggled silently, his cries muffled by a pillow pressed against his face and held there by Fukujiro's forehead as he worked to tie the boy.

The tying was finally done, and Minoru pleaded half-audibly from under the pillow: 'Ouch! You're killing me. I won't yell; just take away the pillow.'

So that the boy could not flee, Fukujiro straddled his body. He took away the pillow, but kept his right hand near Minoru's face in case he cried out. With his left hand he grasped the boy's hair and, giving it small tugs, said: 'All right, let's have it! Who's the dark horse you're stepping out with? Come on, out with it!'

Minoru was suffering. His hair was being pulled; his bare chest and arms were chafed by the rope. Yet even with Fukujiro's old-fashioned accusation ringing in his ears, this fanciful youth never once imagined that the ever dependable Yuichi would arrive here to rescue him. He thought of practical ruses that he had been taught by worldly experience.

'Stop pulling my hair and I'll tell you,' Minoru groaned. When Fukujiro let go his grip, the boy slumped as if dead. Fukujiro was seized with panic and shook the boy's shoulders. 'This rope is killing me,' Minoru gasped. 'Untie the rope and I'll tell you.' Fukjiro turned on the light at the head of the bed. He untied the rope. Minoru applied his lips to the sore places on his wrists. He kept his head down and said nothing.

The momentum of Fukujiro's faint-hearted outburst was by this time half-spent. He saw Minoru's firmness, and thinking

354

now to bring him around by tears, he bowed his head to the floor before the naked boy who sat cross-legged and begged forgiveness for his violent behaviour. On the boy's white chest the pink rope marks were still visible. Naturally, this theatrical display of pain, too, had an indeterminate ending.

Fukujiro feared having his own conduct discovered, so he decided against calling in a private detective agency. Beginning the next evening, however, he neglected the shop and again went on the trail of the one he loved. He found no trace of Minoru. He gave some money to a trusted waiter and set him to the task. This clever, faithful fellow reported triumphantly that he had seen the face of Minoru's companion and had been able to ascertain that he was named Yuchan.

Fukujiro went about to the various hangouts, which he had not visited for a long time. One of his old acquaintances who had not yet freed himself of his bad habits came by, and, taking him along, Fukujiro was able to inquire about Yuchan's identity at many quiet coffee houses and bars.

Yuichi was under the impression that his own affairs were not known beyond a very small circle, but in this inquisitive little society which had nothing to talk about but itself, intimate information concerning him had spread far and wide.

The middle-aged men of that street were jealous of Yuichi's beauty. They were willing to admit that they would be happy to make love to him, but this youth's cold way of turning people away plunged them into jealousy. The same was true of young men not so beautiful as Yuichi. Fukujiro easily garnered a number of details about him.

In the prattle of these persons the malice of women abounded. When it came to information they did not have, they would display a paranoiac kindness and introduce Fukujiro to some other individual in possession of new gossip. Fukujiro would meet with that person, who would then introduce him to another, who would also put himself out gossiping. In a short time, Fukujiro met ten men he had never seen before.

If he had known about it, Yuichi would have been amazed. Not only was his relationship with Count Kaburagi discussed, but even his affair with Kawada, who was so careful about appearances, was bandied about in detail. Fukujiro relentlessly searched out everything from the identity of Yuichi's in-laws to his home address and telephone number. When he returned to his shop, he pondered various low stratagems that cowardice leads men into.

28

Hailstones from a Clear Sky

Even when Yuichi's father was alive, the Minami family did not have a cottage. His father did not like to be tied down to the same place whether avoiding the heat or avoiding the cold, so while he, always busy, remained in Tokyo, his wife and child spent summers in hotels in Karuizawa, Hakoné, and the like, and he visited them on weekends. At Karuizawa they had many friends, and summers passed there were busy. About that time however, Yuichi's mother noticed his predilection for being by himself. Her beautiful son, his age, his robust health, and his physique notwithstanding, preferred to spend summers in Kamikochi or places where he would meet as few acquaintances as possible, rather than Karuizawa, where he had company all the time.

Even when the war became intense, the Minami family was not in a hurry to evacuate. The head of the family was not concerned about anything like that. A few months before the air raids started, in the summer of 1944, Yuichi's father died at his Tokyo home of a cerebral haemorrhage. His resolute widow refused to give in to the urging of those around her and stood her ground in her Tokyo residence, guarding her husband's ashes. Perhaps her spiritual power threw the fear of God into the incendiary bombs; the house was still standing when the war ended.

If they had had a cottage, they could have sold it at a high price and tided themselves over the post-war inflation. Yuichi's father's estate besides the present house, amounted in 1944 to 2,000,000 yen in savings, negotiable securities, and personal effects. The widow was only upset that she would have to sell her valuable jewels to a broker for a song in order to get through the emergency. She managed, however, to get the help of a former subordinate of her husband, a man who knew his way around in matters of this kind, who took care of minimizing the estate tax, then skilfully went through the negotiations over the securities and the savings accounts and overcame the hazards of the emergency currency regulations without a hitch. When the economy was stabilized, they still had a savings account of 700,000 yen and the economic acumen of Yuichi, brought up in this confused period. Then the kind adviser left this world with the same illness as Yuichi's father. His mother blithely turned over the household accounts to her old maidservant, whose old-fashioned incompetence, and Yuichi's amazement when he found the crisis she had precipitated, has already been told.

For these reasons the Minami family had no opportunity to take summer vacations after the war. An invitation from Yasuko's family, who had a cottage at Karuizawa, to spend the summer there made Yuichi's mother happy, but fear of leaving Tokyo and her attending physician even for a day stifled her joy. She told the young couple: 'Why don't you take the baby and go?' This suggestion was made, however, so glumly that Yasuko considerately announced that it would not do for her to leave her sick mother-in-law alone. That reply was just what the mother-in-law wished; it made the old lady very happy.

When guests came, Yasuko greeted them with fans, cold towels, and cold drinks. Her mother-in-law praised highly the filial devotion of her daughter-in-law, which made Yasuko blush. It was enough to make Yasuko fear that guests would think these goings-on a mere manifestation of her mother-in-law's egoism. She fabricated irrational explanations, such as that she was really trying to get the newborn baby acclimatized to the hot Tokyo summer. Keiko perspired and developed prickly heat, so she was always sprinkled with talcum powder, which made her look like candy dusted with confectioners' sugar.

Yuichi's free and independent spirit hated favours from his in-laws, and opposed accepting the offer of a summer vacation. Yasuko was schooled in the gentle art of politics and concealed her sympathy with her husband's feelings behind the façade of filial piety towards her mother-in-law.

358

The family passed the summer days peacefully; Keiko's presence made them forget the heat. She still did not know how to smile, though, and never once broke her earnest, animal expression. She had begun to show an interest in the turning movements and the rattling noise of her windmill at about the time she was first taken to the shrine. Among her presents there was also a music box, which came in handy.

The music box came from Holland, a model of an old-time farmhouse with a front yard filled with flowering tulips. When you opened the front door a woman in Dutch dress, wearing a white apron and holding a watering can, came out and stood in the doorway. While the door was open thus, the music box played. The tune seemed to be a strange, countrified, Dutch folksong.

Yasuko liked to play the music box for Keiko on the pleasantly breezy second floor. On summer afternoons, her husband, weary with homework that dragged on and on, would join in playing with his wife and child. At such times the breeze coming through the garden trees and blowing through the room towards the northeast seemed even cooler.

'She understands, doesn't she? Look, she's listening!' Yasuko said.

Yuichi studied the infant's expression. This baby has only insides, he thought. To her the outside world hardly exists. To her the outside world is her mother's nipple in her mouth when her stomach is empty, the vague alternations of light between night and day, the beautiful movements of the windmill, or the soft monotone of her rattle and the music box; nothing else. When it comes to her insides, though, well now! The instincts, the history, and the heredity of the first woman are combined in her, and later she will only have to spread them like a water flower in its wet environment. Only the task of making a flower bloom will remain. I shall bring her up as a woman among women, a beauty among beauties.

The scientific method of raising children, with its fixed feeding times, was going out now, so when Keiko became peevish and cried, Yasuko soon gave her the breast. Her breasts, naked and exposed in the bodice of her thin summer dress, were very beautiful. The blue line of the veins ran clear in a circle about the delicate, white skin. When bare, however, her breasts were always perspiring, like fruit ripening in a hothouse. Before she cleaned the nipples with a piece of gauze soaked in boric acid solution, Yasuko always had to wipe away the perspiration with a towel. Before the child's lips could reach out for them her breasts were already dripping. They were always hurting from being overfull.

Yuichi looked at those breasts. He looked at the summer clouds floating by the window. The cicadas buzzed incessantly, so that at times the listening ear forgot the racket. When Keiko had finished nursing, she slept under her mosquito netting. Yuichi and Yasuko looked at each other and smiled.

Suddenly Yuichi was struck by a jarring sensation. Was not this what we call happiness? Or was it nothing more than the helpless relief of seeing what you have feared come to pass, before your eyes – fulfilled. He felt the shock and sat as if stunned. He was amazed at the certainty to all outward appearances that all the end results were before his eyes – at the innocence of it.

A few days later, his mother suffered a sudden setback. To make matters worse, she, who usually would have sent at once for the doctor, now stubbornly refused treatment. That this talkative old widow should go all day without opening her mouth was strange, one had to admit. That evening, Yuichi ate dinner at home. When he saw the colour of his mother's skin, her twitching expression when she tried to smile, and her almost complete lack of appetite, he postponed his departure.

'Why aren't you going out this evening?' she said with studied pleasantness to her son, who seemed to be lingering around the house for ever. 'Don't worry about me. I'm not sick. If you need proof of it, I'm the one who knows best about my own condition. If I don't feel right, I'll call the doctor. I'm not afraid to bother anybody.'

Yuichi, however, made no move to go, so the next morning the sagacious woman changed her tactics. From morning on, she was in high spirits.

'What about yesterday?' she said to Kiyo in a loud voice. 'Yesterday, for all I know, was proof that I haven't graduated from the menopause yet.'

360

The night before she had slept almost not at all, but the state of excitement brought about by lack of sleep, and the fact that her mind had churned all night long, showed this great act of hers to good advantage. After supper Yuichi went out free of worry.

'Call me a taxi, please,' she said to Kiyo. 'I'll tell him where I want to go when I get in the car.'

Kiyo started to get ready to go with her, but the old lady restrained her, saying: 'I don't need anyone with me. I'm going alone.'

'But, ma'am—' Kiyo was thunderstruck. Since Yuichi's mother had become ill, she had almost never gone out alone.

'Is my going out alone so strange? Don't take me for the Empress Dowager, now, please! Didn't I go to the hospital alone the other day when Yasuko had the baby? It didn't matter then.'

'Yes, but then there was nobody but me to mind the house. And don't you remember that you promised me yourself that you would never go out alone again?'

Yasuko listened to this argument between mistress and servant and went to her mother-in-law's room with an anxious look on her face.

'Mother, I'll go with you if you think it isn't convenient for Kiyo to go along.'

'It's all right, Yasuko; don't worry' – her voice was gentle, yet tinged with feeling. It was almost as if she were talking to her own daughter: 'It's a matter of my husband's estate, and there's someone I must see a little while. I don't like to talk to Yuichi about things like this. If he comes home before I do, please tell him that an old friend came by to meet me in his car. If, on the other hand, he comes home after I do, I won't say anything, and you and Kiyo please be sure not to say anything either. Promise me that. I've worked out my own way of dealing with this.'

After she had enjoined them to silence, she hurriedly went out to her taxi and departed. After two hours, she returned in the same cab. She went to bed, seemingly exhausted. Yuichi came home very late.

'How is Mother?' he asked.

'Very well. She went to bed much earlier than usual – about nine o'clock,' Yasuko, faithful to her mother-in-law, answered.

The next evening when Yuichi went out, his mother once more hired a car and prepared to go out. On this second night, she stubbornly and silently went through it all again. Kiyo brought in her Kanze sashpin and flinched as her mistress seized it from her hand. The old lady's eyes, however, aglow with a threatening fever, did not so much as notice Kiyo's existence.

For two successive nights she went to Rudon's in Yura-kucho, on the watch for Yuichi as her one and only piece of evidence. The frightful anonymous letter she had received the day before yesterday had encouraged her to go herself to the mysterious restaurant indicated on the enclosed map. She must see with her own eyes the person in question, as evidence that its information was not false. She decided to go alone. No matter how deep the root of the unfortunate thing that was undermining this family, it was a matter for the mother and her child to resolve. Yasuko must not be brought into it.

Rudon's was amazed at having this peculiar guest for two consecutive nights. In the Edo period, the male prostitutes, while they usually served homosexuals, were commonly patronized by widows. Nowadays, however, that custom was forgotten.

The letter told about the strange customs and the argot of this place. The widow Minami exerted herself to the utmost, and succeeded miraculously from the first in acting like a person who knew her way around. Without in the slightest betraying her amazement, she mixed sociably. The Master, who came over to greet her, was charmed by the presence of this refined old woman and her uninhibited discourse. He could not help trusting her. Then too, above all, this woman did not seem reluctant about parting with her money.

'That's a curious customer,' said Rudy to his boys. 'Look how old she is; she knows everything. She doesn't seem to be a person you need to be wary about; the other guests can enjoy themselves without worrying about her.'

The second floor of Rudon's was at first a bar employing women, but Rudy changed his policy and fired the women.

Now, beginning early in the evening, men danced together on the second floor and watched dances by half-clad boys in women's clothing.

On the first night, Yuichi did not appear. His mother was determined to wait there on the second evening until he showed up. She did not like saké, but she offered it unstintingly to the two or three boys waiting on her table, besides whatever else they liked. After thirty or forty minutes, there was still no sign of Yuichi. Then something one of the boys was saying made her prick up her ears.

The boy said to his friend: 'What's up? Yuchan hasn't been around for two or three days.'

'What are you so worried about?' asked the boy he had spoken to.

'I'm not worried. There's nothing between me and Yuchan.'

'That's what you say.'

The widow asked casually: 'Yuchan must be famous around here. He's a very handsome fellow, isn't he?'

'I've got his picture. I'll show it to you,' said the boy who had spoken first.

It took considerable time for him to produce the picture. From the inside pocket of his waiter's coat he took a dusty, dirty packet. It was a jumbled bundle of calling cards, ragged folded slips of paper, several one-yen notes, and even a movie programme. The boy approached a floor lamp and carefully inspected the articles one by one. The unlucky mother, who did not have the courage to go over them minutely, closed her eyes.

'Let it be a man who is not at all like Yuichi,' she prayed in her heart. 'Then there will still be some room for doubt. I will have a happy moment of stalling for time. Then I can end up believing that every line of that awful letter – there being no evidence – was an outright lie. Let that picture be of a man I have never seen.'

'Here it is! Here it is!' the boy shouted.

The widow Minami held her presbyopic eyes at a distance and looked at the calling-card-size photograph in the light of the standing lamp. The surface of the picture shone in the light and was hard to see. Finally, at an angle the face of a smiling young man in a white polo shirt was clearly visible. It was Yuichi.

That was truly a moment to take her breath away, and Mrs Minami completely lost all heart to confront her son. The indomitable will power she had maintained until then was broken. Distracted, she handed the photograph back. Her ability to laugh, to speak, had vanished.

On the stairs there was a sound of footsteps. A new guest was coming up. Two boy friends who were necking in one of the booths sprang apart when they saw that the guest was a young woman. The woman noticed Yuichi's mother and went in her direction, approaching with serious countenance.

'Mother,' she said.

Mrs Minami's face went white. She looked up. It was Yasuko.

The rapid conversation that passed between mother-in-law and daughter-in-law was pitiful to hear. 'What are you doing in a place like this?' the mother asked. Yasuko did not reply. She only tugged at her to go home.

'But who would think of meeting you in a place like this?'

'Mother, let's go home. I came to get you.'

'How did you know where I went?'

'I'll tell you later. But now let's go home.'

The two quickly paid the check, left the place, and got into the mother's waiting car.

The widow leaned back on the seat and closed her eyes. The car started off. Yasuko sat on the edge of the seat and solicitously watched her.

'You're drenched in perspiration,' said Yasuko, wiping her mother-in-law's forehead with a handkerchief.

After a time the widow opened her eyes and said: 'I know: you've read my mail.'

'I wouldn't do anything of the sort. I got a thick letter, too – this morning. Then I knew where you went last night, Mother. I knew you wouldn't take me with you tonight either, so I started after you left.'

'You got the same letter!'

The widow whimpered like a person in torture. 'Yasuko, I

364

beg your pardon,' she said, weeping. Her reasonless apologies and sobs moved Yasuko and made her cry too. Until the car reached their home, the two sympathized with each other in tears. Yet they exchanged not a word about the real issue.

When they got home, Yuichi had not yet returned. The widow's motive for striving to settle the matter alone had not been based so much on a heroic resolution to spare Yasuko anguish as on a sense of humilation that made her unable to face her daughter-in-law. Once, therefore, this humiliation had dissolved in tears, her only confidante, Yasuko, became at the same time her indispensable aid. The two quickly started comparing the letters in a room far away from Kiyo. Not enough time had gone by to allow the women to begin to harbour hatred towards the mean-spirited, unnamed person who had written them.

Both letters were in the same hand. The contents were identical. There were many miswritten characters; the sentences were clumsy. Here and there were evidences that the writer had deliberately distorted his handwriting.

The letters were written as if a sense of duty had made this report on Yuichi's conduct necessary. Yuichi was an 'absolute phony' of a husband; he was 'absolutely incapable of loving women'. Yuichi was 'bilking his family, pulling the wool over the world's eyes'. Not only that, he paid no heed to the happy arrangements entered into by other people. Although a man, he had become the plaything of men. He had once been the favourite of former Count Kaburagi, and now he was the pet of the president of Kawada Motors. Moreover, this beautiful spoiled child had been continually betraying the patronage of these older lovers. He had loved and left an unbelievable number of young lovers – more than a hundred of them, no less. 'It should be pointed out' that the younger lovers were all of the same sex.

In the meantime Yuichi had come to take delight in stealing what belonged to others. Because of him, an old man whose boy lover he had taken away committed suicide. The writer of this letter was a person who had suffered from the same offence. He pleaded that it be understood that the feeling with which he had sent this letter was one that could not be side-stepped.

'If this letter calls up any doubts, if there should be any qualms over the definiteness of the evidence, I wish you to visit the following restaurant after supper and see with your own eyes the truth of what I say. Yuichi will be in this place at one time or another. If you meet him there you will find the above report verified.'

This was the essence of the letter. The drafting of the detailed map showing the location of Rudon's, with exact information about the persons who visited there, was the same in both letters.

'Did you meet him, Mother?' asked Yasuko.

The widow had earlier intended to say nothing about the picture, but without realizing it she blurted out everything: 'I didn't meet him, but I saw a picture. It was a picture of Yuichi that a very lowbrow waiter there was guarding with his life.' Saying this, she was stricken with remorse, and added: 'But regardless, that's not the same as having met him. We still haven't proved that the letter was in the slightest degree a hoax.

As she said these words her haggard eyes contradicted her words. They seemed to say that in her heart she did not believe that the letter was in the slightest degree a hoax.

The widow Minami suddenly realized that Yasuko's face, so close to her, bore no trace of agitation: 'Why, you seem to be perfectly calm! That's strange. You, who are Yuichi's wife!'

Yasuko was apologetic. She was afraid that her outward composure might be causing her mother-in-law pain. The widow went on: 'I see no reason to believe that this letter is not entirely false. What if it were true? Could you still be calm?'

To this contradictory question she offered an extraordinary answer: 'Yes. Somehow, that's the way I would react.'

The widow was silent for a time. After a while she said, with eyes lowered: 'That's because you don't love Yuichi, I guess. The saddest part of it is that no one would have any cause to blame you for it. It is, rather, a fortunate thing in the midst of misfortune, I cannot help but feel.'

'No!' said Yasuko in a tone almost joyous in its determination. 'That is not so, Mother. It's quite the opposite. That's the very reason why ...'

The widow trembled before her young daughter-in-law.

Keiko was crying; her voice came from the bedroom through the reed screens. Yasuko got up to nurse her. Yuichi's mother was left alone in the eight-mat annex. The smell of mosquito incense deepened her uneasiness. If Yuichi came home, his mother felt she would have no place to go. This same mother who had gone to Rudon's, intent on meeting her son, now feared nothing more than meeting him. 'If he stays away tonight, however filthy the accommodations, how happy I will be,' she prayed.

The widow Minami's pain was probably not based on moral considerations. She merely felt a confusion of spirit from the reversal of all her ordinary thought processes and ideas about the world, through which her natural gentleness could not penetrate. Only revulsion and fear now filled her heart.

She closed her eyes and saw again the scenes of hell she had encountered in the past two days. In them were phenomena she was unprepared for, except for one clumsy letter. In them were phenomena of indescribably bad taste, horror, disgust, ugliness, blood-curdling unpleasantness, an anguish to make one writhe, all that excited revulsion. And what made for a truly unpleasant contrast was the fact that the employees and patrons of the place never altered their ordinary human expressions, the sangfroid with which they met their daily rounds.

Those men act as if they consider themselves proper, she reflected irritably. How ugly is an upside-down world! Whatever those perverts think or do, my way is the proper way. My eyes have not gone mad.

If she had never been so shaken as she was then, she had also never had her self-confidence so bolstered in all her life. That conclusion is not strange. In the fearful and yet uproariously funny phrase, 'sexual perversion', everything was explained. That this hairy caterpillar of a phrase, which no well-bred young woman would utter, pertained to her own son, the wretched mother pretended to forget.

When she had seen the male lovers kissing, the widow had become violently ill and turned her eyes away.

'If they had any upbringing, they wouldn't do such things!' As the word 'upbringing', not less funny than 'sexual perversion', floated through the widow's mind, a pride, that had long been dormant awoke in her.

Her upbringing had been in 'the very best of families'. Her father, affiliated with the rising classes of the Meiji era, loved refinement almost as much as he did medals. In her house all was refined, even the dogs. When her family sat down in their own dining room, even with no guests present, they would say, 'Would you be so kind as to . . .' when they wanted the gravy passed. The time in which the widow had been brought up was not necessarily a tranquil time, but it was a great time. Soon after she was born it saw victory in the Sino-Japanese War. When she was eleven, it met victory in the Russo-Japanese War. Until she became a member of the Minami family at nineteen, her parents required nothing for the protection of this rather sensitive girl but the highly stable moral dignity of the time and culture in which they lived.

When, fifteen years after she had become a bride, she had had no child, she could not appear before her mother-in-law, still living, without humiliation. When Yuichi was born, she breathed a sigh of relief. By this time changes had occurred within the centre of the dignified atmosphere she venerated. Yuichi's father, who had been a great woman-chaser since his high school days, for these fifteen years since his marriage still lived a wild life. The tremendous relief of the time of Yuichi's birth came from the confirmation that the Minami family register would not show that her husband's seed had been sown in questionable soil.

The first thing she had run into was humanity of this kind, but her heart, with its inexhaustible love and esteem for her husband, and her natural pride easily came to terms. Forgiveness replaced resignation, and tolerance replaced humiliation, and taught her a new way to love. This was indeed a love with dignity. She felt that there was not a thing in this world she could not forgive – at least all but indignity.

When hypocrisy becomes a matter of taste, great matters are

easily dispatched and small matters are fraught with fine moral shadings. The widow Minami was not inconsistent at all in con- sidering the atmosphere of Rudon's as simply bad taste. Since it was vulgar, she could not pardon it.

It was reasonable that, given this background, her usually gentle heart should not be inclined in the slightest towards sympathy with her son. The widow Minami also could not help wondering how an ill-bred thing like this, simply de- serving of revulsion, could be related to this pain and these tears that shook her to the depths.

When the feeding was done, Yasuko put the baby to bed and returned to her mother-in-law.

'I don't want to see Yuichi – this evening, anyway,' her mother-in-law said. 'Tomorrow I have to talk to him. Let me do the talking. Why don't you go to sleep, too? It doesn't pay to keep ruminating about it, does it?'

She called Kiyo, and hurriedly told her to prepare for bed. She acted as if something were chasing her. She felt confident that once she got into bed this evening, in the extremity of her fatigue, she could sleep the sodden sleep the drunkard craves from his saké.

*

During the summer, the Minami family used whatever room was coolest for their meals. The next day was sweltering even in the morning, so Yuichi, his wife, and his mother had a meal of cold juice, eggs, and toast on the veranda. During breakfast, Yuichi was always immersed in the newspaper. This morning, as usual, the crumbs from his toast fell audibly on the paper.

The meal was over. Kiyo brought in tea, cleared the table, and left. The widow Minami extended the two letters to Yuichi with almost rude abruptness. Yasuko's heart churned as she watched her, and she looked away. The letters were hidden by the newspaper; Yuichi did not see them. The mother poked the paper with the letters.

'Won't you put that useless paper down? Here are some letters that came in the mail.'

Yuichi dumped the newspaper untidily on the chair beside him and looked at the trembling hand with which his mother held out the letters. He saw the faint smile of tension in her face. He looked at the addresses on the envelopes, then turned them over and saw the blank spaces where the senders' names should have been. He took out a bulky letter and opened it. Then he took out the other.

'They're both the same – the one that came to me, and the one that came to Yasuko,' his mother said.

When he began to read the letter, Yuichi's hand also trembled. The colour drained from his face, and he kept wiping the perspiration from his brow with a handkerchief.

He was barely reading. He knew the contents of the anonymous missive. He was more concerned with the painful process of getting out of his predicament.

He induced a pained smile at the corners of his mouth and summoned all his powers; then he looked squarely at his mother.

'What's this rubbish? This headless, tailless, vulgar letter? Somebody's jealous of me and is trying to cause me trouble.'

'No. I myself went to the low-class dive named in that letter, and I saw your picture there with my own eyes.'

Yuichi had lost his powers of speech. His heart was in turmoil; he could not realize that in spite of the fury of his mother's tone and her distraught look, she was far removed from her son's tragedy, and that her anger was hardly more severe than if she were scolding him for wearing a tasteless necktie. In the first pitch of his excitement, he saw what was in his mother's eyes: 'society'.

Yasuko began to weep quietly. Inured to submissiveness, she usually hated to be seen crying, but now she was not sad at all, and therefore suspected her flow of tears. Usually she restrained her tears from fear of incurring her husband's displeasure; now her tears were meant to rescue him from his plight. Her body had been trained by love and served well in love's behalf.

'Mother, don't go too far!' she whispered brokenly, then rose from her seat. She walked – half-ran – through the house into the corridor, to the room where Keiko slept.

Yuichi sat wordless, motionless. However oppressed he might be, he had to do something soon to extricate himself. He took the sheets of paper piled helter-skelter on the table and ripped them to shreds. Then he crushed the torn fragments into a ball and dropped it in the sleeve of his white splash-pattern robe. He waited for his mother's response. She, however, sat with her elbows on the table, not moving, supporting her downcast head with her fingers.

It was the son who finally broke the silence.

'You don't understand, Mother. If you want to believe all of this letter, all right, but –'

The widow Minami almost shouted: 'What's going to happen to Yasuko?'

'Yasuko? I love Yasuko.'

'But aren't you one who hates women? All you can love are ill-bred boys and rich old and middle-aged men!'

The son was amazed at the complete lack of tenderness in his mother. Truthfully, his mother's fury was directed at her son's blood ties, of which, indeed, half were her own. Thus she could control her tears.

Yuichi thought: Wasn't it my mother who rushed me into marriage with Yasuko? It's pretty rotten that she has to blame it all on me.

Sympathy with his mother, so weakened by illness, kept him from giving voice to that retort. He said in a clear, clipped tone: 'Indeed I love Yasuko. Can't that be taken as evidence that I like women?'

His mother, who was not even listening to his plea, answered in a way that seemed almost a threat: 'At any rate, I must see Kawada and –'

'Please – don't act so gauche. He would think you're trying to blackmail him.' The son's words had their effect. The poor woman muttered something incomprehensible and left Yuichi sitting alone.

*

Yuichi sat alone at the breakfast table. In front of him was a clean tablecloth somewhat dotted with bread crumbs. There was the garden filled with the light of the sun coming through the trees and the voices of cicadas. Only the crumpled ball of paper weighing down his sleeve made it other than a clear, uneventful day. Yuichi lit a cigarette. He pushed back the sleeves of his heavily starched bathrobe and folded his bare arms. Whenever he looked at his own young, bare arms, he felt an exaggerated pride in his well-being. He felt pain in each breath, as if a solid board were pressing against his chest. His heartbeat was faster than usual. He couldn't tell, however, whether this chest pain was not one of anticipated joy. There was a certain cheer in his discomfort. He smoked sparingly at what remained of his cigarette.

He thought: At least now I'm certainly not bored.

Yuichi searched for his wife. Yasuko was on the second floor. He could hear the mellow sound of the music box.

In her room, Keiko lay in her mosquito netting. Her eyes were happily open and directed towards the music box. Yasuko looked up at Yuichi and smiled, but it was an unnatural smile and did nothing to mollify her husband. Yuichi's heart had been open as he mounted the stairs, but when he saw this smile it closed again.

After a long silence, Yasuko said: 'About that letter – I don't think anything of it.' Then she added clumsily: 'I only feel sorry for you.'

These words of sympathy were spoken in the gentlest tone; so much the more deeply did they wound the young man. What he had expected from his wife was not sympathy so much as frank disdain. His wounded pride could not help scheming a reasonless revenge against her.

*

Yuichi needed help. He thought of Shunsuké. But when he realized that Shunsuké was one of those to blame for this turn of events, his hatred rejected the name. He saw on the table the letter from Kyoto that he had read two or three days earlier. She is the only one who can save me, Yuichi thought. He decided to send her a telegram.

Outside, the street shone with a fiendish glare. Yuichi had come out by way of the back door. At the front gate he saw someone who seemed hesitant about entering. At first the visitor walked past the gate. Then he went back. It was as if he were waiting for someone in the house to emerge. When the stranger turned towards him, Yuichi was shocked to recognize the face of Minoru. They ran to each other and shook hands.

'A letter came, didn't it? An awful letter. I found out that my old man sent it. I was so sorry about it I cleared out of the house. The old man put a detective on our trail. He found out all about us.'

Yuichi was not surprised. 'I thought as much,' he said.

'There's something I want to talk over with you, Yuchan.'

'Not here. There's a little park near by. Let's go there.'

Affecting the calmness of an older person, Yuichi took the boy's arm and guided him. Talking rapidly of the difficulties into which they had just been plunged, they hastened their steps.

The neighbouring N— Park had been a part of the grounds of the estate of Prince N—. Twenty years before, the prince's family had broken up and sold his vast land holdings, donating a portion of the slope surrounding the pond to the borough for use as a park.

The view of the pond, covered with water lilies at the peak of bloom, was lovely. But for two or three children chasing cicadas, the park at summer noon was empty. The two men sat down on the slope facing the pond, in the shade of a pine tree. The grassy incline, which had not had any care for a long time, was littered with scraps of paper and orange peel. Scraps of newspaper clung to the shrubbery at the water's edge. After the sun went down, the little park would be crowded with people seeking the cool air.

'What did you want to talk about?' asked Yuichi.

'When this business happened, I decided I couldn't stay in my old man's house any more. I'm going to leave home. Yuchan, will you come with me?'

'With you?' Yuichi hesitated.

'Are you concerned about money? Don't worry about that. Look how much I have.'

His face serious, his mouth slightly open, the boy unbuttoned the back pocket of his trousers. He withdrew a carefully folded roll of bills.

'Keep it for me,' he said, handing it to Yuichi. 'Heavy, isn't it? It's a hundred thousand yen.'

'Where'd you get this money?'

'I broke open the old man's safe and cleaned it of cash.'

Yuichi looked at the pitiful, the niggardly result of one month of dreaming with this boy of adventure. They had turned away from society and dreamed of a youth of daring deeds, exploration, heroic evil, of the brotherly love of comrades-in-arms who face death on the morrow, of sentimental exploits they knew would end in disaster, and of all manner of youthful tragedy. They knew that they had been cut out for nothing but tragedy, that a cruel lynching by a secret society lay in store for them, or the death of Adonis slain by a wild boar, or a dungeon into which evil men had trapped them and where the water rose moment by moment to drown them, or ritualistic ordeals in cave kingdoms in which there was no chance of survival, or the end of the world, or fabulous opportunities to rescue hundreds of their fellows by sacrificing their lives, or glory filled with horrendous perils. Indeed, these were the only catastrophes meant for youth. If such opportunities for catastrophe are allowed to pass, youth must die. What is the death of the body, after all, compared with the unbearable death of youth?

Like many other youths – Why? Because living the life of youth is a never-ending, terrible death! – they spent their youths dreaming of ever new annihilations.

The outcome of these reveries, however, was now before Yuichi's eyes. It was nothing more than an urban incident; it had no hint of glory, nor of the smell of death. This drab incident, appropriate to a ditch rat, might perhaps come out in the newspapers – an item about the size of a sugar cube.

This boy's dreams have the tranquillity of a woman's, was Yuichi's disheartening thought. We're supposed to elope with stolen money and live somewhere, just the two of us. Ah! If only he had had the courage to kill his old man, then I would fall down on my knees before the boy!

Yuichi called forth his other self, the young head of a family. He quickly decided the attitude he' should assume. Compared with the other, pitiful outcome, the alternative of hypocrisy seemed far preferable.

'Suppose I hold on to this,' said Yuichi, putting the roll of bills in his inside pocket.

Innocent trust shone in the boy's eyes, so like a rabbit's, and he answered, 'All right.'

'I've got a little business at the post office. Would you like to come along?'

'Wherever you go ... I've entrusted my body to you too.'

'You sure have,' Yuichi said, as if to reassure himself.

At the post office he sent a telegram to Mrs Kaburagi that read as if it had been sent by a fretful child: 'Need you. Come right away.' Then he called a cab and told Minoru to get in.

'Where are we going?' asked Minoru.

Yuichi told the driver the destination in a low voice. Minoru, who hadn't heard, assumed they were going to some fine hotel. Then, seeing the cab approaching Kanda, the boy thrashed about like a sheep brought back to the fold.

'Leave things to me,' said Yuichi; 'I won't do anything wrong.'

The boy quickly seized upon something in Yuichi's resolute tone and smiled. This hero was now going to show his strength and revenge himself, the boy thought. When the boy imagined the face of his foster father, ugly in death, his body trembled with joy. Minoru dreamed that Yuichi dreamed about him just as he dreamed about Yuichi. Yuichi had a knife. He would impassively cut the old man's jugular vein. As Minoru thought about the beauty of the killer in that moment, Yuichi's profile became in the boy's eyes something that possessed all the perfection of a god.

The cab stopped in front of the coffee shop. Yuichi got out. Minoru followed. On this school street at noon in midsummer there were few passers-by. As the two crossed the street, the sun at the zenith barely made a shadow. Minoru triumphantly lifted his eyes towards the surrounding second- and third-floor windows and scanned them. The people who were looking unconcernedly down on the street were certainly not dreaming that these youths were on their way to kill a man. Great deeds always are carried out at just such obvious times as this.

The shop was quiet inside. To eyes accustomed to the light

outside, it was terribly dark. When he saw the two entering, Fukujiro, who had been sitting by the cash register, suddenly stood up.

'Where did you go off to?' he demanded of Minoru, as if about to grab him.

Minoru calmly introduced Yuichi to Fukujiro. Fukujiro's face went white.

'I'd like to speak to you for a moment.'

'Won't you come in the back? This way, please.' Fukujiro left the register in the care of a waiter.

'Stay here,' said Yuichi to Minoru, stationing him in the doorway.

When Yuichi took the roll from his inside pocket and handed it over to him, Fukujiro was dumbfounded.

'Minoru tells me he took this from your household safe. He gave it to me, and I am giving it back to you untouched. Minoru was not himself, I believe, so please don't be harsh with him.'

Silently and suspiciously, Fukujiro stared at the young man's face. This man before him, whom he had attacked and injured by such a low trick, he had loved at first sight. He quickly thought of a stupid plan. He would confess all and submit to the other's rebuke. It would be a short cut to winning his sympathy.

First he would apologize. He could take his cue ready-made from heroic tales and the songs of minstrels. 'Well, sir, you win!' he would say. 'When I stand before you in your grandeur, my smallest concern disgusts me. Go ahead, punch me, kick me, do what you want with me until you're satisfied, and so on.'

Before he went into his act, Fukujiro had a matter to settle. Now that he had his money back, he must count it. The amount of money that was in the safe he always kept in his head, but it still had to check with the balance in his books. And 100,000 yen was not something one could count in a second. He pulled up a chair to the table, bowed lightly to Yuichi, spread out the money, and began carefully counting the bills.

Yuichi observed the dexterity with which the small business-

376

man counted his money. In the movements of his fidgety fingers there was a dead-earnestness that was aloof from love, anonymous letters, and theft. When he had finished counting, Fukujiro put his hands on the table and nodded to Yuichi again.

'You're sure it's all there?'

'Yes, it's all there.'

Fukujiro had missed his chance. Yuichi was already on his feet. Without another look at Fukujiro, he strode to the door. Minoru had seen all of this unforgivable betrayal by his hero. He stood with his back to the wall, his face pale, and watched Yuichi go. As he went out, Yuichi bowed; Minoru looked away.

Yuichi walked rapidly down the midsummer street. There was no one behind him. A smile tugged at the corners of his mouth. He was filled with an indescribably joyous pride. Now he understood the pride of those who do charitable deeds. When it comes to bemusing the heart, no evil is better than hypocrisy. He knew that, and he was very happy. Thanks to the scene just enacted, the young man's shoulders were now unburdened. This morning's heavy oppression seemed to have lifted. To make the joy complete, he decided on a foolish, meaningless purchase. He went to a little stationery store and bought the cheapest possible celluloid pencil sharpener and a pen point.

29

Deus ex Machina

Yuichi's inactivity was complete. There was no matching his composure during this period of crisis. His calmness, born only from the depths of loneliness, silenced the family. It was almost as if they had decided the anonymous letter was a hoax. That is how calm Yuichi was.

He passed those days serenely, not saying much. The youth planted his feet on his own ruins and with the self-possession of a tightrope walker perused the morning paper at leisure and took a nap when the sun was high. Before a day had passed, the family had lost the urge to resolve the issue and seemed bent only on how to get around the topic. Above all, it was not a refined thing to talk about.

Mrs Kaburagi's reply wire came. It said she was arriving in Tokyo on the Special Express *Hato*, arriving at eight thirty. Yuichi went to Tokyo Station to meet her.

Mrs Kaburagi, carrying a single small suitcase, got off the train and picked out the figure of Yuichi wearing a student cap and white shirt with sleeves rolled up. She saw his face with its noncommittal smile, and, much sooner than his mother would have, observed his distress. Possibly she had never imagined seeing anything like this expression, concealing its burden of despair. She hurried towards him in her high-heeled shoes. Yuichi too made his way swiftly towards her. His eyes still averted, he seized Mrs Kaburagi's bag.

Her breathing quickened. The youth was conscious as ever of her steadfast gaze.

'It's been ages. What's wrong?'

'Let's talk about it later.'

'All right. Don't worry, now; I'm here.'

In truth, there was in the lady's eyes as she said this an unblinking, indomitable strength. Yuichi needed this woman whom he had once so easily forced to her knees. Now in his helpless smile she read the hardship he had undergone. And as she realized that it was not of her making, a feeling of extraordinary courage was born in her.

'Where are you staying?' Yuichi asked.

'I wired the inn that was once our family mansion.'

The two went to that inn, and were greeted by startling circumstances. The well-intentioned manager had made up the second-floor western room of the annex for Mrs Kaburagi – the very room in which she had discovered Yuichi and Kaburagi.

*

The manager came to greet them. This old-fashioned, perspicacious gentleman did not forget to treat Mrs Kaburagi as if she was still a countess. Aware of the awkwardness of the relationship between him, as host, and her, as his guest, and embarrassed that in a sense he had usurped her residence while she was away, he praised his establishment as if it were her home and he the visitor. He slithered around the walls like a lizard.

'The furnishings were so marvellous that we took the liberty of keeping them just as they were. All our guests say that they have never seen such genuine, refined furniture. I apologize about the wallpaper; we had it changed. The gloss of this mahogany pillar, now, is inexpressibly beautiful in a subdued way –'

'But remember that this was once the steward's house.'

'Of course. I'm fully aware of that.'

Mrs Kaburagi offered no objection to being assigned this room. When the manager had gone she got up from her chair and walked attentively around the old-fashioned room, which looked so narrow because of the bed covered with white mosquito netting. Now once again after six months she was in this room into which she had peeped and then fled from home. It was not her nature to see this turn of events as an inauspicious coincidence. Besides, the wallpaper in the room had been rehung.

'It's hot. If you'd like to take a shower . . .'

379

At this suggestion Yuichi opened the door to the narrow book-closet, about three mats in size, and turned on the light. All the books had been removed. A sheet of pure white tiles glared at him. The book-closet had been turned into a moderate-sized bathroom.

As a traveller returning to a land visited long ago discovers first only his old memories, Mrs Kaburagi was attracted only by Yuichi's unspoken anguish, the counterpart of her own pain. She did not see his transformation. He looked for all the world like a child in torment, incapable of doing anything about it. She did not know that he himself saw his distress.

Yuichi went into the bathroom. There was a sound of water running. She reached her hand to her back, undid the row of small buttons and loosened her bodice. Her shoulders, smooth as ever, were half-exposed. She didn't like electric fans, so didn't turn on the one in the room, but from her bag she took a silver-leaf Kyoto fan.

His unhappiness and the happiness I am returning to, what a heartless comparison! she thought. His emotions and my emotions are like the blossoms and the leaves of the cherry tree, made to come out without meeting one another.

Moths were colliding with the window screens. She understood the stifling impatience of the great moths of the night scattering the dust from their wings. Anyway, this is the only way I can feel. At least now I can encourage him with my sense of being happy.

Mrs Kaburagi looked at the rococo sofa on which she had sat so often with her husband. Sat – nothing more. Not even the edges of their clothing had touched; there had been always a fixed distance between them. Suddenly she recalled the memory of their grotesque shapes – her husband and Yuichi, embracing each other. Her bare shoulders felt cold.

What she had seen was accidental – in fact, it had been an innocent intrusion. She had wanted to see the kind of happiness that existed eternally and surely at times when she was not present. Such audacious wishes always invite the most unfortunate results, perhaps.

And now Mrs Kaburagi was with Yuichi in this same room. She was occupying the very place that happiness might have occupied. Instead, here she was. Her truly sagacious spirit soon awakened to the evident truth that for her there was no possibility for happiness, and that Yuichi would never love a woman.

Suddenly, as if she were cold, she reached back her hand and refastened her bodice. She had come to realize that all her charms would be futile. In the old days, if so much as one button were undone, it was because she was conscious of the presence of a man who would be glad to button it. If one of the men she was accustomed to associate with in that period had observed her modesty here, he would certainly have doubted his eyes.

Yuichi came out of the bathroom combing his hair. His damp and glistening youthful face reminded Mrs Kaburagi of the coffee shop where she had seen Kyoko, when Yuichi's face was wet from the sudden rain.

In order to set herself free from memories, she called out to him: 'All right, tell me quickly. Here you've brought me all the way to Tokyo and you haven't yet told me why.'

*

Yuichi gave her the gist of what had happened and asked for help. However, what she caught running through it all was the urgent hope that the authenticity of that letter somehow be disproved. Mrs Kaburagi therefore quickly made a daring resolution – she promised to visit the Minami home the next day. Then she sent Yuichi on his way. She was somewhat intrigued by it all. Her character owed its uniqueness to the fact that in it an inherently aristocratic heart and a whorish heart were naturally combined.

The next morning at ten o'clock the Minami family greeted an unexpected visitor. She was conducted to the second-floor drawing room. Yuichi's mother appeared. Mrs Kaburagi said she would like to see Yasuko too. As if acceding to the visitor's request to be spared an encounter, Yuichi remained in his study.

Her somewhat fuller body in a light purple dress, Mrs Kaburagi had a style that swept all before her. She smiled constantly, so polite and composed that even before she began her story she had filled Mrs Minami with terror, making her fear she was to hear about yet another scandal.

'I hate to mention it, but electric fans and I – oh, thank you,' said the guest, and a hand fan was brought. She held the handle of the fan and languidly waved it and let her gaze flutter about Yasuko's face. This was the first time the two women had sat face to face since the dance the previous year.

Normally, Mrs Kaburagi thought, I would be jealous of this woman. Her heart, however, had become fierce, and, perhaps out of cruelty, she felt nothing more than contempt for the beautiful young wife.

'Yuchan wired me and asked me to come. Last night I found out all about that strange letter. That's why I've come here today. I understand the letter also had something to say about Mr Kaburagi.'

The widow Minami hung her head in silence. Yasuko lifted her hitherto downcast eyes and looked straight at Mrs Kaburagi. Then she said, in a soft but firm voice to her mother-in-law: 'I think I'd better not stay.'

Her mother-in-law, not wishing to be left alone, stopped her: 'But Mrs Kaburagi has gone out of her way to come here to talk to both of us.'

'Yes, but I don't want to be part of any more discussions on the subject of that letter.'

'That's just the way I feel. But when you don't discuss the things you should, you regret it later on.'

The way in which these two women went on exchanging very proper words and at the same time walked circumspectly around one ugly word was ironical in the extreme.

Mrs Kaburagi interrupted for the first time: 'Why, Yasuko?'

Yasuko felt as if she and Mrs Kaburagi were engaged in a clash of wills: 'Well, I just don't have any thoughts now about the subject of this letter.'

Mrs Kaburagi bit her lip at this curt reply. She thought: My, she takes me for an enemy and is challenging me to a fight. Her patience was at an end. She cut short her efforts to help Yasuko's narrow, young, virtuous mind to see that she also was on Yuichi's side. She forgot the limitations of her role and dropped all inhibitions about making high-handed statements.

'I really want you to hear what I have to say. What I have come to report is an auspicious thing of a sort. Some who hear it, however, may look at it as an evil thing, perhaps.'

'Please, hurry and tell us,' said Yuichi's mother. 'I'm in an agony of suspense.' Yasuko did not leave her place.

'Yuchan felt that, besides me, there was no witness who could say that that letter was absolutely without foundation. So he wired me to come. What I have to confess is a bitter pill to swallow. I think, however, that what I have to say will do much to put your minds at ease about that disgraceful lie of a letter.' Mrs Kaburagi's voice broke as she went on: 'Yuchan and I have been having an affair for a long time.'

Mrs Minami exchanged a long look with her daughter-in-law. This new blow took everything out of her. After a time she regained her composure and asked: 'But does that mean recently, too? You've been in Kyoto since spring.'

'When my husband lost his job, he was already suspicious of what was going on between me and Yuichi. So he made me go to Kyoto with him. Just the same, I've been coming to Tokyo all the time.'

'And Yuichi...' The mother fumbled for words but finally fastened on the vague word 'friendly', and somehow managed to say it; 'And Yuichi was friendly with only you?'

'Well —' Mrs Kaburagi looked over at Yasuko as she replied: 'There might have been other women. He's young, after all. That can't be helped.'

Yuichi's mother's face went beet-red; then she nervously asked: 'Those other people, weren't any of them men?'

'My!' laughed Mrs Kaburagi. She took pleasure in letting the vulgar words fall from her lips: 'But I know of two women who have had abortions to get rid of Yuichi's children.'

*

Mrs Kaburagi's confession, candid and bare of superfluous flourishes, had a tremendous effect. This brazen confession delivered before the wife and mother of her lover was far more appropriate and credible in the situation than a maudlin confession meant to elicit tears.

The widow Minami's confusion was more than she could

bear. For the first time in her life her feminine modesty had been attacked there in that vulgar restaurant. As a result her will was paralysed, so that she could see in this most recent extraordinary event which had been provoked by Mrs Kaburagi only its naturalness.

The widow tried to calm herself. It was a respite to allow stubborn, fixed ideas to run through her head: Nobody can prove that this confession is a lie. The best proof of its truth is that – regardless of how men might act – it is impossible for a woman to confess that she has been involved in an affair that never took place. Besides, when it comes to a woman rescuing a man, there is no telling how far she might go. So it is possible that a woman like the former countess would march in on a man's mother and wife and make such an ill-bred admission.

There was in this judgement a marvellous logical contradiction. In short, by her use of the word 'man' and the word 'woman', she was already taking a mutual affair for granted.

If she had been an old-fashioned woman, she would have closed her eyes to an affair like this, involving a married woman and a married man, and covered her ears too; but now she found herself approving of Mrs Kaburagi's confession. She was thrown into terrible confusion because her moral outlook seemed to have become cloudy. She was frightened by the part of herself that leaned towards believing Mrs Kaburagi's entire story and rejecting the letter as a piece of rubbish, and felt a strong urge to cling to the evidence she had gathered verifying the letter.

'Yes, but I saw his picture. I still feel sick when I recall that filthy place and that ill-bred waiter with Yuichi's photograph.'

'Yuchan told me about that. Truthfully, he told me that some of his school friends went in for that sort of thing, and they pestered him so to give them pictures of him that he let them have two or three, and I suppose they got passed around. Yuchan went to some of those places with his friends, half out of curiosity, and when he gave the cold shoulder to a man who kept making passes at him, that man wrote the letter to get back at him.'

'Well, why didn't Yuichi tell me, his own mother, that story?'

'I suppose he was afraid to.'

'I'm not a very good mother, that's certain. Granting what you say, however, may I ask you an impolite question? Is there no basis for believing there was anything between Yuichi and Mr Kaburagi?'

She had been anticipating this question. Nevertheless, she had to struggle to maintain her composure. She had seen it. And what she had seen was not a photograph.

Mrs Kaburagi was wounded in spite of herself. She was not embarrassed about bearing false witness, but she found it painful to betray that fervent pretence she had built over her life since she beheld that sight – the very fervour from which this effort to bear false witness sprang. She was acting heroically now, but she refused to see herself as a heroine.

'Oh, that's a story beyond imagination.'

Yasuko had been silent the whole time. The fact that she had not said a word made Mrs Kaburagi uncomfortable. In truth, the one to respond most honestly in the affair was Yasuko. Mrs Kaburagi's veracity did not seem open to question. But what was the watertight connection between her husband and this other woman?

Yasuko bided her time until the conversation between her mother-in-law and Mrs Kaburagi was finished. In the meantime she was groping for a question that might perplex Mrs Kaburagi.

'There's something I find strange. Yuchan's wardrobe has been steadily growing.'

'Oh, that,' Mrs Kaburagi answered. 'That's nothing. I had them made for him. If you like, I'll bring the tailors over. I'm working, and I like to do things like that for someone I like.'

'Really, you're working?' The widow Minami's eyes rounded. It was unthinkable that this woman, the soul of extravagance, should actually be working.

Mrs Kaburagi informed her straightforwardly: 'After I got to Kyoto, I became a broker of imported automobiles. Recently I struck out for myself as an independent broker.'

This was her only true statement. Lately, she was showing great skill in a commercial arrangement under which she bought cars at 1,300,000 yen and sold them at 1,500,000 yen.

Yasuko was concerned about the baby and left her seat. Yuichi's mother, who until this time had been putting up a brave front for her daughter-in-law's benefit, broke down. She could not determine whether this woman before her was friend or foe. Regardless, she felt compelled to say: 'I don't know what to do. I'm more concerned about Yasuko than about myself –'

Mrs Kaburagi launched forth coldly and bluntly: 'I came here today determined about one thing. It seemed to me better to have you and Yasuko know the truth than to be menaced by that letter. Yuichi and I are going on a trip for two or three days. There is nothing serious between me and Yuichi, so Yasuko doesn't have a thing to worry about.'

Mrs Minami dropped her head at the explicitness of this audacious distinction. At any rate, Mrs Kaburagi's dignity was hard to impugn. The widow abandoned her motherly prerogatives. The intuition by which she divined in Mrs Kaburagi more motherliness than in herself was a correct one. She did not realize that her comment was ridiculous: 'Please take good care of Yuichi.'

*

Yasuko bent over the sleeping Keiko. In the past several days her peace had been shattered, but like a mother who in an earthquake instinctively protects her child's body with her own, she had constantly schemed how to prevent the catastrophe from affecting her child. Yasuko had lost her bearings. She was like a lone island buffeted by rough seas, no longer fit for human habitation.

She was being propelled towards something enormous, more complicated than disgrace; she felt almost no humiliation. The pain that almost took her breath away had come well after the incident of the letter, when the equilibrium she had attained by determining not to believe the contents of the letter was destroyed. While she was listening to Mrs Kaburagi's frank testimony, a transformation in her innermost feelings indubitably came about. Of that transformation, she herself was not yet aware.

Yasuko heard the voices of her mother-in-law and their

guest as they came down the stairs. Thinking that Mrs Kaburagi was leaving, Yasuko got up to say good-bye. But she wasn't leaving. Yasuko heard her mother-in-law's voice and had a glimpse of Mrs Kaburagi's back through the blind as she was conducted into Yuichi's study. She walks around my house as if it were her own, thought Yasuko.

Mrs Minami soon came out of Yuichi's study, alone. She sat down at Yasuko's side. Her face was not pale; on the contrary, excitement had brought a flush to her cheeks.

After a time the mother-in-law said: 'What moved her to come here and tell us a thing like that? She didn't do it for the fun of it, that's certain.'

'She must like Yuichi a great deal.'

'To say the least!'

Now in the old lady's heart, apart from her sympathy for her daughter-in-law, a kind of relief and pride was being born. If it came to the stage of deciding whether she should believe the letter or Mrs Kaburagi's story, she would unhesitatingly choose the latter. That her beautiful son should be sought after by the opposite sex was in her moral outlook a virtue. In short, it made her happy.

Yasuko realized that she and her kind mother-in-law lived in different worlds. She had to take care of herself; there was no other way. From her experience, however, she knew already that, other than letting matters take their course, she had no way of rescuing herself from pain. Placed in such a pitiful position, she crouched unmoving, fixed, like a helpless little animal.

'Well, that's the end,' said the old lady in despair.

'It's not really the end, Mother,' said Yasuko. Her words were stern, but her mother-in-law understood them as being meant to give her courage.

In tears, she thanked her with whatever phrases she could utter: 'I'm such a lucky person to have a daughter-in-law like you. Thank you – thank you, Yasuko ...'

*

When Mrs Kaburagi was at last alone with Yuichi in his study, she breathed the air of the room deeply through her nostrils, like one entering a forest. This air seemed to her more delicious and refreshing than the air of any forest.

'This is a nice study.'

'It was my father's. When I am in the house I can only breathe easy when I'm here.'

'I too.'

Yuichi understood why her echoing phrase came so naturally. She had barged into somebody else's house like a strong wind; thrown propriety, honour, sympathy, and modesty in all directions; indulged herself to her heart's content in cruelty to herself and others; and fervently, for Yuichi's sake, dared superhuman feats. And now she took a breath.

The window was open. On the table was an old-fashioned desk lamp, some ink bottles, a heap of dictionaries, and a Munich beer stein decorated with summer flowers. Across the near foreground, so like a copper plate etching, the scene of the fierce, late summer street unfurled itself, somehow imparting a desolate feeling by the raw wood of the many buildings raised on the ashes of the fires. The capital street-cars descended the hill on the trolley street. After a passing cloud slipped away, the rails in both directions, the foundation stones of the burnt ruins still not rebuilt, and the shards of glass in rubbish piles shone out with a terrific glare.

'All is well. Your mother, and Yasuko, too, aren't going to that restaurant again just to check up on you.'

'All is well, I agree,' said the youth, convinced. 'There won't be a second letter, I suppose. Mama doesn't have the courage to go there a second time, and Yasuko, even though she has the courage, would never do so.'

'You're tired. I think you should take a little vacation somewhere. Without consulting you, I announced to your mother that you and I are going on a two- or three-day trip together.'

Yuichi turned to her as if shocked.

'Let's go tonight,' she urged. 'I can get railroad tickets through a friend. I'll call you later. We can meet at the station. I'd like to stop off at Shima on the way back to Kyoto. We'll take a room in the hotel.' She studied Yuichi's expression carefully: 'Don't worry. I know too much to cause you any trouble. Nothing will happen between us, so relax.'

Mrs Kaburagi again had gauged Yuichi's inclinations; Yuichi agreed to go. In fact, he had wanted for two or three days to extricate himself from this stifling situation. No companion could be as gentle – and as safe – as Mrs Kaburagi.

The youth's eyes displayed his appreciation, and Mrs Kaburagi, who feared as much, hurriedly waved her hand: 'It isn't like you to be grateful to me for a small thing like that. All right? During the trip, if you think of me as anything else but air, I shall be very upset.'

Mrs Kaburagi departed. Yuichi's mother saw her to the door and afterwards followed Yuichi back to his study. While she had been with Yasuko, her eyes had been opened to her role.

The old lady closed the door dramatically behind her: 'Are you going on a trip with that married woman?'

'Yes.'

'I wish you wouldn't. It will be pretty hard on Yasuko.'

'If so, why doesn't she come and stop me herself?'

'You're a child. If you then simply faced Yasuko and told her outright you're going on a trip, you'd cut the ground from under her feet.'

'I'd like to get away from Tokyo for a little bit.'

'If so, go with Yasuko.'

'If I went with Yasuko I would get no rest.'

The woman's voice rose in her excitement: 'Think of your child a little, too, please!'

Yuichi dropped his eyes and said nothing. In the end his mother spoke: 'Think of me a little too.'

This egoism reminded Yuichi of his mother's complete lack of gentleness during the episode of the letter.

The dutiful son was silent for a time; then he said: 'Anyway, I'm going. I've caused that person enough trouble, what with this weird business of the letter. Don't you think it would be mean not to accept her invitation?'

'You're talking like a kept lover.'

'Right. As she says. I'm her kept lover.'

Yuichi pronounced his words triumphantly to his mother, now more distantly removed from him than he could measure.

30

Heroic Passion

Mrs Kaburagi and Yuichi departed that evening on the eleven o'clock night train. By this time the heat had abated.

Setting out on a journey engenders a strange emotion. One is seized by the feeling that he is free not only from the land that he has just left behind him, but also from the time that he is vacating.

Yuichi had had no regrets. Strange to say, it was because he loved Yasuko. As he saw things from the position of his twisted love, his going away on this journey under the many compulsions that forced him to do so was a parting gift to Yasuko. At this time his keen sensitivities had no fear even of hypocrisy. He thought of the words of the pronouncement he had made to his mother: 'At any rate, I love Yasuko. Can't that be taken as evidence that I like women?' With those words in mind, he seemed to have sufficient reason to believe that it was Yasuko and not himself whom he had put Mrs Kaburagi to the trouble of rescuing.

Mrs Kaburagi did not understand these new workings of Yuichi's heart. He was only very beautiful, overflowing with youth and charm; furthermore, he could never love a woman. She – and no one else – had saved him.

Tokyo Station receded in the distance. Mrs Kaburagi emitted a low sigh. If she exhibited even the slightest sign of love, Yuichi's long-awaited rest would certainly be lost. As the train lurched along, their bare arms touched once in a while, but when that happened it was she who quietly withdrew her arm. If Yuichi became aware of her love through even the faintest quiver on her part, he would end up being bored, she feared.

'How is Mr Kaburagi doing? His letters seem fine.'

'He's living off his wife. I guess one would have to say that's what he's always done.'

'Is he still *that* way?'

'Nowadays, since I have found out all about him, he's much more relaxed. When we walk in town and he teases me by saying, "Isn't that kid pretty?" it's sure to be a boy.'

Yuichi said nothing, and after a time Mrs Kaburagi asked: 'Don't you like me to say things like that?'

'No,' said the youth, without looking at her. 'I don't like to hear subjects like that coming from your mouth.'

The sensitive woman saw through the childish fancies this self-centred youth was hiding from the world. It was an extremely important discovery. It meant that Yuichi was still searching for some kind of illusion about her. I must act more as if I don't know. I must never appear to be anything but harmless as a lover, she decided, with some satisfaction.

The exhausted pair slept after a time. In the morning, at Kameyama, they changed to the Toba Line. From Toba they took the Shima Line, and over an hour later arrived at the last stop, Kashikojima, an island connected with the mainland by a single short bridge. The air was remarkably clear. The two travellers stepped down into an unfamiliar station and sniffed the sea breeze coming across the numerous isles of Ago Bay.

*

When they got to the hotel on the top of the hill on Kashiko-jima, Mrs Kaburagi asked for only one room. Not that she anticipated anything at all. Mrs Kaburagi did not know what to make of this difficult love of hers. If one could call it love, it was a love *incognita*. In no play, in no novel, had its like been drawn. Everything had to be worked out by her, tested by her. If she could sleep one night in the same room with a man she loved so much, not looking forward to anything happening, when day dawned, thanks to this arduous ordeal, a still soft, feverish love would be given form and be forged into steel, she thought. On being shown into the room and seeing the two beds side by side, Yuichi was taken aback, but then soon was embarrassed that he had doubted her.

The day was fine, refreshing, not too warm. Guests who came to the hotel during the week usually stayed over. After lunch they went to the beach on Shima Peninsula, near Goza

Point. They got there in the big motor launch that went from the back of the hotel along the inlet from Ago Bay.

Mrs Kaburagi and Yuichi wore light shirts over their bathing suits. The tranquillity of nature was all about. The surrounding seascape was not so much that of island upon island floating on the water, but of numerous islands crowded together. The shoreline was jagged in the extreme, and the water seemed to be stealing far in upon the land, eating away at it. Thus the singular calm of the view was like that of the very centre of a flood above which only the broad hills majestically stood forth. To the east, to the west, as far as the eye could see, all the way to the unexpected mountain passes, the coruscating sea extended.

Since during the morning a number of guests had had their swim and returned, there were only five people in the boat with Yuichi and Mrs Kaburagi when it went out in the afternoon. Three were a young couple and their child. The other two were a middle-aged American couple. The boat threaded among the pearl rafts that floated everywhere on the calm surface of the deep-cut bay. The rafts were used to hold the baskets which, immersed deep in the sea, held the pearl-bearing oysters. Since it was already late summer, the women pearl divers were nowhere to be seen.

They had folding chairs placed on the deck in the boat's stern and sat down. Yuichi was struck with admiration at his first view of Mrs Kaburagi's bare body. Her flesh combined elegance with ripeness. All was sheathed in fine curves; the beauty of her legs was that of a woman who had sat on chairs since childhood. Particularly beautiful was the line from her shoulder to her forearm. As if she meant to reflect the sun's rays, Mrs Kaburagi did nothing to protect her slightly tanned skin, which showed not the least sign of ageing.

The roundness from her shoulder to her wrist – in the shifting shadow of her hair flying in the sea breeze – was like the bare arms of noble ladies of ancient Rome revealed by their gowns. Having been set free of the fixed idea that one must desire this body, from the sense of duty that one must entrap oneself in it, Yuichi understood its beauty well. Mrs Kaburagi had taken off her shirt, and her white bathing suit concealed only her trunk. She watched the islands shining in the sun – so

392

numerous they gave one no time to respond. The islands flowed up to her, then receded. Yuichi imagined the multitudes of pearls beginning to ripen in the baskets suspended into the deep sea from the countless pearl rafts under this late summer sun.

The inlet of Ago Bay branched off into many other inlets, and from one of these the boat emerged and slipped along the surface of the sea, seemingly closed in as before by land. In the green of the surrounding islands, one could see the roofs of the houses of the pearl-industry workers. They combined to form the walls of a labyrinth.

'There's Hamayu!' shouted one of the guests.

On one island, clumps of white flowers were visible here and there. Mrs Kaburagi looked across the shoulder of the youth at the fabled flowers of Hamayu, now past their prime.

Until now she had not loved nature. Only body heat, pulse, flesh and blood, and the smell of human beings had charmed her. But the panorama before her eyes now captured her fierce heart. Why? Because nature seemed to reject her advances.

After they had returned from their swim before supper, the two went to the hotel bar for cocktails. Yuichi ordered a martini. The countess told the bartender to mix and shake absinthe, French vermouth, and Italian vermouth and provide her with a Duchess cocktail.

The two were surprised at the uncanny colours burning everywhere in inlet after inlet in the evening glow. Their drinks glowed orange and light brown, shot through with these rays, then turned crimson.

Although the windows were open everywhere, there was not a sigh of wind. It was the famous evening calm of the Isé-Shima coast. The burning atmosphere, suspended like heavy wool fabric, did not disturb the healthy repose of the youth, exhilarated in mind and body. The joy in his body after the swim and bath, the consciousness of renewal, the beautiful woman beside him knowing everything and forgiving everything, just the right degree of inebriation: these divine favours were flawless; they made it easy for the one beside him to feel unlucky.

All in all, this man must have had something of an experience, Mrs Kaburagi could not help thinking, as she gazed at the youth's now serene eyes, storing up not one atom of ugliness that might have existed in his memory. This man continually lives in this moment, in this spot, with his innocence intact.

Mrs Kaburagi now understood well the grace that constantly and happily surrounded Yuichi. The way he was snared by grace was like the way a man is snared in a trap. You have to be cheerful, she thought. If not it would be as before, nothing more than repetitions of unhappy encounters heavy as stone.

In this trip to Tokyo and the succeeding excursion to Shima, her firm self-sacrifice was valiant. It was not simply restraint. It was not self-control. It was living in the consciousness in which Yuichi lived, believing only in the world that Yuichi beheld, guarding against allowing her own wishes to twist anything in the slightest. Thus a long hard apprenticeship was necessary before she could impart about the same meaning to the vilification of hope and to the vilification of hopelessness.

Nevertheless, these two people who had not seen each other for a long time had a thousand and one things to talk about. She told a story about the recent Gion Festival; Yuichi told the story of Shunsuké's uneasy trip in Kawada's yacht.

'Does Mr Hinoki know about this recent letter?'

'No, why should he?'

'Well, you seem to consult Mr Hinoki about everything.'

'I wouldn't tell him about something like that.' Yuichi thought regretfully of his few remaining secrets and went on: 'Mr Hinoki doesn't know anything about that.'

'I wouldn't think so. In the old days that old man was an incorrigible woman-chaser. But the strange thing was the women did nothing but run away from him.'

Sunset was over. The wind began to spring up faintly. Even though the sun was down, there was still a clear glow off the water. The sheen of the water still reached all the way to the mountains, betraying the presence of the sea. The shadows were deep on the surface of the sea close to the shores of the islands. The olive-green shadows on the water contrasted with the sea that still gorgeously reflected the light. The two got up and went to supper.

*

The hotel was far from a settlement, and when the evening meal was over there was nothing to do. They played some records, and leafed through some bound volumes of picture-magazines. They carefully read the travel folders of the airlines and hotels. Thus Mrs Kaburagi lowered herself, becoming like a nurse to a child who wants to stay awake doing nothing for ever.

Mrs Kaburagi perceived that what she had once imagined to be pride of conquest had turned out to be nothing more than childish caprice. If this discovery was not distasteful to her, neither was it disappointing. For she recognized that the joy Yuichi alone seemed to be taking in this deepening night, his placid contentment, the peculiar pleasure he took in not doing anything, was based entirely on the awareness that she was there beside him, in all her solicitude.

After a time Yuichi yawned. Then he said reluctantly: 'Shall we go to bed soon?'

'I'm sleepy; I can hardly keep my eyes open.'

But Mrs Kaburagi, who should have been sleepy, started babbling when they got to the room. It was a babbling that was beyond her control. Even when they had resting their heads on the pillows of their separate beds, and turned off the lamp that was on the little table between them, she kept up her cheerful, feverish monologue. Her topics were innocent, innocuous, enervating. Yuichi's answers came from the darkness at long intervals. Finally, he was silent. Wholesome sleep took the place of words. Mrs Kaburagi, too, ceased talking. For more than thirty minutes she listened to the youth's regular breathing. Her eyes were wide awake; she couldn't sleep. She lit the lamp. She picked up the book on the night table. She was startled, then, by the rustle of bedclothes as of someone turning in sleep, and glanced towards the neighbouring bed.

In truth, until this time Mrs Kaburagi had been waiting. She was tired of waiting, disillusioned with waiting, and then – even though she had seen clearly since that strange peeping that waiting was impossible – she still waited. Yuichi, however, who had discovered the one person in the world he could relax with, the one woman who was willing to talk to him, with supreme trust stretched out his happily tired body and slept. He turned. Though he was sleeping naked, he was too warm, and pushed the blanket from his chest. The circle of light at his head made his face, cut with deep shadows under the eyes, and his loosely covered, rising and falling chest shine like a bust carved on an ancient coin.

Mrs Kaburagi altered her dream. To be more exact, she shifted from the subject of the dream to the object of the dream. This subtle shift of vision, this shift from one chair to another in her dream, this small unconscious change in attitude, led her to give up waiting. She moved across to the other bed, like a snake writhing across a stream. Her hands and arms trembled as they supported her bending body. Her lips were directly opposite the face of the sleeping youth. She closed her eyes. Her lips could see well enough.

Endymion's sleep was profound. The young man did not know who was cutting off the light across his sleeping face, or what a feverish, sleepless night was pressing close. He did not feel the stray hairs brushing his cheek. He only opened his lips slightly, exposing the glistening rows of teeth.

Mrs Kaburagi opened her eyes. Their lips had not yet touched. It was now that she opened her eyes to her resolution of valiant self-abnegation: If our lips so much as touched, in that moment something would leave with a flutter of wings, never to return. If I wish to maintain between this youth and me something like music that never ends, I must not move a finger. Night and day I must hold my breath, careful never to disturb so much as a particle of dust between us. ... She regained her control and returned to her bed. She pressed her cheek against her warm pillow and looked fixedly at that form, like a bas-relief in its circle of golden light. She turned off the lamp. The vision persisted. She turned her face towards the wall; it was near dawn when she finally slept.

This heroic ordeal was crowned with success. The next day Mrs Kaburagi awoke with a clear head. In the eyes with which she looked at Yuichi's face deep in the sleep of morning, there

396

was a new, resolute power. Her emotions had been refined. She picked up her pure white, wrinkled pillow and playfully threw it at Yuichi's face.

'Wake up! It's a lovely day. You can't sleep all day.'

This late-summer day was much pleasanter than the day before, filled with promise of being a day to remember always. After breakfast, they packed lunches and drinks, hired a car, and set out to do some sightseeing around the farthest reaches of the Shima Peninsula. They would return to the hotel by boat from the beach where they had bathed the day before. From the village of Ugata near the hotel, they went through wilds of burnished earth, from which scrubby pines, hemp palms, and tiger lilies sprang here and there, and finally reached the port of Nakiri. The view from Cape Daio, over which a giant pine towered, held them breathless. As they stood buffeted by the wind, they saw the white clothing of the pearl divers at their task, looking like whitecaps breaking upon the sea. They saw on a cape to the north the Anori lighthouse standing like a tall stick of chalk, and the smoke from the pearl divers' fires rising on the beaches of Cape Oi.

The old lady who was their guide was smoking a handmade cigarette of chopped tobacco rolled in a camellia leaf. Her fingers, yellow with age and nicotine, trembled as she pointed to the end of misty Cape Kuni in the distance. There long, long ago the Empress Jito had gone with many court ladies on a boating excursion and held court for seven days.

Hearing this ancient, useless lore of travel was wearisome. They returned to the hotel no more than an hour before the time Yuichi was to depart. Mrs Kaburagi, who did not have good connections to Kyoto this evening, stayed behind, planning to leave the next morning. About the time the evening calm began, Yuichi left. Mrs Kaburagi saw him off as the trolley stop just below the hotel. The trolley came. The two shook hands, after which Mrs Kaburagi drew back abruptly, made her way to the railing outside the station, and waved good-bye. She waved for a long time, cheerfully, showing no emotion whatever, while the scarlet evening sun shone on her cheek.

Yuichi was alone among a carful of peddlers and fishermen.

His heart was filled with gratitude towards this mistress of noble, disinterested friendship. Gratitude welled up in him; it made him feel envious of Kaburagi, who had taken this perfect woman as his wife.

31

Problems Spiritual and Financial

When he got back to Tokyo, Yuichi ran directly into trouble.
During the short time he had been away, his mother's kidney
trouble had taken a turn for the worse.

Unaware what to strive for, what means to use in resisting,
the widow Minami, half blaming herself, had no recourse save
to become gravely ill. With marvellous facility, she became
dizzy and often for a very short time lost consciousness. Thin
urine welled from her constantly; the symptoms were certainly
those of kidney atrophy.

When he arrived home at seven in the morning and opened
the front door, Yuichi knew from the expression on Kiyo's face
that his mother was critically ill. The moment he entered, the
heavy odour of illness struck his nostrils. The joyful memories
of the trip were suddenly frozen in his heart.

Yasuko, exhausted from nursing her mother-in-law late into
the night, was not yet awake. Kiyo went to prepare his bath.
Yuichi made his way upstairs to the bedroom he shared with
Yasuko.

The high windows had been open throughout the night to let
in the cool air, and the rays of the rising sun now streamed in
and lit the skirt of the mosquito netting. Yuichi's bed was laid
out. The linen pads had been carefully arranged. On the pallet
next to his Yasuko was sleeping with Keiko.

Yuichi lifted the netting and slipped in. Softly he lay down
on the padding of his own bed. The baby opened her eyes. On
her mother's outstretched arm she lay, soberly and with wide
eyes observing her father. The scent of milk came to him
faintly.

The infant suddenly smiled. It was as if drops of smile dripped from the corners of her mouth. Yuichi poked her cheek

lightly with his finger Keiko, her eyes unwavering, continued smiling.

Yasuko started to turn over, rather painfully, then stopped and opened her eyes. She saw the face of her husband, unexpectedly close to her own. Yasuko did not smile at all.

During those few moments while Yasuko was awakening, Yuichi's memory moved swiftly. He remembered the sleeping face that he had so often gazed upon so intently, the sleeping face that he had dreamed of – immaculate possession that he would not harm for the world. He remembered her face filled with surprise, joy, and trust that time in the hospital room during the night. Yuichi could expect nothing from his wife when she opened her eyes. He had merely returned from his trip during which she had remained behind in despair. But his heart, accustomed to being forgiven, yearned; and his innocence, accustomed to being trusted, dreamed. In this instant his emotions were like those of a beggar who asks for nothing, yet who has no other skill save that of begging.

Heavy with sleep, Yasuko's eyelids opened. Yuichi saw a Yasuko he had never seen before. She was a different woman.

She spoke in a sleepy, unvarying, yet not at all ambiguous tone. 'When did you get back? Have you had breakfast? Mother is very sick. Did Kiyo tell you?' she asked, as if reading off a check list. Then she said: 'I'll fix your breakfast quickly; won't you wait on the veranda?'

Yasuko arranged her hair and dressed hurriedly. She came downstairs with the baby in her arms. She did not entrust the child to her husband while she prepared breakfast, but laid her down in the room next to the veranda where he was reading the newspaper.

The morning had not yet warmed up. Yuichi blamed his uneasiness on the night journey, so hot that he had slept almost not at all. He clicked his tongue as he thought: I now understand clearly what they call the unimpeded pace of misfortune. It has a fixed speed like that of a clock ... But one always feels like this when he hasn't had enough sleep! It's all the doing of Mrs Kaburagi!

*

The change in Yasuko as she opened her eyes in the extremity of fatigue and discovered the face of her husband before her was a surprise mostly to Yasuko herself.

She had formed the habit of closing her eyes and sketching in her mind down to the last detail the picture of her suffering and then opening her eyes and seeing it before her. That picture was beautiful, magnificent. This morning, however, this was not what she saw. There was only the face of a youth, outlined by the rays of the morning sun, shining through a corner of the mosquito netting, giving the impression of an inanimate figure of clay.

Yasuko opened a can of coffee and poured hot water into the white china coffee pot. In her hands there was an unfeeling quickness; her fingers did not tremble in the slightest.

After a while, Yasuko placed Yuichi's breakfast before him on a wide silver-plated tray.

It was a delicious breakfast to Yuichi. The morning shadows were still abundant in the garden. The whitewashed railing of the veranda shone with dazzling late-summer dew. The young couple silently ate breakfast together. Keiko quietly slept. The sick mother had not yet awakened.

'The doctor said Mother should be taken to the hospital sometime today. We've been waiting for you to come home to make arrangements to have her admitted.'

'All right.'

Yuichi looked attentively at the garden. He blinked as he observed the morning sun lighting the treetops of the pasanias. The mother's grave illness drew the young couple together. Yuichi had the illusion that now Yasuko's heart was once again firmly his, and he took advantage of the moment to employ the charms any husband would use.

'It's good to have breakfast, just the two of us, isn't it?'

'Yes.'

Yasuko smiled. There was an impenetrable indifference in her smile. Yuichi was dismayed. His face turned red with embarassment. Then he poured out these words – a transparent, insincere, overdramatized outpouring, perhaps, but at the same time, perhaps also a heartfelt, sincere confession couched in words that he had never before uttered to a woman. 'While I

401

was away,' he said, 'all I thought of was you. It's become clear to me what with all our troubles of the last few days that you mean more to me than anyone.'

Yasuko remained calm. She smiled a light, noncommittal smile. It was as if Yuichi's words were those of an unknown country. She looked at his lips as if they were being moved by someone talking on the other side of a thick pane of glass. His words did not come through.

*

However, Yasuko had already resolved that she would settle down, bring up Keiko, and never leave Yuichi's house until she was ugly and stricken in years. This virtue, born from hopelessness, had a power no sin could influence.

Yasuko had forsaken the world of absolutes; she had left it completely. When she had been in that world, her love yielded to no evidence. Yuichi's coldness, his abrupt rejections, his late homecomings, his overnight absences, his secrets, the fact that he never loved a woman – in the face of such evidence the affair of the anonymous letter was a trivial matter. Yet Yasuko had remained unmoved, because she lived in another world.

Yasuko did not step off her world on her own initiative. She was dragged off it. Yuichi, who as a husband was perhaps too kind, had deliberately enlisted the aid of Mrs Kaburagi and wrenched his wife out of the quiet of love's realm, out of the unrestricted, limpid realm in which she lived, where impossibilities could not exist, and dragged her into the disorderly world of reciprocal love. Yasuko was now hemmed in by the evidence of that world. There were with her there things she had known all along, things familiar to her, with which she was hemmed in by the dull, dumb wall of impossibility. She had only one method of dealing with it all. That lay in not feeling anything – in not seeing, in not hearing anything.

While Yuichi was away on that trip, Yasuko had donned the arts and artifices of this new world in which she was forced to live. She had to go so far as to treat herself resolutely as a woman without love – even of herself. She had turned into a deaf mute, outwardly adjusted; she served her husband his breakfast wearing a stylish apron in a yellow checked pattern.

'Would you like some more coffee?' she said. She said it without effort.

A bell rang. It was the hand bell beside the pillow in Mrs Minami's sickroom.

'She must be awake,' Yasuko said. The two went to the sickroom. Yasuko opened the shutters.

'Have you come home at last?' the widow said, not lifting her head from the pillow. Yuichi saw death in her face. It was swollen with dropsy.

*

That year there were no typhoons of consequence between the 210th day and the 220th day. Of course there were several typhoons, but they all just missed Tokyo, causing no severe wind or water damage.

Yaichiro Kawada was extremely busy. Mornings he was at the bank. Afternoons he held conferences. His executives huddled with him in conferences over the question of how to invade the sales network of a competing firm. At the same time he was negotiating with an electrical supply company and other subcontractors. He was involved in negotiations with directors of a French auto company now visiting Japan, working towards agreements on technical cooperation, patent rights, and commissions. At night, as a rule, he entertained his banking associates at geisha houses. Also, based on intelligence reports his labour relations chief brought him periodically, he had come to understand that strike-breaking preparations on the part of the company had been quite unsuccessful and that the union was developing momentum towards a strike.

The tic in Kawada's right cheek was getting worse. It was the only emotional weakness in his otherwise imperturbable exterior, and it threatened him. Hidden behind his proud, German, never downturned face; behind his fine nose; behind the clear line of the cleft of his upper lip; behind his rimless glasses, Kawada's sensitive heart moaned and bled. At night, before he went to sleep, he would read a page from a collection of Hölderlin's early poetry. He would peer at it stealthily as if reading an erotic passage, intoning: '"*Ewig muss die liebste Liebe darben...*"' It was the last verse of the poem 'To

403

Nature'. ' *"Was wir lieben ist ein Schatten nur. . . ."* He is free,' groaned the wealthy bachelor in his bed. 'Just because he's young and beautiful, he thinks he has the right to spit on me.'

The twofold jealousy that makes the love of the ageing homosexual unbearable came between Kawada and his bachelor's sleep. Take the jealousy of a man whose woman is unfaithful and combine with it the jealousy that a woman past her prime feels towards a young, beautiful woman, and combine with that doubly intricate product the peculiar consciousness that the person one loves is of the same sex, and you have an exaggerated, absolutely unforgivable humiliation in love. If a prominent man experienced something as enormous as this at the hands of a woman, he would be able to endure it. But nothing could do more harm to the self-respect of someone like Kawada than to have the humiliations of love for a man thrown into his face.

Kawada recalled how one day when he was young he was seduced by a rich merchant in New York's hotel Waldorf-Astoria. Then he remembered the night of a party in Berlin, when he and a gentleman he knew got into the man's Hispano Suiza and headed for his villa in the suburbs. The two men in swallow-tail coats embraced in the car oblivious to the headlights of other cars. Their perfumed hardboiled shirt fronts rubbed against each other.

It was the last flourish of Europe before world panic. It was the time when an aristocratic lady and a Negro, an ambassador and a villain, a king and an actor in American action films slept together. Kawada recalled the boy sailors of Marseilles and their shiny, white, prominent chests, like waterfowl. Then he thought of the beautiful boy he had picked up in a café on the Via Veneto in Rome, and of the Arab boy in Algiers – Alfredo Jemir Musa Zarzal.

And Yuichi surpassed all these! Once Kawada found time to meet Yuichi. 'Do you want to see a movie?' he said.

'No, I don't want to see a movie,' Yuichi said.

They passed a billiard parlour, and Yuichi, who didn't play much, suddenly went in, for no good reason. Kawada didn't play. For all of three hours, Yuichi idled around the pool table while the busy captain of industry sat in a chair under a faded pink curtain waiting disgustedly for the one he loved to end his fit of bad temper. The blue veins in Kawada's head pounded; his cheeks quivered; his heart shouted out loud: 'Here he keeps me waiting in a poolroom in a chair with the straw coming out of it! I, who am never kept waiting by anybody! I who don't mind keeping callers waiting for a week!'

The wrecks of this world are of various kinds. A bystander might have looked at the destruction Kawada predicted for himself as a quite luxurious one, after all. It alone, however, was to Kawada at this moment the most frightening destruction possible, and with good reason he concentrated on avoiding it.

Kawada was fifty years old, and the good fortune he hoped for was to look with contempt at life. This was at first glance a very cheap good fortune, one that society's men of fifty come to entirely unconsciously. The resistance to life of the homosexual who refuses to be subordinate in his work, however, audaciously floods the world with this sensitivity wherever there is space, awaiting the chance to permeate the world of men's work. He knew that Wilde's famous pronouncement was nothing more than sour grapes: 'I have put all my genius into my life; I have put only my talent into my works.'

Wilde was forced to say that, of course. The homosexual of promise, whoever he is, is one who recognizes that certain manliness within himself, and loves it, and holds fast to it, and the masculine virtue that Kawada recognized in himself was his ever-ready nineteenth-century predilection for diligence. A strange trap for one to be in! As in that long-ago warlike time, loving a woman was an effeminate act; to Kawada any emotion that ran counter to his own masculine virtue seemed effeminate. To samurai and homosexual the ugliest vice is femininity. Even though their reasons for it differ, the samurai and the homosexual do not see manliness as instinctive but rather as something gained only from moral effort. The ruin Kawada feared was moral ruin. The reason that he was an adherent of the Conservative party lay in its policy of protecting the things that should have been his enemies: the established order and the family system based on heterosexual love.

Yuichi's shadow flickered over every part of his social life. Like a man who makes the mistake of looking at the sun and wherever he looks thereafter sees an after-image of the sun, Kawada saw Yuichi's image in the sound of the door of the president's office where Yuichi had no right to be, in the sound of the phone, even in the profiles of young people in the street outside the car window. That after-image was no more than a ghost. Since the idea that he should part with Yuichi first entered his mind, that empty wraith had gradually become monstrous.

In truth Kawada had half-confused the emptiness of his fatalism with the emptiness of his heart. In the decision to part company, he showed he preferred the alternative of quickly and cruelly killing his passion to living with the fear that he would someday find the passion withered inside him. Thus, at parties with nobles and famous geisha, the pressure of the rule of majority that young Yuichi too had felt, crushed the haughty heart of Kawada, which should have been abundantly equipped to resist it. His many uninhibited dirty stories had been the toast of the banquet hall, but now this not necessarily time-honoured art filled Kawada with self-repugnance. Of late his taciturnity froze the very heart of the company's social director. Even though it seemed that under the circumstances parties would go much better if the president did not appear, Kawada's sense of duty always urged his presence.

This was the state of Kawada's mind. One night when, after a long absence, Yuichi suddenly appeared at Kawada's home and Kawada happened to be there, the delight of the unexpected meeting upset his resolve to call it quits. His eyes could not get enough of looking at Yuichi's face. Even though mad imaginativeness usually left his eyes clear, now the same thing made him drunk. Strangely beautiful youth! Kawada was drunk with the mystery before him. With Yuichi, it seemed, this evening's visit was purely a whim, but even so, there was no one like him at underestimating his own miraculous powers.

The night was still young, and so Kawada went out for a

drink with the youth. They went to a not-too-noisy high-class bar – under these circumstances, of course, not an 'in' one – a bar where there were women.

It happened that four or five of Kawada's close friends were there drinking. There were the president of a well-known drug company and some of his directors. This man, Matsumura by name, winked slightly, and, with a smile, waved to them.

Matsumura, second of his family to become president of the firm, was not much over thirty. He was a notorious dandy, self-important, and he was one of the fellowship. He paraded his vices, proud of them. Matsumura's pet notion was to convert all the people under his control to the heresy, or if he couldn't do that, to win their approval. Matsumura's diligent and industrious old secretary was a loyal man who strove to believe that nothing was as refined as homosexual love. He berated himself that he was so plebeian as not to possess so refined a nature. It was Kawada who was placed in an ironic position. When he, so circumspect in these matters, appeared with this beautiful youth, his friend and his colleagues stared at them openly over their drinks.

After a time, when Kawada went to the men's room, Matsumura nonchalantly left his place and sat down in Kawada's chair. Before the waitress at Yuichi's side, he pretended to be talking about business and said magnanimously: 'Oh, Mr Minami, there's something I want very badly to talk with you about. Can you have dinner with me tomorrow night?'

Just that much was said, with eyes never wavering from Yuichi's face; each word, every syllable, was pronounced with deliberation, like placing a stone in the game of Go. Yuichi said 'Yes', before he realized it.

'Will you come? Good. I'll meet you tomorrow evening at five o'clock in the bar of the Imperial Hotel.' Above the din, the feat was completed in a stroke, with all the naturalness in the world. When Kawada returned to his seat, Matsumura was already back at his own table, chatting away.

Kawada's acute sense of smell, however, quickly picked up a lingering odour like that of a cigarette that had been stamped out. It was quite painful for him to act as if he hadn't noticed it; if the pain continued long he would be in a bad temper indeed. He feared that he would create suspicion in Yuichi and then, finding it all too much to bear, would have to confess the reasons for his moodiness. So he suggested they leave, and, after an amiable farewell to Matsumura, they went out, much earlier than expected. Kawada stepped to the car and told the driver to wait there while they walked to another bar.

Then Yuichi told him what had happened. The youth walked along the rutted pavement, and, hands in the pockets of his grey flannel trousers and head down, said, as if it mattered little: 'A while ago Mr Matsumura asked me to meet him at the Imperial Hotel bar tomorrow; he wants to have dinner with me. I couldn't say anything but yes. What a pain!' He clucked his tongue. 'I wanted to tell you right away, but it was hard to do so in that bar.'

Kawada's joy on hearing this was unbounded. This haughty man of affairs, given to modest joys, said 'Thank you', with heartfelt appreciation. 'I'm afraid I made a real problem out of wondering just how long after Matsumura asked you, you would tell me about it. And since you couldn't talk about it in the bar, I'd say you got it in the shortest time,' he said. It was a compliment heavy with logic, a sincere confession.

At the next bar, Kawada and Yuichi laid their plan for the following day, for all the world as if they were making a business deal. Matsumura and Yuichi had no business connections whatever. Matsumura, moreover, had desired Yuichi before this. The implications of the invitation were obvious.

'Now we're accomplices,' Kawada said to himself, with joy he could hardly contain. 'Yuichi and I are accomplices! How closely our hearts will beat together!'

Kawada's tone was matter-of-fact, no different from that he used when in the president's office. He was careful when the waitress was near and instructed Yuichi as follows: 'Now we know how you feel. You don't want to go to the trouble of calling Matsumura to call things off. Here's what let's do.' (Kawada always said 'Do this', in the corporation; he was not a man ever to say 'Let's do'.)

'Matsumura is master of his domain, so it's no good to treat him unceremoniously. Granted, circumstances were what they were and you gave your consent. Why don't you go to the place agreed on? Accept his invitation to dinner. Afterwards, say, "That was a fine meal; now I'd like to buy you a drink." Matsumura will come along without a care in the world.

'Then let's work it out so I happen to be at the same bar you go to. I'll be waiting beginning at seven o'clock. Now what bar is good? Matsumura will be on his guard for places I go to, and won't come, so it will not seem right for me suddenly to appear accidentally at a bar I've never been to. It must all be carried out very naturally. Oh, yes. There's the bar *Je l'aime*, where I've gone with you four or five times, in this neighbourhood. That's fine. If Matsumura balks, lie to him – tell him something such as it's a bar I never go to. How's that? That looks like a great plan that has us protected on three sides.'

Yuichi said: 'Let's do it.' Kawada realized he would have to arrange to cancel his business engagements for the next evening the first thing in the morning. The two did no more drinking for the time being. Their pleasure that night was boundless. Kawada wondered how he had ever thought even for a moment of breaking off with this young man.

*

The next day at five, Matsumura was at the bar in the grill of the Imperial Hotel, waiting for Yuichi. His heart was filled with all manner of sensual anticipation, glutted with conceit and confidence. Matsumura, though a company head, dreamed of nothing more than being an interloper, and slightly shook the glass of cognac he was warming in both hands.

Five minutes after the appointed time, he tasted keenly the pleasure of being kept waiting. The guests at the bar were almost all foreigners. They talked endlessly in English that sounded like a dog barking deep in its throat. When it occurred to Matsumura after another five minutes that Yuichi might not appear, he tried to feel in the next five minutes what he had felt five minutes before, but the next five minutes were already altered.

This five-minute period was a time for vigilance. Yuichi had indeed come and was in the doorway. He was hesitating, it seemed, about whether to come. The feeling that he was there filled the place. When that five minutes was past, the feeling evaporated, and a new feeling, that he was not there, replaced it. At about five fifteen, determined once more that he must try to wait, Matsumura's heart repeatedly prompted him to change his mood. When twenty minutes had gone by, however, even these measures no longer helped.

He was battered by uneasiness and disappointment, busily trying to reconstruct at least the intolerable feeling of anticipation that caused his present anguish. I'll wait a minute more, Matsumura thought. His hopes were hitched to the circuit of the second hand as it approached and went past the sixty mark. Thus Matsumura, in a way unusual to him, waited and wasted forty-five minutes.

About an hour after Matsumura resignedly left the place, Kawada interrupted his work early and headed for the *Je l'aime*. There Kawada tasted, though at slower pace, the same agony of waiting that Matsumura had undergone. The punishment of his long wait, however, was many times that of Matsumura; the cruelty of it was beyond comparison with what Matsumura had suffered. Kawada waited in the *Je l'aime* until it closed. His pain, aggravated by his imagination, expanded and deepened with each moment. He refused to resign himself to it; his pain could do no more than mount.

In the first hour the breadth of Kawada's dreams was beyond limit. They're taking a long time over the meal. He was probably asked to some Japanese-style restaurant somewhere, Kawada thought. Perhaps it was a restaurant attended by geisha. This idea seemed plausible; for a man like Matsumura would be punctilious about having geisha present.

A little more time went by. His heart, labouring to minimize his fears that it was becoming far too late, suddenly exploded into a series of new doubts: Yuichi was lying, wasn't he? No, that can't be. His youth couldn't stand up against Matsumura's cunning. He's naïve. He's innocent. He loves me; there's no doubt about it. It's only that he couldn't get Matsumura to come here by his own power. Or perhaps Matsumura saw through my plans and, of course, wouldn't fall for the trick. Yuichi and Matsumura must be at another bar now. Yuichi must be waiting for the chance to slip over where I am. I must be patient a little while longer. Thinking thus, Kawada was assailed by regret.

Oh, my, just out of damned vanity, I've gone and made Yuichi fall into Matsumura's clutches. Why didn't I just have him turn down the invitation? If Yuichi didn't like phoning and calling it off, I could have called Matsumura and done it myself, whether it was proper or not.

Suddenly a wild fancy ripped at him: Right now, in a bed somewhere, Matsumura is hugging Yuichi, for all I know!

The logic of each surmise gradually broke down into fragments. The logic that held Yuichi pure of heart and the logic that revealed him as impossibly low contradicted each other painfully. Kawada sought relief from the phone at the counter. He phoned Matsumura. Though it was after eleven, Matsumura wasn't home yet. He did what was forbidden and called Yuichi's home, but he wasn't there. He asked the number of Yuichi's mother's hospital and, throwing common sense and tact to the winds, implored the hospital operator to check the hospital room. Yuichi was not there either.

Kawada was beside himself. After he got home he couldn't sleep. At two o'clock in the morning, he called Yuichi's home again. Yuichi had not yet returned.

Kawada could not sleep at all. The next morning was a clear refreshing, early fall day, and at nine he phoned Yuichi once more. And now Yuichi answered. Kawada had few hard words to say to the youth when he came to the phone, but he asked him to come to his office at ten-thirty. This was the first time Kawada had asked Yuichi to the company. On his way to work in the car, Kawada's heart mulled over the very masculine decision he had arrived at during the night: 'Once you decide a thing, never deviate from it. Whatever it is, hold to your decision!'

Kawada entered his office at ten. His secretary greeted him. He called the director who had attended last night's banquet in Kawada's stead, but the man had not yet arrived. Instead, another director dropped in to pass the time of day.

Yaichiro Kawada closed his eyes in vexation. Although he had slept not one wink, he had no headache. His racing mind was clear.

The director leaned at the window and toyed with the tassel of the window shade. He said in his usual loud voice: 'I've got a hangover; my head is splitting. Last night I was out with some fellow, and we drank until three o'clock this morning. At two o'clock we left Shimbashi and then woke up all the bars in Kagurazaka. Who do you think it was? It was Matsumura, of Matsumura Pharmaceuticals.' Listening, Kawada's jaw dropped. 'Your body just can't take running around with fellows as young as that,' the director went on.

Concealing his interest, Kawada asked: 'Who was Matsumura running around with?'

'Matsumura was alone. I'm an old friend of his father. He goes out with me as if he were dragging his old man around. Yesterday I deliberately got home early, thinking I'd take a quick bath, when he called and asked me out.'

Kawada was ready to let out a bleat of joy, but a stubborn second thought held him back. This lucky intelligence did not make up for last evening's torture. Also, Matsumura could have asked this trusted director to make a false report that Yuichi was not along. One could not say that was not the case. 'When once you decide a thing, never deviate from it.'

The director then brought up various topics connected with their work. Kawada gave astute answers that surprised himself. The secretary came in and announced a caller. 'It's a relative of mine, a student,' said Kawada; 'he's looking for a job, but his grades are pretty bad.' He frowned. The director decided to leave, and then Yuichi came in.

In the fresh light of the early autumn morning, youth alone shone from the young face. Without a single cloud, without a hint of shadow, that face ever reborn from morning to morning clutched at the heart of Kawada. This youth's face belied his exertions of the night before, as well as his betrayal, and showed no hint that it might have made another person suffer. It knew no recompense; even if it had participated in a killing the night before, surely it would not have changed. He wore a blue blazer, from which the creases in his grey flannel trousers fell straight as an arrow. He approached Kawada with perfect composure.

412

Kawada himself opened the argument, with a clumsiness of which even he was aware: 'What happened last night?'

The beautiful youth showed his manly white teeth and smiled. He sat down in the chair indicated to him and said: 'That business of Matsumura's was a pain in the neck, so I didn't go to meet him. So I didn't have to meet you either, I figured.'

Kawada was accustomed to explanations like this, full of contradictions.

'Why didn't you have to come to meet me?'

Yuichi smiled again. Then, squirming so that the chair squealed, like a rude schoolboy, he said: 'Day before yesterday, and yesterday too?'

'I called your home I don't know how many times '

'That's what the old girl says.'

Kawada showed the reckless valour of one who had been beaten and cornered. Suddenly he changed the subject to Yuichi's mother's illness: 'Are you having trouble meeting her hospital expenses?'

'Not particularly,' the youth answered.

'I won't ask where you stayed last night. I'll just give you a gift for your mother in the hospital. All right? I'll give you what you think you need. If you're satisfied, just nod.' Kawada's tone became all business.

'And from now on, I want you to stay away from me altogether. You won't hear any more from me. I beg of you from now on not to put me in any ridiculous predicament or interfere with my work.'

He snatched a cheque book from his pocket and, wondering whether he should give Yuichi a few minutes' time to think, sat irresolute, looking up stealthily at the youth's face. Until this time it was, in fact, Kawada who had been looking down. The youth's eyes were lifted. In this instant Kawada waited for the youth's explanation, or apology, or appeal, and at the same time feared all of them. The youth, however, sat silent and proud, his back straight.

The sound of a cheque being ripped from the book broke the silence. Yuichi looked at it; it was for 200,000 yen. He silently slid it back with his fingertips.

Kawada tore up the cheque. He wrote a larger sum on another. He slid that towards Yuichi. Yuichi again refused it. This absolutely ridiculous and solemn game was repeated a number of times. When it rose to 400,000 yen, Yuichi thought of the 500,000 yen he had borrowed from Shunsuké. Kawada's behaviour excited only his disgust, and the youth had considered bidding Kawada up and then taking the cheque and tearing it to bits before his eyes and saying good-bye with a flourish. When the figure of 500,000 yen flickered in his mind, however, he came to his senses and waited for the next figure to be named.

Yaichiro Kawada's proud forehead was not bowed; a twitch ran like lightning down his right cheek. With the last cheque in tatters before him, he wrote another and handed it across the desk. It was for 500,000 yen.

The youth held out his fingers, folded the cheque slowly, and put it in his breast pocket. He stood up, and with a smile that showed he bore no hard feelings, bowed.

'I appreciate all you've done for me for so long a time. *Sayonara.*'

Kawada did not have the power to get up from his chair. Finally he reached out his hand and said: '*Sayonara.*' As they shook hands Yuichi noticed that Kawada's hand shook severely. Yuichi did not allow compassion to get the better of him, which was lucky for Kawada, who would have died rather than be pitied. His natural emotions, nevertheless, were tinged with feelings of friendship. He preferred elevators, so he didn't go down the stairs, but pressed the button in the marble pillar.

*

His prospective employment with Kawada Motors had gone up in smoke, and his social ambitions were back where they had started. With the 500,000 yen, Kawada had bought back his right to look at the world with contempt.

Yuichi's ambition was made of extremely fanciful stuff, but the collapse of his dreams promised to interfere with his return to reality. Broken dreams, to a greater extent than dreams still in force, are apt to treat reality as an enemy. The possibility of filling the yawning gap between his dreams of his powers and his occasional sober estimates of his powers seemed blocked for the time being. Moreover, having learned to see, he recognized that it had been blocked from the beginning. For detestable modern society has a way of frustrating dreams; this is one of its chief powers.

To be sure, Yuichi had learned to see. Without the interposition of a mirror, however, it was difficult to see youth in the very middle of youth. The fact that the negations of youth end in abstraction while the affirmations of youth have a sexual leaning seems to stem from this difficulty.

Last night, on a sudden gamble, he had broken his appointments with both Matsumura and Kawada and spent a pure evening drinking with a school friend until morning. But this so-called purity was only physical.

Yuichi looked at his own position. Once he had smashed his way out of the cage of the mirror and forgotten his own face and come to regard it as something that did not exist, then for the first time he had begun searching for the position of the seeing person. He had been set free from the childish ambition of dreaming that society might supply him with some kind of image that would be a substitute for the image that the mirror had reflected. Seeking this in the very middle of youth, now, he was impatient to complete the difficult operation of basing an existence on something he couldn't see. A decade ago, his body could have accomplished this operation with the greatest of ease.

Yuichi felt Shunsuké's spell. He must first return the 500,000 yen to Shunsuké. Everything else had to come after that.

A few days later, on a cool evening, the beautiful youth visited Shunsuké's home without any previous notice. It happened that the old man was at work on a manuscript he had been carrying about with him for several weeks. This autobiographical essay Shunsuké Hinoki had titled 'On Shunsuké Hinoki'. He had not realized that Yuichi would be visiting him, and he was reading over the unfinished manuscript under the desk lamp. He was marking it here and there with a red pencil.

32

Grand Finale

That morning, Yuichi had done nothing of consequence. His employment examination for Yasuko's father's department store was a week away. Thanks to his father-in-law's good offices, his job was already assured. As a matter of form, however, he had to take the test. By way of preparation, it was important that he pay a visit to his father-in-law, as a matter of business courtesy. It would have been well to do it sooner, but his mother's worsening health provided a useful excuse for postponement.

Yuichi was not in the mood to visit his father-in-law today. He had in his wallet the cheque for 500,000 yen. Yuichi set out for the Ginza alone.

The city trolley stopped at the Sukiyabashi Station and seemed not to be going any farther. The passengers flowed out on to the street and hurried in the direction of Owari Cho. Into the clear autumn sky, black smoke mounted in thick clouds.

Yuichi got off the trolley and mingled with the crowd, hurrying with them. The Owari Cho crossroads was already filled with people. Three red fire engines had stopped in the middle of the throng. They threw long streams of water where the black smoke was mounting.

A big cabaret was on fire. From this side the view was cut off by the two-storey building near at hand, but every now and then rising spires of flame flashed in the black smoke. If it had been night, the smoke, enclosing innumerable sparks which would then have been visible, would have been a shapeless black. The fire had already moved to the surrounding stores. The second floor of the two-storey building near by was already burning. Only the outer walls seemed to remain.

The eggshell paint of the outer walls, however, was still its vivid and clear everyday colour. The crowd shouted praises for the courage of one of the firemen, who had climbed to the roof half surrounded by flame and with his fire axe was breaking down the roof. The sight of these little black human figures gambling against death seemed to strike the hearts of the crowd with pleasure – a pleasure not unlike that lewd one.

A building under renovation near the fire was surrounded with scaffolding. A number of people were on the scaffolds guarding against the spread of the fire.

The fire unexpectedly made little sound. Explosions – the sound of the ridge-pole burning and falling, and the like – could not be heard here. There was a dull, buzzing sound, but that was from a newspaper's red, single-engined aeroplane circling overhead.

Yuichi felt something like fog playing about his cheek and took cover. An old, rotten hose belonging to one of the fire trucks, which was conducting water from one of the hydrants at the curb, was sending up a spray of water out of a hole that had been repaired. It cascaded down on the street like rain. The spray wet the window of a drygoods store. It made it difficult to see the employees inside the store as they crouched among their personal effects and the portable safe they had brought out, worrying about the spread of the fire.

The water from the hoses ceased every once in a while. The streams in the sky visibly withdrew and drooped downward. In those intervals the black smoke kept drifting off at an angle, seeming without end.

'The National Guard! The National Guard!' the crowd shouted.

A truck pushed in upon the crowd and stopped. From its rear a contingent of white-helmeted guardsmen descended. It was only a unit of policemen brought to control traffic, but the fear it excited among the crowd was laughable. Perhaps the crowd felt stirring within itself seditious leanings that might have brought out the National Guard. Before the advancing phalanx of guardsmen, their clubs at their sides, the people surged in retreat.

Their blind power was awesome. Individuals one by one lost their will; they had been taken over by the agencies of a power outside themselves. The pressure to mount back on the sidewalk pushed the people standing in front of the stores back against the display windows.

At one store, a youthful group standing in front of a large, expensive, single-pane store window, spread their arms out wide and shouted: 'Watch the glass! Watch the glass!'

Like moths around a flame, most of the crowd was impervious to the dangers of the glass.

As he was being pushed about, Yuichi heard a sound like firecrackers. The crowd had trampled on some balloons that had been torn from the hand of a child. Then Yuichi noticed, under the stampede of feet, a blue wooden sandal that was being sloshed about like a bit of flotsam.

When finally Yuichi managed to free himself from the mob, he found himself facing in a strange direction. He redid his disarranged necktie and walked away. He didn't look again in the direction of the fire. The extraordinary energy of the mob scene, however, had stirred in him an inexplicable excitement.

Since he had no place to go, Yuichi walked for a time and finally went into a theatre that was showing a movie he did not especially want to see.

*

... Shunsuké laid down his red pencil.

His shoulder was very stiff. He stood up and, striking the shoulder, moved to the large library next to the study. About a month earlier Shunsuké had disposed of about half of his collection. As he got older his books had come to seem useless to him. He kept only those that he particularly liked, took down the empty shelves, and had a window cut through in the wall that had so long blocked off the light. In the north window, so close to the foliage of the magnolia tree, he had two clear panes of glass installed. The cot he had kept in the study for naps he moved into the library. There, Shunsuké would make himself comfortable and riffle through the pages of the books lined up on a small table.

Shunsuké entered the study and looked for something on the shelf of original works in French literature, which was up

418

fairly high. He soon found the book he was looking for. It was a special edition with rice-paper pages of *Musa Paidica* in French translation. *Musa Paidica* is a collection of poems by the Roman poet Straton, of the time of Hadrian. He followed in the steps of the Emperor Hadrian, who loved Antinous, and he wrote poems only about beautiful boys:

> Let the cheek be fair
> Or dipped in honey shades,
> Of flaxen hue the hair
> Or black with every grace;
> Let the eyes be brown
> Or let me disappear
> Into those flashing pools
> Of deepest black.

He of the honey-coloured skin, the black hair, and the jet-black eyes must have been born in Asia Minor, as was the famous Eastern slave Antinous. The ideal youthful beauty dreamed of by second-century Romans was Asian in nature.

Shunsuké again took Keats's *Endymion* from the shelf. His eyes moved over the verses he had almost committed to memory.

Just a little more, the old author thought.

Already nothing is missing of the material that visions are made of; in just a little while it will be complete. The image of adamantine youth will be ready. It's been a long time since I felt palpitations like this or such reasonless fears just before completing a work. In the moment of completion, that final supreme moment, what will appear?

Shunsuké stretched himself diagonally across the bed and idly turned the pages of the book. He listened to the sounds about him. All over the garden the insects of autumn were chorusing.

In a corner of the bookstacks the *Complete Works of Shunsuké Hinoki*, just brought out last month, stood, all twenty volumes in a row. The stamped-gold characters shone forth in dull, monochromatic brilliance. Twenty volumes of repetition of the same sneer of boredom. As a man might, purely out of politeness, chuck the chin of an ugly child, the old author idly cupped his hand and caressed the rows of characters on the spines of his collected works.

On the two or three small tables around the bed, a number of books were scattered – seemingly open to the page last read – their white pages open like so many dead wings.

There was a collection of the poems of Ton-a of the Nijo school, a *Taiheiki* opened to the pages dealing with the Great Priest of the Shiga Temple, a copy of *Okagami* handed down from the Retired Emperor Kazan, a collection of the poems of the Shogun Yoshihisa Ashikaga, who died young, and a sumptuously bound combined edition of the *Kojiki* and the *Nihonshoki*. In those last two works the theme is endlessly repeated that so many young and beautiful princes have had their lives cut off in the flower of their youth, with the exposure of some foul love affair or insurrection or plot, or have ended their lives themselves. Prince Karu was one. Prince Otsu was another. Shunsuké loved the blighted youth of ancient times.

He heard a sound at the door of the study. It was ten p.m. There was no reason for a caller to come this late. It must be the old housekeeper bringing up tea. Shunsuké answered without looking up. It wasn't the old servant who entered. It was Yuichi.

'Are you working?' he asked. 'I headed up here so quickly the housekeeper was too surprised to do anything to stop me.'

Shunsuké came out of the library and looked at Yuichi standing in the middle of the study. The beautiful young man's arrival had been so sudden that it seemed as if he had appeared out of all the books Shunsuké had been poring over.

The two exchanged the salutations appropriate to the great length of time since they had last seen each other. Shunsuké conducted Yuichi to an easy chair and went to get the wine bottle he kept for company in the library cupboard.

Yuichi heard a cricket chirping in a corner of the study. The room was just as he had first seen it. On the knick-knack shelves surrounding the window on three sides were many pieces of ancient pottery; their position had not been changed in the slightest. The beautiful totem doll of ancient crafting was where it had been originally. Nowhere were flowers of the season visible. The black marble mantel clock was still gloomily carrying the time. If the old maidservant neglected to wind it, her old master, who had very little to do with everyday affairs, would not touch it either, and in a few days the clock would run down.

Yuichi now took a look around him. This study, he felt, had a mysterious history. After he had known his first joy, he had visited this house; in this room he had been read a passage from the *Anointment of the Catamite* by Shunsuké. He had come into this room stricken with the fear of life and consulted with Shunsuké on the abortion for Yasuko. Now he was here, captive of neither the joys of the past nor the troubles of the past, serene and undisturbed. After a time, surely, he would return the 500,000-yen to Shunsuké. He would be relieved of a heavy burden, freed of all control over his person. He would leave this room, surely, without ever having to come back.

Shunsuké brought a bottle of white wine and glasses on a silver tray and placed them before his guest. He sat down on the window seat fitted with the Ryukyu-patterned cushions and filled Yuichi's glass. His hand shook visibly, spilling some wine, forcibly reminding Yuichi of Kawada's hand a few days before.

This old man is in seventh heaven, I've come on him so quickly, Yuichi thought. There's no need to bring up the business of the money right away.

The old man and the youth drank a toast. Shunsuké lifted his eyes for the first time and looked at the face of this beautiful young man he had not been able to look at until now. He said: 'Well, how are things? How is reality? Has it pleased you?'

Yuichi smiled ambiguously. His youthful lips twisted with the cynicism he had learned.

Shunsuké went on without waiting for an answer: 'There might be anything. Things I can't express, unhappy things, shocking things, wonderful things there might be. But, after all, they're not worth a thing. That's written on your face. You've changed inside, I suppose. But to outer appearances, you haven't changed a bit since the first time I saw you. Your exterior is not affected at all. Reality couldn't leave a single chisel mark on your cheek. You have the gift of youth. That will never be conquered by something of the likes of reality.'

'I've broken with Kawada,' the young man said.

'That's good. That man has been eaten up by his own idealism. He was worried about your influence on him.'

'I had an influence?'

'That's right. You can never be influenced by reality, but you constantly exert an influence on reality. You have turned that man's reality into a fearful idea.'

Kawada's name had been mentioned, but Yuichi quickly lost the opportunity to mention the 500,000 yen in the lecture that name provoked.

Who is this old man talking to? To me? Yuichi wondered. If I didn't know better I'd be breaking my head trying to figure out Hinoki's crazy theories. Does he think he's talking to me, when I'm not the least excited about these artificial things that get him all wrought up?

Unconsciously, Yuichi's eyes moved to a dark corner of the room. The old author seemed to be talking to another person behind Yuichi.

It was a quiet night. Other than the voices of insects there was no sound. The gurgle of wine being poured from the bottle rang clear, with the smooth weight of jewels. The cut-glass goblet shone.

'There. Have a drink,' Shunsuké said. 'It's an autumn evening. You are there, the wine is here, there's not a thing more this world requires. Socrates listened to the cicada's voice and in the morning by the little stream lectured to the beautiful boy Phaedrus. Socrates asked questions and answered them himself. He discovered the roundabout method of arriving at truth through questioning. But you'll never get a question from absolute beauty in a natural body. Questions and answers can only be exchanged between things in the same category. Spirit and body can never engage in dialogue.

'Spirit can only inquire. It can never get a reply – outside of an echo.

'I did not choose to be in the position of questioning and then answering. Asking is my fate. There you are, beautiful nature. Here I am, ugly spirit. That is the eternal schema. No algebra can bring about the mutual exchange of those terms. I don't have any intention of deliberately belittling my own spirit. Spirit has many quite wonderful things about it.

'But, Yuichi, my boy, love – at least my love – doesn't have even the hope of Socrates' love. Love is born from nothing less than hopelessness. Spirit against nature – the demonstration of spirit in the face of such an incomprehensible thing as love.

'Then why do I inquire? To spirit, there is no way of proving oneself save in inquiring of something else. Spirit that does not inquire leads a precarious existence . . .'

Shunsuké paused. He turned about and opened the bay window, looking through the screen and down into the garden. There was a faint rustle of wind.

'The wind seems to be rising. Autumn is getting on. Is it hot in here? Since it's hot, leaving it open won't . . .'

Yuichi shook his head. Shunsuké closed the window again and then, looking the youth in the face, resumed his lecture.

'There we are. Spirit constantly formulates questions. It must store up inquiries. The creative power of spirit lies in its ability to create questions. Thus the supreme objective of spirit is in the creation of the question itself – in short, the creation of nature. But that is impossible. Yet the march towards impossibility is the method of spirit.

'Spirit is – well, it is the drive to pile zero on zero endlessly in order to arrive at one.

'Let's say I ask you: "Why are you so beautiful?" Can you answer? Spirit from the beginning anticipates no reply.'

His eyes stared fixedly. Yuichi tried to return the stare. Yuichi's power as one who sees, however, had been lost, as if he had been put under a spell.

The beautiful youth was looked at – willy-nilly. What towering impoliteness there was in that look! It turned its object to stone, it robbed him of his will, it reduced him to nature.

Of course, that look wasn't directed at me, Yuichi thought, in terror. Mr Hinoki's look was undoubtedly directed at me, but the thing Mr Hinoki was looking at was not me. Another Yuichi who is not me is in this room.

That was nature itself, the Yuichi who yielded nothing to

the ancient statues in their perfection – Yuichi saw clearly the sculptures of the beautiful youths beyond his powers of seeing. Another beautiful youth clearly existed in that study – a youth who never shrinks no matter how much he is stared at.

The sound of wine being poured into a glass brought Yuichi to his senses. He had been dreaming with his eyes open.

'Drink,' said Shunsuké, bringing his glass to his mouth and going on with his talk.

'So, beauty, do you see, is on this side, yet unreachable. Isn't that right? Religion always puts the other side, the future world, over there in the distance. Distance, however, in man's concept, in the long run is something that can be traversed. Science and religion only differ in respect to the distance. The great nebula six hundred and eighty thousand light-years away, similarly, can be reached. Religion is the vision of reaching; science is the technique of it.

'Beauty, on the other hand, is always on this side. It is in this world, in the present, firm; it can be touched with the hand. That our sexual appetites can taste it is beauty's precondition. Sensuality is, therefore, essential. It confirms beauty. However, beauty can never be reached, because the susceptibilities of sense, more than anything else, block attainment of it. The method by which the Greeks expressed beauty through sculpture was a wise one. I am a novelist. Of all the rubbish that has been invented in the modern times, the profession I have chosen is the worst. Don't you think that for the expression of beauty it is the most bungling and low-class of professions?

'Right here, a thing that cannot be touched. When I say this, you must know what I mean. Beauty is the nature under man's nature, under man's condition. Among men, it controls men most deeply. It is beauty that defies mankind. Thanks to beauty, spirit cannot get a moment of decent rest.'

Yuichi listened. He felt as if, close by, the sculpture of the beautiful youth was listening intently in the same way. In the room the miracle had already occurred. After the miracle had occurred, however, only a commonplace quiet occupied the place.

'Yuichi, my boy, in this world there are times known as the

supreme moments,' Shunsuké said. 'They are moments of the reconciliation of spirit and nature, the conjunction of spirit and nature in this world.

'Their expression is nothing if not impossible for human beings while they are alive. Living men can taste those moments, perhaps, but they cannot express them. That goes beyond human powers. Do you ask: "Then human beings cannot express superhuman things?" That would be a mistake. Human beings in truth cannot express the ultimate in human conditions. Human beings cannot express the highest moments that occur to human beings.

'The artist is not capable of everything, nor is expression capable of all. Expression is always being pressured to make alternative judgements. Expression or action? The action of love, now – without action man cannot love. So he expresses it afterwards.

'The truly important problem, however, is the thing in which expression and action might be possible simultaneously. Of these, man knows only one. That is death.

'Death is action, but there is no action so supremely unitary as this – oh, yes, I made a mistake.'

Shunsuké smiled.

'Death does not go beyond truth. Suicide might be called death through action. A man cannot be born of his own will, but he can will to die. This was the basic proposition of all the ancient suicide philosophies. However, there can be no doubt that in death, the action known as suicide and the expression of all that is life can come simultaneously. The supreme moment must wait for death. This can be proved in reverse, it seems.

'The highest expression of the living – occupying at best the second highest position – is the total form of life minus *alpha*. To this expression add the *alpha* of life, and life is complete. Why? Even while expressing it men go on living – undeniably their lives are excluded from expression, but they are only simulating a temporary death.

'This *alpha*, how men have dreamed about it! Artists' dreams are always connected with it. The fact that life dilutes expression, robs the real preciseness from expression, everybody is aware of. The preciseness that the living conceive of is only one form of preciseness. To the dead, for all I know, the sky we think blue may glimmer green.

'It's a strange thing. When living men are driven to hopelessness in trying to express this, again and again it is beauty that comes rushing in to save them. It is beauty that teaches that one must stand one's ground firmly among the impressions of life.

'And now we see that beauty is bound by life and sensuality. It teaches men to have faith only in the validity of sensuality. In that respect, indeed, we may understand how beauty is logical to men.'

When Shunsuké had finished speaking, he laughed softly and added: 'Well, that's all. It wouldn't be right to have you fall asleep. There's no reason to hurry tonight; after all, you haven't been here for a long time. If you've had enough wine . . .'

Shunsuké saw that Yuichi's glass was still full.

'Well! Shall we play chess? Kawada taught you how, I suppose.'

'Yes, a little.'

'Kawada was my teacher, too. Of course, he didn't teach us chess so that we could play on into an autumn night in this way. This board, now –' He pointed to a fine old board with pieces arranged in their places.

'I found it in an antique shop. Chess is now perhaps my only debauchery. Can you stand it?'

'I don't mind.'

Yuichi did not deter him. He had forgotten that he had come here to return the 500,000 yen.

'I'll give you the white men.'

On either side of the chessboard the unfinished glasses of white wine shimmered. Then the two men were quiet; only the faint click of moving pieces broke the silence.

As they sat thus, the presence of another person in the study made itself evident. Yuichi looked over his shoulder several times towards the invisible statue that was observing the moves of the chessmen.

There was no way of estimating what time they spent in this

way, whether long or short they did not know. If the 'supreme moment', as Shunsuké had called it, were to come in a moment of unawareness like this, it would surely go by unnoticed. One game was over. Yuichi had won.

'Well, I lose,' the old author said. In his face, however, delight flowed. He wore a peaceful expression Yuichi had never seen before.

'Maybe I had too much to drink and that beat me. Let's try a return bout. Maybe I'd better sober up . . .' As he said this he poured some water into a cup from the pitcher in which thin slices of lemon had been floating. He stood up, holding the cup: 'Excuse me just a moment.'

He went into the library. After a while he lay down on the bed in a position in which only his legs were visible. His serene voice called to Yuichi from the study: 'If I just doze off a little, I'll sober up. Wake me in twenty or thirty minutes. When I wake up I'll play you that return match. Wait, now.'

Yuichi moved to the window seat. He stretched his legs comfortably and toyed with the chessmen.

Afterwards, when Yuichi went to wake him, Shunsuké did not answer. He was dead. On the table near his head, held down by his wrist watch, was a slip of paper on which something had been hurriedly written:

'*Sayonara.* There's a gift for you in the right-hand drawer of the desk.'

Yuichi awoke the housekeeper; the family physician, Dr Kumemura, was called. The doctor heard all that had been going on. The cause of death was uncertain at first; finally it was put down as suicide, brought about by a lethal dose of Pavinal, which Shunsuké had been taking daily to relieve the neuralgic pains in his knee. Yuichi was asked whether a note had been left. He produced the slip of paper. When the right-hand drawer of the desk was opened, they discovered a legally executed will. In it nearly ten million yen in personal and real property and other assets in the estate were left in entirety to Yuichi Minami. The two witnesses were the head of the publishing firm that had published the complete works, an old friend of Shunshuké, and the head of his book publishing department. They had accompanied Shunsuké to a notary in Kasumigaseki a month before.

Yuichi's plan to return the 500,000 yen debt had failed. To make matters worse, he was depressed by the thought that his entire life would be bound by the ten million yen through which Shunsuké had expressed his love for him, though under the circumstances depression was inappropriate. The doctor phoned the police station, and the chief inspector came, along with a detective and a coroner, to look into the matter.

Yuichi replied to all questions during the investigation. The doctor put in friendly words, and there seemed to be not the slightest suspicion of collusion in regard to the suicide. On seeing the will, however, the assistant police inspector inquired closely into the nature of the relationship with the deceased.

'He was a friend of my dead father and brought my wife and me together. In this respect he was a second father to me and went to much trouble on my behalf. He always treated me with great affection.'

With this single perjury, Yuichi's eyes streamed with tears. The chief investigator took these tears with professional detachment. He was convinced of Yuichi's complete innocence.

The ever vigilant newspapermen came in, badgering Yuichi with the same questions.

'Since he made you his sole heir, he must have loved you a lot, didn't he?'

That word 'love' among these words that had no ulterior intent pierced Yuichi's heart.

The young man sat with a serious look on his face and made no reply. Then he remembered he had not informed his family, and he went to call Yasuko.

The night was over. Yuichi did not feel tired. He was not sleepy, but he was tired of the mourners and the newspapermen who had been crowding in since early in the morning, so he told Dr Kumemura he was going to take a walk.

It was a very clear morning. He went down the hill and looked at the trolley tracks stretching away in twin, freshly gleaming rails through the silent street. Most of the stores were still closed.

Ten million yen, the young man thought, as he crossed the

broad street. But watch out! You get hit by a car now and you'll spoil it all.

A flower shop had just opened its doors. The array of plants and blooms leaned forward with a damp, depressed air.

Ten million yen – you can buy a lot of flowers with that, the young man thought.

A nameless freedom hung heavily in his chest, heavier than the long night's gloom. Uneasiness made his steps clumsy as he hurried along – an uneasiness brought on by his staying up all night, one might say. The Government Line Station came into view; he could see the early working people gathering towards the ticket gate. In front of the station two or three bootblacks had already lined up.

First, get your shoes shined ... Yuichi thought.

FOR THE BEST IN PAPERBACKS, LOOK FOR THE 🐧

In every corner of the world, on every subject under the sun, Penguin represents quality and variety – the very best in publishing today.

For complete information about books available from Penguin – including Puffins, Penguin Classics and Arkana – and how to order them, write to us at the appropriate address below. Please note that for copyright reasons the selection of books varies from country to country.

In the United Kingdom: Please write to *Dept E.P., Penguin Books Ltd, Harmondsworth, Middlesex, UB7 0DA.*

If you have any difficulty in obtaining a title, please send your order with the correct money, plus ten per cent for postage and packaging, to *PO Box No 11, West Drayton, Middlesex*

In the United States: Please write to *Dept BA, Penguin, 299 Murray Hill Parkway, East Rutherford, New Jersey 07073*

In Canada: Please write to *Penguin Books Canada Ltd, 2801 John Street, Markham, Ontario L3R 1B4*

In Australia: Please write to the *Marketing Department, Penguin Books Australia Ltd, P.O. Box 257, Ringwood, Victoria 3134*

In New Zealand: Please write to the *Marketing Department, Penguin Books (NZ) Ltd, Private Bag, Takapuna, Auckland 9*

In India: Please write to *Penguin Overseas Ltd, 706 Eros Apartments, 56 Nehru Place, New Delhi, 110019*

In the Netherlands: Please write to *Penguin Books Netherlands B.V., Postbus 195, NL–1380AD Weesp*

In West Germany: Please write to *Penguin Books Ltd, Friedrichstrasse 10–12, D–6000 Frankfurt/Main 1*

In Spain: Please write to *Longman Penguin España, Calle San Nicolas 15, E–28013 Madrid*

In Italy: Please write to *Penguin Italia s.r.l., Via Como 4, I-20096 Pioltello (Milano)*

In France: Please write to *Penguin Books Ltd, 39 Rue de Montmorency, F-75003 Paris*

In Japan: Please write to *Longman Penguin Japan Co Ltd, Yamaguchi Building, 2–12–9 Kanda Jimbocho, Chiyoda-Ku, Tokyo 101*

BY THE SAME AUTHOR

'Mishima's characters are observed with the sharpest of eyes and with maximum chill . . . a most beautiful writer of prose – clear, eloquent, visual' – *Financial Times*

Thirst for Love

Before her husband's death, Etsuko had already learnt that jealousy is useless if it cannot be controlled.

So when she arrived as a young widow at her late husband's family farm near Osaka, Etsuko resolved to hold her emotions in check, silently tolerating the nocturnal embraces of her father-in-law as she nursed a new secret passion. Jealousy, love, passion, hatred – she could control them all as long as there was hope . . .

Death in Midsummer and Other Stories

Death, homosexuality and the spiritual emptiness of post-war Japan: these are the often shocking subjects which Mishima explores.

'Mishima achieved a fusion of thought, vision and expression that has been equalled by only a handful of writers this century anywhere in the world' – *Sunday Telegraph*

The Sailor Who Fell from Grace with the Sea

'He had the economy of means to create enormous myths – his novels are compressed visions' – Arthur Miller

The Sailor Who Fell from Grace with the Sea is one of Mishima's finest achievements, a chilling revenge tragedy shot through with glittering eroticism.

After five years of widowhood, elegant Fusako consummates her two-day relationship with Ryuji, a naval officer convinced of his glorious destiny. From the beginning, they are spied on by Fusako's son, Noboru. He is thirteen, precocious and dispassionate. 'No. 3' in a sinister élite of schoolboys who, eventually, devise their own plans for Ryuji . . .

Also published

THE TEMPLE OF THE GOLDEN PAVILION
SEA OF FERTILITY
YUKIO MISHIMA ON HAGAKURE